5-27-2009

To Erin and Larry,
Hope you enjoy
my debut Novel.
Best Wishes,

SNAKES IN
THE GRASS
FRANK SULLIVAN

iUniverse, Inc.
New York   Bloomington

Snakes in the Grass

iUniverse books may be ordered through booksellers or by contacting:

iUniverse
1663 Liberty Drive
Bloomington, IN 47403
www.iuniverse.com
1-800-Authors (1-800-288-4677)

ISBN: 978-0-595-52529-4 (pbk)
ISBN: 978-1-4401-4098-3 (dj)
ISBN: 978-0-595-62582-6 (ebk)

Printed in the United States of America

iUniverse rev. date: 4/23/2009

IN MEMORY

In memory of my dear friend, Dr. Marcus Rosa,
who inspired many of the stories in this novel.
1918 – 2008

These are the stories of my friend, Dr. Marcus Rosa, a physician and surgeon who lived in Brazil during formative and difficult political times. He was the personal physician to villainous dictators and leaders of military coups. To me, he was a friend, tutor, and neighbor. He took great delight teaching Portuguese to me and he told his stories in mixed English and Portuguese during weekly language lessons.

I do not know the truth of his stories. Were they all true? Who knows? When one recalls a lifetime of challenges, some events are blown out of proportion and others are forgotten. During my Portuguese lessons, Marcus retold many stories, usually rendering additional details with each reiteration. He led an amazing life and he was happy to share his adventures with me.

The beginning of the story is based in fact, at least from his perspective. To mold his stories into an engaging account, I have added my own fiction to weave a narrative. This story is a work of fiction, and indeed, I have used a pseudonym for my friend to avoid trespass upon the privacy of his family.

ACKNOWLEDGEMENTS

To my wife, Linda, for her love, support, dedication, and patience with everything I do.

To my children, Michael and Michelle who are a daily inspiration to me.

To my brother Paul for his positive encouragement and technical suggestions.

To Ellen Gardner, Jerry Diehl, Julie Chaffee, and Skip Bryant for their technical suggestions.

FOREWARD

During my first trip to Brazil, I felt I landed on a different planet. Certainly, there are the typical southern hemisphere differences: water in a toilet bowl drains in a counter-clockwise direction, and the night sky has the Southern Cross but no Big Dipper. The constellation Orion is in the northwest sky instead of the southeast sky. The terrain is vastly different. Green is the predominant color and plants grow everywhere with little or no attention. Animals are different. Brazil has no large wild mammals such as elk or deer. The wild cats have been hunted to near extinction. The wildlife is all in the rivers. Alligators (technically caiman) are plentiful, as are piranhas. At home, we fish quietly to prevent scaring the fish away. Here, you hit the water with your fishing pole to make a lot of noise to attract the aggressive fish. The Amazon basin was once a saltwater ocean so there are marine relatives such as freshwater bottlenose dolphins and stingrays.

Socially, the people are friendly and outgoing. Try reading a book alone on a park bench and someone will invariably come up and start a conversation. The bureaucracy in Brazil is extensive and makes life challenging. All people pay their monthly bills at the bank, making it impossible to use banks at the first and end of the month. The court system is vastly different. Attorneys do not argue cases on behalf of clients; the litigants are the only ones allowed to speak at trials. The attorneys for both sides sit quietly and speak only when the judge asks them a question. Portuguese, not Spanish, is the language of the land. In the big cities, some young people know English. Outside of São Paulo and Rio, one seldom hears English spoken.

Food in Brazil is plentiful and relatively cheap. Wonderful and exotic fruits and vegetables vary by season and unfortunately, many cannot be exported because of a short shelf life. Every big city has its share of McDonalds and Brazilians line up there for lunch. Breakfast consists of only coffee and cheese breads. Cheese breads, made from cheese and tapioca or manioc flour, are usually served as a half-baked glob. Only real natives can truly enjoy these. The national dish is feijoada, a stew of beans, sausage, and pigs ears. The best feijoada includes all the parts of the pig that the butcher didn't want. If you overindulge at a *churrasaria*, steak house, you will wish you were a vegetarian. The staff will keep bringing barbequed meat on a spit until you refuse to eat any more. For drinks, a beer is usually cheaper than bottled water. Cachaça is the national liquor and is rum made from sugar cane. Its affects usually leave one with a tremendous headache the next morning. The food and water in the urban areas is clean and fresh so there are no real dangers and one should try anything on the menu that looks good.

In writing this book, I made several concessions for the benefit of the American reader. Most activity in the novel occurs within Brazil or America. Rather than confuse the reader about the actual facts of metrics and foreign currency, I have used non-metric references for distances and measures. References to Brazilian currency have been converted to its equivalent value in today's dollar. Since this is an epic story occurring over several decades, one would have to reference Crusados, Cruzeiros, Novo Cruzeiros, and Reals to mention a few that mean "dollar." Additionally, the hyperinflation of the Brazilian currency in the 1980's and 1990's meant that no one really knew the value of money. During this tumultuous time, consumers were adding an extra zero to the prices of goods on a weekly basis. Therefore, any references to actual currency of the day would have been meaningless and confusing to the reader.

While this novel is fictitious, there is a basis in truth to the starting point of the journey. My hope is that the reader will enjoy and discover Brazil, the star of South America.

PROLOGUE

With swift determination, Ramon destroyed all the evidence. He knew that just one single shred of evidence would send him to the gallows, or worse, life behind bars in some godforsaken prison sunk in the Amazon jungle. Eleven murders in one day was a record for Britania and probably all of Brazil.

Pieces of glass were flying everywhere. Ramon's only tools included a sledgehammer and a pair of eye goggles. Hundreds of glass cages yielded large piles of sharp glass on the floor. Sweat poured from Ramon's forehead and trickled around the eye goggles.

The constant ringing of the telephone up on the first floor made Ramon anxious. The hospital was closed now that its owner was murdered. The ringing phone could be anyone but Ramon's gut told him it might be Vanessa Noqueira. Three days ago, he put her on a bus to Brasilia. Was she safe? Did she make it all the way to her sister's home? Did she need his help, or was she in some sort of trouble?

The phone rang again and Ramon sprinted to the nurse's station on the first floor. Out of breath he answered, "Vanessa?"

"No," replied the caller. "I am Dr. Castanovas and I'm calling for Dr. Noqueira. Is the doctor in?"

Still winded, Ramon asked, "What is your business with Dr. Noqueira?"

"I've been working months with Dr. Noqueira to set a time when I can come to Goiania to certify his serpentorium. Every time I call him he is too busy to see me, but we must complete this by the end of the year."

"Doctor," replied Ramon. "I have some very bad news to share with you. Dr. Noqueira was murdered three nights ago."

"That's horrible. I'm sorry to hear that. Who will be taking Dr. Noqueira's place in charge of the Templeton Institute?"

"Sir, you don't understand. There is no Dr. Noqueira, there is no laboratory, and there is no Templeton Institute. There is no longer anything here for you to certify."

An astounded Dr. Castanovas asked, "Can you please give me a name and a telephone number of a contact person there in Goiania for Dr. Noqueira in case we need to do any follow up?"

"No, there is no one left here," Ramon said as he hung up the phone without saying goodbye. After hanging up the phone, Ramon wondered why Dr. Castanovas thought that Dr. Noqueira's laboratory was in Goiania. Ramon guessed that Dr. Castanovas only had the Templeton Institute mailing address for wire transfers to the Bank of Goiania. If Dr. Noqueira was not sharing information about the location of the laboratory, then Ramon was not going to disclose that the Britania Hospital had just closed. Ramon's instincts told him that one more government investigator was not needed in Britania.

In the basement of the hospital, Ramon continued his cleanup work in the secret laboratory. Yesterday he boxed up most of the indigenous snakes and returned them to appropriate places in the nearby jungle or in the cooler highlands. He euthanized and buried all the exotic specimens. When all the glass cages were in small pieces, he boxed it all up and used a gurney to take the boxes to the hearse. He drove to a secluded tributary of the Araguaia River and dumped all the pieces knowing that they would quickly be churned back to sand in the fast moving water. No one would question, or even remember, Ramon driving around in the hearse because that was part of his job—to go get dead people and take them to the crematorium. And lately, he had been putting many miles on the old hearse.

Ramon returned to the secret laboratory and removed the hidden door and a section of wall to the lab. He opened it all back up to make it look like it was entirely the pathology laboratory. He worked for three days and nights straight with little sleep to get it done. After he finished all the carpentry work, he washed down all the floors, ceilings, and walls with three applications of chlorine followed by a bath of soapy water. Even the world's best forensic laboratory would find nothing in the basement. The nurses completed their work in closing up the hospital on the first day after the tragedy so Ramon used his key to access the hospital when no one else was around.

CHAPTER ONE

The old man caught me staring at his scarred face. All summer I wondered if he would tell me how he got the scar over his left eye that ran from his eyebrow to the bottom of his nostrils. I wondered how many people refused to talk to him because of his deformity.

"Machete," offered the frail old man. "It was a college hazing gone wrong."

"Marcus, among other things, you were a plastic surgeon. Couldn't you fix your own face?"

"I've had plenty of surgeries done and this is the best that can be done with it. My face was nearly cleaved in two so it's much better than it used to be. Frankie, did you study your list of verbs from last time?"

"Yes, a little. There are so many I will never get them straight." The old man calls me Frankie, something that I never let happen in the States. However, in Brazil that is the correct pronunciation. I should have gone by my middle name in Brazil because Alan is the same in English and Portuguese. As for my last name, the L's become an "eh" so Sullivan is pronounced Sue-eh-vahn. Marcus is my neighbor, friend, and volunteer language coach.

He asks, "Did you bring something new to read?"

"Yes, I have a new magazine and a fresh bottle of wine," I answered while pouring some cold wine for him. My price for Portuguese lessons

1

from my old neighbor was an occasional bottle of wine and paying attention to his stories. He especially liked telling stories that completely threw us off track from the lesson of the day.

In his garden terrace, Dr. Marcus Rosa declared, "In my country we drank only the best port wine." The stubborn man has lived in Brazil for over 80 years and he still considers his home country to be Portugal. He speaks with great reverence about Portugal, but of Brazil, he scoffs about the continuing struggles of the country. The greatest struggles in Brazil involve government corruption and illicit drugs. Of the government corruption, Dr. Rosa howls, "There are just stullers here; they are all just a bunch of snakes in the grass!"

While I challenge and tease him about his "home country," there is truth in what he says about the stullers in government. His English is perfect, yet he prefers to use the word "stullers" instead of thieves. In Portuguese, there is not the same "th" sound and it is as difficult for him to use as it is for me to make the "gszhr" sound that I've never mastered. Therefore, I let him use his made up word "stullers" and I know exactly his meaning.

I've been coming to Brazil for a dozen years and my Portuguese is *horrivel*, horrible. I stay only for the winter months and when I return to the States, I don't practice Portuguese so I forget everything until the next trip. I started coming to Brazil for my import business and over the years, business has gone from mediocre to bad. I used to make money from the devalued Brazilian Real by selling products at a premium for dollars. With the global economy, I now receive no discount on the products I buy in Brazil. I still make the annual pilgrimage because it gets me out of the snow in Colorado.

I own a condominium on an island near the town of Essenada. Dr. Rosa is a neighbor who owns a flat in a nearby building in the same complex. The office staff at the complex introduced us. Dr. Rosa did his internship and residency in Chicago so we had many things in common and became instant friends.

During language lessons, the old doctor loved to revisit his younger years to tell me stories of his experiences as a doctor in the jungle. Many of his stories were about a friend, another doctor, who developed a hospital from nothing. Dr. Rosa had a twinkle in his eye when he told these stories and I know he had a sense of both pleasure and remorse in the memories.

Dr. Rosa sank deeper into his rattan chair and sipped his wine. In an almost trance like state he took us back decades ago to tell about his itinerant practice serving the backcountry bordering the area served by the Britania Hospital. Dr. Rosa became very close friends with Roberto Noqueira, the Peruvian doctor who built the hospital out of an abandoned garage ten years earlier.

Every month the two men met to trade stories over an evening of excessive drinking. The men were physicians and it became a contest to tell the most outrageous stories. Both doctors were outcasts in the medical society of Brazil. They had the bad luck of being born outside of Brazil so their assignments were deep in the interior. The government of Brazil reserved the best jobs for those born within its borders.

Despite appearances from his old physical injuries, Dr. Rosa was a kind and generous soul. He told Dr. Noqueira, "Yesterday a patient told me this good story about three snakes who met in the jungle one day. The first snake was a Coral Snake and she asked the other two snakes what they did after they bite someone. The Lancehead Snake said she doesn't do anything special and she usually just slithers away. The Coral Snake replied that she usually bites children since they pick her up because she is so pretty. She said she likes to stay to listen to the wailing of the parents and sometimes she bites them too. The Cobra Snake was listening to all this and when the two first snakes stopped talking, she explained that she has to bite and then race away really fast before her victim falls on her and kills her."

Roberto replied, "That's funny and not far from the truth. This past week I treated a child bitten by a Lancehead and I wasn't sure that I could save him. He finally pulled around but I spent most of the week with him."

Marcus replied, "No, I never treated so many bites and poisons in my whole life since I moved here."

"So what made you leave the luxury of the big city to move to the jungle to treat malaria and snake bites?"

"Everything. My practice was literally sucking the life out of me. The 48-hour shifts were killing me. Look at me—I look a lot older than 55."

"No, you're just ugly. You can't blame that on old age," joked Roberto who thought his joke may have struck a raw nerve but he couldn't retract it with grace.

"Seriously, the stress of big city life and the OB/GYN schedule were sucking my life away. I needed a major change and I guess I got what I wanted."

"Yes, but you won't make the same money that you made in Rio de Janeiro."

"No, but the government stipend isn't bad. By the time you take away the high expenses of city life, I come out about the same. You must do pretty well. Look at that hospital of yours."

"Yes, I do ok. I make the same government stipend as you, but I make a little more selling prescriptions."

"Oh come on, you didn't just buy a new x-ray machine and add two new patient rooms from your earnings on prescriptions."

"Yes, I did! Vanessa and I live very cheaply here. The town gave us our house and we pay almost nothing for food. My patients who can't pay in cash for their prescriptions keep us stocked in produce and you keep me stocked with wine so I pay for nothing."

"You are very lucky. I have to pay my own expenses to travel my circuit and since I travel I can't carry around a supply of many drugs to sell."

"Why don't you flash your government card when you board the boats or when you enter a bus?"

"Oh, I do. No, I'm talking about general expenses of food and lodging on the road. I seldom pay for a hotel but I always pay for my food unless a family invites me for dinner."

The lovely Vanessa Noqueira came out to the veranda and sat beside her husband. Roberto met Vanessa at a medical conference in Brasilia when he was new to Britania. Vanessa is a *Carioca*, a native of Rio de Janeiro. She has long black hair and fine features. She looks very young and she wears the same size clothes she wore in high school. Vanessa quietly scolded the men, "If you continue drinking so much, you won't enjoy the chicken I've been cooking. I'll bring you some coffee and I'm taking away the wine."

"Vanessa," Roberto pleaded as she left the veranda with the bottle of wine.

"Your wife is a great cook. Noqueira, you're a lucky man all the way around."

"Yes, I am. I just wish we could have some children of our own. We try but Vanessa can't seem to get pregnant and every year she misses our chances fall. Marcus, you need to get yourself a wife."

"I have a wife. She is in São Paulo and I've not seen her since we divorced years ago."

"Then you are a free man and you should take a young beautiful wife. It will make you feel younger."

"Maybe, someday. I can't have a wife while I'm a traveling practitioner. If you take me on as a partner then I could have a wife."

"The Britania Hospital is too small right now to support both of us. When the time comes to take on a partner, I will definitely pick you."

After dinner, the two men continued their storytelling and to surpass Marcus, Roberto told a true story he seldom shared. "My friend Tad was a physician and sometimes I would cover his practice so he could have some time off. On this particular day, we were fishing in separate boats on a tributary of the Araguaia River in a section of slow moving water. We were certain that there were some big fish in this quiet part of the river. The area we fished was a huge deep eddy. Big trees from the nearby shore hung over the river making that part of the river very dark. The water contained a high concentration of tannic acid from decaying vegetation which made the water the color of black coffee."

"We moved our boats about 100 feet apart so we both could cast lures without getting tangled. Tad just asked me if I had any significant plans for the remainder of the year. I suppose he was getting ready to ask me to cover him for some holiday. I told him I was excited about getting to go to a medical conference in Rio de Janeiro in October. I was telling him all about the conference and he never said anything back to me so I looked his way and he was gone."

"There was no sign of him. He didn't jump in the water and swim to shore. I know he didn't jump or fall in the water because I would have felt the ripples in the water or I would have heard him. I had my back to him as I was speaking and when I turned to him, he simply vanished. I yelled for him but there was never a reply. I looked all over the river and there was no sign of him anywhere. After yelling until I because hoarse, I went to his boat and pulled up the anchor. I put the anchor in my boat, and rowed to shore. I walked up and down the shoreline and there was no finding him."

"I drove his car back to town and went to his house thinking perhaps he did slip into the water and went home to play a joke on me. I told his wife we were fishing and he disappeared. She became very hysterical thinking that her husband had drowned in the river. I tried to assure her he could not have drowned because he never fell out of the boat, he just vanished."

"I was asked by the police to stay in the nearby village until they finished an official inquest. The next day the police chief took me out to the spot on the river and I showed him where we were fishing and told him all about our trip, how long we were on the river, exactly where our boats were, and all the specifics about that day. They did a 'living autopsy' but that showed nothing unusual. The man didn't have a million dollar life insurance policy; he had no debts, no reason at all to escape his life."

"Finally they concluded that a giant Anaconda Snake came out of the trees from above and ate the man in one bite. They concluded that during the attack the big snake's mouth covered his face so he couldn't scream for help."

After listening to the story Marcus suggested, "That's crazy. I've never heard of such a thing except in the movies and that's pure fiction."

Roberto responded, "It may be in movies but it's true in real life. The giant Anaconda is really a giant and it would be no great feat for one to have taken my friend off his boat. Let me show you a magazine I have. It's in my study and I'll be right back."

Roberto brought back a stack of old National Geographic magazines. Roberto flipped through the pages and after a few minutes shouted, "Here, here, don't you think an animal this size could have easily eaten my friend in a second?"

Marcus studied the color photo and replied, "Is this a real photo or is it a fake?"

Roberto replied excitedly, "This magazine would never print the photograph of a fake. It's real. They found this dead giant Anaconda in the Amazon that died from choking on an adult alligator. It was 120 feet long and 18 feet in circumference. This monster was living near a native village when they found it."

Marcus continued to study the photograph and couldn't believe its size. There was a Brazilian army soldier on its back and the soldier was straddling it like riding a horse but his legs were parallel to the animal like someone doing the splits. Even if this man was small in stature, the giant snake could have eaten several men in one gulp. He replied, "Without the photo I would never believe that such an animal could exist. That monster was probably eating cattle at night."

"Yes," replied Roberto. "He had to eat a lot of things to reach that size. So, it's very possible that my friend was taken up into those trees and eaten by a giant Anaconda. The police organized a search for a giant Anaconda in the area but they found none. By the time they started looking, the beast was probably far away or perhaps just hiding nearby in the river."

A doubting Marcus asked, "If such a snake really exists, how would you escape from one if you encountered it? It's so large it would pounce on a human in a second. There would be no chance of outrunning it."

"I agree," answered Roberto. "I think if you saw one of these in the wild, there would be no escape. Fortunately, giant Anacondas of this size are very rare. I think they call it a 'sport' which means a mutation of sorts that sets the animal apart from others of the same species."

"Yes, I see this issue is dated 1958, so that is probably the largest giant Anaconda found since then. Without the photograph and story, I never would have believed that such an animal could exist on this planet. It really is a monster. I wonder how many people it ate during its lifetime."

Roberto explained, "It choked to death eating a large adult alligator so I suppose it ate people. People would have been easier for it to chase down than alligators. Additionally, humans would have been easier to digest than a whole alligator."

"After seeing that, I will be having nightmares all night long."

"Yes, and when you are traveling on the river you'd better keep a sharp eye out."

"Yes, I will. I do have to get up early tomorrow to catch an early boat. I'll see you in the morning before I leave. Thanks again for your hospitality. Good night."

CHAPTER TWO

Brazil was making a major push to get people out of the *favelas,*
slums, and into the sparsely populated areas of the interior.
When answering a recruitment call, Dr. Rosa had no idea
where he might end up. The government health department told him
he was responsible for the general health of the population for the
state of Tocantins and a small portion of the northern part of the state
of Goias. His territory was a large triangle of land bordered by the
Rivers Tocantins and Araguaia. There were no large cities within the
boundaries of his territory, just small villages and towns. The capital
city of Goias State is Goiania and it is a six-hour bus ride from the
southernmost part of his territory. Brasilia is another three-hour bus
ride beyond Goiania.

The government paid Dr. Rosa a monthly stipend and in exchange,
he was required to provide the general health care for the citizens within
his territory. A large part of his job was keeping records of all reported
cases of malaria, yellow fever, dengue, typhoid, hepatitis, typhus,
and cholera. In addition to the standard diseases, he also reported a
wide range of little-known tropical diseases. He was free to treat any
disease or conditions to the extent of his abilities. Dr. Rosa's skills
were especially suited for jungle work since he was a trained OB/GYN
with extra training in general and plastic surgery, ophthalmology, and

family practice. The government paid him the same amount whether he treated one or one thousand patients per month.

When Dr. Rosa first arrived in Tocantins State, he took out his maps and drew up a schedule to visit every community in the state on a rotation of four weeks. He made his rounds by bus and riverboat so transportation from village to village took up most of his time. On each of his monthly visits, Dr. Rosa would bring the Noqueiras an unusual gift from one of the jungle villages he visited. The Noqueiras were glad to have his company and Dr. Rosa always stayed with them when he visited. Vanessa was glad to have the company of an outsider.

Britania is a farming community in the highlands of Brazil. The farming and ranching is limited by what the poor clay soils can sustain. Around Britania, most of the large ranches used the land only for grazing. Typical of Brazilian farming, large tracts of land are burned and planted. The "slash and burn" method of farming yields a good crop the first year, an average crop in the second year, and dismal yields in the remaining years. The ash neutralizes the soil and provides good nutrients but it is soon washed away by wind and rain.

Britania is the commercial center for this large rural area. The town has a population of over 10,000 and provides all the shopping needs for famers in the large surrounding area. There are several supermarkets and many smaller specialty markets, three banks, and a host of other stores and shops.

When Marcus pressed Roberto again for the two of them to share the workload of the growing hospital, Roberto explained "There just isn't enough work for two doctors at the hospital yet. To be honest with you, it may be years before we need two doctors. Britania isn't growing much because we are so far from other commercial centers. Marcus, I will save all the plastic surgery and all the eye surgery cases for you. I'll schedule them to coincide with your monthly visits."

"Thanks Roberto, I will appreciate the opportunity to spend some additional time with you and Vanessa."

During one of his monthly visits, Marcus reported directly to the hospital and the nurses told him that Dr. Noqueira was sick at home. The nurses already scheduled Marcus to do several eye surgeries and the full workload of Dr. Noqueira. At the end of a very long workday, Dr. Rosa went to the Noqueira home and found Dr. Noqueira nursing a broken foot. In addition, the beaten doctor also had cuts and bruises on his battered face. He had a badly blackened eye and a large cut across his left temple. Vanessa was frantic.

Marcus asked, "Who did the stitches? I recognize the handiwork!"

Roberto Noqueira laughed saying, "It's a lot easier to put stitches in someone else than to do your own. It's looking pretty good by now; you should have seen me yesterday."

"So what happened to you?" Marcus asked.

After the customary glasses of wine were poured, Dr. Noqueira explained, "Several weeks ago the big rancher here, Carlo Roberio, approached me asking me to sell the hospital to him. His oldest son has just graduated from medical school and Carlos wants Augusto to stay here to practice in Britania. Carlos figures that if he gives Augusto a hospital, the son will stay and not return to Rio to practice medicine. I told Carlos that I would not sell and I told him that Britania is a one-doctor town so he hired some guy to come get me. Last night when I left the hospital, out of the dark comes this guy I've never seen. He grabbed me around the neck, threw me to the ground, and then started kicking me in the face. I was certain he was going to kill me but he left me on the ground there by my car. I went back inside the hospital and put in my own stitches."

Shocked, Marcus asked, "Did the police catch the guy?"

"No, I won't be bothering the police about this. This is a matter between Sr. Roberio and me. Besides, Roberio has enough money to pay off all three of our policemen, our mayor, and anyone else who has a problem with what he does."

"Who is Carlos Roberio and how is it he seems to own this town?"

"Carlos Roberio owns one of the largest farms in the state. His land begins six miles west of town and extends all the way over to the lowlands of Mato Grosso. His ranch produces most of the cattle for the area and he has large tracts of land for coffee and soybeans. He has over a hundred men working his fields and he has never done a day of labor in his entire life. He manages one person who manages dozens of farm supervisors. He paid almost nothing for that land. Actually, his father stole the land in the big land grab of the 1950's by bribing some officials in the government. When they got the land, they cut out the hardwood for timber and then burned the remaining land after chasing away or killing off the Indians living on the land. When Carlos was a teenager, he used to brag about how many Indians he killed on his land every week. He has so much land that by working it as a corporate entity, he has made millions from it."

The injured doctor confessed, "I have another problem. I've made an enemy out of the local pharmacist, Davis Lemas. He overcharges our people so I've been selling drugs from the hospital instead of sending patients to him. He diagnoses and treats patients without consulting me, so it's only fair for me to be a pharmacist. I'm pretty certain he has joined forces with Carlos Roberio and I don't think they will stop until they run me out."

Marcus was shocked and tried to persuade his friend to leave town, "They don't have that right and should not have power over you. However, I can see you are outnumbered and have no resources for fighting them. I think you should move your entire hospital over to Itapirapua or São Luis de Montes Belos. Both communities are more prosperous than Britania and both are closer to Goiania and Brasilia. I know a tract of land over in Itapirapua that is for sale for a bargain and it would be a great location for your new hospital. I'll even help you move your medical equipment and beds over there."

"No, I can't do it. I've got too much invested in this hospital to just give it up. Besides, I can't build a new hospital overnight. Ramon, my maintenance man, and I have been working years to get my hospital in its present condition. I just can't walk away from everything that we've worked so hard to build."

"Yes, it will be a lot of hard work to move, but it's better to move than to be permanently planted here. At the very least, let's go over to Itapirapua and look at the location that I have in mind for you. If you don't like it, then let's run over to São Luis and check things out there."

"No, I'm staying here. I won't be bullied into leaving my property behind."

"Then please take my shotgun that I use to chase off the bandits. I'll leave the gun and some shells with Ramon and you be sure to have him drive you home each night and pick you up each morning. They shouldn't bother you if you stick together. And try to get away from the hospital before dark each night. You don't want them coming out of the shadows again so don't give them the opportunity."

"Oh great, besides being beaten, I'll also accidentally shoot myself. No thanks!"

Vanessa Noqueira had been quietly listening to the men's conversation and now felt compelled to add her opinion. "Roberto, we can't stay in this community if it's not safe for us. Why do you want to stay if the community wants us to leave? We need to do as Marcus suggests and move to Itapirapua. You can't live in this town and go around having a nightly shooting match with your enemies."

Marcus continued his description of the property in Itapirapua and listed all the reasons why they should move. He made his best arguments to encourage the Noqueiras to relocate and to do so quickly. The Noqueiras listened with interest and it seemed that Marcus was making progress in getting Roberto to consider the move.

Dr. Rosa stayed a few more days in Britania to help Dr. Noqueira get caught up with his surgeries and until the injured doctor could navigate on crutches. When Dr. Noqueira was not around, Dr. Rosa had a private conversation with Ramon. Ramon was a hard-working young man who was the sole builder and maintenance man of the hospital. Ramon Gobbey was in his early twenties, outgoing, and always had a good word for everyone. Nothing about his personal appearance drew attention to him other than his cheerful personality. He was slender and average in height so he looked like any other young man from rural Brazil.

Dr. Rosa gave Ramon a burlap sack containing his shotgun and a large box of shells. He told Ramon, "Don't be shy about using the gun if Roberto is attacked again. Drive the doctor home in the evenings before sunset and pick him up in the mornings. Dr. Noqueira must never be left alone. You've been promoted Ramon. Your most important job now is providing security for Dr. Noqueira."

"I'll try my best," replied Ramon. "But you know Roberto is very stubborn. I know he will give me the slip and go off on his own."

"You can't let that happen. You have to be a part-time spy and keep track of him every minute. Maybe by my next visit they will decide to move the hospital to another town." Dr. Rosa left Ramon and Britania to continue the circuit through his assigned territory.

CHAPTER THREE

Unknown to Marcus and even to Vanessa Noqueira was a secret held only by Dr. Noqueira and Ramon. The secret was the reason why Dr. Noqueira refused to move his hospital to another town.

The real luxury of building your own business from the ground up is what you can do from the ground up. When Roberto and Ramon built the patient rooms for the hospital, they built the rooms over a very large basement. In the basement, there were several storage rooms. In one corner of the basement was the pathology laboratory where tissue samples were stored. Lining the far wall of the pathology lab was a shelving unit with many glass jars. Each jar contained formaldehyde and a single tissue sample. The door to the pathology lab could be locked from either side. Once inside the pathology lab, a hidden latch was pulled and the entire wall of shelving pulled away to reveal a hidden doorway to a much larger room.

In the center of the room, there was a worktable and two chairs. The table contained a variety of specialized equipment. Strong lights mounted over the table gave a clue to the delicate nature of the work performed in this area.

In the large room, there were six long rows of wooden shelves. All of the shelves contained multiple glass boxes. Each glass box contained a heavy lid and inside each box resided one or more of Brazil's most poisonous snakes, the secret reason for Dr. Noqueira's success and the reason why Dr. Noqueira could never relocate his hospital.

In this hidden laboratory, the two men would milk the venomous snakes for their toxins, which they would then send to locations around the world. Pharmacies, research laboratories, and zoos from all over the world would turn the venom into antivenin by injecting tiny amounts into horses or lambs. Over a long period, the animals developed antibodies to the venom and the final product would save lives.

The pharmacies also have other commercial applications for the dangerous venom. A number of pharmaceutical products have been derived from snake venom. The venom of the Bothrops pit viper led to the discovery of Beta Blockers for cardiovascular disease. Many analgesic and anesthetic medications owe their development to snake venom. Research is also ongoing for the application of various types of venom on nerve diseases such as Epilepsy and Parkinson's. Other researchers are working to develop new drugs for cardiovascular disease, pulmonary diseases, and viral or bacterial infections.

While Dr. Noqueira and Ramon worked in the secret laboratory, they talked as they worked on the easy parts of their job. While applying labels to vials, Dr. Noqueira asked, "Ramon, of the 2,700 different species of snakes in the world, what percent do you think are poisonous?"

"Probably about the same percent as here in Brazil—about half of them."

"No," answered Dr. Noqueira, "Only a little more than ten percent. There are only about 300 species that are dangerous to humans."

"Yes," answered Ramon. "But how dangerous? Probably some of those 300 hardly do anything while some others kill so fast there is no chance of saving someone from a bite. Like the Green Darters, they kill so fast that victims don't even have the time to say ouch before they die."

"You're correct about that. Some snakes do very little harm while others kill instantly. It all depends on the toxicity of the venom and the volume. For the Green Darters, volume doesn't matter because of the very high toxicity. Some of our big snakes produce so much volume that a single bite could kill 40 people if administered in individual doses."

"Who would want to take a dose of venom?"

"No one, I'm just making the point. Those big snakes like the Bushmaster inject way more venom than necessary to kill a human."

Ramon asked, "What makes victims die differently? Green Darters kill instantly but Jararacussu victims take five minutes and then they start melting away. I'd rather die by Cobra, you just fall asleep."

"That's the difference in the kinds of chemical compounds in their venom," answered Dr. Noqueira. "Most snakes have a combination of compounds in their venom which kills the prey and helps in the digestive process. Your little Green Darters have only neurotoxin in their venom. It's the fastest toxin and it goes straight to the central nervous system and shuts everything down. It's very similar to electrocution."

"And Jararacussus, what do they have?"

"Their venom is mostly Cytotoxins, which break down cell membranes. That's why their victims melt away. It's great venom for a snake that eats larger animals."

Ramon offered, "That explains why a Jararacussu can eat another snake its same size or larger. As soon as the head goes in the snake, its already being digested. Makes sense. And Cobras, what do they have?"

"Mostly hemotoxins and cardiotoxins, plus another compound that is a sedative. That's why victims fall asleep."

While the men worked in the secret laboratory, they walked past the glass cages and there was always the loud tap, tap, tap sound made by the more aggressive snakes striking the side the glass. The loudest strikes were made by the strongest and most aggressive snakes. The large aggressive snakes were the Neotropical Rattlesnake, Bushmaster, Jararacussu, and Gray Cobra. These snakes were always on the lookout for something to attack. Most of these monsters were also the most poisonous. An important exception was the smallest snake. The tiny Green Darter was the most deadly and it never made a sound.

In terms of being a successful business, the secret laboratory was a smash hit. It brought the men cash from industrialized countries. All customers of the laboratory had the ability to pay and they always paid in advance of receiving their shipments.

The advantage of making the laboratory a secret, hidden, enterprise was not to throw off the tax collector. Mostly it was based on the history of the two men working together. They had the space available for the laboratory in the basement of the hospital. The space was convenient for use by both of the men. However, "Snake Laboratory" and "Hospital" are not two things that one can mix under the same roof. Patients would never come to a hospital if they knew the basement was full of deadly snakes. If the residents of Britania got wind of the secret laboratory, they would mount a protest to have it closed down. That sort of enterprise belongs out in the jungle, away from people. Once the laboratory was in business as a secret, its status could not be changed.

Roberto and Ramon each had their own areas of expertise in the snake business. Ramon was the snake handler and he was responsible for collecting all the specimens. It was his job to keep his captives well nourished and healthy so they would provide a potent quality of venom.

As a child, Ramon grew up on a nearby farm and his childhood hobby of collecting snakes led him to his part-time career as a snake curator. His knowledge of snakes included everything about their diet, temperament, and handling.

Ramon's mother died before he was a teenager, leaving his father as the sole caretaker of the family farm. When Dr. Noqueira and Ramon first starting making antivenin, it was Ramon's horse on the family farm that helped them develop their first antivenin. Soon, more horses and some lambs were added to the farm and Dr. Noqueira paid Ramon's father for their care and feeding.

Ramon and Roberto spent some time each weekend at the Gobbey farm. Dr. Noqueira checked on the animals and kept a logbook on the progress of each animal. Each animal could be used to make only one antivenin and then it was retired as a laboratory animal. The retired animals were given away except for Ramon's horse named Storm, a big black gelding. While Roberto was checking the livestock, Ramon would wander through the forest looking for fresh specimens for the snake laboratory. On several occasions, Roberto joined Ramon for a walk through the jungle but Roberto was nervous being in the snakes' habitat. He preferred the snakes being in glass cages where he knew they couldn't strike him. The doctor did have a scientific curiosity about the natural habitat of each species and he wanted to see where each kind of snake lived and what it ate in the wild.

In the business partnership, it was Dr. Noqueira's job to find buyers for the raw serum and antivenin. Dr. Noqueira also handled the business end of the project, by doing the invoicing, billing, and accounting. He invested in labeling equipment and used only first quality glass vials imported from Italy. The packaging of the product looked first rate, even by American and European standards. His competition was the large government sponsored laboratory in São Paulo so he had to make his product superior in every way to earn the respect of repeat customers.

Their only competitor, São Paulo's Instituto do Viperidae was a constant thorn to Dr. Noqueira. The Instituto was funded by the taxpayers of Brazil. Thus, the people there had more money than they needed. With too much money and too many workers, the management of the Instituto felt compelled to reach out to others in the serum business. Dr. Vitor Castanovas was the scientist in charge and he felt that he had to come to Goiania to control and license Dr. Noqueira's operation. Dr. Noqueira was normally a very serious and respectful person, but Vitor Castanovas brought out the worst in him. The two professional men fought like jealous children.

Dr. Noqueira answered his weekly call from Vitor, "No, I'm not available this week. I am busy all week. I must prepare for a lecture I am giving to the University of Columbia in Medellin. Yes, I will be there for a couple weeks and when I return, it will not be good at all because I will need to catch up on business. Why don't you try calling me again in four weeks?" Dr. Noqueira could not resist telling lies to Dr. Castanovas because it was so much fun to provoke the scientist. Dr. Noqueira would always tell Vitor he had just spoken at this conference or that, just to agitate the self-important scientist. At least once, during every conversation Roberto would inject that he was a "real doctor," just to further irritate him. Roberto imagined that the self-important Dr. Castanovas looked like a lab rat, with a short little mustache and thick glasses.

On the other end of the line Vitor was getting angry, "Now listen here, Noqueira, it's my job to come certify your operation. If you won't cooperate with me, then I will just have to shut down your laboratory."

Roberto replied, "I have a better idea. Why don't I certify your operation? After all, I am the renowned medical doctor who is the authority in all such matters in all of Latin America. I think it would be much more appropriate for me to certify your operation."

Vitor angrily snorted, "No, you are not the authority. I am! And if I do not get to inspect your laboratory by the end of the year, I shall have it ordered to be shut down."

Roberto replied while laughing, "Why Vitor, if you wanted a tour why didn't you just ask? What, do you need me to show you how to do something? You do not need to bother coming all the way here. Just call and ask me, I will tell you anything you need to know. Ok, I actually do have business to complete so I must go. Talk to you next month. *Tchau.*"

Dr. Noqueira was not sure how long he could keep offending Dr. Castanovas that way. He smiled just thinking about all the grief that he was giving the scientist. At first, Dr. Noqueira worried that Dr. Castanovas might actually come to the laboratory but with each phone call, Roberto could see that the bureaucrat was just so much hot air. Roberto wished that Dr. Castanovas had never found him. Actually, the scientist really did not find him. Dr. Castanovas was under the impression that Dr. Noqueira worked out of Goiania and Roberto did not correct him. Castanovas latched on to him because most research laboratories require the same serum from two separate sources for cross validity. Obviously, one of Dr. Noqueira's customers had passed on the address for the Templeton Institute's "home office" used for the receipt of international money transfers.

In the laboratory, Dr. Noqueira really did have work to do. He was busy getting another large shipment of serum ready to ship to locations around the world. Because the serum had a short shelf life after harvesting, it was refrigerated and fresh venom was quickly sent to buyers each week. For outgoing shipments, Roberto or Ramon would take the vials packed in ice to Goiania by taking the midnight bus. Ramon ended up making most of the bus trips to Goiania. People often asked Ramon why he was carrying packages to the bus station so frequently. He just told them that he was taking tissue samples to the pathology laboratory in Goiania. Very often, he did have to deliver tissue samples and usually there was at least one package for the pathology laboratory.

It was easy for Dr. Noqueira to keep his nighttime job a secret. His customers all lived in time zones different from Brazil so he made sales calls to contacts in other countries during the night. He told Vanessa he was working late at the hospital and he told the nurses in the hospital that he was working in the pathology lab. He instructed the nurses not to disturb him in the lab except by paging him on the PA system.

His international customers paid by wire transfer to his bank in Goiania, in care of The Templeton Institute. Dr. Noqueira thought that the made up name had a sense of respectability to it. After all, anything that sounded English immediately drew a positive response from people in most nations around the world.

Once per month Dr. Noqueira took the midnight trip to Goiania. He followed Ramon's routine delivering the refrigerated boxes to the airport. While he was there, he also did his banking and reconciled the account receivables. Because he had to wait for the bank to open, he could not take the early bus back to Britania so he missed an entire day of work at the hospital. He left his nurses in charge of things and he told them that he had a standing appointment with the pathologist in Goiania. This was not stretching the truth too much as, indeed; he usually met with the pathologist during his trips.

Upon his return, Dr. Noqueira split the proceeds evenly with Ramon. This was the most money Ramon had ever seen and was more money than any working person in Britania had ever seen. Ramon was quickly becoming a very rich man even by North American standards. Dr. Noqueira insisted that their partnership split the profits evenly, for if there were no Ramon, there would be no laboratory. Most partnerships in Brazil fail because one of the parties becomes greedy and wants to do everything and take all the money. Their partnership was successful because each partner brought separate skills and talents, which the other partner could not do. Both men realized this as a strength of the partnership but it was a liability in case anything bad happened to one of them. Dr. Noqueira had neither skills nor interest in going into the jungle to collect snakes. Ramon, on the other hand, had neither skills nor interest in trying to sell the product and do the business tasks.

The only task that both men enjoyed doing was milking the venom. For the big snakes, this was a two-person job and they would take turns handling the fangs. When they first started, the two men practiced snake-handling techniques with non-venomous snakes before handling the dangerous ones. Each man had to know exactly what the other was going to do. When handling snakes that kill instantly, there was no time to depend upon verbal communication. They had practiced the drill and had it down instinctively.

Ramon kept his newfound wealth a secret and he spent only the money he earned as a laborer for the Britania Hospital. He trusted no one and kept the money hidden in a large hole below a floor tile in the kitchen of his apartment.

Dr. Nogueira also lived modestly, spending for himself only the money from his government stipend. All of the earnings from the Templeton Institute went to pay for the expansion of the hospital, the new medical equipment, and the medications he gave out to patients.

Ramon's secret earnings were kept hidden and had no impact on the Britania community. Dr. Nogueira's secret earnings did have an impact on the community and that impact would adversely affect him.

Carlos Roberio saw the continuing improvements and new construction at the Britania Hospital as a sign of its financial success. With every new improvement made to the hospital, Carlos became more and more convinced that his son should own the successful hospital and stay in Britania. Carlos' motives were to keep his eldest son, Augusto, close to home rather than returning to Rio de Janeiro to practice medicine. Augusto was indifferent. He would just as soon return to Rio de Janeiro, but if his father was going to buy him a successful hospital then he could see himself as the big fish in the small pond. This was especially true for Augusto if the hospital was handed to him with no effort spent on his part.

At the secret laboratory, one of the most unusual and quiet residents of the laboratory was not a single snake but rather a colony of snakes. Actually, it might be better described as a "hive." The Green Darter is a tiny pit viper native only to the States of Goias and Tocantins. It thrives only where the jungle meets the high savannah plains. Green Darters live on very small rodents and insects so they prefer to build their hives in grasslands. When grasslands meet the jungle, there exists the tiny rodents that they prefer to eat. These are ground snakes and they are never found in trees in the jungle. Green Darters are the smallest of all the deadly snakes and tiny is a good description for them because they never reach more than a foot in length. In their hive, they look more like a seething mass of yellow-green worms. Their vivid yellow-green color is perfect camouflage for their environment because it matches the color of the grasslands of Goias and Tocantins.

They get their darter name from their hunting behavior. In the grasslands, they quickly dart about in search of prey. Pit vipers do not get their name from living in pits, but some, including Green Darters do live in underground burrows. Pit vipers are so named because of the heat sensing pits on both sides of their face, just above the jaw line. These heat sensors tell the snake where to strike. While their eyesight is good, their eyes give them no direct sight. Since their eyes are on the sides of their heads, they see all around but not directly ahead. Pit vipers, bothrops, and rattlesnakes all have large triangular heads because the venom glands in the head take up so much room. Large triangular heads are not a requirement for a snake to be venomous. Some of the most poisonous snakes, like the Coral and the Green Darters, have narrow heads.

Farmers and ranchers in the states of Goias and Tocantins know all about Green Darters and when they see a dead animal in their pasture, they are immediately suspicious and very careful. If there are two or more dead carcasses together then the rancher is certain that he has a Green Darter problem. The ranchers know they cannot do a detailed check while on horseback because the Green Darters will strike the horse and it will immediately fall and dump the rider on the ground to be bitten as well. When there are dead carcasses, a single ranch hand makes the inspection on foot wearing thick leather boots.

Upon finding a colony of Green Darters, the rancher must take steps to get rid of it before it expands and makes new colonies. Livestock must be kept out of the infected field. The next step is to burn the entire affected field to be certain all the Green Darters are killed. Ranchers in Brazil are accustomed to using flame-throwing equipment because they burn off their fields every few years anyway. The regimen for burning out Green Darters is a little more intense. After the initial burning, the field is continuously burned for three days by adding diesel and napalm. Next, the field is allowed to cool for a day so the soil can be tilled with equipment and the burning process is repeated. This process is expensive and costs the ranchers several thousand dollars for each colony discovered. It's a process that must be done or the land is useless for agricultural purposes.

Dr. Noqueira spent months calling his contacts trying to sell the venom of the Green Darters. Despite his calls to all his current customers and cold calls to new prospects, he was turned down repeatedly. Everyone was too afraid to handle a toxin that would kill instantly. Most of his colleagues thought the venom was useless for the purpose of making antivenin since any victim would be dead before the antivenin could be given. Dr. Noqueira was certain there would be medical applications to a dilute form of the venom. However, the pharmaceutical companies were all too afraid to handle the deadly toxin. They cited "what ifs" of needle sticks or a broken container. They did not want their researchers dying on the spot and no one could blame them.

Dr. Noqueira thought he might have better luck selling the Green Darter venom if he had an antivenin to sell with it. Since the Green Darter venom works so quickly, the antivenin would have to be given prior to handling the snakes. He tried to dilute Green Darter venom to one part per thousand for an antivenin but all he could do was kill off horses. Using his best titrating skills, he kept diluting the venom but each time it killed the animal. Finally, he was using one part per several million and the animal did not immediately die. Unfortunately, on the visit to the farm the following weekend, he discovered the horse staggering around and he had to euthanize it. That's when Dr. Noqueira decided that they didn't have enough horses and the right equipment to attempt to make an antivenin of the Green Darter so they gave up.

CHAPTER FOUR

D r. Noqueira was about to give up trying to market the Green Darter venom and the discussions he had with the companies made him think that he shouldn't be handling the snakes either. He knew that the "what ifs" also applied to him. One bite to him or Ramon and the entire laboratory would cease operations. It would mean the closure of the secret laboratory and the liquidation of the cash held by the Templeton Institute if either man died while handling the Green Darters.

Unexpectedly, a call came from a foreigner wanting to buy the deadly toxin, "My name is Max Schuman and I own a research laboratory here in Frankfurt. A colleague of mine, Hubert Stein, suggested that I call you because he was interested in your highly toxic venom but he doesn't have the facilities for properly handling it."

"Yes, Sr. Stein buys a lot of venom from us and he has always been happy with our product."

"Can you tell me, Dr. Noqueira, is this venom stable as a dry substance or is it toxic only in its original liquid state?"

"We have done limited trials here, but it is toxic in a powdered form. It takes a little longer to enter the bloodstream of course, but the results that we see point to it being as effective in a dry and stabilized form."

"Doctor, we will need a lot of the venom in both dry and liquid form. Can you produce 100 vials by this time next week and what will be the tariff for such an order? Maybe you should make it 75 vials liquid and 25 vials powdered."

"Yes, certainly we can ship that to you by the end of next week. For 100 vials, the cost will be $27,000 plus shipping. Are you sure that you need so much?"

"Yes, 100 vials will do for now. No, I wouldn't trust that kind of shipment. Please, just hold it and I will send my courier to you. That way I can be assured of its safe arrival to my laboratory. Just give me the details where I should send my courier."

The conversation ended and each man had managed to withhold their secrets without resorting to telling too many lies. Max Schuman didn't mention that his laboratory was a weapons manufacturing plant. His interest in the venom was not as a pharmaceutical but as an advanced weapon. The lethal venom applied to a bullet guaranteed that an assassin's bullet would be a kill no matter how insignificant the wound. Such a weapon would forever change the world. Bulletproof vests would be outdated overnight. Max Schuman stood at the threshold between the east and the west and he would sell his deadly product to the highest bidders. Max stood to make more money off the development of this weapon than anything else his plant had made and sold during the cold war.

Dr. Noqueira didn't mention that his laboratory was a secret and that he had no intention of letting someone walk in and "purchase off the shelf." However, the doctor was desperate to make a sale on the Green Darter venom and he would have to work around it. He would have Ramon set up some kind of dummy showroom in the basement of the hospital before the courier arrived.

A week later, Dr. Noqueira received a call from Otto Monk who said he was staying at the hotel in Britania. Max Schuman sent him to pick up a parcel for delivery back to Germany. Dr. Noqueira told Otto that the order was not yet complete and it would be the next day before the order would be ready. The two men arranged to meet at 10 a.m. the next morning at the Britania Hospital. Dr. Noqueira and Ramon were so busy getting the vials of venom ready that there was no time to build any kind of reception area in the basement. The German courier would just have to come into the secret laboratory after all.

The two men met at the front door of the Britania hospital precisely at 10 a.m. and shook hands. Dr. Noqueira thought that Otto looked more like a hit man than a courier. The doctor did not trust Otto from the moment they met. On the way to the basement laboratory, Dr. Noqueira explained he had just a few of the snakes to milk to finish the last vial. Ramon was not present because he was busy with his hospital duties and only one man could milk the tiny snakes. The doctor explained that the liquid venom had to be extracted at the last minute because it had to be fresh and kept on ice until its arrival in Frankfurt. Otto was ushered into the laboratory and asked to have a seat while the last vial was completed. Otto refused to sit and instead paced the room checking out the big snakes and occasionally tapping the glass cages to make an aggressive snake strike.

"Please don't do that. It makes them crazy," the doctor warned.

"Here is the payment in cash," Otto said as he slapped a large envelope on the table.

Still pacing, Otto asked, "What do you feed these big snakes?"

"Mostly rats and rabbits," the doctor replied. He could feel that Otto was now standing directly behind him and he heard Otto make some sort of noise. While handling one of the tiny deadly snakes, Dr. Noqueira looked up with just his eyes to see the reflection of Otto on the glass cages. He could clearly see that Otto had a pistol and it was aimed directly to the back of his head. With one quick motion, the doctor took the Green Darter from the vial and plunged the snake's fangs into the thigh of the hit man standing behind him. Otto didn't make a sound. No grunts, no sighs, nothing. Otto hit the concrete floor and was dead before he landed.

The metal pistol hit the floor with a loud clang as Dr. Noqueira gasped to catch his breath. While he correctly guessed the true nature of the hit man, he was still shocked that someone would come into his work place and try to kill him. He took a few minutes to collect his thoughts and then went over to Otto and placed a towel over his face. With his right foot he stomped on Otto's face as hard as he could, being certain to smash the dead man's nose into his brain. Dr. Noqueira was also the medical examiner for the region and he would simply tag Otto as a car accident victim and would have Ramon haul him off to the crematorium in the morning. The doctor went to the morgue and returned with a gurney to haul Otto away.

After Otto was safely stowed away, Dr. Noqueira called Max Schuman with the intention of using as many obscene words as he could. When Max answered his phone the doctor yelled, "You lousy bastard, you son of a bitch, you sent your courier here to kill me. You no good piece of shit."

In a completely calm voice Max replied, "I'm sorry you're upset. Please, slow down and tell me what happened. I have no idea what you are shouting about." Max knew exactly what the other man was saying because he was the one who ordered Otto to come home with the venom, the cash, and no witnesses to the transaction.

"Your son of a bitch courier just tried to kill me in my own laboratory. I was finishing your order and I saw him point a pistol to the top of my head so now he is dead," shouted the outraged physician.

Calmly Max reassured Dr. Noqueira, "Oh my. That was never my intention. I simply arranged for Otto to pick up the vials and bring them back to me. Perhaps he foolishly became greedy and decided to keep all that money for himself. Surely you cannot hold me responsible for his very poor judgment."

"I swear, if I ever find out that you knew anything about this, then I will come to Germany and personally hunt you down."

"You need not worry yourself about that. I swear I knew nothing about any attempt at killing you. Why on earth would I want to do that! You are my single source for this exotic venom and if I were going to kill you, then I would have no other source. Now, why would I do such a thing?"

Feeling his blood pressure wane, the doctor replied, "I have no idea why. I've never met you and you are a stranger to me. All I know about you is that one of my good customers referred you to me. I have no idea what your motives are."

"Oh, Dr. Noqueira, my motives are the same as any other laboratory researcher. My motives are to make the world a better and safer place. Surely you understand that I had nothing whatsoever to do with this bad thing that happened there. Let us conclude our current business deal so we can move on to continue a trusting business relationship. Without my courier, I will need you to ship the venom, as you originally wanted to do. To smooth things over and to pay for your shipping costs I will wire to you today an additional $10,000 for your troubles. Is that acceptable?"

"Yes, of course it is. The shipment will leave Brasilia tomorrow morning and will arrive in Germany before noon the next day."

"Thank you and please put this all behind you and consider it an unfortunate mistake made by someone I should not have trusted so well. Otto was my sister's husband so I will need to make the arrangements to receive his body here in Frankfurt."

Thinking quickly the doctor replied, "He will be cremated and the remains will be sent to you."

"Yes, that is acceptable. Please keep a record of your expenses related to this and I shall have that amount also wired to your account. Now, is there anything else we need to do to conclude this transaction?"

"No, there isn't," replied the doctor.

"Then goodbye for now," and the phone went dead on Max's end.

Otto was taken to the crematorium, his ashes were sent to Max Schuman along with a phony death certificate, and a bill for services rendered. The event was over and Dr. Noqueira was safe at least for the time being. He still had a sinking feeling in his gut that the whole transaction with Max Schuman was not right. He thought of telling Ramon about it but he really didn't want to involve Ramon in a murder scheme. After mentally reviewing every detail, he felt Ramon was better off not knowing anything about it.

Reluctantly Dr. Noqueira told Ramon, "I just have a bad feeling about working with the Green Darter venom. It's just too dangerous for us to handle. I'm afraid you'll have to euthanize the hive and clean out their cage."

Ramon agreed but when Dr. Noqueira was not around, he put the hive in a metal bucket with a secure lid and drove ten miles out to the countryside where he harvested the hive. He quickly found their burrow and it was unoccupied so he carefully removed the metal lid from the bucket and released the hive back into their burrow. Although very dangerous as a single snake, the hive was not dangerous. Since they had been juggled around in the car during their ride, the hive was now bound in one tight ball. Even when the ball of snakes landed in the burrow, they remained tightly packed together as a defense mechanism.

Three evenings later the two men worked in the lab to get a big shipment ready to send out. They had shipments going to the United States, Canada, Thailand, South Africa, Spain, and Russia. There were many cartons going to different locations in the United States. After expenses, the two men would be splitting around $120,000 from the shipments. With this much money, Ramon could buy a nice house for himself. For Dr. Noqueira it meant a couple more patient exam rooms and more medications for his patients. It was a nice profit for all the hard work put into the project.

Dr. Noqueira attached the labels while triple checking the lot numbers and the contents. There was no margin for error in this dangerous business, not with handling the snakes, and not with mistakes about venom content. Ramon put the vials for each location in separate zip lock plastic bags and adjacent to those he placed another zip lock bag of ice. Once he arrived in Goiania, he replaced the ice with dry ice.

After midnight, Ramon was on the bus to Goiania. Ramon placed the parcels in the cargo hold of the bus. He would sleep until the bus arrived in Goiania around 6 a.m. After the bus arrived in Goiania, Ramon woke a sleeping taxi driver friend who took him over to the plant that produces the dry ice. The driver waited until Ramon finished repacking with dry ice. After all the boxes were sealed, Ramon loaded up the taxi and they drove to the airport.

Ramon's friend waited while he checked in the express airfreight. His driver friend knew that Ramon had to be back to the bus station before 8 a.m. to make the return bus to Britania. By 10 a.m. that morning all the boxes would be at the airport in Brasilia and by noon the next day they would all arrive at their international destinations. Frequently Ramon had to rush over to the pathology lab to deliver a tissue sample after his work was complete with the air shipments. In this instance, he and his driver friend had to rush to catch the bus before it left for Britania. By 8 a.m. Ramon was on the bus—the man who worked as a carpenter and laborer by day would soon be back in Britania."

CHAPTER FIVE

D r. Rosa left Dr. Noqueira and Vanessa to continue his rotation to the northern part of Tocantins where the Rivers Araguaia and Tocantins meet. He did his usual month long rotation through the villages and then started his return south to Goias and Britania. As he got closer to Goias, he purchased some gifts for the Noqueiras as he always did. He was excited when he arrived in Britania because he would soon see his friends. Right after he got off the bus, he heard an old man shouting his name. He recognized the man as a patient for whom he performed eye surgery. The old man came running after him. For a moment, Dr. Rosa thought the man might be angry over some additional loss of sight after the operation.

"Doctor, Doctor, I have awful news for you," panted the old man. Several other villagers were joining the old man and Dr. Rosa wondered why he was being attacked.

"Your friend, Dr. Noqueira was murdered last month, just a few days after you left," continued the old man.

Another villager added, "When he was leaving the hospital, late one night, someone came and shot him."

"Yes," continued an old woman. "It was tragic! They shot him three times in the face. Awful!"

The first old man now found his wind and could continue his

explanation, "Mrs. Noqueira called the police at 3 a.m. when he didn't come home. The police found him inside his car at the hospital."

Remembering his last conversation with the Noqueiras, Dr. Rosa was at a loss for words. The tragedy was predictable; dealing with it was something else. He asked, "Where is Vanessa Noqueira?"

"She has disappeared," continued the old woman. "No one has seen her since the murder took place. I think she ran away for her own safety."

All this happened only a few days after Dr. Rosa last saw the Noqueiras. He was mad that Ramon had not followed his instructions. At the time, he did not know that Ramon had gone to Goiania that night to deliver shipments of venom. In fact, he knew nothing about the secret laboratory then and he would not know anything about it for years to come.

Ramon returned in the early afternoon from his bus trip to Goiania only to find the town in a complete uproar over the shooting death of his friend and business partner. The moment the townspeople told him of Dr. Noqueira's death, he knew instinctively he was also being watched. He was certain that both he and Vanessa Noqueira were remaining targets.

A hundred ideas were swirling in Ramon's mind. He had so many questions, so many concerns. He wanted to stop to mentally review and focus but he didn't have time. He needed to act quickly. Ramon was a one-task kind of guy, not complicated, just straightforward and simple. Now he was in a box, and to survive he had to mentally multitask and process his thoughts quickly. If he failed, Carlos Roberio would kill him and Vanessa.

His first concern and the one that kept recycling in his mind was getting Vanessa out of town before she became the second victim. Secondly, he knew he was out of the snake venom business permanently and he had to remove the lab quickly before anyone found it. Finally, he didn't want to admit it, but this was a kill or be killed situation. It wouldn't take Carlos Roberio and Davis Lemas very long to come in and take over the hospital. Ramon knew he had many details to perform and very limited time.

Normally Ramon used Dr. Noqueira's car but now it was full of blood and useless. It would take days of cleaning before it would be suitable to use to take Vanessa out of town. The car would need to have all of the upholstery cleaned and dried. Besides, it was a crime scene and couldn't be used even if it were clean. Ramon knew he would be the one cleaning and mopping up the blood of his dead friend, employer, and business partner. The body of Roberto Noqueira was lying in a bed in his hospital waiting for the police to arrive from Goiania. Then there would be arrangements for a funeral and Vanessa would demand to be present. There were too many details and much too little time.

Dr. Noqueira saved the life of Henri Bella, an eight-year boy dying from a leg infection. Ramon knew Henri's father and he thought the father might want to be helpful in this time of need. He called Mr. Bella and explained that he needed to borrow Mr. Bella's car for the day. He promised to return it the next day with a full tank of gasoline. Mr. Bella could read between the lines and he told Ramon to come get his car.

On his walk to Mr. Bella's house, Ramon ran into Wescley Silva, the delivery boy for Davis Lemas. Wescley looked guilty and needed absolution for his sins. He stuttered as he started his conversation with Ramon, "Man, I'm really sorry. I thought you knew that Davis and Carlos Roberio were going to kill Dr. Noqueira. I should have called you to warn you, but your doctor got a big warning with the beating. He should have moved away after that."

Ramon wanted to strangle Wescley on the spot but he realized that the boy was a pawn in the events and would not have played a role in the death of Dr. Noqueira. Ramon asked, "You're confirming that Carlos and Davis were responsible?"

"Sure," stammered Wescley. "They brought in an outsider to do the shooting. You should leave town as soon as possible. They don't want any loose ends around and that's what they consider you to be."

"Thanks Wescley," Ramon said. "We never had this conversation—never. Do you understand?"

"Sure Ramon. It's just between the two of us and it never happened. I promise."

"Ok, I've got things to do. Promise me that you will stay away from Davis Lemas and the Roberios for the next few days. Ok?"

"Sure. Are you going to get even?"

"Even doesn't come close. You should go somewhere for the next few days. Take your parents away to visit your relatives." Ramon walked away quickly and turned back to see young Wescley looking at the ground. He thought Wescley looked lost and sad.

After borrowing the car, Ramon rushed over to the Noqueira home to get Vanessa. She was there, stunned and crying. Ramon told her she must pack immediately and he would help her get her things together but they must act quickly. While they threw some of Vanessa's belongings in a suitcase, Ramon explained that her life was in jeopardy and she had to leave town immediately. He explained he would drive her to Itapirapua and from there she would take a bus to Brasilia to stay with her sister.

Ramon quickly threw Vanessa's things in the back seat of the car while Vanessa jumped in the passenger front seat. Between the seats was the burlap sack containing the shotgun that Ramon was supposed to use. Ramon drove to his father's farm first and left the shotgun there. He gathered up four PVC pipes that were each six feet long. The pipes were capped off on both ends and one end had a small hole from which a long length of cord extended. The cord for each set was neatly tied up.

Ramon didn't take the main road out of town; instead, he drove to a side road that also went to Itapirapua. The side road had several advantages. It was a dirt road and if anyone were following him, he would be able to see a cloud of dust. There was also a high hill on the road about midway to Itapirapua. If anyone were following from a distance, Ramon would stop at the top of the hill to watch for them and set up an ambush.

By the time they reached the hill at the midway point it was getting to be twilight. There was a pullout on the edge of the dirt road and a trail to a scenic lookout. Ramon pulled the car into the pullout area making sure that his high beams flashed the tall trees in the distance. He told Vanessa, "Go to the opposite side of the road and hide in the bushes over there. No matter what, stay there until I come get you. You must be totally quiet the entire time no matter what you might hear from this side of the road."

"You're scaring me. What if something bad happens to you?"

"Nothing is going to happen to me. Go now," Ramon answered as he looked down the dirt road watching a fast moving car leave a wake of dust.

With Vanessa hidden in the brush, Ramon got out the four PVC tubes and walked down the path towards the scenic outlook. Two hundred feet ahead Ramon found the ideal tree with large overhanging branches. He climbed the tree with his PVC pipes under his arm and took a position on a branch over the trail. Now it was nearly dark but he had plenty of light for his purposes. The men coming after him would be using flashlights and pointing them to the trail. This was playing in his favor.

Ramon unscrewed the cap without the hole on the first tube being as careful as possible. Pointing the tube to the ground, he slowly released the tension on the rope from the opposite end of the tube. Out slid one very angry Jararacussu. The snake's tail was tied to the cord with some extremely sticky hospital tape. While holding the pipe, he let the Jararacussu slide to a position a little lower than an average man's height. He tied a slipknot around the tree branch and repeated the process for three more snakes. Any men running down the path to catch Vanessa would get what they deserve.

Soon after the last snake was in position, he saw the tailing car stop. Two men got out and came towards his position. As Ramon guessed, they had flashlights pointed to the trail. Ramon could hear them talking about how much money they were going to earn from Carlos Roberio for doing the job. The men were laughing quietly and Ramon thought to himself, "Here, get a big laugh out of this."

Ramon gave the first snake a slight swing, just in time for it to strike the first man. The big snake struck him through the eyebrow. Since the snake was upside down, the fangs were pointing out through the man's forehead and the big snake could not extract itself from the screaming man's face. His buddy pointed his flashlight to the face of the screaming man and tried to shoot the big Jararacussu but instead shot his friend squarely through the brain. Ramon swung the second snake and it bit the shooter in the side of his neck. The shooter started firing his pistol madly into the air and Ramon jumped quickly to the tree trunk to avoid the barrage of bullets. The shooter fell to his knees and made no more sounds.

Ramon loosened the tension on the cord for the big snake that was still stuck in the dead man's forehead. With the Jararacussu completely on the ground, it was able to extract itself and Ramon pulled the cord up to return the snake to its PVC tube and did the same for the other snakes. With all the snakes safely stored away, Ramon dragged the dead men several hundred feet into the jungle. Animals would devour them and their chances of ever being found were slim. Ramon walked to the other side of the road and found Vanessa shaking in the bushes.

Vanessa shook all the way to Itapirapua. She could not be consoled. This was too much for her. She was a doctor's wife from a good family and the events of the day overwhelmed her.

Ramon's preference would be to drive Vanessa directly to her sister's house in Brasilia but there were too many things back in Britania that he had to do right now. He waited at the bus station in Itapirapua until Vanessa was on the bus for Brasilia. After the bus pulled away from the platform, he returned as fast as he could in the old Fiat.

Back in the snake laboratory, Ramon did a mental inventory of the weapons at his disposal. The entire collection consisted of over 400 snakes from 60 different species. All of the snakes were poisonous but some could only be counted on to destroy a limb or provide a lifetime brain injury. Right now, he was interested only in the inventory of the most deadly species. He mentally calculated that he had these deadly killers at his disposal: Coral Snakes, Rainforest Hoghead Pit Vipers, Side Stripped Palm Pit Vipers, Brazilian Gray Cobras, Lancehead Bothrops, Neotropical Rattlesnakes, Bushmasters, and Jararacussu Bothrops.

One by one, he made a mental analysis of which snakes would best suit his purposes. He needed three deadly killers that would guarantee a deep strike and an instant kill. He ruled out the Coral snake because it is frequently too shy to guarantee an aggressive strike. All of the other snakes on his mental list were aggressive and since they were not fed yesterday or today, they were especially agitated. The Rattlesnake had to be deleted from the list because it gives a warning. Ramon also eliminated the Gray Cobra because death by Cobra is too pleasant—the victim lapses into a sedated condition before dying—much too kind for the Roberios. Of those aggressive snakes with the capacity to kill immediately, only the Jararacussu could deliver the kind of menacing death Ramon was seeking. Its venom is almost completely cytotoxic so victims literally melt away in their own pool of blood. He had enough Jararacussu snakes in inventory to do the job but he gathered up a few Bushmasters just in case he needed more ammunition. Both the Bushmasters and the Jararacussu have mean, nasty, aggressive personalities and they will strike anything that comes near them. The toxicity of their venom was about equal, in the range of killing 30 to 40 humans per strike if diluted and given out in individual doses. Even the very dangerous Green Darters would also be collected from their burrow in the wild and used.

Ramon instinctively knew that his movements were being watched and he was fully aware he was the next target on the Roberio list. Ramon had a big advantage over the city men hired by Carlos Roberio. Raised in the jungle, he had stealth skills that others did not possess and he was able to complete all of his tasks that night without being noticed.

The next morning Carlos and Augusto Roberio each took separate cars into Britania to do their business errands for the day. They had planned to meet up with Davis Lemas for a celebration lunch at a quiet restaurant on the edge of town.

On the way into town, Carlos Roberio felt something brush his ankle and he swatted at it thinking it was a bee. When he reached down he got stung but not by a bee. He howled and quickly pulled up his hand to see two bloody bite marks on the back of his hand. In a panic, he started kicking at the floor of the car and the Jararacussu bit him a couple times on his legs and ankle. Carlos was screaming in pain. He pulled the car to the side of the road intending to extract the snakes from his vehicle. The pain from the bite was so intense it felt like someone stuck a red-hot poker through his hand. When he turned off the ignition key, blood was already pouring out of his ears and nose. He licked sweet blood from his lips and he could feel strands of tissue falling from the inside of his upper lip. At the same time, blood was pouring from his eye sockets. His pain was extreme and now he could not yell because his vocal cords and throat tissues had started to melt away. He knew he was dying quickly and painfully yet he had no time to mentally process the event or even to think that his death was a revenge killing.

That afternoon, locals found Carlos Roberio dead at the wheel of his car. His body was not recognizable since his facial features were merely bloody goo and the rest of him had melted into the seat fabric of his car.

Dr. Augusto Roberio was a little luckier; he lived a few seconds longer. His father had already left for Britania a few minutes earlier and Augusto was getting in his car when he saw the tail of a snake on the floor of his car. He grabbed the tail intending to fling it out of his car. In the process, the Jararacussu caught his upper leg with only a partial bite. When the young doctor saw that it was a Jararacussu he immediately put his belt around his leg as a tourniquet and ran back to the house. The young doctor probably didn't stand a chance one way or another, but his run back to the house only pumped the small amount of venom more quickly through his entire body.

Augusto ran to the kitchen and grabbed a sharp knife and drew a deep cut across the bite wound. The two maids were witness to all this and they could not help. After all, Augusto was the doctor and he should know how to save himself. The maids held each other, prayed, and crossed themselves hoping God would save the young doctor. While the doctor's actions may have saved him from the bite of some other snake, it was too little, too late, to save him from the bite of a Jararacussu. His actions only prolonged his death agony even more. Augusto went through the same horrific bleed out that his father just experienced only it took a little longer for death to come. The maids watched in horror and screamed as Augusto finally melted away into a bloody mess on the cold tiles of the kitchen floor.

Mrs. Roberio and the children left the house earlier in the morning than Carlos and Roberio. She was taking the children in to Britania for a picnic along the river. On the way to town, she stopped and picked up the young nanny, Monica Lopes. Katia Roberio was the second Mrs. Roberio for Carlos. The first Mrs. Roberio, the mother of Augusto, met a premature death many years ago. The four young children by Katia represented a second chance for Carlos. He was proud of Augusto but Carlos always imagined that he would have a large family to inherit his large estate. Monica Lopes would have her hands full that day helping Mrs. Roberio take care of the four young children. There were three boys aged eight, six, and five, and the baby girl of the family was still a toddler.

Mrs. Roberio made several stops in town and then they were off to have their picnic at a clearing on the edge of town by the river. At the picnic site, the adults were busy unloading the car and the children were running in all directions. No one noticed the man who passed by their picnic blanket. Easter was just the previous weekend and now on the picnic blanket was a small Easter pail topped with Easter chocolates and tiny toys. Stuffed into the bottom of the pail was the obligatory fake green Easter grass. Some of the Easter grass seemed to be moving as if it had a life of its own. The boys stopped fighting long enough to notice the Easter pail. They ran to the Easter pail hoping to grab all the chocolates. In the scramble, the pail fell over and suddenly all three children were lying silently on the ground. The toddler saw this as her invitation to get some of the candy and soon after she reached into the pail, she fell silently to the ground.

Monica and Katia saw that the children were all silent and on the ground and they thought the children were playing a game to get their attention. When the women went to the picnic blanket they started to tickle the children but there was no response. The women picked up the limp children and within seconds, they too were silent and lifeless on the ground.

Ramon regretted having to kill women and children but he knew that the children would grow up to seek revenge on Mrs. Noqueira. Ramon could not risk any Roberio family member surviving and seeking revenge. He would not allow a Roberio the chance to someday hunt down and kill Vanessa Noqueira. In Brazil, when bad things happen to parents, the children are responsible to avenge bad deeds even generations later. There would never be safety for Vanessa unless Ramon took quick and decisive action to wipe out all the Roberio family members. Monica Lopes was an unfortunate accident in the events of the day.

Ramon thought if there were no surviving Roberio family members there would be no heirs to Carlos' estate. He hoped the land might find its way back to the indigenous people who were run off by the Roberios. He also thought that he was just kidding himself. He feared that the mass snake attacks would put fear in the minds of the townspeople and Britania would fold up and blow away. The other negative scenario was that some corrupt government official in Brasilia would sell the

Roberio Ranch to another land grabber. He feared the Carlos Roberio legacy would just be repeated by someone else.

Time was running short and Ramon had to finish his last important task of the day. The Pharmacist, Davis Lemas, was mad about being stood up for his lunch appointment with the Roberios. He ate lunch alone in the designated restaurant waiting and hoping the Roberio men would arrive late. When they failed to show up, he was angry. He paid his bill and went to his car. It was a hot day and he left the windows rolled down to keep the car cooler. He pulled out of the parking lot of the restaurant and cranked up the car stereo. It was the loud music that drew onlookers to the Lemas car stopped by the side of the road on the way to the center of town. Inside was a dead man, or at least they thought it might be a man. Davis Lemas had turned into the same kind of slimy corpse as the Roberio men.

All the snake attack rumors panicked the locals. To make things worse, the newspapers in Goiania and Brasilia made it sound like Britania was under constant attack by snakes. One by one, cars loaded up and people pulled out of Britania. When the people left, the businesses followed. Soon Britania was nearly a ghost town. The town lost its doctor and hospital so there was no medical care available. By the end of the month after the attacks, all but a few of the businesses relocated to Itapirapua or São Luis de Montes Belos. Homes and shops were closed and boarded up. Property in Britania was almost worthless. Even the squatters refused to come to Britania or to the Roberio Ranch fearing for their lives.

The mayor of Britania realized that suddenly he was the mayor of an empty town. The snake attacks destroyed Britania. Most alarming of all were the corpses of two adult females and four children lying in the open in the park by the river. Word had gotten out that their deaths were caused by an attacking hive of Green Darters and no one would go near the site. Mayor Marcel Braga had already phoned all the local contractors and found none willing to retrieve the bodies. If the snakes had killed so many, then everyone thought that the entire area was heavily infested with Green Darters. Weeks passed and Mayor Braga spent all his time making contacts trying to find someone willing to risk their life to go to the park and bring out the remaining bodies of the Roberio family.

The mayor eventually realized that the park would have to be treated the same way that the farmers treat their fields when infested with Green Darters. However, he was not going to be the one to tell the bad news to the parents of Monica Lopes, the nanny on that fateful spring day. Since the entire Roberio family had been killed, the Lopes family members were the sole surviving relatives of the disaster. He knew the Lopes family would fight burning the corpses and burying them in the park. Mayor Braga telephoned Alan Alves, the mortician in Itapirapua and asked the mortician to speak to the Lopes family about his plans. The mayor could offer Mr. Alves only a paltry sum for his time, but the generous Mr. Alves agreed to speak with the family.

During their meeting, the Lopeses were shocked to hear that the remains of their daughter would lie forever unmarked in a communal grave with the Roberio family members. Mr. and Mrs. Lopes demanded that Mr. Alves find a way to retrieve the remains of their daughter. Mr. Alves explained that Mayor Braga had been working weeks to find a contractor who would go in to retrieve the bodies. He explained to them that all the contacts thought it was too dangerous to go into the park. Mr. and Mrs. Lopes continued their protest to Mr. Alves. Finally, he suggested that they try to find someone willing to do the job. He gave them a month to find someone and told them if they could not find someone, then the plan to burn the field should proceed.

Only a week later Mr. Alves received a call from Mr. Lopes. Tearfully, Mr. Lopes explained that he could not find anyone to retrieve his daughter's remains. Regretfully Mr. and Mrs. Lopes gave in and agreed that the mayor's plan was the only available option.

Alan Alves reported to the mayor that the Lopeses approved the burning plan but they also asked that it be done respectfully. The mayor didn't respond verbally, but thought, "respectfully, hell, how about carefully!" The mayor had control of a small village budget that would be even smaller next year due to the shrinking taxpayer roll. Clearing the picnic field would wipe out the recreation budget for the next five years, or the town could turn off all public lighting at 7 p.m. Take your pick, he mused.

Mayor Braga was able to find a rancher willing to come to town to burn the picnic field. It would be a costly six-day event of literally burning money as more and more fuel burned the field. Midway through the operation the rancher brought in a backhoe operator who dug a trench for the burned bodies. Most of the bones were quickly moved into the hole and buried. A few smaller bones lay scattered around the trench site. Next, the topsoil was tilled over the entire field and the fires were started again. When the equipment operators moved out of the field, they got off the equipment by jumping as far away as they could to avoid being bitten by a stray Green Darter. The mayor had the *bombeiros*, firefighters, waiting to pressure spray their equipment to make sure that none of the tiny snakes were lodged in any mechanical crevice.

Black smoke rolled over the town of Britania as if it were a sign of bad things to come. Mayor Braga wrote a city check to Alan Alves for the paltry sum of $25. The Mayor was embarrassed to pay Mr. Alves such a small sum for the time he spent, but he was thankful that he did not have to confront the Lopeses himself.

CHAPTER SIX

The week following the murder of Dr. Noqueira, Ramon was out of a job. Well, actually he was out of two jobs. The nurses volunteered their time to close down and shut off things at the hospital. Ramon spent several days trying to wash the blood out of the seats of Roberto's car. Since the police held the car for a week, the bloodstains were permanent—he would have to do something else. He wouldn't sit in the car because it still looked awful. He put a blanket over the front seats and that helped a little bit but there were still bloodstains on the headliner and the floor carpets.

The police questioned Ramon about Roberto's death. From them, he learned that a homeless man in a nearby village had $500 on him. The police said they were sure that he was the man who shot Dr. Noqueira but they could not hold him since there was no evidence. The police said that they told the homeless man to leave the area. Ramon did not say anything but he was certain that the homeless man left the area $500 lighter.

The police did not say anything to Ramon about the snake attacks but Ramon knew that they were thinking the same thing as everyone else in town. Wherever people gathered, there were whispers about the tragedy of the Roberio clan. Had Vanessa Noqueira stayed in Britania she would have been known as the "voodoo widow." Everyone was certain that she had engaged a Quimbanda priest to seek revenge on the Roberios for killing her husband. Few villagers could actually blame Mrs. Noqueira for doing such a bad thing because most of them would have done the same given the circumstances.

In other parts of the world, Quimbanda might be called black voodoo. Few people realize that Quimbanda really does work. However, it's not magic that makes it work. Ignore all the trappings of Quimbanda, in their little storefronts in the big cities—it's all just window dressing. Beware though, it is dangerous and not to be dealt with on a whim.

When you visit a Quimbanda priest, he will ask you many questions about your enemy or your intended target. You will have to answer all his questions in detail and you will have to explain the status of your victim, how much money they make, where do they live, and how many relatives. This questioning goes on and on for several hours. While you are speaking to the priest, he is mentally calculating the maximum it will cost to have your target killed. In Brazil, it's not uncommon to have an enemy killed for a few hundred dollars. After you have paid a large sum of money to the priest, he makes a very big deal about delivering a death sentence to your victim. He appears personally, in public, in front of the victim and announces that a death curse has been placed. In the days of black slavery, this theatrical death sentencing actually killed victims just from the fear of knowing they were going to die. Now it's rather risky behavior on the part of the priest because some victims just pull out a handgun and shoot the priest dead. Obviously, now the death sentence is seldom practiced.

If your intended victim does not die on the spot from fright, the priest has to go find and pay a hit man to deliver on the curse. During that long conversation of questions and answers with the priest, he had calculated the worst-case scenario for each murder. If your victim was out of the country, then you paid for round trip airfare and related expenses to have your bullet delivered to your victim. Not all Quimbanda curses are death sentences. Many people just want their enemy run out of town for good, or they want some bad misfortune to happen. In this case, the Quimbanda priest may run around doing the evil deeds himself.

Quimbanda priests are an unusual lot. There is a saying in Brazil that the Quimbanda are one part assassin, one part detective, and one part air. The reference to air means that no Quimbanda priest has ever been charged with murder. After the deeds are done, the priests just vanish into thin air. As for the detective part, the priest will check out your story before killing any of you enemies. If a person has been wronged, then the priest will complete the mission. If the priest finds out that you lied, then you might end up being the assassin's target. For this reason, people don't mess around with Quimbanda priests. If you are ever investigated by a Quimbanda priest, it's best to stick to the facts and give them politely and quickly to the priest. As for the assassination part, the priests justify it as "Divine Intervention," and they are doing sacred work by delivering people to the devil. The saintly part of their work is the result of a bizarre and unfortunate marriage of Christianity and native African beliefs.

The opposite of Quimbanda is Umbanda, or white magic. While Quimbanda works with the negative side of the universe, Umbanda works with the positive. It's far easier to employ Quimbanda because it's easy to do bad things to people. If you walk up behind someone on the sidewalk at an intersection and shove them into oncoming traffic, that's an easy deed. Not much thinking, not much planning, not much effort—easy peasy. However, making sure that someone has a certain success in life, now that's a difficult task.

Sometimes Quimbanda and Umbanda can achieve the same outcome. The difference is in the details. Let's suppose that you have a daughter trying to get into the University of Rio de Janeiro. There are three students wait listed before your daughter. If you employed a Quimbanda priest, he would do some awful deeds to take the three other students off the waiting list. However, if you employed an Umbanda priest, he would just visit the Registrar's Office and give a clerk some money to put your daughter's application on top of the other three student applications. Same outcome, different execution, so to speak.

In Britania, with all the "voodoo widow" rumors flying around, Ramon knew that Vanessa's emergency trip to Brasilia was a permanent arrangement. She would never be able to return to Britania and in all likelihood she didn't want to because her only family was in Brasilia. Even though Vanessa was in Brasilia, Ramon was not sure that she was safe. He would have to go there to make sure that she was in a safe place. With no hospital, no laboratory, and no snakes, Vanessa was the only thing that he had to take care of right now.

Ramon emptied out his savings account from the large hidden hole in the floor of his apartment kitchen and packed two large suitcases full of money. He shoved his clothes and personal belongings in a duffle bag and loaded up Dr. Noqueira's car. His plan was to go to Brasilia to return the car to Vanessa and he thought he would stop along the way in Goiania to have all the upholstery replaced. When he arrived in Goiania, he found a shop that gave him a good price for the upholstery job but they needed the car for two days. He would have to stay a couple nights in Goiania. While waiting around in Goiania, Ramon needed a safe place to store two suitcases of cash. While the men were working on the interior of the car Ramon decided to take the suitcases over to the bank that Roberto used.

Edmar Falco, president of the Goiania Bank, had followed all the events in Britania and he was waiting for Ramon to arrive. The bank president overheard Ramon introduce himself to the teller and he walked up to Ramon and led Ramon into his office. In the usual custom in Brazil, within 30 seconds of sitting, a bank staffer quietly brought in a demitasse of hot sweet coffee for Ramon. Mr. Falco explained the assets of the Templeton Institute. Roberto and Ramon were the sole and joint owners of the savings and checking accounts. The Templeton Institute had only two directors on the board—Roberto and Ramon. Ramon was already aware that he had signing authority for the checking account but he did not realize there was a large savings account as well. There was less than $100,000 in each of the bank accounts. Mr. Falco explained that Roberto also had several safety deposit boxes. Since all the assets of the Templeton Institute were held jointly, Ramon was now the sole owner.

Ramon pointed to his two suitcases and explained that he had some family antiques in the suitcases and needed enough safety deposit boxes to hold everything in them. Ramon asked if there might be some vacant safety deposit boxes adjacent to Roberto's boxes. The bank president went to a key cabinet with a note containing some numbers written on it. He pulled eight keys from the cabinet, wrote the numbers on his piece of paper, and handed the keys to Ramon. The president briefly suggested that Ramon should be investing any money instead of holding cash.

In the privacy of the bank vault, Ramon placed all his cash in the safety deposit boxes. He also held the keys to Roberto's boxes so he opened them and was shocked to see them all stuffed with cash. Ramon had never counted his own money and now with Roberto's money he had twice as much. It would take hours, if not days, to count all the money and he didn't have the time to deal with it. On his way out of the bank, Mr. Falco motioned for him to return to his office. Ramon returned to his seat and was told that he really should meet with Roberto's attorney, Thomaz Rocha. Ramon agreed and the bank president picked up his phone, dialed Mr. Rocha's number and told the attorney that Ramon Gobbey was on his way over to see him.

Thomaz Rocha was a short, stocky man in his early forties with gray hair. He greeted Ramon with a big smile and a bone-crushing handshake. He expressed his condolences to Ramon and told Ramon that he read all about the events in Britania. He told Ramon that he knew that Dr. Noqueira was secretly supporting the Britania Hospital with proceeds from the Templeton Institute. It was clear that Mr. Rocha did not know exactly how the Templeton Institute earned its money. The attorney once saw some names on some of the international wire transfers and guessed that Roberto and Ramon developed veterinary medications.

Mr. Rocha told Ramon, "You're legally free to close the Templeton Institute corporate books but you might wait awhile to see if the corporate structure has some future use to you. Legal and filing fees to maintain the corporation are only $100 per year. You don't need to make any decisions right away. There might be some alternate purpose for the Templeton Institute some day and keeping the corporation intact would give you options."

Ramon asked, "And about taxes, are they current or in arrears?"

Mr. Rocha advised, "The corporation is current with all its tax filings and everything else is in order."

After the meeting with Mr. Rocha, Ramon was relieved to learn that Dr. Noqueira had not been using the corporation as a tax dodge. He was still a little confused about a couple of things. He was not aware of the vast amount of cash in the safety deposit boxes and secondly, he didn't understand why Dr. Noqueira paid him his full half of the proceeds. The doctor should have been withholding taxes from Ramon's half. Somehow, things just didn't add up for Ramon and he was uncomfortable about not knowing the answers. He didn't know how much money Dr. Noqueira left for Vanessa but he was upset thinking that he might be the only beneficiary. Ramon was puzzled that Roberto had all that cash in the safety deposit box. Ramon thought that Dr. Noqueira was spending all of his money on improvements to the hospital. The only thing he could guess was that Dr. Noqueira had been lucky on some investments along the way.

Dr. Noqueira owned the Britania Hospital but had the title under the name of the Templeton Institute. In addition to all the money in the bank, Ramon was now the owner of the hospital. With no doctor, the empty hospital was not worth much.

Ramon went over to check the status of Roberto's car and the upholstery shop was finished with it. It looked like a new car, at least from the inside. Ramon knew that Vanessa would refuse the car but at least it now had some resale value. Ramon could sell it in Brasilia and give Vanessa the cash from it. Ramon stayed that night in Goiania and left the next morning to drive to Brasilia.

Ramon found the home of Vanessa's sister in Brasilia and determined that it was in a good part of town. For now, Ramon would have to rely on Vanessa's sister and brother-in-law to provide security for her. With the entire Roberio clan out of the picture, risk to Vanessa was greatly reduced. Ramon took an apartment close to where Vanessa was staying and he met with a neighborhood real estate broker. He asked the realtor to locate three houses in the neighborhood, which would be good for rental income. He told the broker to find houses within a four-block radius of Vanessa's current address.

His thinking was that Vanessa could live in one of the houses near her sister and then rent the other two houses. He figured that the two rental houses would provide a good income for her since she had only herself to support. His motivation for doing this was solely guilt. He didn't know if Roberto left her access to any assets but since she fled quickly she had no property. The house in Britania would soon be worthless. It was the large savings account that troubled him the most. Ramon thought he had no right to that and it should have been left for

Vanessa. At least he could provide for her this way and he was devoted to helping her in the future.

After Ramon closed the deals with the real estate broker, he had the two of the rental houses sparsely furnished. The third one was closest to Vanessa's sister and he had that one completely furnished with everything she would need. When he was finished with the project, he visited Vanessa. He met her sister and brother-in-law. The sister looked just like Vanessa but was a little older. The brother-in-law was big and strong so Ramon felt good about having Vanessa live near them.

He asked Vanessa to take a walk with him and they walked to the closest house that Ramon had furnished completely. Ramon went to the front door, unlocked it, and asked Vanessa to enter. When she entered the foyer, Ramon said, "Here are the keys to your new home. I had this one completely furnished for you since it is so close to your sister's house. Since it's less than a block away you can visit her several times a day, yet still have your own home."

"Ramon, you did not need to do this. It's too generous, why did you do it?"

"Guilt, honestly. I was supposed to be guarding Roberto and we know what happened the moment I had to leave town."

"Don't blame yourself for what happened. Really, it was all Roberto's fault. I begged him to leave Britania. He was just too stubborn to leave."

"Here are the keys for two more houses about another block away. You can earn a good income from the rents on those houses. Here is the business card of the realtor who has been helping me. He will help you find good tenants for the houses. Call on him anytime you need help with the houses."

"Ramon, you are a good man," Vanessa said as she wrapped her arms around him. She held on to him tightly and cried for a long time. Ramon walked Vanessa back to her sister's house and he was happy with his decisions about Vanessa.

Soon after Ramon had Vanessa situated he decided it was time to move on. In his spare time, he had already toured around Brasilia and he wanted to explore the rest of Brazil. After all, he had all the money he needed and he didn't have to work. There was no longer anything for him to take care of. After working day and night in two jobs for so many years he thought it was time to take care of Ramon.

On his last night in Brasilia, Ramon walked over to see Vanessa Noqueira and to say goodbye. Just before he approached the corner to her house, he jumped when he heard a loud bang. He muttered to himself, "Fuckin little shits. Why do parents give their kids fireworks when it's not a holiday?"

As soon as he turned the corner, he saw a man holding a pistol and Vanessa was lying dead on the sidewalk. He raced to the gunman and wrestled the pistol away, throwing it into the street. Ramon had the gunman on the ground and he had his hands securely around his throat. Ramon shouted, "Who paid you to do this?"

"Sergio."

"Sergio who?"

"Sergio Roberio."

Ramon didn't need any more information from the gunman. The gunman grabbed Ramon's throat so Ramon raised the man's head and slammed it forcefully to the concrete sidewalk. The man's body went limp and he made no sounds.

The police arrived and determined that Ramon fought in self-defense. The cops asked Ramon if he knew why the gunman killed Vanessa and he speculated that it was a robbery even though the gunman had no cash on him. Ramon had to deal with Vanessa's sister and brother-in-law so he stayed in town to attend her funeral. After the funeral, he asked Vanessa's sister to keep the properties he purchased for Vanessa.

Before the funeral, Ramon had additional business in Brasilia. He found that Sergio Roberio was the brother of Carlos Roberio and he lived in Brasilia. He wondered if there were any additional siblings of Katia or Carlos Roberio hiding around Brazil. Ramon had the money so he hired a private investigator to find all remaining heirs to the estates of Carlos and Katia Roberio. A quick investigation showed that Sergio was the only remaining heir. Sergio had long ago severed close relations with his brother. While they both grew up on the Roberio Ranch, Sergio had no fondness for country life.

Ramon had mixed emotions about what to do with Sergio. Sergio, the estranged last heir to a fortune, would be an easy target to frame.

Ramon could set Sergio up to take the fall for the murders of the entire Roberio family. Ramon could not decide—kill Sergio, frame Sergio. Some seek guidance in God; Ramon sought his answer in a bottle. Normally he wasn't much of a drinker but today he started the afternoon with several beers. On the way to his apartment, he purchased a bottle of *Cachaça,* cheap and potent liquor made from cane sugar. The next morning his head was pounding from mixing beer and too much cheap liquor. The liquor did help bring about a decision. Framing someone is too messy, too complicated, and there are too many ways to foul it up. Sergio would soon die a quick death.

Sergio Roberio was happy with his newfound wealth. As the brother and only surviving member of the Roberio clan, Sergio stood to inherit the very large Roberio Ranch. Sergio's plan was to let people forget about the snake attacks in Britania and then he would sell the Roberio Ranch for millions. He would use the money to buy an island on the Green Coast north of Rio. He was certain that the ranch would bring in enough money that he would have difficulty spending it all during his lifetime.

Sergio Roberio was nervous about the events that unfolded in Britania. In the murder of Dr. Noqueira, his hands were dirty and he was nervous for three reasons. He supplied the hired gun to kill Dr. Noqueira. His brother paid him well to send a gunman to Britania. He couldn't be certain that the hired gunman would escape discovery. If the police caught the man, Sergio didn't know if the gunman would point the finger to him or not.

The second reason that Sergio was nervous was the one that made him lose sleep. At his family's funeral, there were whispers that Mrs. Noqueira hired a Quimbanda priest to kill all the people responsible for the death of her husband. Some of the people in Britania did more than whisper about the curse placed by Mrs. Noqueira. Some came right out to Sergio and asked him where he thought he could run to escape the Quimbanda curse. Sergio believed in Quimbanda and he worried that the hand of death was after him.

Thirdly, Sergio was nervous about the gunman that he sent to kill Mrs. Noqueira. With Mrs. Noqueira gone, would the Quimbanda priest still come after him? Who attacked and killed his gunman?

Sergio had plenty to worry about. He planned to keep a low profile and changed his routine to throw off any Quimbanda priest who might be tracking him. Normally, every Monday, Wednesday, and Friday, Sergio worked out at his health club in the morning for two hours. Sergio didn't want to change his fitness routine so he decided to leave his car at home and instead took a taxi to the club. At the club, he planned to ask a friend for a ride home.

Sergio was a bachelor in his late thirties and he thought that a good physique would deliver a beautiful wife to him some day. After a vigorous workout, Sergio was in the locker room changing clothes when he reached into his gym bag and fell dead onto the concrete floor. No one questioned the incident because everyone felt that the man had overdone his exercise routine and he had been stressed by the recent deaths in his family. The gym manager briefly thought it was curious that there was no gym bag present after the witnesses reported one but he just figured that someone had stolen the dead man's belongings. There was no investigation into the death because it was so obvious that Sergio died from a heart attack at the gym.

Sergio and his hit man drove Ramon's body count to thirteen. Thirteen murders would certainly mean the death sentence if he were caught. Mentally he compared murder to drowning. You can get the gallows for one murder or thirteen. The same is true for drowning. You can drown in seven feet of water, or seven thousand feet of water, numbers really don't matter.

CHAPTER SEVEN

After the sad events in Brasilia, Ramon made a beeline for the beaches of Copacabana and Ipanema. He wanted to be as far away from Britania and Brasilia as he could get. The free loving city of Rio de Janeiro was a bit of culture shock for Ramon. It was the largest city he had ever visited and the congestion wasn't much to his liking but he did like the beaches. For there, on the beaches he was free to play *futvolei*, volleyball without use of hands. Better yet, he enjoyed watching the Carioca women in their tiny "dental floss" bikinis. Carioca is the name for natives of Rio de Janeiro. The female Carioca spends most of her day at the gym and therefore has the body of a goddess. Of course, here we are talking solely about the young females. Unfortunately, modesty does not come with age in Brazil and it's common to see seventy-year-old people in bikinis.

The dress codes in restaurants and businesses around the beach are non-existent to very casual. Some of the better restaurants may ask the men to wear a shirt but the women are eagerly greeted when they arrive in the tiniest bikini. Ramon would later confess to friends that his favorite hangout in Copacabana was the frozen food section of the supermarket on the beach. There he was able to watch young women in bikinis lean over the frozen food to reach for items.

During his stay in Rio de Janeiro, Ramon met some American men who were working as contractors installing television and satellite receiving equipment in the city. He hung out with them at one of the beach kiosks after work. The company they worked for was a big American based multinational firm. Ramon met the crew's boss one day and had a long talk with him. Gary Bennett was a smart investor and he told Ramon that his company was in a position to make a lot of money from locations like Brazil. The American explained that communications technology was exploding and if Ramon had any money to invest, he should consider buying some stock in the company.

Ramon agreed with his new American friend and called Mr. Falco in Goiania. He told the banker to use the remainder of the large savings account to purchase shares of the multinational communications company as well as several other "blue chip" American stocks.

Ramon Gobbey was living in Rio, had his own apartment, and was living the life of an easygoing bachelor. He was trying to find meaning in life, trying to find a good girlfriend, and trying to find out what he would do for the rest of his life. He worked at several different odd jobs, keeping most of them only a few weeks. He thought of going to São Paulo to work for the reptile institute that competed with Dr. Noqueira but he knew he couldn't do that. He knew that he would never handle another snake. It had to be that way. No one knew his secret and he was not going to reveal his past.

Ramon applied to several hospitals trying to get a job as a janitor or maintenance mechanic but he never received calls for interviews. Since coming to Rio, he briefly made deliveries for a pharmacy, an appliance store, and a grocery store. Working dead-end jobs at least gave him some opportunity to meet people his own age.

Until recently, his girlfriend was Andressa. She was petite, brunette, attractive, and fun to be around. Several dates ago, Andressa's father loaned Ramon his car. Ramon bought some fresh shrimp and put it and his fishing gear in the trunk of the car. He and Andressa spent the night fishing off Leme Rock on Copacabana Beach. The next night when he went to pick up Andressa, her father was furious with him. The father took Ramon to his car and started yelling, "You little bastard, you spent the entire night having sex in my car. I can't get the smell of it out of the car."

Ramon had to work hard to keep from laughing. In his most

serious voice he said, "Sir, I'm very sorry. We did not have sex. The smell is from shrimp bait I put in your trunk and some of it must have spilled on to the carpet of your trunk. I will take your car and go clean it up right now."

Ramon returned the car with a fresh smelling trunk. Andressa's father now spoke to him differently; he was disrespectful and rude. Ramon didn't know if the father was mad because he didn't screw Andressa, or if he was still mad about the shrimp. In any event, there were too many girls out there to waste any time on a girl with a crazy father. Ramon moved on to find other girlfriends.

One night Ramon unlocked his apartment door and entered the dark apartment as usual. Before he could reach for the light switch, a hand came from the shadows and suddenly there was a knife held to his throat. After the lights came on there was a man sitting in his chair in his living room. The man behind him now had Ramon on the floor and was busy tying his hands and feet.

With Ramon completely tied up, the man in the chair introduced himself as Max Schuman. Very calmly Max explained, "If you want to live, you will cooperate with us. You were a hard little son-of-a-bitch to find. We've already been to your father's farm in Britania and we've examined the blood levels of the livestock on your farm. We know that you were the person helping Dr. Noqueira. It took a lot of investigative work on my end to tie all the pieces together. In Britania, there was so much for us to piece through. I think that you personally were responsible for destroying the entire town."

"If you've hurt my father you can go to hell," yelled Ramon.

"I have no intention of hurting anyone except you if you don't cooperate. Since Dr. Noqueira is dead, I have no source for the Green Darter venom, which I now need. I require more venom for the products I make. I had hoped to synthesize it in our laboratory but we have had no such luck. You, young man, are going to harvest some venom and some snakes for me to take back to Germany."

"Those snakes are all back in the wild now. You can't just go out in the field and start milking them—you need equipment. It's been nearly three years since those snakes were put back in the wild, by now they could be anywhere."

"I've brought everything you will need to do the job. Tomorrow we will fly to Goiania and then rent a car to go to Britania. We will set up a lab in your father's house and you will be busy all week milking as many Green Darters as possible. I will take a box of snakes back to Germany in hopes of keeping them alive there."

The next morning Max and his thug named William drove Ramon to the airport where they all boarded a plane for Goiania. During the night, Ramon tried to remember the details of the Green Darter venom package he mailed so long ago. He did remember that it was mailed to Germany but that's about all he could remember. This kidnapping must have something to do with the reason why Dr. Noqueira ordered him to destroy the Green Darters.

During the flight to Goiania Ramon asked loudly, "How long is the prison sentence for someone who kidnaps someone and transports them across state lines?"

Calmly Max replied while pointing to the passenger cabin door, "The door is there, you can leave any time you want."

"Why do you need me? Can't you go do this yourself—you've already been to Britania? Go find the snakes for yourself."

"We know that you are the snake expert. Cooperate with us and I will make it well worth your time and energy. It's going to be a short little visit and you'll get to spend some time with your papa. Besides, you should see the current state of affairs in Britania. You really did a number on that town. There isn't anything left there. You think I am the bad guy here. If I am the bad person then you are the devil. I've just interrupted your playtime in Rio a little. You, you destroyed an entire town in very little time."

Ramon was silent. He had no reply. Max was correct about him. In the long car ride over to Britania form Goiania, Ramon had time to come up with a good plan. He remembered a Green Darter hive that he had to access from just one direction because vines covered the ground from the other direction. The ground vines made it too dangerous to cross because one fall on the ground and the snakes would be able to bite. He would send Max and William around the dangerous side hoping that one or both would trip on the vines and fall. If one man was left standing he would simply toss a bucket full of Green Darters on him. If that didn't work, there would be plenty of time to get rid of the two men while they slept in his father's house. Ramon was sure that Max had something to do with Dr. Noqueira telling him to get rid of the Green Darters. Perhaps the doctor and Max had already had a previous dispute.

When they arrived at the farm, Ramon did not want to worry his father so he introduced Max and William as customers who were going to help him harvest some Green Darters. Max proceeded to take over the kitchen of the old farmhouse, turning it into a laboratory. Max and William also unpacked their gear, which included heavy leather boots, snake-handling tools, vials for the venom, and a sturdy wooden box for taking snakes back to Germany.

While Max was unpacking, Ramon went out to the old barn to collect his tools. He found his favorite old metal bucket with a lid that he had used so many times with the Green Darters. He also saw some of Dr. Noqueira's old logbooks and assumed that Max and William had already read them.

He now knew how Max tied him to Dr. Noqueira but he was still puzzled to know how Max found out about his revenge killing of the Roberio family. Max could only be guessing because there was no real evidence.

Before returning to the farmhouse, Ramon picked some apples and went to the pasture. There were four horses in the field but only one was his horse. Storm immediately saw him and came running up to him. He gave Storm an apple and the other horses came up wanting food too. Ramon was just 14 years old when his father gave Storm to him. He named the big horse Storm because he was black, like a big storm cloud. Storm became the first laboratory animal for the secret laboratory. Dr. Noqueira knew that Ramon loved Storm so he gave the big horse only a minute injection of venom and spread the venom injections out over time so it would have no adverse effects on the horse. Storm produced their first antivenin, which was from Gray Cobra. They never used Storm again as a test animal.

Back in the farmhouse Max insisted, "We must start collecting snakes today so Ramon here can collect the venom. We don't want to rush the toxin collection process and have anything bad happen to our snake expert."

Ramon replied, "The last time I returned the Green Darters they were in a hive about 8 miles from here. It's easy to get to so we should get started."

Out at the field Ramon led the others to the hive location. He did as he planned and pointed to the hive telling the other two men to go around the other way and he would meet them on the other side of a large tree. Unfortunately, the ground vines were gone but the hive was still there. Max and William watched as Ramon gathered the hive and put it in the metal bucket. Ramon closed the lid and tightened the heavy latch so it was completely secure.

Max's wooden box was still in the rental car so Ramon asked William to go get it so he and Max could look for another burrow. After William brought over the heavy box, all three of them looked around the brush for another hive. They spread out in their search and soon Max shouted out. Max found a dead calf on the ground and he wanted Ramon to check it. Ramon turned the carcass over and found another colony inside the abdominal cavity. The hive did not stay in a tight ball and quite a few of the snakes managed to slither away, making the men quite nervous about their whereabouts. Ramon scooped up the hive, put it in the wooden box, and secured it well.

With these snakes, it would take Ramon two or three days to complete the milking. He figured that he had about half the snakes needed for the amount of toxin Max wanted. He had very mixed emotions about what to do with Max and William. He wouldn't think twice about killing both of them, especially if they were planning to kill him or his father. On the other hand, Ramon wouldn't mind being paid if Max kept his word. In his mind, he kept mulling over, 'trust Max, kill Max.'

That night Max tried to assure Ramon, "I'm sorry I had to kidnap you to do this but I didn't think there was any other way. I know you wouldn't have done it unless I brought you here. Last time I paid Dr. Noqueira around $30,000 and I will pay you the same amount once we are safely in Germany. Last time Dr. Noqueira and I had a falling out of sorts. It was an unfortunate misunderstanding. Did he ever tell you about it?"

"No, all I recall is that he made me get rid of the Green Darters after I sent your shipment of venom. What happened?"

"Oh, the details are not important. I received the venom and he received the payment so actually the transaction was completed." This time Max did not intend to kill off the witnesses to the transaction. The lethal bullets were selling well and Max was not certain if his researchers would ever be able to synthesize the venom so he needed Ramon around to deliver future shipments.

Max went on to explain himself, "I will need future shipments of this volume and I do hope that I can count on you to deliver. Please keep me informed of your whereabouts so I will not have to spend so much time looking for you in the future. For each shipment, you will be paid $30,000. By Brazil standards, you can live on that for a long time. You could use the money to help your father fix up this farm. You could go to America and get a good college education. That kind of money should have some positive influence on your life. I just want you to be assured that I need your future services so you don't do anything drastic like killing us while we sleep on your porch tonight."

"Yes, I did think that you deserved to be killed. However, the money can always be put to some good use. How do I know that you will actually pay me once you return to Germany?"

"Well, if I cheat you on this order, you probably will kill me the next time I show up wanting more venom. In that event, I would not blame you in the slightest."

"I should probably tell you that you are wasting your time taking live snakes back to Germany. They live on a very limited diet of native rodents found only in this state of Brazil. Taking them back to Germany will just mean that you will have a box of dead snakes soon. Besides, if you get caught in Customs, they will put you in jail forever."

"Yes, you are probably right. As long as I can count on your help in the future I will just return with the venom."

"What kind of pharmaceuticals are you making from the venom?"

The real Max replied with a smirk, "Oh, it's definitely life altering, very promising."

The next two days Ramon worked long hours milking the tiny snakes. It took dozens of snakes to produce a few drops of venom. As a break from the work, he took Max and William with him to find the last several hives they needed. It didn't take Ramon long to find new hives. He knew exactly where to look and soon they had all the necessary snakes. It took Ramon the rest of the week to complete the process and when he finished he returned all the hives to their own burrows. With the work completed, Ramon gave Max a slip of paper with his account number at the bank. Max reiterated his promise to wire the money soon after his return to Germany.

William carefully packed the vials in bubble wrap and placed them in the sturdy wooden box for the trip back. They brought with them vial labels that were preprinted indicating the material was antibiotics for dogs just in case Customs decided to open the box.

Ramon explained that he would like to stay awhile to help his father and would be returning to Rio in about a week. Max handed an airline ticket to Ramon saying, "Here, you will need to call them right now and have this changed to the date you want to use for your return to Rio. Since you will be on your own to get to Goiania, here's $500. That should be more than enough for you to rent a car, or take a bus and blow the rest on some girl."

Ramon was surprised by Max's generosity but he was not going to change his mind and return to Rio with them. After spending a week with the two men, he was ready for them to leave and he really did need to stay awhile to help his father.

His father was getting on in years and Ramon needed to find someone locally who could check in on his dad to help with cleaning and meals. The father was a good repairman and could fix everything. Fortunately, he passed those skills on to his son. Now the old man was to too frail to do much manual labor so Ramon also needed to find a handyman to take care of things around the farm. The pasture fence needed repairing soon or the horses and sheep would be gone. It would be no big loss if the animals ran away but Ramon needed to have someone take care of his Storm. If the animals ran off, Ramon was worried they might be slaughtered for food. Dr. Noqueira explained to him that the animals did not retain any venom in their tissues but rather they retain antibodies to the venom. Still, it probably would be better if the laboratory animals were not eaten.

Ramon spent most of the week at the farm helping his father. He took Storm for long daily rides and felt guilty that he wasn't around to exercise his horse more often. In the barn, he found the logbooks that once belonged to Dr. Noqueira. He couldn't believe that he was so careless to have left the logbooks in the barn. He was positive that Max and William read the logbooks.

Ramon took the logbooks out behind the barn, placed some dry wood over them, and started a fire. As the books burned, he recalled the hectic days after Dr. Noqueira was murdered. No wonder he forgot to burn the logbooks.

After Ramon completed all the repairs at the farm, he had some time to catch his breath and relax. Ramon also wanted to take his time to visit Britania without Max around to scold him. He needed to know if the remaining locals knew that he was responsible for the snake attacks or was it only Max who discovered his secret.

Walking around Britania gave Ramon the full sense of what he did to the community. The condition of the town shocked him. On the main street, there remained only a small run down mercado. Only a dozen of the houses were occupied and the rest were vacant and boarded up. As he feared, his nice hometown was now an empty ghost town where the jungle had taken back the once landscaped yards. He went to the park by the river and there was a rusting sheet metal fence blocking the view to the river and of the decaying bones of the Roberio children. Usually squatters fill in where there is vacant land in Brazil but they still avoided Britania and the Roberio Ranch because it was a plague-infested area.

The Britania Hospital where he worked double duty was slowly decomposing. People from other villages scavenged building materials from the hospital so now it was missing doors and windows.

When he walked down the empty main street, a young man approached him. It was Wescley Silva. Wescley was nervous and he spoke first, "Ramon, I haven't spoken to anyone about our meeting when you warned me to leave town after Dr. Noqueira's murder. Obviously, you made the arrangements to send a Quimbanda priest to take out the Roberio clan. No, don't answer that, I already know. It's ok."

"Wescley, I'm sorry. I didn't know it would have this impact on the town."

"Man, it was a big bomb you sent here. Now, there's no employment, nothing. I'm taking care of my parents and they refuse to leave so

I'm stuck here with them. If it were not for them, I'd be in Rio right now."

"Wescley, I promise you that things will get better in Britania and people will return. It may take a couple of years but people will return."

"No, I disagree. Every month it gets worse. I don't think there will ever be any hope for Britania. Your Quimbanda priest also killed the town when he killed Carlos and Davis. You were lucky to get out of here with your life. It's a wonder you and Mrs. Noqueira weren't killed in the cross fire."

"Wescley, here, take this money to help with your parents. Be patient and trust me, things will get better here." Ramon didn't tell Wescley that Vanessa escaped only to be killed in Brasilia. Wescley was already depressed and looked like he didn't need another bit of bad news.

CHAPTER EIGHT

Following his misadventures with Max Shuman, Ramon went back to Rio de Janeiro. He and his American friend Gary Bennett were having a late afternoon beer break at one of the beach kiosks on Ipanema Beach when Gary suggested, "Why don't you come along next month when I return to America. You can hang out at my place and the change would do you good. It would make you learn English very quickly. It won't cost you a thing besides your airfare and visa."

"That sounds like fun," Ramon replied. "Will I have to sleep on your porch or do you have space for me?"

"I've got plenty of space. I have a three-bedroom apartment on the beach in Fort Lauderdale. I have a guest bedroom and the other bedroom is for my work and fishing gear. I have a nice home office where I do a lot of my work. It's a nice place. I just lock it up when I leave and it's always there when I return from these overseas assignments. There is only one thing that I need to explain. My girlfriend may be moving in with me and if that happens then we will need to find another place for you to stay. I'm really serious about this girl and I'm sure she is the one. We would already be living together except her work is in the opposite direction from mine. She works as an executive and works 60 hours every week so we only see each other on the weekends. You will just need to give us some privacy on Friday and Saturday nights."

Ramon asked, "Do you think I will be able to get a tourist visa?"

"One thing is certain," replied Gary. "If you don't bother going down to the American Embassy to apply for one, you will never know."

The next day Ramon went to Centro Rio and waited in a long line at the American Embassy. He paid his fees but to continue the application process, he had to return with a valid airline ticket. He left the Embassy and called Gary to find the exact flight information for his return and then went over to the American Airlines downtown branch and booked the same flight. He went back to the Embassy and stood in the same long line. He was lucky to get through the line before closing and he showed his airline ticket. The clerk said she had to keep his passport overnight, but he could pick up his visa and passport after ten o'clock the next morning.

The next month, Ramon flew to Miami with Gary. Fortunately, Gary's description of the apartment was correct and there was plenty of room for him. Gary spent lots of time on the phone in his home office. Gary was a consultant to several companies. When he was in the States, his phone was always ringing. Gary spent some time each day at a company south of Fort Lauderdale but Ramon could not go along because of the company's security restrictions. When there was actual fieldwork required, Ramon got to tag along. That left lots of time for Ramon to kill at the beach in Ft. Lauderdale.

Ramon was happy to help Gary with his household chores but wondered why he didn't have a maid to do his washing and cleaning. When Ramon asked about it Gary replied, "Are you kidding? All they do is put your things in the wrong place and then you can't find anything. Besides, you spend too much time filling out forms for tax withholding, FICA, unemployment compensation and a ton of other red tape. I'd be spending more time filling out forms then the maid would spend working. Besides, I have you here to help me. And, you would be bored if you didn't have something to do. So, here is a list for groceries and places to go for me tomorrow. Let's take my old jeep out and I can see if you can drive it well enough."

Ramon passed the driving test so he was allowed to use Gary's old jeep. Ramon was totally lost driving around but he figured if he got too lost he would just stop and ask for directions. Gary showed him where to go to do errands. At least with Gary's second set of wheels Ramon would have some freedom to drive around and check things out for himself. Ramon didn't mind being a slave to Gary, after all, Gary was not charging him for food or rent so he was happy to do Gary's errands while he was at work. Doing Gary's errands also meant that he had to use English and it was a great way to learn.

Ramon couldn't cook meals very well because he didn't have the ingredients that he was used to using. Mostly his maid cooked his meals in Rio, but his father also taught him how to cook everything. It took Ramon over a month to find out that milk was in the cold section at the grocery store. Gary kept asking for milk for his cereal in the morning and Ramon had to tell him the store was always out. He kept looking for milk stored on pallets in cases of one-liter cartons but could never find them. After he discovered the milk, he wondered why American milk was so bad that it could only be kept refrigerated and then it only had a shelf life of a week. The liter cartons in Brazil had a shelf life of six months and did not have to be refrigerated except after they were opened. Ramon did discover frozen microwave dinners at the grocery and these became a quick favorite since they required no preparation. Gary always growled when he served them but Ramon liked them because they were all so different. Still, without fresh pig ears, he could not prepare his favorite dish of beans.

After Ramon was in the States almost three months Gary explained to Ramon that major things were about to happen back in Brazil. Gary explained that the news agencies were reporting Brazil would soon turn over its military leadership to an interim appointed President and real elections would be held. Gary came right out with his concern, "Ramon, I know you have some money. I suppose that you have some inheritance from the family coffee plantation, or however you got your money really doesn't concern me. What I need to tell you is that your money in Brazil might become worthless overnight. In these government conversions, the insiders issue new money to themselves first and then declare all other currency obsolete. If you have any money in the bank in Brazil you need to go withdraw it and convert it to U.S. dollars right now."

Ramon replied, "Yes, I do have some money in the bank in Brazil. You should know that I came by my money by myself and I did so honestly and by difficult and dangerous work. No, my parents were never rich and to this day, my father is a poor farmer. No, I am not a drug dealer. Now, I'm not sure that I can just go get my money. Remember that I'm on a tourist visa so if I leave I can't come back."

"Let's check that," Gary said. "Bring me your passport and let's read the restrictions on your visa."

Gary read the fine print on Ramon's visa and said, "You're fine. It's a tourist visa but you have unlimited access to come and go for a period of five years. You are only in trouble if you stay here more than ninety days at any one time so you are soon approaching that. It just means that before ninety days are up you need to go to Mexico or the Bahamas and have your passport stamped and then you are good to return for another ninety days. I'm not sure that you really do need to return to Brazil. Do you have a banker there who you can trust to wire your money in dollars to the U.S.?"

"No, bankers in Brazil cannot be trusted so I need to fly there to get it. Besides, it's in a safe deposit vault and I have the only key."

"You will still need to do some work regarding your money before you bring it back. Foreigners are not allowed to have bank accounts in the States. I will check with my rich friends who do some offshore banking and ask them about their resources."

Before Ramon left for Brazil, Gary had the information about offshore accounts in the Cayman Islands. He had no first-hand knowledge of this bank but his friend assured him that it was a legitimate bank and could place Ramon's funds in any major currency or in stocks of the major exchanges. Gary handed Ramon the telephone number for the Cayman Islands Bank and Ramon called to set up an account. The bank faxed back a confirming account number and gave Ramon his access code verbally. Their fax also contained all the specifics on receiving an inbound wire transfer. Ramon put the fax copies with his passport so he would have them available for his use in Brazil.

Ramon paid a lot of money for the first available flight to Rio de Janeiro. From there he flew to Goiania to collect his cash. He stayed overnight in Goiania and the next morning he went to a department store to buy four very large suitcases. He was self-conscious showing up at the bank with four large suitcases but he explained to Mr. Falco that he needed them for the antiques stored in the safety deposit boxes.

He could have made the bank visit with hired armed guards but that would really be drawing attention.

When he opened his first vault box, he was happy with what he saw. The entire contents of the first box were in U.S. $100 bills. Ramon had forgotten that long ago he had the bank convert some of his currency to U.S. one-hundred dollar notes because they took up less room in his hidden vault in his kitchen floor. Ramon counted out $20,000 in U.S. notes and returned them to a vault box. He would keep that vault box and surrender the rest. He thought he would keep the $20,000 as a safety net in case anything bad ever happened to him.

His three other vault boxes all contained Brazilian notes so he carefully packed them in his suitcases. The four vault boxes owned by Roberto also contained only Brazilian notes and he packed them in the remaining suitcases.

Ramon left the bank after surrendering the keys for the vault boxes he no longer needed. Mr. Falco helped Ramon carry the four large suitcases out to a waiting taxi that took him to the airport for his return to Rio de Janeiro. At the airport in Rio, Ramon purchased four strong locks for his suitcases. He also paid to have all the suitcases wrapped in plastic shrink-wrap for additional security.

With his business in Brazil completed, Ramon returned to the United States to continue his tourist visit. During the flight, he completed the required Customs forms and had to ask the flight attendant for a form "#4257- Declaration of currency over US $5000." He whispered his request to the flight attendant who then shouted to her co-workers that she needed a "4257." Ramon felt that having to ask for the form was like making an announcement over the public address system to everyone on the plane, "Hey, I'm carrying around more than $5,000 cash in U.S. currency." Ramon slumped down into the seat hoping he could avoid detection of onlookers.

He considered himself lucky to have gotten out of Brazil with the cash. Now he just needed to make it through Customs going back to America. At least he had his passport stamped and now he was good to stay an additional ninety days in the States. He just hoped that he didn't get mugged taking his suitcases out of the airport.

CHAPTER NINE

When Ramon arrived in Miami, Gary was waiting for him to clear Customs and he helped Ramon load the four large suitcases into the trunk and back seat of his white Saab. Ramon told Gary his stomach hurt from being so nervous about carrying the money. Gary said, "No, that's just your stomach telling you that you need some food. You didn't eat any of that disgusting food on the plane did you?"

"No, I was too nervous to eat."

It was still early in the morning so Gary suggested, "Let's go grab some breakfast at the diner and you can tell me about your trip."

The two men took a quiet corner table in the diner and Gary probed, "So, you obviously didn't wire the money to the Cayman Islands. What happened?"

"I asked about that and Brazil keeps records of such transactions and you have to pay a heavy tax when you wire money from your account. I didn't want a paper trail so I brought it all back with me except for a small emergency fund that I left in US dollars at my bank in Goiania. On the plane last night with the customs forms, they make you ask for a form declaring when you are carrying more than $5,000 in US funds. That made me nervous because it tells everyone on the plane your business. So, I'm still nervous with all that cash setting out there in your Saab."

Gary inquired, "So how are you going to get the cash to your account in the Caymans?"

"I guess I will have to mule it there myself. I could really use your help when I go there to the bank in case there are things they tell me that I can't understand. I doubt that the bank staff speak Portuguese."

"See, aren't you glad I brought you to the States to learn English?"

"Yes, but my English is not good enough yet to understand business or legal matters. Those aren't subjects I talk about with the girls on the beach."

Gary asked, "What help are you looking for? What are your plans?"

"I thought you could go with me to the Cayman Islands this weekend. You will need to take off a weekday from work so you can go to the bank with me."

The two men changed the subject briefly while the waiter walked to their table. Gary ordered a large breakfast and Ramon ordered coffee and toast. After the waiter left, Ramon continued, "I'll call the bank today to be sure there is not some bank holiday this Friday or next Monday and then I will call you at work. Can you get either of those days off?"

"Sure, either day will work. I'm sort of between projects right now so your timing is good."

Ramon asked, "Do you want to make a four-day weekend out of it?"

"No, let's just do three. When you call the bank, you should ask for an appointment with the bank president. Since you are making a big deposit, he should be there to meet you and to help you. It would be good for the two of you to meet personally. So make that a priority when choosing the Monday or the Friday."

Ramon replied while mentally reviewing their proposed schedule, "No, a Monday will not work out. We don't want to spend the entire weekend in the Caymans babysitting the suitcases. We will have to go to the bank on a Friday. If I can't get an early morning flight then we may have to fly out on Thursday night. Is that ok with you?"

"Sure, that works," replied Gary.

On Friday afternoon, Gary and Ramon made the deposit to the Cayman Islands Bank. Ramon walked in by himself to meet Nanette

Spencer, the bank president. Nanette was in her early forties but showed no sign of her age. She was black and wore her black hair straight in a Jackie Onassis flip. Her black business dress was tailored and she wore large black beads around her neck. Her glasses were large and rimmed in heavy black plastic. Mrs. Spencer invited Ramon into her private office.

Ramon explained that he had many Brazilian notes and some American notes for counting so Mrs. Spencer took him to a private counting room and called in three tellers to wait for the money. Ramon went back out to the taxi waiting in front of the bank. Gary was in the cab making sure that it didn't drive away with the four large suitcases in its trunk.

While the tellers counted the money, Ramon had a good visit with Nanette Spencer. She made some good recommendations about placing the money in stock of various multinational companies. Ramon asked the president, "I just want to be certain, will I have access to my money whether I am in the States or in Brazil?"

Mrs. Spencer replied, "Yes, you will have instant access from any country in the world that allows wire transfers. That's an easy transfer to either Brazil or the United States."

"And what about annual taxes?" inquired Ramon.

"In the Cayman Islands you only pay a small tax on your annual earnings," answered Mrs. Spencer. "If you want to sign and date this form, it gives us custodial power for your account. The custodial power is only for the purpose of filing and paying your tax on the earnings. It doesn't give us any more control over your account than that. Most of our clients choose this option. The bank charges only $50.00 for each tax filing and that is much less expensive than hiring an outside accountant."

After waiting several hours in a small room with windows looking into the counting room, Mrs. Spencer came in and handed Ramon a note showing the total in U.S. dollars of $10,874,173.00. Ramon asked, "May I please have $5,000.00 back with $2,000.00 in Cayman notes and the rest in U.S. bills? Please deposit the balance in my account."

"Certainly, Mr. Gobbey," replied the executive. "We will get that for you right away. Is there anything else that we can do to help you?"

Ramon paused and asked, "Can you tell me about the privacy of my funds. Will anyone in the United States or Brazil be able to find out how much money I have?"

"Never," replied Mrs. Spencer calmly. "That is the beauty of banking in the Cayman Islands. We are the Switzerland of Latin America. Our government will never probe into your business nor will it let the government of other nations find your information. The government of the Cayman Islands does not allow subpoenas from other nations, so there is absolutely no way for anyone to know your business unless you tell them. Our government gets much of its operating revenue from the taxes we just discussed. If we had no privacy, we would have no accounts. Without these large accounts, funding for our government would end. Please understand, there is no way that our privacy laws will ever change."

Ramon added, "And what about the privacy of wire transfers to and from your bank?"

"Wiring money into your account is absolutely confidential on this end," assured Mrs. Spencer. "However, you need to remember that Brazil charges a tax on wire transfers out of their country so that will leave a paper trail. Now, about receiving wire transfers coming into America or Brazil, both counties require notification to the government of any transfers over $5,000 at one time. In Brazil, you will not be caught if you wire $4,000 every ten minutes forever. In the United States that would create a red flag and the government will be notified. If it is any help, the notifications only tell where the money is going into Brazil or the United States. It does not tell where the money came from. As I said, your account information here is absolutely confidential."

Ramon asked, "What about accessing my funds through a checking account here?"

"Unfortunately, your checks would only be good for use on the Cayman Islands," replied Mrs. Spencer. "However, many of our clients pay for major items with an international money draft which we can mail to you by overnight services. That is a way to get around the notifications on the wire transfers. Another option is for you to carry an international credit card. We can issue one with almost any limit. It is generic so no one will be able to tell that it originated in the Cayman Islands and it cannot be traced back to your account here."

"Perfect," Ramon replied with a smile. "I will do the international money drafts instead of wire transfers. Just to explain, Mrs. Spencer, I am no drug dealer. My money comes from dangerous and difficult work. My concern for confidentiality is for my own safety. In Brazil, if people know you have money they will kidnap you to get it. I want to live discreetly so I must be certain that my banking is kept confidential at all times."

Mrs. Spencer held up her hand to Ramon and said, "There is no need to explain yourself. Our clients all have different reasons for wanting private banking and it is our job, and our pleasure, to supply that service. About the credit card, should I have one mailed to you and what limit would you prefer?"

"Yes, please," replied Ramon. "A credit card with a $10,000 limit would be nice."

As Gary and Ramon got ready to leave the bank, Mrs. Spencer stood and shook hands with both of them. She gave Ramon a deposit receipt and her business card, telling him, "Please, call me any time, day or night. If you need anything, or have any questions, I am at your disposal." Ramon thanked her and the two men left the bank.

Ramon was all smiles as he left the bank. He got 100% of everything he needed from Mrs. Spencer. Ramon was relieved to have his cash out of Brazil and for once earning money instead of sitting dormant. Ramon had never counted his money and was surprised that he had over ten million dollars. He thought that was good earnings for nine years of work with Dr. Noqueira.

With the rest of the weekend to kill, Gary and Ramon rented a charter for some deep sea fishing and caught a couple good sized Marlin which they brought up to the side of the boat and released. On Saturday night, Gary drank too much and didn't remember which lady from the bar he took back to his hotel room. Ramon had one drink at the bar and spent the rest of the evening talking to a pretty blond down at the beach.

On Sunday morning, Gary was still hung over and could barely walk to the taxi waiting to take them to the airport. He slept the entire time on the plane back to Miami and his breath smelled like tequila. Unfortunately, Ramon had the seat next to Gary and had to suffer while Gary snored. Ramon paid for the hotel rooms, the charter fishing, and everything else for the weekend so he was happy to be returning with less than the $5,000 he obtained from Mrs. Spencer. At least he wouldn't have to fill out the form 4257 on this flight.

That night back in Florida, Ramon was not feeling very well. Maybe it was the food he ate in the Cayman Islands, or maybe he picked up a bug along the way. Before bedtime, he felt like he might have a fever so he took some aspirin to kill it. That night Ramon was up half the night and for the other half he had the worst nightmares in his life. During the nightmares, the young Roberio children taunted him and called him a child murderer. The worse of it came from their nanny, Monica Lopes, "You little bastard, are you very happy there counting your vast amount of money in your bank? Why did you have to take my life away? Why is your life so much more important than mine? What are you going to do with the rest of your life?" In the nightmare, Monica was much angrier but that is all Ramon would allow himself to remember.

Then there was the nightmare from his father telling him, "Remember, the good is in the sweat of the land. You know what to do. It's all about the land."

In the morning Ramon apologized to Gary and told him he was so sick he couldn't do any errands. Ramon told him, "Just tell me how to reach you today in case I need you to take me to a hospital. I'm serious. I thought I was going to die last night."

"Hey buddy, what the hell happened to you in the Caymans? Did you get something serious from that girl you were kissing? Maybe she gave you hepatitis. If you don't get better soon maybe you should go see a doctor."

"I hope it's just a bad case of flu so you should stay away from me, but come get me or call an ambulance if I call you today."

Handing Ramon a slip of paper Gary said, "Ok, you can call me at this number today but I warn you I will be in meetings all day. I will tell the secretary to pass on any calls from you. However, I can't come home to take care of you. I'm stuck there all day so it will be early evening before I'm home. Call me if you get really sick. The only thing I could do is to call the nearest ambulance for you. I have some medication for flu and I'll leave that out for you."

The following day Ramon felt just fine. His sickness passed as quickly as it came. He unpacked from his trip and caught up with washing clothes and he cleaned the apartment. Gary had left out a grocery list so he took Gary's jeep to the store. When Gary gave him his first driving lesson for American driving he warned Ramon that the old open jeep was fine for doing errands but he shouldn't take it on the freeway or drive it fast. The old jeep was pretty much a rust bucket but Ramon liked driving it because it was open. It was also great for catching beach girls. The old upholstery smelled like mold but that's a given for an open car in the tropics.

By now, Ramon had mastered grocery shopping. If he stuck to the same store, he pretty much knew where everything was located. There were just so many choices for food it was ridiculous. He wondered why Americans needed 800 different kinds of cereal but had only one kind of banana.

A few days later when Ramon was at the apartment, he answered the phone and was surprised that it was Thomaz Rocha on the other end. "Ramon, I'm sorry I couldn't reach you any sooner. I found your phone number for America only because I happened to be talking to your banker, Mr. Falco, here in Goiania. I'm afraid that I have horrible news for you. Your father passed away three days ago. We didn't know how to contact you so they went ahead and cremated his remains. I will have the mortuary hold them until your next trip back home."

Wiping tears from his eyes Ramon replied, "Yes, that will be fine. On what day did he die?"

Rocha replied, "It was Sunday, the 25th."

Ramon tried to be thoughtful and asked his attorney, "Will you please have someone go to his home and box up any papers that look important and place them in storage for me? As for the farm, will you please contact a real estate broker and have it placed for sale? And of the horses and sheep in the pasture, can you please have someone give those away to some children in the area? You must tell their parents that the animals must never be eaten. Those animals were my pets and they need to remain pets so please find some families who will take them on that condition. As for my horse, Storm, I want to keep him. Will you please find someone who will board him? If you will pay them on a monthly basis I will reimburse you upon my return."

"Don't worry about a thing," the attorney replied. "I'll take care of everything. Do you have any idea when you might be returning?"

"I have some things to do here and I'll need to book a flight to Rio. I should be back there by the end of next month at the latest."

As he was saying goodbye to his attorney, it hit him like a big rock thrown against the side of his face. The 25th was day the he returned from the Cayman Islands. That was the day he was so sick and that was the night he had a conversation with his father during his nightmares. A cold chill ran entirely through Ramon as he realized that he had a deathbed visitation from his father who was 5,000 miles away.

The next week the men traded cars so Ramon could take Gary's Saab to the dealership for an oil change and periodic maintenance. Ramon was at the dealership all morning waiting and to kill time he flipped through weekly news magazines. While skimming pages, one image caught his immediate attention. In the section called "Transitions" there was a photo of Max Schuman. The obituary said that the German industrialist died during a workplace accident. The notice went on to describe Max as a notorious arms dealer and a major supplier of weapons to covert operations around the world. There was no doubt in Ramon's mind how Max died. Max was no pharmaceutical researcher—he was a weapons dealer. Undoubtedly, he died while making a weapon out of the Green Darter venom. Ramon looked up from the magazine to see how many people might notice if he tore the page out of the magazine. The waiting room was full of people but he tore the page out anyway and left to check on the progress of the Saab in the service bay.

That night he told Gary that he needed his help, "I have to confess to you that I told you a small lie about how I made my money. I was a drug dealer."

"I knew it, I knew you were a drug dealer," Gary exclaimed.

"No, no, not in the sense that you are thinking," said Ramon. "In Brazil my business partner and I had access to some of the rarest and deadliest chemical compounds on the planet. We sold these compounds to pharmaceutical research companies around the world. The work was very dangerous and we were paid very well for the compounds. Unfortunately, before we ended the business, one of the shipments was contaminated and I fear at least one man has died from exposure. He owned a laboratory in Frankfurt and I must go there to make certain the product is destroyed."

"Why don't you just call the police there and tell them to go destroy it."

"I don't think they would pay any attention to me. Besides, they would never know how to handle it safely. I need to go there personally to make sure that it's all destroyed properly."

Walking to the telephone, Gary explained, "Well, little buddy, you're in luck. I just happen to know a technician in Frankfurt who can help you get around and who can translate for you. You'll have to use your English though."

Gary dialed and waited for an answer, "Hey, Greta, this is Gary Bennett. Would you be up for doing a little industrial espionage? It might involve some wiretaps, a little breaking and entering—just your kind of thing. My friend's name is Ramon Gobbey. I'll have him call you back as soon as he makes his airline reservations. Just treat him nice and take it slow. His English isn't very good yet and he doesn't know two words of German. Just make sure he gets his job done and put him on his plane back to the States. You'll be paid well so don't worry about that. Just call your work and tell them you're going to be out sick for a couple of days."

After hanging up with Greta, Gary turned to Ramon and said, "You're in good hands. I've used her for corporate surveillance on quite a few occasions and she is always right on top of things."

Ramon smiled and said, "Yeah—on top of things!"

"Well, yes, that too. She is a young woman and she has needs. You may have to pay her in more than just cash."

"No problem." Ramon said with a wide grin. He was just hoping under his breath that Gary wasn't kidding about Greta. He didn't want to walk up to a sign with his name on it at the airport and find an old ugly woman standing behind it. Ramon thought if that happened, he would definitely have to do something to pay Gary back.

Ramon thought for a minute and then started shouting, "Wait! Wait! I can't go to Germany wearing shorts and flip-flops. That's all I own. I have to go there to look and sound like someone very important. If I show up in my sandals and shorts they will laugh at me. Also, I think it might be really cold in Germany right now."

Gary assured him, "Don't worry about it. We'll leave for the airport a couple hours early. I know a place along the way where you can buy an expensive suit and they do instant alterations. Just go pack your toothbrush and underwear and we'll get you a dark business suit on the way."

At the tailors, the clerks gave up trying to teach Ramon how to tie a knot for his silk tie. They tied one good knot and then showed him how to loosen it up to take his shirt off keeping the tie in place. With his dark suit, tie, and shiny black shoes Ramon looked the part of someone very important. "The Germans will be fooled," thought Gary.

After the fitting, Gary drove Ramon to the Miami airport and dropped him off for his direct flight to Frankfurt. Ramon couldn't get a ticket so he was going to fly standby and take any available seat for the red eye flight. He figured if he didn't get on the flight he could just take a shuttle back to Ft. Lauderdale and try again the next night. Fortunately, there was at least one empty seat on the jumbo jet so Ramon boarded after all the other passengers. The next morning Ramon was a little intimidated at the Frankfurt Airport Customs. Every few feet there were armed guards with machine guns and dogs. Ramon just had his small carry-on so he passed through Customs quickly.

Outside of Customs, there was a long line of people holding placards with names. Ramon beamed when he saw a sign with his name on it but the smile quickly disappeared. Holding the sign was an old, fat, ugly woman wearing a black leather full-length coat. He murmured to himself, "Oh piss, I'm really gonna get even with Gary for this. This is why Gary didn't describe her to me." Ramon went around the barricades and tapped the fat woman on the shoulder. Without saying a word, the woman grabbed the sleeve of his new suit coat and dragged him to the nearest door. Right outside the door, she pointed for Ramon to get in the back of a car and she went to the driver's side. In the back seat was a beautiful blond girl who beamed, "Hi Ramon, I'm Greta." Ramon couldn't hide a big smile.

As they drove away, Ramon told Greta all the facts that she needed to know. His explanation was similar to the one he recently gave Gary about chemical compounds that contained a deadly viral contamination. As soon as he told Greta the name of Max Schuman, Greta shouted in German to the driver. The fat woman yanked at the steering wheel turning the car quickly in a different direction. There was a verbal exchange between Greta and the fat woman and it was quickly giving Ramon a splitting headache. He thought when Germans talk to each other they were always yelling and spitting at one another. The German language certainly did not have the rhythm and poetry of Portuguese nor was it succinct like English.

Greta explained to Ramon that the news of Max Schuman's death was a big deal in Germany and in all likelihood, there would still be police investigators on the scene. Greta was going to have the driver go past the building that housed Max's operation so they check out the security. The fat woman pulled alongside a vacant concrete building in an industrial park on the fringe of Frankfurt. There were no police cars around so they were able to take their time studying the building. Greta got a good look at the locks on the doors. Yellow police tape covered the main door and Ramon wondered if every country in the world used the same yellow plastic tape for crime scenes. Greta saw what she needed and loudly shouted instructions to the driver. The fat woman stepped on the gas and they left the industrial park.

On the drive to Greta's apartment, the fat woman stomped on the brakes at every stoplight and then gunned the car as fast as possible when the light turned green. Ramon asked, "Have you ever thought of giving your driver some driving lessons?"

"Don't worry about her. She will never change."

Once they were in Greta's apartment, Greta showed Ramon around. Ramon noticed that there was only one bedroom and he had plans to sleep on a bed.

Greta asked, "Ramon, are all the men in Brazil as handsome as you?"

Ramon blushed. He always thought of himself as being only average in looks. He smiled at Greta because he thought she might like him. Ramon replied, "No, I'm the ugly one."

Greta looked at his small carry-on case and said, "Did you think that we are going to do a covert operation tonight wearing a suit and tie?"

Ramon replied, "No, I wore the suit in case I have to talk to someone else who is very important."

"Oh, and do you think I'm very important?" purred Greta while pushing him to the sofa.

As their lips met, Ramon replied, "Yes, yes, you are very important."

"That's good, because we have all afternoon to kill. And these two very important people need to find something to occupy their time until dark."

Greta smelled great and she tasted even better. Ramon forgot to protest when she quickly removed his skillfully knotted silk tie. Seconds later, their clothes littered the living room floor. The afternoon went by too quickly and after dark, the two retrieved their clothes from the floor.

Greta fixed a couple sandwiches and called her brother. He lived nearby and was slightly larger than Ramon. She asked him to bring over a pair of black jeans with a belt and a black T-shirt.

In German, the younger brother asked, "Are you going fishing with a new boyfriend tonight?"

She replied, "Why yes, I am. And, he's very cute. When are you coming over?"

"Give me 30 minutes. Does he need some tennis shoes to complete the ensemble?"

Greta looked at Ramon's small shoes and replied, "No, there's only so much we can do. See you soon."

Just after Greta and Ramon finished their meal, Greta answered a knock at the door. Greta introduced her brother Matthew to Ramon. The men shook hands and Matthew shoved the folded clothes into Ramon's arms. Matthew spoke only German, "Please tell him not to get any stains on my jeans."

Greta teased and replied in German, "I don't think that would be possible. I just drained him this afternoon."

"I'm free tonight if the two of you need a chaperone," offered Matthew.

"Yes, I do think that we could use your help on a little surveillance job at the industrial park. I see you came dressed for action tonight so you can stay in the car and keep a look out."

"No way Sis, if there's an inside job then I'm your man," Matthew asserted.

"Ok, then you can break and we will enter. Ramon has to get inside to look for some very specific contaminated products and you wouldn't know what to look for. I need you in the car with the radio just in case anyone shows up."

Ramon changed into the clothes that Matthew brought while the siblings talked. He had to tighten up the belt and roll up the pant legs and he thought he was ready to go. The shiny dress shoes looked out of place but there was nothing he could do about that. He just hoped that he wouldn't fall on his ass while wearing them.

On the way to Max's industrial building Greta and Matthew discussed the best ways to break into the building. Greta wanted to enter through the roof and Matthew argued for a quick break-in at the front door by picking the lock. Greta warned, "There is a sophisticated alarm system and if you enter at the front door it will go off and the guards will be there in no time."

"Not if I cut the power to the entire building," offered Matthew.

Greta asked Ramon, "Will that poison of yours be affected in any way if we turn off the electricity to the building? Will anything bad happen if it's frozen and thaws out? Can you think of any bad outcomes if we shut down the power so the security alarm will not go off?"

Ramon replied, "No, actually that might be the best thing to help kill it. But don't the two of you know that alarm systems now have redundant power sources? So killing power to the building won't prevent the alarm from going off."

"Don't worry about that. We have a nice little tool which we quickly plug into the alarm system and it shorts everything out," Greta assured Ramon.

According to plan, Matthew picked the lock and Greta jumped into action and immediately silenced the alarm system with a high voltage battery tool she carried in her backpack. Matthew returned to the car to keep watch. The concrete industrial building had no windows so Greta was able to use some very large and bright battery powered floor lamps to light up the rooms. Ramon did an initial survey of the building and was surprised how big the building appeared once he was inside. The warehouse was enormous and it would take them all night to look for the vials Max purchased.

Ramon asked Greta to call her brother to come into the building. With Matthew there, he drew out a picture of the vials and the label and asked them to start searching the warehouse for anything that looked remotely like his drawing. He asked them to mark the locations of any small caliber ammunition they might find. With Greta and Matthew searching the warehouse, Ramon was free to explore the Research and Development Laboratories of the facility.

There were three labs and the first two looked like they had nothing to do with Ramon's product. In the third lab, Ramon had the wind sucked from his lungs when he walked into it. There was police tape all over the floor showing where bodies were found. Many more people died here than just Max. Shaking, Ramon ran to get Greta from the warehouse. "You've got to come help me. I found something but I need your help reading German," Ramon said as he tried to catch his breath.

Greta followed Ramon into the lab and said in English, "Oh my. What happened here?"

"Looks like a lot more people died here than just Max Schuman," Ramon offered. "Here, here is one of my vials I sold to Max Schuman. It's labeled veterinary antibiotics and it has a deadly contamination. Use only your rubber gloves when handling any of this. Please read these logbooks and look at their set up over here and tell me what they were trying to do."

Greta studied the lab instruments on the counter and then read the logbooks. She was careful not to touch any of the instruments in the lab and she wore her rubber gloves when handling the logbooks. After a long five minutes Greta said, "Ramon, you've been a very naughty boy. You sold Max a deadly poison and he was using it to develop an aerosol weapon. From the logbooks, it looks like they wanted a weapon that could be placed in a closed building like a skyscraper or an airport and the aerosol would kill everyone there. Looks like they completed the project. It's a good thing they all died before selling it."

"Yeah, just like a bunch of dead rats," replied Ramon. "Max told us he was a pharmaceutical researcher and we didn't have the resources to check him out properly. Why hasn't your government come in here yet and cleaned this all out?"

"Maybe because it's too dangerous. My bet is that someone else has purchased the whole deal. There is a new Max waiting on the sidelines and he owns the police. That's the only logical reason," Greta whispered.

"I believe you," Ramon replied in a hushed voice. "Let's gather up everything harmful here and pile it up by the back loading dock. We will need to bag these logbooks and I need to go burn them myself. They are far too dangerous to be left here."

Greta and Ramon found Matthew in the warehouse busy tagging boxes of small ammunition. After looking it all over Ramon said, "I have no idea which are poison bullets and which were not. None of them are labeled, 'Poison Bullets.' All of the small ammunition is suspicious and will need to be hauled over to the loading dock."

Greta suggested, "Matthew and I will work in the warehouse. Before you start hauling anything out of the contaminated lab, you need to put on one of those hazmat suits from the first lab and wear a respirator. I'll help you get into the suit. Only you should be in the lab. There is no sense of all three of us dying from exposure to Max's poison."

"That makes me feel so much better," answered Ramon.

Ramon spent the next few hours carrying items from the contaminated lab to the loading dock. He found nine full vials and two partial vials of Green Darter venom so he carefully triple bagged them and put them in a cushioned box and took it to the loading dock. Ramon bagged up the logbooks in triple plastic bags and put them in the trunk of Greta's car. Matthew found a large cart to use to haul the cartons of ammunition to the loading dock. When all the items were on the dock, Greta asked Ramon, "Now what do we do with all of this?"

Ramon replied, "We light a big bonfire right here."

"No, you can't do that. This place will spend days blowing up and firefighters will be killed. It has to be disposed of in a proper manner," warned Greta. "I have an idea. Ramon you will get to make use of that suit you brought. Matthew, I will need you tomorrow as well. You will need to call your employer to tell your boss that you have the flu. Here's the plan. Early in the morning, we appear here as Interpol Agents and we will call in a 'Code Red' to the Hazmat Team. Matthew and I will be in disguises because this is our home city. Ramon, all you need to do is to shout orders to me in Portuguese and I will translate. The louder you shout at me the better. The three of us will all be Interpol Agents and I have two friends who will paint their car tonight to look like

Frankfurt Police. I will have them here tomorrow wearing city police uniforms and they will escort us in and out and we will be here to give the Hazmat Team instructions on how to handle Max's lab."

"Wow, do you really think all that is going to work?" Ramon asked. Without waiting for a reply, he added, "In the best-case scenario all that ammunition needs to be burned. In fact, everything in the building needs to be burned and then the building needs to be burned and torn down and the concrete parts need to be hauled to a landfill for hazmat."

Cheerfully, Greta replied, "No problem. Tomorrow morning when you are yelling and screaming at me in Portuguese, I will just translate all of that to the chief of the Hazmat Team. Watch for a double wink of my left eye and that will mean that I'm talking to the chief and he will be the one we will need to impress. If we do a good job in front of the chief there will be no trace left behind of Max's laboratory."

Back at her apartment, Greta went to work calling her friends who would be city police in the morning. She put Matthew and herself in disguises and then took Polaroid pictures for Interpol identification badges. She made Ramon put his suit and tie back on for a photo for his identification badge as well.

A few hours later, Greta's friends pulled up in the phony squad car. Ramon was messing with his silk tie and Greta tied it for him again. After a quick check of dress codes and identification badges, they were all off to the industrial park. On the way there, Greta smiled at Ramon and said, "Ok, this is your day. I hope you are a good actor. Just remember that you have to be shouting and screaming at me as if you are in a horrible panic. We didn't get to practice that but I think you will do fine."

Before they got to the industrial park they called the Hazmat Team for a Code Red to Max's building. They parked and waited out of the area so they would arrive just when the Hazmat Team pulled in. When the big truck used by the Hazmat Team arrived the Interpol Agents were there shouting at them to break down the door at the loading bay. The Hazmat Team members quickly attached a chain to the door and to their truck and the door was off in a couple seconds. Greta was in fine form as she sprung to the loading bay with Ramon on her heels.

Greta had her audience so she gave the double wink to Ramon and he quickly started screaming orders to her.

Greta screamed to the chief in German, "All this in the loading bay is contaminated with a lethal virus that can kill the entire city. All your men must be wearing air compressors and they must carefully take these items over to that field and burn it all. It's explosive. Does your team know how to handle burning ammunition?"

The chief nodded and reached for his radio and called for more equipment. Ramon continued his loud rant and Greta translated to the chief telling him that the glass vials in the cushioned box contained the deadly virus and it needed special handling in its destruction. Greta screamed and pointed to the box, "This is the material that is so deadly it might kill half of Germany. Do you understand?" The chief nodded again and spoke quickly into his radio.

Ramon continued his screaming and now added waving his arms madly for extra emphasis. Greta translated, shouting to the chief, "All the material in the warehouse is explosive and the rest of it will need to be taken to a military firing range and burned. You must evacuate all areas for at least a half mile radius before you start any burning."

Almost out of breath, Ramon continued his shouting to Greta. This time she informed the chief, "The virus is so dangerous that the entire building needs to be burned for at least 24 hours, then knocked down, and the parts need to be disposed of in a hazmat landfill."

At this, she could see the chief raise his eyebrows. She wasn't sure that the chief believed her until he reached for his radio again and called for more equipment. Ramon was still screaming and was starting to lose his voice.

By now, the parking lot of the industrial building was filling with heavy equipment owned by the Hazmat Team. When he saw all the equipment Ramon smiled knowing that the job was done. Also arriving were vans owned by the local news stations. They were pulling up and taking videos of everyone and everything. That was Greta's cue to get her team out of there. The imposters all managed to be wearing sunglass and holding their hands over their faces as if they were shielding their eyes from the sunlight. In the paper the next morning, there was a front-page story with a photo of Greta. She was there wearing sunglasses with her hand over her face and she was pointing at something. A black wig hid her long blond hair and over that, she wore an Interpol baseball cap. The photo in the paper was a very realistic action shot but it gave no clue to the identity of the Interpol Agents on site.

The photo caught the attention of Peter Strubble, Director for Interpol in Munich. He called Erik Bittel, the agent in charge in Frankfurt to congratulate him on successfully removing the dangerous plant. The agent confessed, "I had no involvement in that whatsoever and I was about to call you to find out why I wasn't asked to participate."

Director Strubble replied, "Well, it's obvious that it was our people who did this. Please ask around there in Frankfurt and find out which agents were in charge. I'd like to be debriefed."

"So would I," answered Agent Bittel. The two ended their conversation promising to call the other with any information about the raid. The next day, there was a huge drug raid in Frankfurt and the Interpol agents quickly forgot about Max's industrial plant.

The fake squad car dropped off the three Interpol Agents but by now, they had changed clothes and were civilians again. Ramon told Greta, "I need to change back into my casual clothes and then you need to take me someplace secure where I can burn those logbooks. They are still in the trunk of your Audi."

Greta offered, "My grandmother owns a farm out in the countryside. We can go there next but before we do why don't you call your airline for the day you want to return." Greta said it that way hoping that Ramon would stay around for a few more days. Ramon didn't understand Greta's clue and he called to reserve a ticket for the evening flight back to the States.

At the farmhouse, Greta introduced her grandmother to Ramon in German, "Grandmother, come meet my new boyfriend. Don't you think he's cute? I just adore him. He is from Brazil."

The old grandmother answered, "Yes, he's very handsome. Why don't you marry him?"

Greta replied, "Yes, I think I will."

"Greta, you always liked the boys who were tall, dark, and handsome."

"Yes, I will have to settle for two out of three but I think he is so cute it makes up for us being the same height."

"Don't worry about such nonsense. The two of you make a perfectly beautiful couple. You just need to get busy and have some children so I am alive to see my great-grandchildren."

Greta wondered, "Yes, but how do I know for sure he is the right one?"

"If I were 40 years younger, we'd be fighting over your handsome young man. Look how he smiles at you! Those dimples, Greta, he is delicious. And permanently tan. My grandchildren will be beautiful. You can't let him get away."

Greta showed Ramon a metal barrel used for burning farm trash. The two gathered some newspapers and gasoline and were about to start the fire when the grandmother shouted at Greta. Greta told Ramon, "We must bring in and fold her laundry from the clothes line first. She doesn't want her laundry smelling like smoke. Come help me fold sheets." The two completed the laundry task and then returned to burn the logbooks. Ramon lit a match and set the logbooks ablaze and the two of them found a bench near the barn. Greta held Ramon's hand and asked, "How many people could have been killed from those vials you sold to Max Schuman?"

Ramon answered earnestly, "Let's see, he last purchased 20 vials from me. Each single drop could kill 800 people. There were around 200 drops per vial, which makes 160,000 dead people per vial. That, times 20 vials makes a little over 3 million dead people. What we sold to Max was deadly only in the bloodstream. God knows what he did to it to make it stable as an aerosol. If he made it more potent in his process, then it might have been capable of killing millions more. If he made it a hundred times more potent then he could have killed off countries. If he made it a thousand times more potent then he could have killed off half the population of the world."

Greta asked, "Why in the world were you selling such a thing?"

"It's a product for medical research," replied Ramon. "In a very dilute form it could just sedate a patient. Many of our compounds were processed into medicines used as general anesthesia for surgery. There actually has been much good accomplished from the products we sold. We just had no idea that Max Schuman was making weapons. He told us he was a medical researcher. In the end, Max got what he deserved. And now there will be no trace of anything that Max produced."

Silently, Ramon wondered to himself, about the numbers he just quoted to Greta. Ramon worried and got that sinking feeling in the pit of his stomach. With Max's resources, it would not be difficult to increase the potency of the venom. He was giving himself a panic attack just thinking about the consequences. He also worried and wondered if Max had time to sell any of the venom or the new weapon to anyone else. The logbooks were burning and Ramon prayed that the laboratory personnel kept only the one set of books.

Ramon got up and poured more gasoline on the fire. After the logbooks were ashes, Ramon and Greta waved goodbye to her grandmother. Ramon and Greta had just pulled away from the driveway of the farmhouse and did not see the chickens that came to peck the ground around the bin used for burning. Ten of the chickens passed by the bin and suddenly half of them were dead on the ground.

When Ramon and Greta returned to the apartment, they both smelled like smoke so they took a shower together. After showering, they spent the rest of the afternoon as they had the day before. Ramon had fallen for Greta and he loved her more than woman he had ever dated. For Ramon, it was more than a sexual conquest. He had deep feelings for Greta and he knew he was in love with her. He wished that Greta felt the same way about him.

That evening as Ramon dressed for his return flight Greta was upset that Ramon was not staying a few more days. She was too proud to let Ramon know how she really felt about him. She gave him a hint to stay longer but obviously, he didn't want to stay longer. She guessed that he didn't feel the same way about her. Ramon heard no such invitation and felt that Greta was ready for him to leave.

Just before they left the apartment, Ramon asked Greta for her bank account number and if she had wire transfer instructions for him. "You mean you're not going to pay me before you leave?" Greta asked.

"Well, you know Greta," teased Ramon, "Secret agents never carry around cash through Customs." Greta gave him a playful shove and handed him a note she had previously written. It contained her bank name, account numbers, and her full name. Circled at the top of the note was "US$10,000.00"

Ramon glanced at it and said, "Well that's a nice round number," as he hugged Greta and gave her rear a firm squeeze. She responded by planting a deep kiss and hugged him back. Two hours later, Greta dropped Ramon off at the departures area for his airline.

While parked in the unloading area, Ramon gave Greta a deep long kiss and said, "Auf Wiedersehen."

Greta returned the long kiss and whispered, "Auf Wiedersehen."

While driving back in her little black Audi, Greta was mad at herself for tearing up so much that she could barely drive.

CHAPTER TEN

Ramon slept for 20 hours after his return from Germany. He was exhausted. Too much had happened in the last month and he needed some down time to recover. He had been kidnapped, his father died, his kidnapper died, he just took two red-eye flights, he fell in love, he participated in a successful covert operation, he yelled at the Germans so much that he still couldn't speak.

When Gary got home that night, he discovered Ramon sleeping. Gary kicked the bed and yelled, "Get up you lazy bum. Get up and come tell me what happened in Germany."

Ramon got up, took a shower, and then found Gary working in his home office. Gary was on the telephone so Ramon waved and went to the kitchen to find a microwave dinner that he ate on the patio. Gary was all smiles when he came out to join him on the patio. Gary asked, "So, how did it go? How was Fräulein Greta?"

"Greta was awesome. I'm in love," Ramon said in a horse voice.

"Why can't you talk? Cat got your tongue, Greta got your tongue?"

"Yes, Greta got my tongue and a few more things to boot!" Ramon boasted with a big grin. "I was yelling all morning at the German Hazmat Team. I lost my voice and I can barely speak."

Gary inquired, "Was Greta everything I said she would be?"

"You didn't tell me anything about Greta at all. At the airport, there was a fat, ugly woman and I assumed she was Greta. I was ready to get you for that but then the old woman shoved me in the back seat of a car and there was beautiful Greta. Like I said, I'm in love."

"Hey buddy, you'd better not use the L word around Greta. If you do, she won't have anything to do with you. She's a chick who likes the chase. So what are you going to do now?"

"I've got to go to Brazil to take care of my father's affairs. Meet with the attorney, the real estate agent—that kind of stuff. I wish I didn't have to. I'm not ready for another red-eye flight so soon."

"Then don't go right now. Wait a week to rest up and then go. While you are relaxing you can catch up on my errands, house cleaning, and shopping."

"Ok, ok," Ramon replied. "And you wonder why I can't catch an American beach girl. It's because I'm too busy doing your errands. It doesn't matter because I love Greta, but there's no way a Trans-Atlantic relationship would ever work. If she ever moves here to the States let me know and I will come see her."

A week later, Gary drove Ramon to the airport. Gary figured that he wouldn't be seeing Ramon anymore unless they met up in Rio. Ramon was returning to Brazil in his new suit and with the few possessions he owned.

Soon after Ramon left for Brazil, Gary received a call from Greta. She was calling for Ramon and wanted him to know that she received his wire transfer. Gary gave Greta the phone number that he had for Ramon in Brazil. Greta went on, "You should have seen the operation I did with Ramon. It was wonderful. We saved the world! I got my picture on the front page of the newspaper."

Gary replied, "Greta, when you are in a covert operation you're not supposed to get your photo in the newspaper."

"Oh, it was great. I will send you a copy of it. You'll get a kick out of it. I had Ramon screaming at me in Portuguese and I was yelling at the Hazmat Chief. It's a wonder I didn't give the poor fellow a heart attack. After every time we yelled he was on his radio ordering more equipment and in no time we had the entire place surrounded with Hazmat trucks. They have already torn down the building and hauled it away."

"Sounds like you had a fun time. Did you like Ramon?"

"Yes, he stole my heart. I should call him and tell him about the money transfer and about the building being torn down so quickly."

The number that Gary gave her was the telephone number to Ramon's apartment in Rio but she never got through to him. Ramon had moved on to start the rest of his life.

The future Mrs. Gary Bennett was busy planning her wedding. Gary proposed and Cathy accepted. They set their wedding date for the following year. The couple had many issues to resolve before the wedding. Housing and employment locations accounted for most of their anxiety. Cathy was not ready to cancel her lease nor was Gary willing to give up his apartment. The two compromised and agreed to a four-month trial living together at each of their apartments in rotation. If they couldn't agree to one of their existing locations, then they would look for an apartment in between.

Gary thought it was a waste to keep his empty apartment in Ft. Lauderdale and the matchmaker in him had ideas. He called Greta in Frankfurt, "Greta, do you still have a valid work permit for the States?"

"Yes, why?"

"I've taken on a big project and I need to clone myself. I'm wondering if you might be open to coming over to help me on it if I can beat your current salary."

"Sure Gary, what did you have in mind?"

"I have seventeen installs to do next month. All of them are medium or large companies and I can't come close to finishing the work on schedule even if I put my crew on overtime. I'm vacating my apartment for the next two months because Cathy and I are combining households. You can stay for free in my apartment. In addition to the free lodging I'll pay for your round trip airline tickets."

"Yes, I'm ready for some new adventures. When do you want me?"

"As soon as you can book a flight over."

"I really should give my employer a two-week notice. I don't need to burn any bridges here. I will be coming back to Germany and will need a good reference. I'll look into flight schedules and timing and I'll call you back tomorrow."

Gary then went on to the next part of his plan. He was determined to get Ramon married off to Greta. Gary knew that Ramon and Greta were perfect for each other and he knew that Ramon really did love her. A man never admits to being in love unless he is ready to take the big leap. Greta herself sounded lovesick when he spoke to her on the phone. Now it was just a matter of getting the two of them in the same place at the same time.

Finding Ramon in Brazil proved to be difficult. Ramon was no longer at his apartment in Rio. Gary remembered that Ramon was from a small town called Britania and he tried to remember the name of his banker. Gary remembered that his banker was in the capital city of the state where he lived. Gary pulled out an old, worn world atlas and looked for the city. Yes, he found Goiania and he remembered Ramon telling him that he was going to see his banker at the Bank of Goiania.

Gary called the bank and asked for the bank's president. Mr. Falco was not willing to hand over any phone numbers to an unknown caller but he did suggest calling Thomaz Rocha, Ramon's attorney.

The attorney was glad to be of assistance and told Gary that Ramon was staying out at the family farm and gave the phone number to him. Gary called the number, "Ramon, you're hard to find these days."

"Gary! What's up man?"

"You asked me to call you if Greta was ever coming to the States. You said that you would be interested in seeing her if she comes here. I'm pretty sure she will be here in two weeks."

"Wow, that's great. How long is she going to be there?"

"Minimum of a couple months. I hired her to help me complete some projects. She will be staying at my place. Cathy and I are getting married so we are combining households. I won't be there so you're welcome to come up and hang out with her."

"Wow, me and Greta shacking up at your place! Are you really sure you want to do that. I mean we'll be doing it all over the place. On your kitchen table, on your patio, everywhere."

"Ok, I asked for that. Just thank me later on your tenth wedding anniversary."

"I'm just giving you a hard time. Thanks for getting us back together. I confess I do want to marry Greta and I'm ready to settle down. It's just the logistics that's the problem. We're like you and Cathy except our locations are half a world apart. One way or another we will find some solution and figure out where we are going to live and what we're going to do with the rest of our lives. I'll be back there in a couple of weeks. I have some business matters here that I need to work on, and then I'll leave."

Married or not, Ramon had decided what he wanted to do with the rest of his life. Before leaving for Miami, Ramon met with his attorney, Thomaz Rocha. During their meeting, Ramon asked about the status of the Roberio Ranch and he asked the attorney to investigate if it could be purchased. Ramon explained that he was disappointed by the condition of Britania and he wanted to do some good for the people there. He asked Thomaz, "Do you know any high-ranking Senators in the State Government?"

"Certainly, I have some good contacts," answered the attorney. "What do you have in mind?"

"I'm thinking of purchasing the Roberio Ranch and giving it all away as farms to poor people who want to learn how to farm. I know that the government is interested in getting poor people out of the big cities and back to the land. This may be an opportunity for the government to help start a project that they will like. I'm not thinking of just dumping poor people out in the jungle. The government has already tried that, around Manaus, and it was a big failure. No, I'm talking about plotting out several thousand farms large enough to sustain successful farmers. I would have to hire people to teach them how to farm. There will be enormous infrastructure costs so you will need to negotiate an extremely low price for the ranch. I cannot spend more than five million dollars on it. For the project to be successful, I will need the entire ranch for that price, or hopefully less."

The attorney cautioned, "The Roberio Ranch is more than three and a half million acres. Do you have the kind of money that would sustain such a project?"

"No," replied Ramon honestly. "I will have to stage it over time. That is such a large project, it will take time to find people who want to become farmers. I know it's a project that will be several years in development. My plan is to farm some of it in soybeans to raise the cash for infrastructure expenses."

Mr. Rocha pressed, "Wouldn't you better off just investing your money? Why do you want to give away all your assets?"

"No, I'm not giving everything away. I will still be a millionaire. I want to bring life back to Britania and I want something good to come from the Roberio Ranch," answered Ramon.

"I will call my primary contact and let you know what I can find out. I doubt that the government will sell that much acreage at such a small price. You know, there are whole countries that have less land than the Roberio Ranch."

"See what you can do and keep me informed. I'm returning to Miami so please call me there. I will leave the number with Mrs. Pedrinho."

Ramon had to know if Greta felt the same way about him. His feelings were a little hurt because Greta did not beg him to stay with her in Frankfurt. Before going to Miami, he needed to make certain the romance was mutual. Ramon told Gary that he didn't want to carry on a Trans-Atlantic relationship, but that is what he started when he called Greta in Germany. He knew he had to act boldly or lose Greta. He called saying, "Greta, my heart aches for you. I need to know if you feel the same way."

"Yes, Ramon, I've been thinking of nothing but you since you left. My heart was broken when you didn't stay longer in Germany after I hinted for you stay here."

"Greta, I'm sorry. I would have stayed longer but I didn't hear any invitation so I assumed that you were finished with me. I'm sorry my English isn't better. If you only hint about something then I will never understand. I'm sorry I didn't understand you."

"Don't apologize. I should have been more direct. It's all my fault."

"No, I should have been paying more attention to you. It doesn't matter now. I just had to know that you felt the same way about me."

"Yes, Ramon, I love you."

"And I love you."

"Gary is putting me to work in Miami in two weeks. Will you come see me?"

"Yes. Gary just called me. He is trying his best to get us together. Yes, I will be there in two weeks to see you."

"Ramon, I tried calling you but I never got through. I wanted to tell you that I received the money transfer. They destroyed and hauled away Max's warehouse in only a few days after we called in the Code Red."

"That's great news. I can hardly wait to see you in Miami."

"Yes, I will also be counting down the days."

"I will call you every night until we meet again in Miami. I love you Greta."

"And I love you Ramon."

In Fort Lauderdale, Ramon kept his promise to Gary. He and Greta did do it on the kitchen table and everywhere else in the apartment. They were madly in love and could not keep their hands off each other. Ramon couldn't bear to be away from Greta when she went to work. Greta's job meant that she was gone every weekday but they had the nights and weekends alone in the apartment. Except for receiving occasional phone calls from Thomaz Rocha, Ramon really didn't have anything to do to occupy his days at the apartment. He no longer roamed the beaches in search of blonds—he had his very own and wasn't interested in chasing beach girls.

Late one morning Ramon answered the door and an older woman barged right in. She announced that she was Marsha Bennett, Gary's mother. She went straight to the liquor cabinet; poured herself a cognac, and asked Ramon if he wanted one. He declined thinking he'd better stay sober for her visit. She asked Ramon to join her on the patio. "Ramon, dear boy, Gary has told me all about you. Now, when is the wedding?"

"We haven't set a date yet. Actually we haven't even had the time to discuss getting married and I haven't proposed yet."

"Life is short—you'd better get on with it before she finds someone else she likes better."

Marsha's bluntness made Ramon blush. Marsha was acting just like a Brazilian matron but he wasn't used to American women being so bold. "Yes," replied Ramon. "I've been waiting for a holiday or some special occasion to ask Greta."

"Rubbish. Just pop the question to her. You know she will say yes. Do you have a ring picked out already?"

"No, not yet."

"Ok, then we have one more place to add to our errands today."

"Errands?" Ramon thought to himself, "Oh god, she is Gary's mother and she is having me do errands. Wow, that nut sure didn't fall far from the tree!"

"Yes, errands. We're going shopping. Gary tells me that you can't cook and it's silly for you to be here stuck in this apartment all day with nothing to do. At the very least, you should have a nice meal ready for Greta when she gets home. Tonight you will make her an excellent romantic dinner and afterwards you'll pop the question. She will say yes, and then you can start planning your wedding date. See how simple that is?"

"Did Gary ask you to come over today to coach me in making a proposal?"

"No, he just described you as a 'lost cause who needed someone's help since he doesn't have his own mother to push him.' I brought for you two week's worth of recipes for dinner menus. Just rotate them and you will be serving the same dinner only twice per month. We're going shopping and I'll teach you how to buy groceries. We'll come back and I'll show you how to prepare meals. Tonight you'll have dinner ready for Greta when she gets home. Be thinking about how you want to give her the ring. This is so exciting!"

"Did you do this to Gary and Cathy?"

"No, it was much worse. That took me forever!"

Ramon drove Marsha in Gary's old jeep to the supermarket he knew best. Marsha spent a couple hours showing Ramon things to buy now and food to buy later. After the supermarket, Marsha directed Ramon to the nearest megamall. On the way there, Marsha probed, "How long have you been saving up for Greta's ring and how much can you afford to pay?"

"My whole life and whatever it takes."

"No, be serious about this. Greta will be wearing that ring for the rest of her life so it has to be one that she will be proud to wear.

Anyway, the place we're going to only has expensive rings so Greta will like anything you buy there."

Ramon's new surrogate mother-in-law lead the way to an expensive mass merchandising jewelry store and made a big commotion to get the attention of all the clerks. Within seconds, she had several clerks and the manager waiting on them. Ramon protested and wanted to escape but Marsha had his exit blocked. He knew he would not be leaving the store without wedding rings. He protested, "I don't even know Greta's size or the style she likes."

"No problem," assured the store manager. "We'll resize any ring and if she doesn't like the style you select, you can exchange it for another ring."

After looking at every wedding set in the store, Ramon selected a traditional engagement and wedding band set. The store manager quoted a price and Marsha went into action. After just twenty minutes of brow beating by Marsha, the manager's final price was less than half his original quote. Ramon smiled at Marsha and was glad that she was with him to make the purchase. Ramon gave the store manager his credit card from the Cayman Islands Bank, which he had never used before. To his surprise, the charge went right through with no problems.

Marsha helped Ramon make a splendid dinner and she asked Ramon, "So, are you going to put the ring in the bottom of a champagne glass?"

"No, I'm a simple guy. I'm just going to kneel and beg her to marry me."

"That sounds wonderful to me. You both will remember it forever. Call me any time if you have questions on how to prepare any of those meals."

"I will," answered Ramon as he opened the door and gave her a parting, Brazilian-style-air-kiss on one cheek.

Ramon was exhausted from all the shopping so he grabbed a cold beer from the refrigerator and went to the patio to enjoy it. The dinner was in the oven and Greta would be home soon. Ramon put his feet up on another patio chair and fell asleep. Two hours later Greta woke him and asked if he was trying to burn down the apartment. Ramon ran to the kitchen and saw smoke coming from the oven. His wonderful romantic dinner was ruined. Closing the oven door, he announced to Greta, "We're going out to dinner tonight. There is a new steakhouse that just opened over by the beach, let's go try it."

Greta protested, "I'm too tired. I worked all day and my feet are killing me."

"We have to go out tonight since I just burned all the food. I'll give you a foot massage and then we'll go. I'll drive so you don't need to do anything except enjoy the food."

After eating their meal, Ramon kneeled beside Greta and asked her to marry him. Greta hugged him and said "Yes, yes, yes, I love you Ramon."

When Ramon slid the engagement ring on her finger Greta could barely speak. "That is the largest diamond I've ever seen."

"Is it too big?"

"No, diamonds are never too big. I love it."

"Seriously, if you don't like it they will exchange it for any other style."

"No, I love it and I love you."

"You're just saying that because I picked it out."

"Yes, I love it because you picked it out."

On the way back to the apartment, Greta asked Ramon, "When should we get married?"

"It doesn't matter to me. How much planning time do you need and where do you want to get married?"

"I don't need any planning time. I'm ready to get married now. I can't decide where. I only have my grandmother, brother, and my best friend in Germany. You don't have any family in Brazil. Why don't we get married here in Miami? Can we afford to fly three people over from Germany? They would love it. We have to check about the license and that kind of stuff first so maybe we should plan on having the wedding in a month."

"Ok, then it's set. We'll have our wedding in Miami next month. And yes, we can afford to fly people over from Frankfurt."

Ramon and Greta were married the next month in a tiny Catholic Chapel in south Ft. Lauderdale. Greta's grandmother and brother Matthew flew over along with Greta's best friend who served as her maid of honor. Greta also flew in a couple more girlfriends and a cousin. Still, it was a small wedding party. Gary Bennett was best man and Cathy helped with planning the event. Marsha Bennett beamed with pride at the outcome of her intervention.

The happy couple left Miami to honeymoon in Jamaica. They had a wonderful time on the beaches. They spent their days snorkeling and fishing and in the evenings, they took long romantic walks on the beach.

Since neither of them carried passports from the United States, they were free to take a ship over to Cuba where they spent several days enjoying a different world. Near the end of their perfect honeymoon Greta got serious and asked Ramon, "Are we going to live in Fort Lauderdale forever? I mean, that wouldn't be bad for me but you don't have anything to do there."

"I've already warned Gary that I am stealing you away. I will never be able to get a work permit in the States. Maybe I could get one in Germany since you will be making me a German citizen. I don't have your skills so I don't know what kind of job I can get. I can make you a Brazilian citizen and get you a job there. Plus, I will have a job in Brazil. You may not like being a farmwife. It's not very glamorous but I think you will be too busy raising our children to miss your career. If you get too bored on the farm, in time I will be able to give you a real job."

"Children, I can't wait. How many can we have?"

"How many do you want?"

"At least three, maybe four. Is that alright?"

"Yes, you're going to make a wonderful mother to our happy children."

"If we're going to live permanently in Brazil, can we have my car shipped there? Also, I will need to return to Frankfurt to pack all my things and close out my apartment. Will you go there with me?"

"Yes, yes, we have plenty of time for all of that. I was expecting a protest about living in Brazil. You know, I don't live on the beach. I live on a farm in the interior."

"Ramon, it doesn't matter where you live. I just care that I will be with you."

"Just relax Greta about getting all the moving done. There is no rush. We have all the time in the world to get everything done. We'll grow old together and have great grandchildren some day."

Ramon and Greta spent the next week packing their things and cleaning Gary's apartment so Gary could cancel his lease. They booked roundtrip tickets to Frankfurt and one-way tickets from Miami to Rio. In Frankfurt, Ramon and Matthew helped Greta pack up all of her possessions for shipment to Brazil.

Greta asked, "Ramon, I'm going to the car wash to clean my Audi before it gets shipped. Do you want to go with me or stay here and help Matthew?"

"No, I'm good to go, let's go clean your little Audi."

After washing the exterior of the car, they pulled it over to the vacuum station. Ramon went to work scrubbing down the interior and cleaning windows and Greta used the vacuum to clean out the trunk of the car. Ramon was busy and he didn't pay any attention that the vacuum had shut off many minutes ago. Finally, he did notice that Greta wasn't there to give him some instructions on his next chore. He went around the Audi and found Greta face down in the trunk of the car. Her body was limp and her face was deep purple. Ramon put his clinched hand to his mouth to keep from screaming. He ran to nearby people asking if they spoke English. One man answered in the affirmative and Ramon shouted to him, "My wife had a stroke, please call an ambulance right away."

The emergency technicians gave Ramon the bad news right away. There was nothing anyone could have done to save Greta. After they left with Greta's body, Ramon went over to the man who spoke English, "I need your help. My wife just died in that Audi and I want it taken to a smelter to be incinerated. It killed my wife so I must destroy the car."

"Sir, your wife wasn't killed by the car. She just happened to be working on it when she died. If you feel that bad about it, I will gladly give you 500 marks and take if off your hands. Do you have the paperwork for it?"

"No, but I will give you 500 marks if you get the car to a smelter for me. There is one catch and that is that I have to watch the car melt. Can you help me?"

"Sure, for 500 marks you can have my whole afternoon. I'll go call the towing company."

"Couple more things. Call her brother, Matthew, and explain what happened and tell him to meet me at the hospital but tell him I will be a little late getting over there. Then you need to give me a ride from the smelting plant back to the hospital. Ok?"

Ramon's German helper drove to the smelting plant following the tow truck. "You know you really don't need to do this. That is a really nice little Audi and I would love to have it for my daughter."

"No, you don't want it. It's a killer car. How bad would you feel if it killed your daughter?"

"How many people has the car killed?"

"This is the first."

"Sir, you are distraught over the situation and I can't blame you. Don't you think you are over reacting and taking it out on the car when the car had nothing to do with it?"

"No, the car has to be punished."

Ramon noticed the German rolling his eyes. If the German thought he was crazy that was just fine. At the smelting plant, the German talked to the men in charge and they all were shaking their heads in unison. The German came back to his car and explained to Ramon that they couldn't melt down the Audi right now because it had to go through the compactor first and then wait a week until they were ready to melt the cars in the queue. Ramon counted out the rest of his cash and handed it to the German saying, "Here is all the money I have. It's 600 marks. Go ask them if they will crush it and melt it right now."

The German walked back to the men and after a few minutes of discussion, the German handed over the money. In a matter of a few minutes, a huge electromagnet picked up the Audi and delivered it to the crusher. From the crusher the big magnet picked it up again and delivered the Audi remains to a conveyor sending scrap into the smelter. Ramon sat in the German's car and rocked back and forth as the Audi disappeared into the smelter. He noticed that all the men were watching him and Ramon sensed that they all thought he was completely crazy.

The German was very quiet and didn't say anything while driving Ramon to the hospital. Ramon's severe anxiety was caused by his bride's death and by knowing that the crushing process may have leaked some of Max's poison into the air. Ramon knew that Greta died from exposure to a minute trace of Max's poison. Greta's trunk is where Ramon stored the logbooks from Max's warehouse.

Ramon had triple bagged the logbooks before putting them in the trunk of her car. Now he recalled that after he placed the heavy books in the bags, he sat the bagged logbooks on a lab stool to tie the knot. That small amount of exposure transferred the poison to Greta's car trunk. That recklessness on his part killed his bride. He killed Greta. By the time Ramon got to the hospital, he not only acted crazy but he looked very crazy as well.

Ramon's mind was wheeling and quite out of control. He knew if a minute exposure could kill, then Max's aerosol wasn't just a killer for a building. It was a global killer.

At the hospital, Matthew was not happy to see Ramon. Matthew ran up to him and shoved him against the wall. Shouting in German, he grabbed Ramon by the collar, threw him to the floor, and started kicking him as hard as he could. Matthew knew that Ramon killed his sister and he was going to get his revenge on the spot. Security guards broke up the fight. The guards put Ramon in a taxi but he had nowhere to go. Ramon told the cab driver, "Airport hotel." He had no money to pay the driver and fortunately the front desk staff was happy to add the cabbie's fare to his hotel bill and they paid the driver.

Ramon couldn't go back to Greta's apartment to gather his things. Crazy looking Ramon checked into the airport hotel looking like a beaten, homeless drunk. He had no cash and only his credit card to get him back to Miami. As soon as he got to his room, he locked the door and fell on the bed. He cried as he had never cried before. He sobbed all night long and by morning his face was swollen and hurt from crying. He called the airlines and changed his two return tickets for the first available flight out the next day. He called Gary Bennett and sobbed as he told Gary what happened.

While waiting in line to board his flight home, two armed police approached him and arrested him on the spot. Normally Ramon would have been embarrassed to be dragged handcuffed through a public place but crazy Ramon didn't care. In fact, crazy Ramon was shouting and screaming like a mad man who needed to be locked up. The passengers in line looked relieved to see Ramon dragged away.

At the police station, Ramon guessed that they were going to book him for Greta's murder and the murder of 13 other people back in Brazil. They might add another 30 years to his sentence for his role in developing the world's most toxic substance. Why bother with years in prison. He figured they would just execute him for all the murders and just be done with him. Ramon sat in his chair and mumbled nonsense as he tried to figure out the reasons for his misery.

Interpol Director Peter Strubble and Field Supervisor Erik Bittel entered Ramon's interrogation room. Director Strubble was holding photocopies from the newspaper about the hazmat raid on Max's warehouse. Director Strubble started the interrogation, "Your brother-in-law is not very happy with you. He came directly to us to explain your role in the removal of Max Schuman's warehouse. At the time, we were confused which agents were responsible for that. Now we see that the agent pictured here is really your wife. Or I should say, was your wife."

Agent Bittel added, "We searched Max's home and went through all his financial records. We're certain that he sold some of his deadly aerosol to someone in Italy. From the paperwork we found, it looks like he called your poison trilex. Does that mean anything to you? We want you to help us locate and destroy that cache of poison. If you help us, we'll not pursue any prosecution and we'll forgive god-knows-what."

Only a small part of Ramon's mind was listening to the offer made by the Interpol agents. The rest of his mind was still trying to figure out why the love of his life was stolen from him. Which of his many past sins was responsible for Greta's death? As Ramon rocked in the chair, he replied to the agents, "Was it this? Was it this? Was it this? Was it this? Was it this?"

Director Strubble turned to Agent Bittel and ordered, "Have him locked up in the mental ward and put him on suicide watch. Get a doctor in as soon as possible and get him medicated. He isn't any help to us in his current condition."

A week passed and Ramon's medications brought him back, more or less. The medications took all the pain away. The drugs removed all mental pain as well as some physical feelings. Ramon couldn't feel his nose and his hands were numb but at least he wasn't still crying. His bruises were gone and he looked and acted mostly sane.

This time the police escorted him to an office in central Munich. He waited in the lobby with his escorts until Agent Bittel took him to Director Strubble's office. The Director offered, "Look Ramon, we're sorry for how things turned out for you. We know that you were only trying to fix things when you pulled that raid on Max's plant. Here's the problem. Max sold some of his aerosol weapon to someone in Italy. We know that because his financial records show the sale. The problem is that the company that purchased the aerosol has about 20 different locations where they do business. Are you following any of this?"

"Yes, and you want me to pull another raid to destroy this location. You are the police, why can't you figure it out and just go get it? Why do you need me?" Ramon caught himself starting to rock and tried to pull himself together so he wouldn't look the part of a complete psycho. Looking and acting normal were still foreign for Ramon. The medications took away most of his sensory abilities and rocking gave him some physical comfort. He was cogent enough to realize he couldn't start rocking in front of the Interpol men.

"There is a problem with the Italian government," explained Director Strubble. "They don't believe the aerosol weapon exists and they're not willing to cooperate. We have to go there covertly to search for it."

"Do you realize the potency of that poison? A very minute trace of it killed my wife. Something much smaller than a fraction of a speck of dust was all it took. If you go in there and start blowing up buildings, you will spread it over a wide area. Are you going to be responsible if you kill off all mammals in Europe and half of Asia? Oh, you won't care because you will be dead too. Tell me, exactly what are you going to do once I call you from Italy and tell you to come get it out of some laboratory?"

"We'll call in the hazmat specialists and we'll treat it the same way we cleared Max's warehouse."

"And how will you be able to do that? You just said that the Italian government isn't going to cooperate. Do you have covert hazmat teams to send in?"

"Yes, as a matter of fact we do. We'll pull it off just like you pulled of being an Interpol agent. You're not the first to play that game. Help us and we'll send you back to Brazil in style and give you a six-figure bonus if you're successful."

"Six figures in reals, dollars, or marks?"

"Dollars. Even if it turns out to be a wild goose chase, we'll transport you back to Brazil at the very least. We'll get counseling for you to deal with your wife's death. Our doctors will monitor your medications until you are weaned completely off all of them. You help us and we'll help you."

"What help will I have from your office?"

"You'll have three agents assigned to you. They will be with you 24/7."

"You mean they will be watching me 24/7. You still think that I'm crazy."

"Your doctors call it an acute psychotic break. Yes, you're crazy but you're getting better every day."

"And how can you trust a crazy person? If I find the laboratory how do you know I won't just let the poison escape?"

"You won't do it. You went to Frankfurt to fix things. We know you will do the right thing."

"Let's get to work then. I assume you have some files on the company you suspect. Can I get started by reading through those and when do I meet my new colleagues?"

Director Strubble opened his office door and three agents entered. "Ramon, these are agents Derring, Vlosic, and Zendt. They will give you everything you need. Please, go with them and they will share their information and files with you."

The three agents shared a conference room two floors below the Director's office. All of their research was in a big mess on the conference table. Ramon grabbed a handful of papers and started looking through the papers while the female agent, Derring, told him what little they knew about a possible transaction between Max Schuman and an Italian company. Of the three agents, only Derring spoke English and very poor English at that.

The Italian connection was weak. It wasn't known if the Italian company was a front for another operation similar to Max's or if they were just passing the product on. Agent Derring couldn't explain the details of the Italian company. Either she didn't do any research, or she couldn't explain her thoughts in English. During the briefing, Ramon pretended to be taking notes and on a separate piece of paper he wrote: Director Strubble—Urgent—must see you now, Ramon.

Ramon asked Agent Derring, "Where are the restrooms around here? I need to take a break."

"Agent Vlosic will take you there."

"No, just point the way and I will find it myself."

"Agent Vlosic has to watch you."

"What? Why? Vlosic is going to watch me take a piss? You people are crazy, not me!"

Agent Derring gave instructions to Vlosic and he escorted Ramon to the men's room. Vlosic lead the way and as Ramon passed by the desk of a young secretary, he dropped his note in front of her and kept walking.

Twenty minutes later Director Strubble entered the conference room and asked Ramon what he needed so urgently. Ramon turned to Derring and asked, "Can the three of you give us a little privacy? I have something to discuss with the Director." Agent Derring motioned to the others and the three field agents left the room. Ramon got up and closed the door.

The normal, careful and methodical Ramon was not in the room. This Ramon was in a panic and spoke loudly and rapidly. "Strubble, what the hell is this mess?" Tossing some of the papers in the air he yelled, "What, you don't have money to buy file folders? What kind of operation is this? This stuff is all in German and Italian. I can't read any of it. You do realize that we're dealing with the most poisonous substance on the planet? You give me no helpers at all and instead I get three guards who won't even let me go to the restroom by myself. I need help. Lots of it. Right away and the right kind. This is Europe—you've got translators all over the place. Please, get some clerks in here who can translate all of this quickly into English or Portuguese for me. Another thing, I need real agents. Smart ones to help me and not those idiot guards. Get me agents who all speak English, Portuguese, or both. Another thing, I need access to you night or day and I have to be able to reach you within a few minutes. I can't go around your office passing notes like a schoolgirl. Are we on the same page with all of this?"

"Ok, I see your point," admitted a sheepish Director Strubble. "You've got to give me some time. It will take a while for me to find the kind of agents you need."

"You've got a building full of people! Go grab some staff who are working on other things and get them working for me. What could be more important than this?"

Director Strubble left the room without saying anything and Ramon hoped he didn't get the bureaucrat too mad. He watched as Strubble made his way around the large outer office and it looked like he was recruiting staff to help find translators. Within minutes two young clerical workers came into the conference room, gathered all the papers and left. They didn't say a word but they smiled at Ramon as they left. Ramon took that as a sign of progress.

Slowly, file folders made their way back to the conference room. The material was neatly filed and translated. Finally, Ramon had some real work to accomplish. Even Director Strubble stuck his head in to check on Ramon and asked if he needed anything.

"Yes...food...lunchtime...Chinese," Ramon mumbled without taking his eyes off the papers.

Ramon spent all afternoon reading the translated reports and newspaper clippings about the company suspected of dealing with Max Schuman. By evening, Agent Vlosic was back and he motioned for Ramon to follow him. Vlosic took him to the basement of the building, opened a door and gave him a slight shove. The door locked behind him and he was alone in a cell, or rather a hotel room without windows. There was a television, a nice bathroom with shower, and plenty of cameras to monitor his every move. He even found new clothes in his size in the closet. There was a knock on a small door and Ramon opened it to find his supper. After eating, Ramon kicked back on the bed and turned on the television hoping to find some news. Ramon fell asleep but was soon wakened by someone calling his name.

"Ramon, I'm Dr. Venturi. Do you remember me?"

"No."

"I took care of you when you first entered the hospital. How are you feeling now?"

"Tired."

"Are you having any trouble sleeping?"

"Not until you woke me up."

"Here, I am changing your medications. These pills are not as strong and you will be back to your normal self very soon. You can't stop taking the medication immediately or you will have some severe withdrawal headaches. Do you understand?"

"Yeah," replied a sleepy Ramon.

"And do you know what the date is today?"

"Yeah."

"Yes, then what is today's date?"

"It's the 15th unless it's past midnight and then it's the 16th."

"Very good."

"Hey doc, you're wearing some cologne, right?"

"Yes, is it too strong? Sometimes patients taking so much medication have a heightened sense of smell."

"It's alright. It just made me think of something. How did you apply your cologne?"

"Well, I use a little spray of 4711 every morning. It's a cologne we make right here in Germany. Maybe you should buy some as a souvenir of Germany."

"I think I just overlooked something from my work upstairs. Do you think you could convince the agent outside to take me back to the conference where I worked all day?"

"I'll ask, but it's completely his call. You really do need to get your sleep."

Agent Vlosic escorted Ramon back to the conference room where Ramon flipped through files as fast as he could go. He was looking for one thing that he knew he missed while reviewing the material earlier. When he found the single sheet of translated material, he read it more closely this time. It reported that the suspect Italian company owns a perfumery near a small village in Tuscany. This time, Ramon had already made the connection. Seconds later, he had Director Strubble on the phone. "I know where Max sent his shipment and I know where it's going next. You'd better start waking up your agents all over the world. You've got a big problem."

"I'll leave home and be back down there in 90 minutes."

"No, don't do that. Get on the phone right away from your home. I don't have anything to show you anyway."

"Then what do you have?"

"I connected the dots."

"Ramon, you're not making any sense."

"It makes perfect sense. Tonight I went back and read some of the translated material I skimmed over today. Among many other things, that Italian company owns a perfumery in Tuscany. You'll find everything there."

"Ramon, it's almost midnight. You'd better start connecting those dots for me."

"It's so obvious I missed it at first. Don't you get it? Aerosol weapons, vials of poison. Aerosol perfumes and colognes, vials of the same stuff. They already have a distribution system for it. All they have to do is change the contents and ship as usual. Or, they might be really smart and use some other company's label."

"Ramon, please slow down and explain this. You're still not making any sense."

"It was Greta who told me how they were going to use it. When we were in Max's warehouse, she said that the weapon was designed to kill off all the people in a big building like a skyscraper or an airport. It's the airports. All over the world, everyone is going to die at the same time in all the big airports. You've got to have agents all over the world go to every big airport that has a gift shop, perfume shop, and especially duty-free shops. It's probably already been shipped. You've got to act fast on this or millions will die."

"Ramon, back up. You said this will happen at the same time all over the world. What are you talking about?"

"Well, not instantaneous, but faster than you or anyone else can stop it once it starts. Ok, let's pretend I own the perfume company and I want to kill the world, or most of it. I'm very smart so I steal some other company's label and put it on my deadly bottles of perfume. I only need Max's formula in one aerosol bottle as the tester that I send to every duty-free shop at every airport. I send them a harmless case of perfume and tell them it's their free case to sell and I enclose a coupon for 90% off on their next order. With the free case, I send along one spray sampler, which is really the poison. I send along instructions telling them they can only get the discount if they follow the rules and display the perfume and tester on a certain day of the month when they open for business. Within hours or minutes some poor victim will use the tester and bang, kills everyone."

Director Strubble alerted his network of agents who organized a recall of all perfumes sent to any airport location around the world within the last month. Every airport shop in the world returned perfumes to the Interpol laboratory in Munich. Soon they had a large warehouse of perfumes needing testing.

The three field agents met with Director Strubble concerning the perfumery in Tuscany. Strubble ordered, "The three of you will pose as tourists to conduct a raid on the laboratory. You'll take Ramon along with you."

Vlosic suggested, "Ramon should be locked up in his cell. He will blow the whole thing and once we do free him, he will probably run to the press to spill his guts."

"Vlosic, realize you're dealing with a very toxic substance. Take Ramon with you. He can be your bird in the coalmine. Let him lead the way and if there is any problem at all, the three of you can escape."

Agent Derring agreed, "I'm all for that. Let him die since he created this mess."

At noon the next day the three field agents and Ramon drove up to the perfumery in Tuscany. The perfumery was in an ancient stone building previously used by the winery surrounding the property. The agents made no comment that the place looked deserted. Ramon noted that the house next to the perfumery building also showed no signs of activity. Additionally, a lawn sprinkler in front of the house gushed at full blast, saturating all the ground around it. The runoff water made a small gulley going across the dirt road in front of the house. Ramon's gut and the clues told him that the facility had not been in use for some time.

Agent Derring told Ramon, "We're just going to have a quick look around. You're going to lead the way and let us know if there is anything unusual. Here, wear this respirator."

"You didn't pack full hazmat outfits?"

"No, we don't need them for this surveillance. We're just going in and out. Five minutes maximum in the building."

"Agent Derring, you don't understand the toxicity of this substance."

"We'll be fine for the short amount of time we will be there."

"Tell Agent Vlosic that he can't go in because he has a full beard and the respirator won't give him any protection."

Agent Derring answered for the bearded agent, "He knows how to wear a respirator."

Ramon was about to tell Agent Derring that she didn't have her respirator on tight enough and Agent Zendt was wearing his respirator loose around his neck. She wouldn't listen to him so Ramon thought, "Ok, the three of you will just have to be my canaries in the coalmine."

Ramon led the way into the perfumery and very slowly opened the front door. If trilex was present, he didn't want to stir it up. He moved slowly through the lobby with the same thought in mind. Agent Derring was behind him shoving him to hurry up. The production laboratory was sealed off from the lobby by a wall of glass. Ramon entered through the tightly sealed glass door. Ten steps into the laboratory Ramon thought he saw a foot sticking out from behind a counter. He heard a thud and looked behind to see Agent Vlosic dead on the floor. A second later, the two remaining field agents also fell dead onto the concrete floor. Ramon grasped his respirator and shoved it to his face as hard as he could. He then slowly stepped out of the laboratory and just as carefully exited the lobby of the perfumery.

Still holding the respirator tightly to his face, Ramon walked over to the gushing lawn sprinkler and scrubbed his hair vigorously for ten minutes. Then he took off all his clothes and shoes throwing them as far away as he could. He scrubbed his naked body for another ten minutes. Finally he put his face and respirator directly in the nozzle of the sprinkler and continued to let the water wash around the edge of the respirator. He then ripped off the respirator and gave it a long toss. While holding his breath, he put his unprotected face directly into the path of the water nozzle. He held his breath for as long as possible in the gushing water and then ran upwind from the area. Upwind took him straight across a vineyard and up a hill. Ramon stopped running when he was a mile away. Winded, naked, and in the middle of a large vineyard, he saw a farmhouse in the distance and walked to it.

Ramon wrapped himself in one of the towels drying on the clothesline and knocked on the door of the farmhouse. An old woman answered the door and she was shocked to see a half-naked man on her doorstep. Ramon asked, "Do you speak English?"

The old woman could only reply in Italian. She motioned for Ramon to stay outside and then he heard her talking on the phone. Maybe she was calling for the police. Within minutes, the old woman's daughter showed up with some clothes and shoes. Handing them to Ramon, in English, she said "Here, go behind the house and change into these clothes."

When Ramon returned, the middle-aged woman said, "Hi, I'm Berta. How is it that we have a handsome young man running around naked in our vineyard?"

"It's too long a story to explain. We're all in great danger and must leave the area immediately. If you have other family members please go use your mother's phone right now. Call them all and tell them to go to Spain, or Africa, or somewhere far away from Italy."

"You're just trying to scare us to steal our money or our car."

"No, I promise. I'm just scaring you to get you to leave with your family. And, you must take me with you."

"Why?"

"Because I don't want to die. The longer we stand here the greater the danger. Please, we must go now. Please, get your mother in the car and let's go."

"But I have to get my husband and children."

"Can your husband pick up your kids and met us at the airport in Florence?"

"Yes, but he has go get them out of school. Florence is a two-hour drive away."

"Good, then we must get started."

At the airport, Ramon saw gift shops and thought of the delivery system for the trilex but he didn't say anything to his rescuers. He had managed to scare them enough for one day. Berta's husband maxed out his credit cards and paid for Ramon's flight to Lisbon. Berta's family went to London because they had extended family living there. Ramon gave Berta the details on how to find out when it was safe to return to their home.

With no cash, no credit cards, and wearing only the clothing from one of Berta's older children, Ramon checked into the Atlantica Hotel in Lisbon with only a promise of payment within two days. Ramon had two urgent collect calls to make as soon as he entered the privacy of his hotel room. "Mrs. Spencer, I'm in a little bit of a jam and need some help," he explained to his Cayman Islands Banker. "I'm at the Atlantica Hotel in Lisbon and I need you to overnight $5,000 to me. I lost my credit card also, so later you can send a replacement to me at my address in Britania."

"I did say to call me anytime, but do you realize it's 3 a.m. here?"

"Yes, I'm sorry. I wouldn't bother you if it were not a true emergency."

"Ok, ok, now that I'm awake tell me where to send the money?"

Ramon ended his call to Mrs. Spencer by thanking her and apologizing again for waking her in the middle of the night. Ramon's next call was to Director Strubble who was still working late at his office in Munich. The Director recognized Ramon's voice and snorted, "Where the hell have you been? I've been waiting all day for a report."

"Yes," said Ramon. "About that, there's a little bit of a problem." Raising his voice Ramon continued, "Your idiot asshole agents can't take advice and they don't know how to wear a respirator. You can go get their bodies inside a very highly contaminated perfumery in Tuscany. I had to decontaminate myself in the yard in front of the adjacent farmhouse. You will need to arrange for some heavy equipment to remove and burn all the soil that is wet from the sprinkler. Follow the gulley to the seepage and dig all that up as well."

"You found the trilex. Great job Ramon. I'll get our other agents in Italy to come get you and bring you back to Munich."

"That won't be necessary, besides I'm not in Italy."

"You have to come back here to Munich so we can settle up. I promised to pay you and arrange for your transportation back to Brazil."

"No, you don't need to pay me. If I come back, you will want me to do one more job for you and then another one. Strubble, just get yourself some good agents who know all about hazmats. Ones who won't be running off half-cocked and ready to kill themselves. That makes twice that I've saved the world from trilex. From now on, you're on your own. Just remember your promise that you're not going to stir things up for me. It's important that you keep my name out of all of this. Will you keep your promise?"

"Yes, I promise. Your name will never come up from any of this."

"Another thing, please put lots of pressure on the people running that laboratory for the recalled perfumes. Have a very long talk with the person in charge and tell him there is a good chance that some of the trilex was shipped out. Any bottle they open has the potential of destroying all life in Europe. Will you promise me you will do that?"

"Yes, of course. Why do you think some of it was shipped?"

"Just intuition. I just saw one dead person in the perfumery. I suspect they were already shipping and some bottles were not sealed well enough. It probably killed one person who was packing bottles and that person dropped an entire bottle which broke on the floor making the environment inside so highly toxic."

Six weeks later, Ramon was in Brazil and curious about the destruction of the perfumery in Tuscany. His call to Director Strubble was put through immediately, "Ramon, I hoped that I might be hearing from you."

"I was just wondering how things ended there. What happened?"

"The Italians cooperated fully," explained Director Strubble. "They tented the whole building and destroyed every bit of it. They brought in some fancy high-temperature, high-pressure incinerators. They burned all the trilex, the perfumery, and all that ground you contaminated. They even burned down the farmhouse. They leveled the whole place and now it's all in a landfill for hazardous materials."

"What a relief," replied Ramon. "I've been worrying about that the whole time since I left Europe."

"If there is a silver lining to trilex, it's that my budget has been increased to staff up for a unit dedicated to find and eradicate weapons like it. How would you like to be in charge of that unit? You'd make lots of money, more than you could ever make in Brazil. You'd be in charge of everything. Hire your own staff, train them, everything."

"Sounds like a great job offer," replied Ramon. "I've just committed myself to a large project here that I need to finish. Thanks for the offer, and thanks for thinking of me."

"Well, think it over and call me if you change your mind. The top position will be open for two more weeks and then I must choose someone to fill it. Of course, I'd prefer to hire you."

"Ok, ok," answered Ramon. "If I change my mind, I will call you. Tell me, whatever happened to the recalled perfumes, did they ever find anything at the airports?"

"Yes, Ramon. It was packaged just the way you said it would be. It's a damn good thing you made me call in all my agents in the middle of the night. You saved the world—that's why you are needed here, working for me. It would be a rewarding career. Just perfect for you."

"Thanks again. I'll have to think about it," replied a weakening Ramon.

"We found three contaminated cases which were shipped out to duty-free shops. Since we found some of it, we did a second recall of the product they labeled. You were right all along. They did steal a label from some other company. The laboratory here in Munich has at least a year of work to finish testing all the recalled products. The delivery system is quite sophisticated and a close visual inspection will show the weapon. However, we're not taking any chances, we're testing everything."

Ramon offered a guess, "So they put a pressurized bottle inside a normal looking spray sample bottle?"

"Exactly! See, that's why you're needed here. I have to be honest with you, seldom do I see a better match between a position and a person. You were made for this job."

"No, that's not intelligence. It's just would I would do," offered Ramon.

"Anyway, the sample bottle was designed to discharge its full contents under pressure once someone hit the spray button. Kind of like a mosquito fogger. Once discharged it would have killed everyone in the airport and all the emergency responders. If it escaped out of the airport, hell, it may have also killed a whole city."

"We were extremely lucky to find it in time," replied Ramon. "Max Schuman's motive was financial gain. These people were out to control the world. I don't know what use they would have for a half-dead planet but that is where they were going."

"We'll never know their motives. We found 23 bodies in the perfumery and we think the people in charge were all killed. Just like Max Schuman and his workers."

"Thank God for big favors. Hopefully that will be the end of trilex forever."

Director Strubble answered, "Yes, thank God. And do seriously think about the job offer. I hope you will join my team."

"Ok," answered Ramon. "I will seriously think about it. Thanks for the update. *Tchau.*"

CHAPTER ELEVEN

While Ramon was in Germany saving the world, Thomaz Rocha was busy negotiating a deal with the state authorities to buy the Roberio Ranch for approximately two million dollars. That was around fifty cents per acre. Mr. Rocha was fearful that Ramon was over-extending himself. Ramon never told Mr. Rocha how much money he had in the Cayman Islands Bank.

Ramon met with Thomaz Rocha upon his return to Brazil. The attorney asked, "How are you?"

Ramon answered, "Tired. I just got back from Lisbon. It was a long flight."

"So how was your holiday?"

"Very pleasant and quite exciting," replied Ramon, telling both a truth and a lie. Ramon never told anyone in Brazil about his marriage. Now, he was in a different world and there was no use to bring up sad memories. "So, you told me on the phone that you might have good news upon my return. How did it all go?"

"I was able to negotiate such a good deal with the state authorities because they were glad to get the property back on the tax rolls. The idle property serves no purpose for the state government and they are happy to see someone willing to risk their life to revive the Roberio Ranch. The government of Brazil has no money invested in the ranch so the politicians were willing to give it away to someone with the funding to turn it back into a productive ranch. I did convey to the state authorities your plan to distribute farms to the poor. The final deal with the government includes a condition that at least 51% of the tillable land be distributed to the poor and up to 49% can be owned by the Foundation for crop production."

Ramon replied, "You were a good negotiator. With the price at only two million, I will be able to get started right away developing the property."

Unknown to Mr. Rocha, there was another reason why he was able to strike such a good deal with the government over the sale of the Roberio Ranch. His contact throughout the negotiations was Senator Paulo Dias, a Senior Senator who frequently paid visits to the President of Brazil. Mr. Dias chose wisely and decided to share the information about a purchaser for the Roberio Ranch and their plans to give most of it away. The President was intrigued and wanted to hear every detail. The President loved seeing the private sector taking on this kind of project. If the project were a failure, he was able to say he had no responsibility for it. Conversely, if it were a success, he could honestly say that he backed it from the very beginning. He told Mr. Dias, "This group will need a lot of money to make the improvements they are thinking about. Give them a very low offer on the sale. If it's more than they can afford, them come down in price. I want to see what happens with this project."

Ramon kept in frequent telephone contact with his attorney after the sale of the Ranch was completed. During one conversation, Ramon asked, "What would be necessary to change the status of the Templeton Institute from a regular corporation to a non-profit corporation?"

Thomaz replied, "Just paperwork. It's easy to do. We just need to submit the request and pay a fee."

"Then please change it to a non-profit status and change the name to the Templeton Foundation. I want the Templeton Foundation to hold title to the Roberio Ranch. Please call me once the title transfer is complete and I will come to Goiania. There is a lot of work we need to do once we get title to the Roberio Ranch."

Ramon realized that his deal left him open to scrutiny by

the government and he realized he had to be very careful about documentation. He asked Mr. Rocha, "Please set up a checking account for the Templeton Foundation through the Bank of Goiania. That account must be solely for this project and must withstand any inspection by the government. There must be a clear paper trail on all matters related to this account. I will fund the account with an international money draft for two and one half million dollars made out to the Templeton Foundation and it will come directly to you within a few days."

While waiting for the land title transfer to the Templeton Foundation, Ramon kept busy at the family farm. After repairing the pasture fence, he retrieved Storm from the stable that was caring for him. The other horses and all the sheep had already been given away. Storm loved having Ramon back and the two spent part of each day out exploring the trails around the family farm. Ramon made some cosmetic repairs to the farmhouse with the intention of getting a purchase offer. Ramon never received any purchase offers so he changed his mind about selling it. The farm was only four miles from the north side of Britania and if he ended up working out of Britania, Ramon thought he might as well live at the family farm.

Some days found Ramon so depressed he could hardly move. Greta's death nearly paralyzed Ramon. From Greta, he had only the memories of their brief and happy days together. Ramon carried much guilt from the deaths of Greta and 13 others. The death of his father also hit him hard. His only friends were all in America or Rio. Britania was deserted. Only a few elderly people lived in Britania. The remaining inhabitants of Britania had no family to help them leave. Ramon wanted to talk to someone his own age. Ramon had only Storm to share his secrets.

Ramon's secrets became an increasing burden. It was something that he could not shed. He had enormous guilt. He killed is bride. He had killed women and children. He was a mass murderer. He realized he might end up making the international headlines someday as one of the deadliest mass murderers. Sure, others may have killed more, but no one had ever committed mass murder in such a style. Ramon thought to himself, "Did I do it to protect Vanessa? Or did I do it to avenge Dr. Noqueira?"

Ramon thought he should just end it all and kill himself. Sharing his thoughts with Storm, he said, "If I kill myself who will be around to take care of you? Who cares if I make the newspaper headlines as a mass murderer? Who do I have left who would be embarrassed for me? Greta is dead. My father is dead. Vanessa and Roberto are dead. Everyone I used to know in Britania is gone. Gary Bennett in America would just get a laugh out of it—he thinks I'm a drug lord anyway. If I just killed myself, no one would ever find me. I would just go to one of the remote Green Darter hives and become one of their burrows. Perfect way to die. So instant that you can't feel pain. Cleaner than a bullet to the brain. Suicide by Green Darter. Storm, do you think I could just bottle that up and sell it to pharmacies? I can see it on the shelf at the local pharmacy, 'Green Darter Instant Painless Suicide, $49.95.' I think a lot of people would buy it."

Now he was making himself laugh. He felt better after talking to Storm. He had a plan to pay for his crimes and he would work his plan. Ramon knew that he could never change what he did to Greta and to the Roberio family. He could only change his future.

Many weeks passed and finally Thomaz Rocha called Ramon at his farm. The paperwork was complete making the Templeton Foundation owner of the huge Roberio Ranch. Ramon told his attorney that he would take the midnight bus to Goiania and would be waiting for the attorney to arrive at his office in the morning.

Thomaz Rocha knew better than to keep a client waiting and he knew that the midnight bus from Britania arrived in Goiania shortly after 6 a.m. By 6:15 a.m. the next morning, Thomaz was at his office brewing some coffee and his wife sent along some cheese breads for the important client meeting.

Ramon was impressed and he smiled when Thomaz met him at the attorney's office at 6:20 a.m. Ramon told Thomaz Rocha, "I want to divide most of the Roberio Ranch and give it away in segments that will sustain farming families. Perhaps 200 to 400 acre parcels will provide very well for families. With the government's conditions on the sale, that means that we will be plotting out 4,000 to 6,000 separate farms."

The attorney stated the obvious, "That will take millions of dollars to accomplish."

"Yes, I know. I grew up in Britania and I've lived there almost my entire life. When I was a child, Britania was a vibrant community. Now, when I go back, there is almost nothing there. All the people I once knew are gone and most will never return. I want this project to breathe life back into the community."

The attorney repeated his concern, "Ramon you do not have the kind of financial capital to take on this big of a project. The mere size of the Roberio Ranch is too big for such an undertaking."

Ramon assured his attorney, "I still have funds beyond the purchase price. I don't have unlimited wealth but I have enough to get this project started. I want the property to start producing some income from crops to help pay for the development. I need your help getting the property back into production."

"Certainly, I am here to help you in any way," replied the attorney.

"First of all, we need to hire someone who is familiar with the layout of the Ranch," Ramon stressed. "I don't have any contacts and I don't know if any of the former land supervisors for the Ranch are still around."

Thomaz replied, "I don't personally know of any remaining supervisors but I will ask around and let you know if I find anyone."

Ramon told the attorney, "Go ahead and give a one year employment contract to an experienced land supervisor, but only if you can find someone good. 'Good' meaning someone willing to work hard, someone who knows the layout of the land, and someone who will be a thoughtful and level-headed person."

As Ramon got up to leave Rocha's office he was having second thoughts and added, "Perhaps I should really be here to interview workers before they are hired. Please search for three good men as candidates and I will choose the one I want. If someone has other offers call me immediately and I will drive over from Britania to meet with them right away."

Still having concerns Ramon added, "You know, I don't know how to explain all of this to you right now but this project is going to be a very big deal for both of us. There will come a time when you will have to bring on more law partners because this project is going to take all of your time. As for me, I want to explain my role to you right now so we start off on the right foot. I want this to be my vocation. I want to work on it daily. I never want to be known as the money person for this operation. I don't want to be seen as the top guy in charge. I'm afraid that's a role you will have to accept right from the beginning. I want to be involved in the daily work and decision-making, and yes, I do want to have the final say in running things. But, people must never know that I am the financier of this project—absolutely never. When we have our interviews you will need to introduce me as a consultant who has been hired for the project. I will be your first employee. Over time we will come up with some important sounding title for me, but for now just introduce me as the consultant hired by the board of directors. For now, you and I are the board of directors. Does this entire conversation make any sense to you?"

"I'm very confused. You want to be in charge, but you don't?"

"I know. I know. It's absolutely confusing. That's why it's important that we discuss it and I need to be sure that you agree with me and can keep our secrets from everyone."

"Yes, of course you can be assured of my trust. I just don't want to make any mistake that will get you upset over my performance."

Thomaz had previously disclosed that he knew Dr. Noqueira received his money from developing veterinary medications so Ramon allowed the attorney's assumption to continue. Ramon explained, "When Dr. Noqueira and I developed those medications, neither of us were seeking personal fortune or fame. We each just wanted to do some good for the people. Dr. Noqueira put much of his money back into the hospital. I saved my money for some cause I knew I would find someday. I don't want to be owned by my money. If it's known that I am wealthy, then I will have to come here in a limousine with bodyguards. I will have to live in an estate surrounded by tall walls and more bodyguards. I can't allow the money to ruin my life. I think I've found my calling and it is to use this property to provide a better way of living for thousands of people."

"There is plenty of time for the two of us to get our communications in synch," continued Ramon. "But from the beginning just make sure that the new employees understand that we all work for an anonymous benefactor. If you are not sure about something just hedge on it and say that you need to check with the board or the anonymous donor—that will buy us time to talk in private. Also, from day one, you need to pay me as an employee. I will turn in timesheets and follow all the rules as the other employees and if you see me doing something wrong you will need to correct me in front of the others, just like any other employee. I will open my pay envelope when they do."

The two men parted agreeing to meet as soon as three potential land supervisors could be located. The Templeton Foundation was formal, legal, and it owned the deed to the massive Roberio Ranch. When Thomaz Rocha cautioned Ramon about being too aggressive in developing it, he was correct in his warning. The size of the Ranch was roughly the size and shape of the State of Connecticut with slightly over 3.5 million acres. The roads through the Ranch were dirt roads so it took a whole day just to drive across it. Rocha did not want Ramon over-extending himself and putting the Ranch into bankruptcy.

Thomaz Rocha worked hard the next week and spent all of his time on the telephone recruiting land supervisors who were familiar with the Roberio Ranch. During his conversations with contacts, someone suggested that Andre Rondon was available and would be a necessary addition to any planning for the Roberio Ranch.

Andre Rondon was one of the great grandsons of Colonel Candido Rondon who first surveyed the entire area in the early 1900's. Colonel Rondon was famous for a couple of other reasons. His work led to the installation of the first telegraph line to span the interior of Brazil. However, his most famous achievement was taking the American President, Teddy Roosevelt, down a previously unexplored tributary of the Amazon River. President Roosevelt narrowly escaped death during that adventure and today the river bears his name. All of the male children and grandchildren of Colonel Rondon lived to become the best land surveyors in Brazil. Land surveying was in their blood and whenever the government needed a survey, it was always a Rondon who got the job. In fact, Colonel Rondon's legacy was so great that Brazil's last state, Rondonia, is named in his honor.

By the end of the week, Thomaz Rocha lined up three good prospects for the land supervisor position. One of the men, Denis Brava had worked on the Roberio Ranch as a supervisor. The other two, Marcio Torres and Dalton Santos had never worked on the Roberio Ranch but they both were land supervisors on other ranches around Britania. All three men were good prospects and all three had extensive experience working farms and ranches around Britania.

When Ramon returned to Goiania, he first met with Thomaz Rocha who had already interviewed all three of the candidates for the land supervisor position. The three men vying for the position were lined up, seated in the waiting room of Rocha's office when Ramon arrived. Rocha's pick for the job was Denis Brava because he already knew the lay of the land on the Roberio Ranch. He told Ramon that the other two men were also very qualified and any of the three candidates would do a good job. They also discussed Andre Rondon and both men agreed that they should bring Rondon on board as soon as possible before he was hired by someone else.

Ramon spent an hour interviewing each man for the land supervisor role. He was trying to determine if any of the men had bad attitudes or poor work ethics. He asked the usual questions but also wanted to know how they had worked as a team with many other people on the large ranches. Rocha had already done some snooping around and had a sketchy background check on each candidate. There were no red flags for any of the men. At the end of each interview, Ramon asked the candidates to wait in the waiting room until all the interviews were completed.

None of the candidates had resumes, but Thomaz prepared a brief description of each man's work history. Ramon matched the notes, to the personalities.

For Denis Brava, Thomaz wrote, "Formerly the head man at the Roberio Ranch. Knows everything there. Doesn't seem to hold a grudge about the tragedy. Solid worker, confident and trustworthy." Denis was slender and in his mid-thirties with black hair and a square jaw. He had the look of someone in charge.

Thomaz wrote for Dalton Santos, "Technically skillful, has supervised both dairy operations and large ranches in the area." Dalton was a short, solidly built man with short, auburn, wavy hair. His looks made him difficult to place for he looked like he might be Australian or European.

The note for Marcio Torres read, "Competent, experienced ranch supervisor. Technically knowledgeable, people in the community like him." Ramon thought Marcio might be a little high strung. When

Marcio was waiting with the group Ramon noticed him chewing his fingernails. Marcio was typical Brazilian in looks, shorter, black hair, brown eyes, and a mix of the races much like Ramon himself.

The note about Andre Rondon simply read, "Hire this guy immediately!" The attorney had underlined the words several times. Ramon knew that getting a Rondon for a major surveying project was a prerequisite. If Andre didn't have a job offer today, he would surely have one by the following day. Andre looked much like his famous ancestor, a Peruvian, short with dark skin, black hair and dark brown eyes.

With all the interviews completed, Ramon asked Thomaz to tell all three that they had jobs as land supervisors. Ramon suggested, "One of them will stand out eventually and we will put one of them in charge of everything. For right now, hire all three as land supervisors with the same pay and work schedules. We will begin our workday tomorrow at 8 a.m. here in your conference room. I want you to introduce me again as the 'consultant' and I will explain some things to them that I have been told to me by our anonymous benefactor."

Andre Rondon dropped by the office to see about his job prospects so Thomaz Rocha asked him to stay for the meeting. Thomaz started the meeting by telling all three land supervisor candidates and Andre Rondon that they were all hired for positions. The attorney explained that an anonymous benefactor purchased the massive Roberio Ranch with the intention of populating it with many farms. He introduced Ramon Gobbey again as the land consultant who would be working with the group on a daily basis.

Ramon surprised everyone by saying that he had spoken to the anonymous donor and wanted the new hires to know, "The Roberio Ranch will now be known as Templeton Farms, a wholly owned subsidiary of the Templeton Foundation. There is a huge amount of work to be done at Templeton Farms and everyone will be working very hard during the next year. Andre Rondon here will be joining our team as the chief surveyor. Our first day of work will begin in the morning so please come prepared for a very long workday."

Before the meeting adjourned, Denis Brava asked, "Can you tell us the name of the anonymous donor who is our employer?"

"If he or she had a name, then there would be no 'anonymous' to the donor," answered Ramon. "All we can tell you is that sporadically Thomaz or I give a verbal report by phone and we are pledged to give no information at all about the donor. Actually, we don't know anything about the donor so there really isn't anything to discuss. Suffice to say that there is sufficient wealth backing the donor that you never need fear missing a paycheck, which probably makes you better off than serving Carlos Roberio."

"Oh, please don't get me wrong," replied Denis. "I was never a fan of Carlos Roberio."

"Sounds like a story to tell, and some day when we are out working the farm you can tell me all about it," said Ramon as the group broke up to leave.

Strong, hot coffee kicked off the planning meeting for all the new hires the next morning. The agenda called for a review of the general principles that Ramon wanted to share with the team. He wanted them to all be on the same track and just as importantly, he needed their feedback on his plans and goals for the use of Templeton Farms.

As for teamwork, Ramon stressed that their employer demanded loyalty to the Templeton projects, confidentiality, honesty, trust, respectful communication and hard work. Ramon shared with the men that his involvement with Templeton Farms would be in its initial development and long term planning. He said that he had no interest whatsoever in being the point person to answer questions from outsiders about the project. He asked Thomaz Rocha if he would serve as spokesman for the time being and Rocha nodded in approval. Ramon clarified that the attorney would have to answer to <u>all</u> outsiders and Rocha replied his agreement by saying, "*Ta, ta, ta.*"

Thomaz Rocha and Ramon emphasized that they would be the liaison between Templeton Foundation Projects and the anonymous donor. Ramon asked the men present to respect his privacy and not to tell others in the community that, "Mr. Gobbey said this or that…" He asked them instead to always use the phrase "the board of directors" when referring to himself, Mr. Rocha, or to their unknown benefactor. Mr. Rocha explained that eventually there would be a community relations person to deal with outsiders, but even then the men had to be silent about what they were doing at the farm.

Ramon continued, "Our first purpose in developing the Templeton

Farms is to provide a decent quality of life to a sustainable number of farmers. Our benefactor doesn't want them suffering from hunger or being worse off than when they lived in the *favelas*. We also want to provide an opportunity for the indigenous people to farm the land, land that was taken away from them. In that regard, we will be recruiting and giving priority to natives for acreages which best match their skills. And finally, it is hoped that our efforts will bring life back to the town of Britania."

Ramon then went on to describe the long-term vision for Templeton Farms. He explained that the vision was a rough plan and he needed the unbiased input from all the men in the room to come up with a final work plan. He said he had been thinking that the land would support up to 6,000 individual farms in the 200-400 acre range. The farms would not be sold, but would be given away to families without financial means. In addition to returning land to natives, the Foundation wanted working poor families from the cities to learn farming. The three land supervisors would be responsible for teaching farming techniques to people who may have never set foot on a farm before. If there were any families left in the area who used to live around Britania, they would also be given a priority.

Thomaz Rocha explained that the financial wealth of the Foundation was not unlimited and the farms would have to produce some revenues to help pay for infrastructure, schools, and ongoing improvements to the community. He acknowledged that people wouldn't come even to a free farm and live in a tent, so some kind of simple house would need to be built on every property. Every farm would need to be fenced and roads would have to be built throughout the Templeton Farms to every home site. The farms would all need wells drilled to provide water for drinking and irrigation. These items would need to be paid for from crop revenues.

Ramon knew that soybeans were a good cash crop and he thought having a communal soybean farm would employ young men from larger families. Since one man can manage 4,000 acres of soybeans, it would be a good source of income with little related expenses. He thought that the communal farm might also plant black beans and rice. These staples of Brazil are dry products and can be stored and shipped. He thought the individual farmers should grow coffee, fruits, vegetables, and tropical nuts. He envisioned a large communal diary since the individual farmers wouldn't have the financial means to buy the necessary dairy equipment. Cash earned from the communal farm and dairy would not go to the individual farmers; instead, it would go to the general overhead and improvement of the community.

Ramon told the group that he and Mr. Rocha would be meeting separately to address the issues of land ownership. Ramon acknowledged the problem that Brazil has with squatters. Since most squatters merely want to be paid off to move away, they were not good prospects as farmers. He also wanted to prevent people from moving in and then selling their farm without producing any crops. Thomaz Rocha agreed and added that they would develop a plan to address all the property ownership issues.

Ramon suggested that the first task would be for the land supervisors to assist Andre Rondon in completing a survey of the land to verify the outer markers of the property. Then they could start dividing the land between the communal farms and the individual farms. At that point, Ramon asked the men to provide their feedback to the plan and Thomaz Rocha kept notes on a blackboard in the meeting room.

Denis Brava was the first to speak and he said the plan sounded great to get the old ranch producing but he had serious reservations about doing such intensive farming on the poor soils of the ranch. He told the group, "After we burn a field and plant it for beans, grass, pineapple, or whatever, we get an excellent crop the first year and almost nothing by the third year. We can't have 6,000 farmers burning their fields every year. If we did that, the bureaucrats from Brasilia would be up here in a minute complaining that we are destroying their air. And it probably wouldn't be fit to live in Britania either."

"Good point," the attorney stated as he wrote out Denis' concerns on the blackboard. "Do you have any recommendations?"

Denis replied, "I'm just saying we can't go into this like farming as usual. We've got to change the way we operate."

Dalton Santos suggested, "Farmers who are irrigating are getting three to four harvests per year. With this intensity of land use, we need to think about irrigation for all the farms."

"More than just irrigation," added Marcio Torres. "We need to change the quality of the soil so burning is no longer needed. We have to give the soil the same thing that burning does. Plus, Dalton is right; we need to irrigate every field in production."

Dalton had another request, "For the entire 6,000 farms we will need at least 80 families who are bee keepers. Honey will be a good cash crop, but the entire farm needs the bees for pollination. Without bee pollination, there will be no nut crops at all and many of the fruits and vegetables need bees to get good yields. We should use some of the dedicated soybean land for clover for the bees. You should consider waiving the needs test to get at least several experienced bee handling families here to train additional families in bee keeping."

While writing on the blackboard the attorney asked, "Where do you go to find some 'bee families' who might be willing to relocate here?"

Dalton replied, "I have some contacts so I will ask around. Do I get a recruiting bonus?"

Andre Rondon added, "I will need help from the others, especially Denis Brava who already knows the area. We need to find the outer boundaries and then we need to physically survey the land to determine what areas are best for specific crops."

Ramon suggested that he and the four new hires start the initial land survey the next morning. He suggested that they drive out to the Roberio ranch house with plenty of petro to fuel up whatever farm trucks might be there and in working order. Denis suggested that none of them might be in working order since they were idle so long the engines were probably ruined on all of them. Denis offered his personal jeep if they couldn't get any of the old farm trucks working.

At the end of their first day of meetings, there was a solid plan in place for Templeton Farms. Areas for the dairy and soybean fields were tentatively laid out on paper. A very large section of land was dedicated for individual farms. There were tentative roads outlined on paper from the beginning of the property in the east to the soybean farm on the western boundary. Every man had his work assignments. For the next two weeks, all of them would be working closely with Ramon and Thomaz.

Ramon was happy with his new hires. Denis Brava was the natural leader of the field staff and he brought general knowledge and leadership. Dalton Santos and Marcio Torres were technical farmers and brought all the specific skills about the agriculture business. Dalton also had experience working with dairies in addition to his vast farming knowledge. Marcio Torres was the youngest and the most energetic and he would be the one capable of juggling the most assignments. Andre Rondon was a capable surveyor and his skills would be needed until all 6,000 farms were plotted and fenced. Ramon was looking forward to a long and rewarding working relationship with the four field men.

BRAZIL

Atlantic Ocean

VENEZUELA

GUYANA

SURINAME

FRENCH GUIANA

RORAIMA

AMAPA

Amazon River

Manaus

PARA

AMASONAS

Tocantins River

Araguaia River

MARANHAO

CEARA

RIO GRANDE DO NORTE

PARAIBA

PIAUI

PERNANBUCO

ALAGOAS

SERGIPE

RONDONIA

TOCANTINS

BAHIA

Palmas

D.F.

Gurupi

Brasilia

MATO GROSSO

Itapirapua

Britania

Goiania

MINAS GERAIS

ESPIRITO SANTO

GOIAS

BOLIVIA

MATO GROSSO DO SOL

Belo Horizonte

Vitoria

Essenada

SAO PAULO

RIO DE JANEIRO

PARAGUAY

Rio de Janeiro

Sao Paulo

PARANA

SANTA CATARINA

ARGENTINA

RIO GRANDE DO SOL

URUGUAY

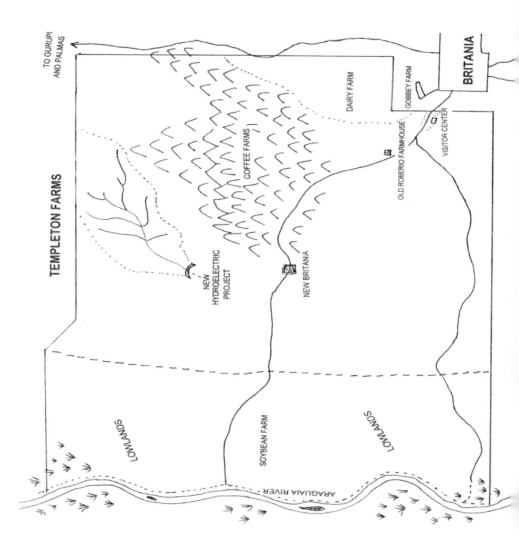

TEMPLETON FARMS

TO GURUPI AND PALMAS

BRITANIA

GOBBEY FARM

DAIRY FARM

OLD ROBERIO FARMHOUSE

VISITOR CENTER

COFFEE FARMS

NEW HYDROELECTRIC PROJECT

NEW BRITANIA

SOYBEAN FARM

LOWLANDS

LOWLANDS

ARAGUAIA RIVER

CHAPTER TWELVE

The four field men and Ramon started their survey of the newly created Templeton Farms at the ranch house formerly occupied by the Roberio family. They found three rusting flatbed trucks and the men wanted to get at least one of them running. Finally, one old Scandia belched black smoke and after running for a while, it seemed to work fine. Denis said, "That's a Scandia for you, just can't kill their engines."

While the men were working on the old trucks, Ramon went to investigate inside the ranch house. Years later, there were still bloodstains on the tile floor where Augusto Roberio had melted away into a glob of bloody ooze near the kitchen sink. People had come into the home to scavenge and it looked like the same kind of shipwreck as the Britania Hospital.

Denis decided that Andre and Ramon would ride with him in his jeep while Dalton and Marcio drove the flatbed truck. That would require more petro, but riding in the open bed of the old truck wouldn't be very comfortable for such a long drive.

Their goal was to reach the western boundary of the property, which was the Araguaia River. Denis was driving and Andre was riding shotgun. Andre yelled back to Ramon in the back seat to explain, "The location of the eastern boundary is known but we need to find at least one of the survey pins on the western boundary. If no survey pin can be found on the western border, then the pins will have to be reset by surveying all across the vast property. My job will be much more difficult if the group can't find any of the western pins."

Late that afternoon they were making good progress and Denis was driving his jeep a little too fast when a giant armadillo ran out in from of the jeep. He stomped on the brakes but still hit the animal, which squealed loudly. The flatbed truck stopped behind the jeep and Marcio and Dalton jumped out. Dalton saw what had just happened and went back to the flatbed to get a shovel. With the shovel, Dalton put an end to the animal's pain. Ramon thought they were going to bury it, but the men proclaimed it to be the evening meal. Because the animal was the size of a big dog, Dalton and Marcio each grabbed an end of the animal. They threw it on the flatbed and tied it down.

The men found a nice clearing for a camp and decided to stop for the night. The Araguaia River was still a few more hours to the west. The field staff strung up hammocks between some nearby trees. Ramon noticed that their camping gear looked like it was covered in tar and it smelled worse. Ramon unpacked his pristine hammock with its set of double mosquito nets. Ramon's gear was not new; he just took very good care of what he had. When Ramon strung up his hammock, the men started laughing at him. Dalton told him, "That lily white hammock is going to be a different color by the time you are finished with this trip."

Ramon asked, "Why?"

Dalton replied, "You'll see."

Denis and Marcio made a fire and were busy butchering the poor armadillo for dinner. Ramon once sampled armadillo and thought it tasted like grease. In this area, there is also the little coati that looks like a raccoon and it also tastes like grease. Ramon wondered to himself why some animals were so disgusting they are only good for buzzard food.

Ramon was busy trying to untangle the strings of his double mosquito net when he saw a big Lancehead Snake out of the corner of his eye. The expert snake handler certainly knew how to safely handle the big snake but in front of this group, he had to assume a different persona. As loudly as he could he started screaming, "Snake, snake,

snake!" and ran away. Dalton came running with his rifle and killed the big snake with just one shot.

Dalton warned Ramon, "You'd better be more careful. That was a Lancehead and it could have killed you."

To continue the charade Ramon yelled, "Hell no. I'm outa here. See you. I'm driving one of the vehicles back to Britania tonight."

Dalton tried to comfort Ramon saying, "You'll be fine if you stay around us. Don't go wandering off by yourself. You would be in more danger driving back by yourself than staying with us. At least we all know what we are doing in the wild."

Denis and Marcio found the dead Lancehead and skinned it. Ramon said, "Oh, great meal we're having tonight! Greasy armadillo and poison snake."

Marcio suggested to Ramon, "Try it, you might like it."

"No thanks," replied Ramon. "Boy, am I glad I brought along my own canned food for the trip. If I had to eat that greasy armadillo, I'd be sick for a month!"

Grease drippings from the armadillo meat were falling into the fire and thick black smoke rose up from the grease. The smell reminded Ramon of burning tires. The snake meat cooked quickly and Dalton passed around snake-kabobs letting Ramon have first pickings. Ramon passed the stick on to Marcio without sampling the charred meat. Ramon opened his can of beans and ate from it. Denis asked Ramon if he was going to share his beans so Ramon passed the beans to his left. When the can came back around to him, it was empty. Ramon was not pleased so he said, "Thanks for that."

Denis teased him and said, "Don't get pissy. Now you're gonna have to eat some real food. Which would you like, snake or armadillo?"

Ramon replied, "Oh hell no, I'm not eating any of that." Ramon knew that by now, the men were probably getting really tired of him but he had to keep up the persona to burn it into their memories.

After the men finished eating, they got ready to go to their hammocks. All the men stripped naked, slathered themselves with grease, and then took turns rubbing the black grease on the backs of each other. Ramon knew the answer but he asked, "What the hell are you guys doing?"

Marcio replied, "It's sulfur grease. If you want to sleep in your hammock, you have to use it. If you don't cover your entire body with it, the mosquitoes will get you and you will get malaria."

Marcio threw his can of sulfur grease to Ramon who dodged it so he wouldn't have to touch it with his hands. Ramon exclaimed, "I'm not touching that stuff! It smells like shit." Ramon was certain by now that the men would be more than ready to drive him back to Britania.

Ramon announced to the group, "I'm not sleeping outside. There are too many damn snakes and mosquitoes. I'm sleeping in the cab of the flatbed." Ramon marched over to the flatbed, closed the windows, and pretended to sleep.

Ten minutes later, he could hear the naked men in their hammocks talking about him. He heard Dalton start, "God, what a little pansy. I bet he has never been camping in his whole life. Do we draw straws in the morning to decide who has to drive him back to Britania?"

Denis answered, "No way. He insisted on coming with us so let him find out what it's like doing work in the wild."

Andre agreed, "It's really important that we locate those survey points on this trip so we can get started with the project. It will kill too much time to have someone drive him back to Britania and then drive all the way back to the Araguaia. I'll talk to him in the morning and try to get him to settle down a little bit."

Denis asked, "Do you guys know what would be really funny?"

Marcio offered a reply, "What, we find out he is really a girl?"

"No," replied Denis. "What if he is really our boss? Suppose that he is the financier of this project. What if Ramon is the 'anonymous donor' and we are all really working for him?"

"That's impossible," answered Dalton. "When Ramon worked for Dr. Noqueira he was just the janitor. A janitor doesn't get the kind of money to buy this property."

"Yes," replied Denis. "But don't forget that he went to America. He had to have money to do that. Maybe he inherited a bunch of money from some relative in America. Or, maybe he met some rich heiress and talked her into buying this property and maybe she is the 'anonymous donor.' It has to be something like that. Someone with millions of dollars didn't just call up Thomaz Rocha and Ramon Gobbey out of the blue and offer them jobs to start a project like this. Ramon didn't even finish his college degree so he isn't even qualified for a job like this. There has to be a connection somewhere."

Dalton replied, "You've really thought this out. If there is something there I'm sure you will uncover it."

The men said goodnight and in the cab of the flatbed Ramon beamed with joy. He had all the men just where he wanted them. Part two of his persona would have to be played out once they returned to Britania.

The next morning the men ate left over armadillo for breakfast. Ramon opened another can of beans, which he did not share with the group. Andre pulled him aside for a little talk, "Now Ramon, you've got to try a little harder to get along with the group. It's vitally important that we complete this part of the survey so we can continue the process. As I was explaining to you on the way over, if we do not find any of the western survey pins, then my work will be set back weeks, maybe even months. The men really don't have time to take you back to Britania so you have to buck up and just hang out with us until we get the job done."

Ramon smiled, "Sure, I'm sorry. I didn't realize I was being a burden. But tonight we need to find something decent to cook, like fish."

Andre replied, "We will be working around the Araguaia River all day today and if you want to find a spot to fish you can do that while we are working."

When Andre walked Ramon back to the group, he asked, "Ramon would like to spend the day fishing on the river for our dinner tonight. Does anyone know a safe place where we can leave him alone for the day?"

Ramon piped up, "Well I don't know—if there are snakes all around then maybe I'd be better off staying with you guys."

All the men assured Ramon that they would find a safe place on the river where he could spend the day. None of them wanted to babysit him another day.

On the way to the river, Ramon made a point of complaining how bad all the men smelled from the sulfur grease. He told them, "You know, when we get back to Britania you guys will need to be washing for days to get that smell off your skin."

When they reached the river, Denis drove to a clearing where he was certain that even Ramon couldn't get in trouble. Denis said that the fishing may not be the best in this spot but the clearing should be safe for Ramon. Dalton kept some of the armadillo meat from breakfast so Ramon could use it for bait. He gave Ramon a couple fishing rods that he brought along and told Ramon to catch a small fish and then use it for bait for a big fish.

The smelly men took off to find survey markers and Ramon fished in earnest to catch the evening meal. He wanted to catch a big fish so he would not have four angry, starving men mad at him in the evening. Ramon had good luck catching some piranhas, which he used for bait. One of the fishing rods that Dalton gave him was as solid as a broomstick and had a six-inch hook on the line. He hooked a big piranha through the back and threw it to the middle of the current. He spent all afternoon drowning piranhas but late in the afternoon, his luck got better. He moved up stream and again threw the piranha into the swift current in the middle of the river.

Ramon sat on a rock by the shore and prepared to wait a long time to catch a big fish. Fortunately, he was holding the fishing rod when the big fish struck. The fish almost dragged him into the river but Ramon pulled back hard hoping that the line would not break. Eventually he pulled to shore a small pirarucu of only 40 pounds but it would be plenty of fresh meat for the men to eat that night.

By the time the men returned in the early evening Ramon had the pirarucu steaks slowly cooking over an open fire. That night Ramon was back in good favor of all the men. They were hungry and exhausted from working hard all day. The pirarucu steaks cooked over the open fire tasted fantastic and the men were thankful. Even Denis came up and slapped him on the back saying, "You're all right after all. Good job."

The men were all exhausted because they worked very hard trying to find survey pins, but none were found. They planned to stay on the river until they found at least one of the boundary points.

Ramon continued to sleep in the cab of the flatbed truck even though he knew he would be more comfortable in his own hammock with its double mosquito netting. Especially now that the cab of the truck smelled of sulfur grease, he wished he were out in the open air. He had to maintain an image so he slept in the truck. That night the truck was parked too far from the men's hammocks to hear what they were saying about him. He supposed they were still talking about him. He knew that it would be a challenge to keep one step ahead of the men.

The next day Ramon walked the river with the other men. He thought another pair of eyes might help in the search. He would put off any further theatrics until after they found the first survey pin. Andre explained to Ramon that the land boundary is the river but the survey pins are found on the higher banks. Andre had maps showing locations of the pins but they were difficult to find because of the underbrush.

That afternoon Dalton found the first pin. Andre was very pleased because it was the pin for the northwest boundary and it was the most important one. Now they just needed to drive south and find the southwest pin and Andre's job would be finished for the time being. The men spray-painted several big X-marks on a large tree and left to drive to the southern boundary.

The group spent all afternoon looking for the southern pin without any luck. Over a fire, they warmed up the remaining fish from the night before. The men were too tired for much talk so they prepared their hammocks and went to sleep right after eating. Ramon went to the flatbed truck and tried to sleep.

By mid morning of the next day, Marcio found the pin they needed and the men also marked it by spray-painting a nearby tree. The men packed up their camping gear and Ramon purposely left his sack containing his last few cans of beans on the ground for someone else to pick up for him. Yesterday when he helped the group look for survey pins, he saw several snakes but he screamed only once when Dalton was within hearing range. He was lucky today. Under the flatbed truck was a small, black, common water snake. When the men were a few yards behind him Ramon started shouting, "Snake, snake, snake."

Ramon pointed to the snake's location near the back wheels and Dalton went over and picked it up. Dalton started lecturing to Ramon, "You really need to learn about snakes so you're not screaming about little guys like this one. He's just a little common water snake. They never bite and they are very tame. They don't mind being picked up at all. This little guy just eats bugs so we want to take good care of these little snakes. They are so tame they make really good pets. Here, why don't you pet him?"

"No thanks," yelled Ramon. "You can give him a toss."

Dalton took the little snake and gently placed it in the grass away from the truck so it would be safe. With their work done, they headed back to Britania taking a different road back so they could get a better idea of the terrain of the property. On the way back, the men discussed which parts of the property would be best for individual farms versus communal farms.

CHAPTER THIRTEEN

In Britania Denis dropped Ramon off at his farm. While both men were there, the neighbor boy came over asking for money for taking care of Ramon's horse. Ramon asked Denis if he could borrow $5 until payday to pay the neighbor boy. Denis opened up his wallet and handed $5 to Ramon. Ramon was beginning to establish the second facet of his persona.

After Denis left, Ramon called Thomaz Rocha in Goiania to update him privately. Ramon disclosed, "I know that the men think that I might be the anonymous donor so we need to come up with some better plans to throw them off. I will be busy borrowing money from them to show them that I don't have any money. We need to come up with some additional information to throw them off the trail. If we can't fool our own employees, how will we keep the identity of the anonymous donor from the press? Actually, that Denis Brava is going to be a constant challenge."

Thomaz replied, "Do you want me to fire him?"

"Absolutely not," Ramon asserted. "The last thing we need is a bunch of yes men. Denis and the others will keep us on our feet. We're going to have to come up with some good stuff or they will see right through it."

The attorney and Ramon continued their discussion throwing various ideas back and forth. Thomaz finally suggested, "I think it's important that we let the men bring up their concerns first. We need to wait to reply at their timing. If we offer up information too soon it will seem contrived. I'm certain that our plan tonight will work. With the press and the government people, we just need to stick to our guns and say that there is an anonymous donor and we fear asking the donor for identity would mean losing all the money for the project. That will scare away the government people. The press will always be trying to uncover some proof so we need to be very careful with our documentation."

Ramon agreed, "Yes, you are right. As for the real work that went on, the team found the necessary western boundary markers and Andre is very happy. As for fieldwork, I think I've done enough of that. The heat and humidity in the lowlands by the river was horrible and to make it even worse the men wore sulfur grease the entire time. The next time you are handing out assignments for field work please make sure you send me on some other kind of mission."

The attorney teased, "Doesn't sound like you're willing to put much sweat into this project. What about the people who will be living and working out there?"

Ramon defended himself, "Oh I've put plenty of sweat into this already. I think I lost 15 pounds while we were in the wild and I don't have any extra to lose. As for people working in the lowlands, seriously, that should never happen. The lowlands must be used for projects that don't require much intervention. Probably a rotation of grazing and soybean fields would be best unless we can think of some other use."

The men rested for a day and at midnight the following day they gathered at the bus station to take the midnight bus to Goiania. It was a routine that Ramon knew well. They were all going to Goiania to meet with Thomaz Rocha for another daylong planning meeting. Ramon made sure to show up without cash. He asked Denis, "Do you have our tickets?"

Denis answered while pointing, "No, you have to go over to the window and buy your ticket."

Ramon answered, "I don't have any cash. I thought Thomaz was sending over tickets."

Denis went to the window and purchased a ticket for Ramon.

Shoving the ticket into Ramon's hand Denis said, "Here, are you keeping a log of how much you owe me?"

"Just remind me on payday. Hey, thanks a lot."

Denis was muttering under his breath and shaking his head. Denis was thinking to himself, "This is the land consultant with all the answers and he can't get himself from point A to point B!"

Ramon was beaming inside because all the other men heard that he didn't have any money and they could see that Denis was practically growling over having to pay for his ticket. The bus was nearly empty so the five men all took seats in the same area in the middle of the bus. Marcio asked Ramon why he was so broke. Ramon was glad to offer up an answer, "You all know that I just inherited my father's farm. My father was poor and didn't leave any money for me. The farm is in bad condition so I've been spending every dime I have getting it ready to show to prospective buyers. Once I sell the farm I will have some money."

Denis was sitting behind Ramon and he offered, "Ramon, you are like a kid with your money. If you get some today, you will spend it all. You need to grow up and manage your money."

From the tone of the words, Ramon could tell that Denis was pissed for having to pay for his bus ticket. Ramon was still beaming inside. At 3 a.m., the bus stopped at the midway point for restroom breaks. Ramon usually purchased a cola from the vending machine so he asked the others for their spare change to buy the cold drink.

In Goiania, the meeting started before daybreak in the attorney's conference room. Thomaz Rocha brewed the coffee well before the men arrived. Mrs. Rocha prepared a nice layout of cheese breads and meats for their breakfast. The men ate breakfast while telling Thomaz stories that happened in the wild.

Marcio knew better, but he had to take his shoes off right there in the conference room of the law firm. His toes were killing him. During their stay in the wild, the four field men encountered white worms. Now they were all infected and like clockwork, the cysts grew to the size that was now irritating their skin. The nasty little worms crawl into the crevices between toes where it burrows into the skin and becomes a painful, itchy cyst. The worm lives in the moist soil of the jungle floor.

Ramon only went barefoot in the cab of the flatbed truck, so he was not infected.

After Marcio started hacking at his toes with his field knife, the other three men followed. Ramon knew right away what they were doing and told them, "Using those field knives is the best way to get a good infection from those white worms."

Denis answered back, "How do you know what they are? I didn't think you knew anything about the jungle."

Ramon replied, "No, I don't know much about the jungle but you forgot that I worked with a doctor for almost ten years. Yes, I was a janitor but I also supplied an extra pair of hands many times for the doctor. Marcio, if you will go clean your feet in the restroom then I will use you to show the others how to properly remove white worms. All I need is a razor blade."

Thomaz offered, "I think I have an unused box cutter blade in a tool kit. Will that work?"

"Sure," replied Ramon. "And how about some alcohol? Do you keep a bottle of vodka in your desk?"

"No," replied the attorney. "But will gin work?"

"Yes, that will be fine," answered Ramon.

Marcio came back to the conference room and dried his feet with paper towels. To show everyone how to properly remove white worms, Ramon made Marcio put a foot on the conference room table. He said, "Denis, you were using your knife to stab directly into the cyst. You can't do it that way. The cyst cannot come out the way it went in because the skin tissue there is all dead. You'll just end up breaking the cyst apart and then you will get a good infection."

With all the others leaning over his shoulder Ramon started cutting on Marcio's foot while explaining the technique to use. "You have to move over slightly from the entry hole and cut into skin that is not dead. Make a tiny incision right next to the dead skin. The cyst cannot be removed from the area of the dead tissue because it has no elasticity. If you poke around in the dead tissue, you will just break up the cyst and mix it with your own dead tissue cells. Then, you get a really horrible infection. So, you gently squeeze the cyst right over to the new hole you just made. Ideally, it would be better to have some tweezers at this point but if you squeeze you can do the same thing. See, out pops the little cyst that's been driving you crazy. Now, just pour a little gin over it. Maybe at break time one of you can run to a pharmacy to buy some isopropyl alcohol. Keep your boots and socks off during the meetings today to give the cuts a chance to air out and I guarantee that none of you will get an infection. That is if you do exactly what I showed you. You must be very careful not to break the cysts."

The men took turns passing around the single box cutter blade and swabbed it off with gin between users. Denis was impressed and said, "Ramon, so what other surprises do you have?"

"If you are fishing in one of the rivers and get a fish hook in you, then come see me. That was the most frequent thing I did when Dr. Noqueira was away. Also, I'm good at killing Bot worms. At least you didn't get any of those on the trip. You must be careful not to get those while working in the jungle. They would be a hundred times more painful that these tiny white worms."

Dalton asked, "So, Ramon, you were a janitor and an orderly at the hospital?"

"No," replied Ramon. "I was just a janitor. But, in a small hospital you have to be flexible and help out in lots of different areas."

The strange smell of sweaty socks and gin invaded the attorney's conference room. Thomaz started, "It's going to be difficult for me to take you men seriously as you sit here barefoot in my conference room, but I will try. Let's get started. I understand that Andre has some exciting news for us."

It was Andre's turn for show and tell and he came prepared with maps. He outlined for the group the next necessary steps in the survey process. Andre Rondon thanked the three land supervisors for helping him and he suggested that from this point on he could hire assistants to help finish the survey with him. He said, "You can hire a whole army of assistants for what you are paying these guys as he pointed to the supervisors." The men got a big laugh out of that because they knew they were all making the same amount of money. Andre added, "But, seriously, these three guys will have a lot of work to do to get all this done in time before new residents arrive. They should be spending their time supervising the construction of roads, houses, irrigation wells, fences, and a lot of stuff we haven't even thought of yet."

Denis Brava nodded in agreement and added, "Before we start the construction phase we should decide which men are going to supervise which projects. There will be some projects like roads and fences that all of us will be involved in and we will all be working to coordinate with Andre to make certain the locations are correct."

In his role as facilitator, the attorney suggested, "Well that leads us into the next phase of our meeting. Since you all have seen the lay of the land we need to firmly set the locations of the individual farms, the soybean fields, and the dairy."

Denis interrupted, "Before we get into all of that I think there are some business issues we need to talk about first. We almost didn't have our land consultant with us this morning because he didn't have enough money for bus fare. Can the Foundation give us all an advance to use for travel and business expenses so we are not spending our own money?"

Thomaz replied, "Well, it's usually done the other way around. Yes, you do spend your own money and then we reimburse when you turn in your receipts."

Denis answered, "Yes, I understand that. But if we do it that way, then there may be times that our land consultant here will be left behind in Britania."

The attorney probed, "How much of an advance were you thinking about?"

"At least $50," answered Denis. "But $100 would be better. We understand that we still have to turn in receipts and that your secretary will have to spend some time reconciling the advances periodically but we really do need it so we won't be wasting time with people stranded."

"That sounds fair to me," Thomaz assured the group. "I'll have my secretary, Mrs. Pedrinho, go to the bank at ten o'clock to get a packet of small notes for each one of you. As long as she is doing that why don't you hand me your bus receipts and I'll have her include that amount in your packets as well."

Ramon and Thomaz could tell that Denis was just warming up. Apparently, there were a lot of issues boiling up under the skin of Denis Brava. Denis added, "I don't mean to be rude, but I'd like to point out that five of us just made a daylong bus ride to get here and it will take a day to get back to Britania. That's 10 extra workdays spent for a one-day meeting. In the future, Mr. Rocha, do you think that you could come to Britania instead?"

"Yes, certainly, I see your point," replied the attorney. "We don't have any space in Britania for a meeting room unless one of you wants to offer up your personal residence."

Ramon interrupted, "Yes, I agree with Denis. Also, if one of the goals of the Templeton Foundation is to put life back in that community, then the Foundation needs to take a leading role in its redevelopment. There are rows and rows of vacant storefront properties all with 'for sale' signs on them. Those people have moved on and started lives elsewhere so they are desperate to sell those properties."

"The Foundation cannot be seen as taking advantage of other people's misfortunes," cautioned the attorney.

"Right now those people will be happy to sell just to get away from the taxes on those storefronts," Ramon argued. "Actually we would be doing them a big favor. If we put our business in the community then perhaps others may see opportunities there as well."

Thomaz asked, "So, are you talking about the Foundation buying a small store front property just so we have a place to meet once in a while?"

Ramon countered, "No, a lot more than that. The properties are cheap right now so why not buy up what the Foundation might need for years to come. The men do need a place to shower and change clothes when they return from fieldwork. I was thinking about the Roberio ranch house for that but it just has too much bad karma. I went into the ranch house when the men were trying to start the trucks. Looters have destroyed it so I think we need to get it knocked down. It needs to be cleared so it won't be in the way of a new farm for one of our residents. However, eventually the Foundation will need to do business out of an office in Britania. Thomaz, you may be living in Britania and working out of an office there so you might want your firm to buy office space there now."

Dalton jumped in and offered, "I agree with Ramon. The Foundation will eventually be doing its business out of Britania so the Foundation should buy sufficient space now for its future needs. It may be years before a bank makes its way back to Britania but I guarantee you that banking transactions are going to be common once there are more than a few dozen families living there. The Foundation may as well plan to install a bank there. The farmers will need loans to buy seed for the next planting and if we can't loan to them then they won't be able to plant. That's going to put us in the banking business whether we want to be or not."

Thomaz relented, "Ok, perhaps I should return to Britania with all of you and we will search for a future home office for the Templeton Foundation. Are there other new business topics?"

"Yes," said Denis still wanting to get things off his chest. "At our first meeting all we talked about was the 'anonymous donor this, the anonymous donor that.' Just between the men in this room can we just come up with a name for the person, like Jane or John?"

Marcio added, "And please tell us the truth. As employees, we should know. Don't you really know who the donor is?"

The attorney took the lead in responding, "If I share with you the information that I have then you must all swear never to divulge a word that I've spoken. Do you swear?"

Dalton and Marcio quickly answered, "I swear."

The attorney pointed to Ramon and Ramon said, "Yes, I swear."

The attorney looked at Denis and said, "We're waiting!"

Denis replied, "Ok, ok, yes, I also swear."

The attorney drew in a long breath for he knew it would be a long explanation, "Ok, you have all sworn your secrecy to me so if any little bit of this gets out you might all be fired by me! Do you understand?"

The men all nodded in agreement and Thomaz continued with as much self-pride as he could muster, "I am the key to all of this. No, I'm not the donor, but I am the link to the anonymous donor. There is a continuous thread, which links me to Ramon and to the Noqueira family. I was the attorney for Dr. Noqueira and Ramon worked for Dr. Noqueira. Somehow the Noqueira family or friends of the family are behind this. I agree with you men that the donor just didn't pull my name and Ramon's name out of a hat. It's that continuous thread that links us both back to the Noqueira family. However, I can assure you that Dr. Noqueira and Vanessa both died without leaving much of an insurance policy. It's someone who has a connection to Vanessa Noqueira. I don't know if she had rich relatives back in Europe or maybe she had a rich friend in America. That I don't know. Now,

I've received three calls and Ramon has received two calls from the anonymous donor. It is a woman who calls but I doubt that the woman who calls is really the donor. The donor is probably some super wealthy person who simply has his personal secretary checking up on us. So, I am the key and I am the one who was chosen to lead this project."

Ramon exhaled and rolled his eyes while saying, "Mr. Rocha, with all due respect! Please, that is just so much conjecture. You are not the key to all of this. I am! When I was in America, I studied urban planning and in one of my classes I had to give a big presentation about my class project. My project was the town of Britania and what happened to it after a prominent family was attacked by snakes. The class presentations were held in a big auditorium and the public was invited to attend so people came and went as we gave our presentations. Someone sitting in the audience heard my presentation about Britania and decided to become our benefactor. America is full of super wealthy people and I was attending school in one of the richest parts of the nation. So, I am the key to all of this. I am the one chosen by our benefactor to lead this project. And, yes, the donor did just pull your name out of a hat, or saw the advertising for your office. Your relationship to all of this is merely coincidental."

The insulted attorney defended himself and Ramon continued talking. Both men were talking at the same time and they were on the verge of yelling at each other.

Denis jumped in, "Whoa, gentlemen! We didn't mean to start a revolution within the management ranks. Ok, we get it. Neither one of you has a clue who the real benefactor is. Can we just agree to call the anonymous donor, 'Jane,' and let's move on to our other business?"

Mrs. Pedrinho opened the door and peeked in saying she had sandwiches for lunch. The men broke for lunch while the secretary spread out food on a table in the back of the room. The secretary was talking to Ramon and Andre was showing Thomaz something on one of his maps. Denis gave that "let's meet in the restroom" look to the other two field supervisors. In the privacy of the restroom, Dalton told Denis, "Jesus! Man! What are you doing? You almost started a war out there between Thomaz and Ramon. I thought they were going to go for each other's throats."

Marcio added, "Boy, that's going to be a touchy subject around the two of them. We need to be a lot more diplomatic around them so they don't kill each other."

Denis answered, "Yes, I thought the two of them were tight but I guess I called that wrong. I wonder how often we're going to have to pull them apart. Especially now that it's all out in the open that they both think they are the chosen leader for this project. Neither one of them can fire the other so we might be in for some heavy storms ahead. At some point we may have to lock both of them in a room and let them duke it out and the winner can be the leader."

Ramon entered the restroom so the conversation ended abruptly. Ramon asked Denis, "So, did you get everything off your chest this morning?"

"Yeah," replied Denis. "How 'bout you?"

"Oh, I think it's just starting," Ramon replied coldly.

Denis looked at Dalton and raised his eyebrows so the three supervisors made a quick exit. In the conference room, Andre was eating lunch by himself when the supervisors returned. Andre put his hand near his face to hide his lips and mouthed, "What happened?"

Denis just pointed his two index fingers together as if the fingers were fighting and made a face. Andre nodded and made a face back without saying a word.

Neither Ramon nor Thomaz joined the men and instead went their separate ways for lunch. Before the afternoon session started, Mrs. Pedrinho brought in envelopes for each of the men with their names written on the outside. It was the $100 cash advance for travel expenses, mostly in smaller bills. Ramon returned before Thomaz and he opened the envelope with his name on it. He took out bus money and the other $5 he borrowed from Denis and handed it to him. Denis tossed back the $8 for the bus telling Ramon. "No, the secretary already paid me back for that since I turned in two bus tickets."

The afternoon session began awkwardly as Thomaz Rocha resumed his role as facilitator. The atmosphere in the conference room was cold and tense. The bare-footed field men fidgeted in their chairs. Ramon and Thomaz knew that a little tension in the corporate setting is good; it reminds workers to be polite and respect boundaries. Too much tension reduces the flow of productive communication, but in this session, all six men would just have to deal with it. The field men never noticed when Thomaz put his fingers around his wrist and scratched at his watch. Nor did they notice when Ramon put his head back and scratched his neck. The two men had just told each other, "Perfect" and "Great job." The field men were being taken for a ride on the corporate ropes course. It would be a character building experience that would help bind all the men together.

Andre apologized up front about taking so much time from the group but he had to have the answers quickly to the locations of the dairy and communal soybean fields. All the men gave their input on exactly how much land to set aside for the communal dairy and soybean farm. After several hours of discussion, the exact location of these items was determined. With Ramon's urging, the hot lowlands were reserved for the soybean fields and this amounted to about 30% of the total acreage of the project. Land for a very large dairy was dedicated in the southeast corner, in the highlands. That put the dairy close to Britania and close to the best roads for shipping milk away to other cities.

Ramon added that there needed to be a small area centrally located within the individual farms where farmers could meet to exchange crops. He suggested that one of the schools be placed there as well. The field men suggested that they also should set aside land at this location for a small village where farmers could buy necessities from a market or two, and perhaps a town hall for a gathering place. They did not want to take away anything from Britania, but they also didn't want the farmers having to go all the way to Britania to buy just a few things.

Denis went to Andre's big map on the wall and pointed out where there were large tracts of virgin jungle. He warned that it would be a big mistake to clear-cut that land to make way for farms. He suggested that Andre's team leave them as natural areas and plan the farms around many of the natural resources.

The group worked late into the evening and by the end of the long planning session Andre had all the feedback he needed to start laying out the individual farm plots, roads, and utilities. Thomaz had reserved rooms for the men at a hotel across the street. It was late and the men went to bed without drinking or partying. They had to be up early the next morning to be at the bus station before 8 a.m. for the bus back to Britania.

Before 8 a.m. the next morning, Thomaz Rocha met the men at

their hotel and drove them to the bus station. Thomaz returned with them to Britania. Right off the bat, the field men knew that they had a problem. Thomaz was setting at the back of the bus by himself and Ramon was setting in the front of the bus by himself.

The field men took a neutral position in the center of the bus. Denis said, "Ok, we have six hours today to get them to kiss and make up. This is that locked room I was telling you about yesterday. I don't think this is going to be easy. Both those men have a lot of pride and both have a stubborn streak. I propose we break into two groups of two. Andre and Marcio, you start with Thomaz. Dalton and I will work on Ramon. I suspect we won't make any progress the first go around so we will regroup and switch teams. Any other suggestions on tactics?"

Andre said, "Someone has to be the leader in charge. I don't see either man giving up that claim. Can we be respectful to both men and put each in charge of certain aspects?"

Dalton added, "How about making one a chief executive officer and the other a chief operating officer?"

Marcio asked, "Isn't that like making one the president and the other the vice-president?"

"I agree," affirmed Denis. "It has to be that way. There's only one president of an organization. We're going to have to convince one of them to step down for the good of the organization. Does it matter which one we push hardest to take the second-in-command position?"

"Yes," replied Dalton. "Don't we need the attorney in the top position? He is the one making all the legal decisions. Also, Ramon needs to grow up a lot more."

Denis suggested, "Then we only need to work on Ramon and ask him to step into the second-in-command position for the good of the project. Let's not ask the attorney to step down. Let's just tell him we want him to share control with Ramon. Tell him his energy is needed on the legal matters and he should not be wasting his time on day-to-day things. That should massage his ego. Also tell him he has to let Ramon facilitate the meetings and he needs to give up the chalkboard."

Dalton and Denis worked on Ramon all morning. Denis explained, "This project is going to mean everything to thousands of people who move here. We can't have it ruined because you and Thomaz refuse to get along. It's bad that Jane didn't appoint a single boss. Maybe Jane is just testing us to see if we are smart enough to figure it out."

"Yes," replied Ramon. "However, I know that I am right and I am the reason why there is a Templeton Foundation. Thomaz Rocha is totally wrong on this issue."

Dalton asserted, "That may be true. Let's say that you are the reason for the funding. We still need a leader for the project. Thomaz will be very helpful in that role since he is the attorney and he has to make all the legal decisions."

Denis explained, "There is more than enough work for all of us. We believe that you need to be in charge of day-to-day operations and let Thomaz tackle the big issues. Thomaz can handle the politicians, the press, the legal contracts, and governmental issues. To be honest, I don't see these as your areas of interest anyway." Massaging his ego, Denis added, "We see you more as a practical, hands-on kind of guy. After all, didn't you come out to the wild with us and help us search for survey pins? I don't think Thomaz would ever do anything like that."

Ramon replied, "Thanks for not telling me that I was a pain in the ass while we were looking for the survey markers."

Walking on eggs, Denis answered, "No, you were great. We could tell it was your first time camping. At least you made the effort to go with us. That's why you need to be part of our team. Do you really want to be setting around in Goiania wasting your time?"

"No, I won't be wasting my time," replied Ramon. "Jane made this project for me and I need to be the one making all the decisions."

Denis saw the signal that it was time to regroup in the middle of the bus so he told Ramon, "Just think it over. You know you've got to do the best thing possible for the future of the community."

The men did their half-time huddle in the middle of the bus. Thomaz accepted his mandate because he wasn't being asked to step down. Ramon seemed to be more inflexible than ever. Andre asked the group if they knew why Ramon was being so stubborn. Denis said, "I think it's all about power, control, and ego. He is certain that Jane wants him to be the leader. We just need to convince him that a vice-president role will provide the satisfaction he needs. I don't know, maybe it's about titles. If we can come up with a title matching his ego, maybe we can win him over."

Andre added, "Ok, I think I have it. Marcio and I will work on him next."

At the front of the bus, Andre and Marcio had their turn talking to Ramon. Andre started, "Ramon, certainly you realize that this is going to be a huge project and it will take all of us working together to get it done. I'm afraid that you will not keep this team together if you dig in your heels on this issue. This is not the battle you should be fighting. There is too much work for all of us to do to be fighting over who they think Jane might want to be in the leadership position."

Marcio added, "If Jane wants anything, it's for us all to work as a team and finish this project without bankrupting her. The more time we waste fighting, the more money we waste. It's time to move on. You've got to work with Thomaz one way or another. You've got to learn to be respectful of the staff and of Mr. Rocha."

Andre continued, "Ramon, you need to be our Chief Executive for Operations. That means you make all the decisions about the use of the land in the Templeton Farms. You will be making more decisions than Thomaz. He will be making the legal decisions. He will decide matters that pertain to the world outside the Farms and you will make all the decisions that affect things inside the Farms. I can't see how it could be any better for you. If there is something else you need, just tell us."

"Ok, ok," relented Ramon. "I'll be your Chief Executive for Operations. And I suppose Thomaz will be the Chief Executive Officer?"

"Yes," Andre answered cautiously. "Are you ok with that?"

"Well," Ramon replied, "I guess I have to be."

Denis and Dalton assured Thomaz that he was vital to the success of the program but they told him he had to learn how to work with Ramon. They told him that his skills were needed in the legal arena and he needed to delegate to Ramon the day-to-day responsibilities. The field men regrouped to the center of the bus and then separately they told Ramon and Thomaz that just the two of them were going to have a private meeting at the back of the bus. The group said they expected the two leaders to shake hands and end their fighting.

Ramon went to the back of the bus and asked Thomaz, "Do you think we were fighting?"

"No," laughed the attorney. "We were just sharing our viewpoints."

Ramon asked, "Do you think I need to grow up?"

"Well, yes, maybe just a little," answered the attorney. "From what I've heard you really gave them a difficult time while you were out in the wild."

"Let's just say that I gave them an experience they will remember forever."

"Well," answered Thomaz. "I wouldn't do that to them again or they will leave you to rot the next time."

"I just wish I had pictures to share of them all naked and greased up. If I did, I bet I would be the top dog now," Ramon teased.

"Oh, you know you are the top dog anyway," Thomaz replied. "I think we really had them worried. Poor Marcio, did you notice in the meeting yesterday he was so nervous he spent the afternoon chewing his fingernails."

"Yes, maybe we've provided a little too much stress. But they all performed with high honors. I'm very impressed with each one of them. If we both get run over by a truck tomorrow, I do believe the Foundation will carry on through these men."

"I agree," replied Thomaz. "I'm really impressed with the leadership skills of Denis. Also Andre is very skilled. Actually all of them are fantastic. I see a lot of energy in Marcio and Dalton. I don't know how we managed it, but we sure ended up with the best possible crew."

"Yes we did," agreed Ramon. "And how about us? I think we need awards for best dramatic acting."

"Maybe that was too dramatic. What are you going to do to make it up to them?"

"Nothing obvious," answered Ramon. "Perhaps a nice clean home office in Britania where they can come in to change, clean up, and have some good food after they've been out in the fields."

"In all seriousness," continued Thomaz, "We can't show the men that the two of us are in constant agreement. Many times, I will need to be firm on an issue because there is some legal consequence. I think its fine for you to voice your opinions but sometimes I need to win an argument. And, there will be times when one of the supervisors or

Andre needs to win an argument. I realize that you want the final say in everything but that's just not realistic."

"After today I do realize that," responded Ramon. "It's part of the growing up that I need to do. Seriously, I've actually gotten something good out of this little exercise of ours. So, did you get your marching orders from our staff? "

"Yes," answered the attorney. "I'm not supposed to stick my head into routine matters and I need to delegate those to you. Consider yourself delegated. I need to share control with you and I need to let you lead the meetings. I'm forbidden from going near the chalkboard. I thought I was good at chalkboarding but they want you doing that! Oh, and I'm only supposed to be doing legal work and I have to start being nicer to you. How about you, what were your orders?"

"Boy, there were so many," answered Ramon. "Where do I begin? Oh, first I have to learn to grow up and shape up real quick. I really do think that Denis will kick my ass if I don't. I'm no longer allowed to be a pompous ass. I have to start acting like a professional person. I need to be nicer and more considerate to the staff and to you. I've been told that I act like a child around money and I need to learn how to manage my money. I'm not sure that last one is going to happen very soon."

"This process certainly displayed our personal weaknesses to everyone," Thomaz confessed.

"Yes," replied Ramon. "But after today, after these men solved the problems between the two of us, they will know that they can solve any problem. Just about anything will seem insignificant to them after they ended the war between the two us."

"I agree," responded the attorney. "They will forever remember how they pulled together to save the Templeton Foundation in its infancy. And, we will never have to answer any questions about the anonymous donor, at least not from these men."

"Amen," replied Ramon.

CHAPTER FOURTEEN

While Ramon and Thomaz were having their post-war meeting at the rear of the bus, the field men were having their own meeting. They had already moved on to tackle the next task. Andre still needed surveying assistants to help him complete the survey of the soybean fields. The land supervisors needed to hire men for irrigation and drainage work to prepare the fields. This had to happen right away so the soybeans could be planted. It became immediately clear that they would also need some temporary housing for the families of the workers they would be hiring. They needed to hire some carpenters to come to Britania to start repairing the boarded up houses.

The men all knew that they wouldn't find more than a few workers in Britania. They decided that each one of them would exit the bus at a different town on the way back to Britania to start recruiting workers. They spread out the towns so each person could take local buses to nearby villages without overlapping their assigned territories.

The field men asked Ramon and Thomaz to join them so they could fill them in on their plans. Thomaz asked them if they had any concerns about choosing a location for the Templeton Foundation Home Office and Denis said, "Just make sure to get office space that is all together so in the future we won't have to be running from one area to another. We just discovered that we are going to need some temporary housing very quickly. We're ready now to hire surveyor assistants, ditch diggers, and carpenters. If you can buy some of those vacant houses very quickly we can move families into them."

Only Thomaz and Ramon exited the bus at Britania. The other men were off recruiting workers. Ramon wanted to show Thomaz two different locations he had in mind for the future Home Office of Templeton Foundation. One was near the fire station and one was close to the hospital. The two men walked the entire area of Britania making notes of potential storefronts and homes to purchase. Thomaz told Ramon that he would be very busy in the following days contacting people with purchase offers. Ramon asked that he try to get possession of one of the home office locations as quickly as possible advising, "Either location is good, so give priority to the owner who will give immediate possession. See if one of them will accept rents until a closing date and that will allow us to get in and start renovating."

Thomaz decided to take the midnight bus back to Goiania so that gave them the rest of the afternoon and all evening to continue their own planning session. Ramon and Thomaz drew up plans for land ownership. They decided that the easiest solution would be to simply have the Templeton Foundation retain title to all the land, and give the farmers a free lease in exchange for crop production. The farmers could do anything they wanted with their crops and they wouldn't have to share any of the crops they produced. This would keep away the squatters but it meant that families could not inherit farms. Providing the free land lease also prevented any farms from being sold for unpaid taxes. Ramon suggested that the communal farm income be used to pay the taxes on all the property.

Ramon had other ideas he wanted to share with Thomaz. He told Thomaz that he was very serious about finding natives to return to the farm but he personally did not want to search the jungle to find recruits. The two men kicked around some ideas and finally Thomaz suggested that Ramon contact the Anthropology Department at the University of Rio de Janeiro to see if some graduate students might be interested in a project.

Ramon also wanted to kick around some spending issues with Thomaz. Ramon said that the project would need to be staged so he had cash from crops to pay for roads, thousands of miles of fence, simple frame homes, wells, schools, and additional people to organize and run the farms. The two men sat down and drew up a timetable that put off actually letting people into the farms until 14 months later. At the fourteen-month timeline, only a few farmers would be installed. Then, every three months a dozen additional residents would be added. That would give time for several cycles of crop harvests before major expenses would need to be undertaken. Ramon wanted to be ahead of the expense curve with the crop revenues.

The third major concern that Ramon shared with Thomaz was one that he knew the attorney could not answer but he thought Thomaz might have suggestions on resources. Ramon asked, "Where can I find a soil expert? Marcio Torres is absolutely correct. We have to do something to stop the reliance on burning and instead amend masses of hard clay soil. If you think of any suggestions, please let me know."

Ramon asked Thomaz if he would mind coming to Britania every other week to join the staff in planning meetings. Before Thomaz left on the midnight bus, Ramon told him that he would fly to Rio in a few days to search for potential resources at the University of Rio de Janeiro.

CHAPTER FIFTEEN

The Templeton Foundation Home Office was an empty shell of a building. Actually, it was six storefronts all in a row with common walls separating them. The masonry walls could all be torn out to make one nice large open space. All of the units were two stories. Only ten days ago, Thomaz and Ramon were in Britania and picked two separate possible locations for the new Home Office. Thomaz managed to convince the owner to give possession before closing. The building was just setting vacant with no prospect for rent. The row of buildings was near the decaying hospital.

The six men met again in the newly acquired conference room of the Home Office. Ramon went to Itapirapua to purchase the table and chairs they were using. It wasn't very much but it was the start of big things to come.

The field men were excited and had lots of news to share. Andre started by saying, "I now have all of the outer boundaries verified and I have a complete outline where roads, schools, and common areas will be placed. The soybean fields and grazing land are dedicated. As we speak, my assistants are busy setting boundaries for new individual farms. We've permanently placed around 30 new farms on the map already."

Denis reported, "We've been busy burning grasslands which will soon become soybean fields. I'm sure we still smell like smoke and sulfur grease. It's a wonder one of us hasn't exploded already."

Ramon interrupted, "Do you really have to burn those fields? Why can't you just plow under that grass?"

"I know you like to buy heavy machinery to solve every problem, but I don't believe that they make plows strong enough to turn over that grass. It has not been used for grazing for three years and you can barely walk through it. We will burn the fields for the first planting and from then on, we can till the harvested crops. We are only working on turning grazing land into soybean fields. We are not touching the areas of native jungle. That's according to plan, right?"

"Yes, certainly," answered Ramon. "Andre, is there a way to keep a record of how many acres are under cultivation in the communal farms, and how much of the total acreage is saved as natural and recreational areas?"

"Not a problem," answered Andre. "We're already keeping those records. I'll start giving you a monthly report of those numbers so you will know our progress."

"Great. Thanks for that. Denis, please excuse me for interrupting. Yes, I should have remembered the condition of the fields, but you will recall that I was too busy paying attention looking for snakes. Please, continue."

Denis smiled and continued, "We have eight teams of workers digging drainage ditches and setting irrigation lines for the soybean fields. In just a matter of days, we will be planting several thousand acres of soybeans. Our mechanics, Marcio and Dalton worked on the tractors and trucks at the old Roberio Ranch and got most of it working so that equipment is slowly making its way out to the new soybean fields. We need to buy up a bunch of seed so we'll be sending the Scandia flatbed out to the surrounding towns for that. What have I missed, guys?"

Marcio jumped in, "Tell 'em about the lake!"

"Oh yeah," Denis added. "We found the most beautiful lake in the northern highlands. It's a really large lake with a natural dam. I had no idea it was there. Andre, please don't put any farms near it. We need to make sure there is never any development around it and it needs to be kept as a recreational area for the residents. We didn't take the time to

159

try to fish it. It might need stocking with some good fish. Ok, I think that's about it from us."

Thomaz asked Ramon to report next, "No, you go first. I insist," replied Ramon.

"Thanks," replied the attorney. "We've been very fortunate to gather up quite a number of these old buildings for our use. Right now, we are sitting in the future Home Office of the Templeton Foundation. Once we get title we will knock out the walls between most of these buildings and we will make it just one building. On the end unit, we will keep a second floor apartment just for you men so you will have a place to come take showers and change when you get back into town. Or, if you come back in the middle of the night and don't want to go home there will be some cots there too. Eventually we'll get it all fixed up and nice for you. There is an exterior stair so you can come and go without disturbing anyone."

"We've also purchased a number of single family homes," continued Thomaz. "Several of them are available right now for families of workers. Most of them need considerable work before we can allow families to occupy them. I will let Ramon know daily which houses become available for renovation."

"On a personal note," beamed the proud attorney, "Across the street I have purchased two adjacent storefronts for use as a branch office for my law firm. Who knows, someday I may be living here instead of Goiania. Ramon, you're up next"

Ramon began, "That's a remarkable amount accomplished in a short time. You guys are going so fast you're going to work yourselves out of a job. Great job everyone!"

"I flew to Rio for several reasons which I will share with you," continued Ramon. "Marcio and Denis are absolutely correct about the need to improve our soils. What can be done to replace the burning cycles? I posed that question to a professor at the University. He said 'damn near anything that is organic can be composted and returned to the soil.' He advised that in hard clay soils like ours, we must not add sand, as we would just be making bricks. When I returned from Rio I mailed a soil sample to him and I talked at length with him just yesterday. He is advising that we compost all the dairy material and till it into all of our fields. We must also improve the ph of the soil with yearly applications of powered limestone. This is not important for fields that have just been burned. Those fields with ash are good for at least two years. But if we plant any of the old fields, this amendment will be needed."

"I need two plots of around 20 acres each for two processing plants," continued Ramon. "We've been busy spending Jane's money, but with her permission. Jane has already told us she doesn't want our farmers living as poor subsistence farmers. So, we're going to help our farmers achieve better yields. We purchased two giant grinders that will grind anything you throw in them—whole trees, cars, whatever. I hope that only organic matter will go into the grinders. The grinders will then dump into very large mulchers where the organic material will decay in a matter of days and then we can till the mulch into the soil."

Marcio asked, "But where are we going to get so much organic matter?"

"I'm glad you asked, Marcio," Ramon said with a smile. "We've also just purchased all of the trash hauling businesses in Goiania. It will be processed over there to remove glass, plastic, metals, and other recyclable material. Then only the organic material will be hauled here to be ground up and then cooked in the mulchers. Also, any vegetation cleared from the fields can be put in the grinders, even logs, it just comes out as sawdust."

Having no chalkboard available, Ramon drew on a piece of paper what the grinders and mulchers looked like. "Here," said Ramon. "I need this kind of elevation in the land to place the grinders so the mulchers can be rotated under them on tracks. We should place one of the plants near the front of the Farms so we don't have to truck the garbage farther than necessary. It should be a location that is accessible but out of sight. They will make a lot of noise so find some place a little secluded. The other plant should be placed somewhere near the center of the property."

"I need someone who is interested in soil augmentation to take on this project and become our expert in soils," added Ramon. Marcio Torres had a big smile on his face and he said, "Me!"

Ramon asked, "Ok, how many people vote to make Marcio responsible for this?"

The men laughed and all said, "Marcio!"

Marcio was happy to have the soil augmentation as his pet project. He volunteered to help with the project in any way and he also added that a plant nursery needed to be started soon. Marcio said, "We need to start the nursery soon so we can test which plants tolerate the native acidic soils the best and which crops will need the most amount of amended soil for growth in a neutral or alkaline soil."

Ramon injected, "Andre, will you please give this man some land for a nursery—give him anything he wants! What else do you need for the nursery, Marcio?"

Marcio answered, "I won't need this for a long time but eventually I will need a good truck and a tree mover by the time the trees get very large. I want to start growing nut trees now so we have them available at a decent size when our residents want them."

Ramon asked, "Can you put some royal palms in your nursery?"

"Sure, if it's a tropical plant I can get it."

"Great," replied Ramon. "Let's get some royal palms going so we can transplant them later. I think in the future there may be a visitor's center at the very beginning of Templeton Farms and it would be a nice touch to put royal palms on both sides of the road before and after the visitor's center."

Denis asked, "Is Jane going to fire you for making her bankrupt?"

"No," answered Ramon. "In fact she also bought us several hundred truckloads of crushed limestone which will be delivered to the property within two weeks. And for that, Andre, I need space for another processing plant. I would put that plant somewhere near the center of the property because we will be trucking limestone all over the place before plantings. This also involves setting up a processing plant because the crushed limestone has to be applied as a powdered spread."

Dalton asked, "Will you be expecting our work crews to construct these three processing plants?"

"They will be needed briefly," answered Ramon. "We only need your crew to prepare the sites, grading, that kind of work. The two plants will be set up by the company that supplied them."

Finally, Ramon also disclosed, "I might be getting assistance from the University of Rio de Janeiro to help in recruiting natives to return to the farm. I talked to the head of the Anthropology Department and there might be a couple of graduate students from France involved in recruitment. The French students are studying the language of natives in the region and this project might be the basis for their doctoral dissertations. If we are lucky enough to get them, I want to make sure that we give them our fullest cooperation. I know for certain that I don't want to be out in the jungle recruiting natives. I think you all remember what fun I was to have along on our survey trip to the wilds."

"We'll never forget that," said Denis. "Dalton wanted to bring you some pet snakes but I wouldn't let him."

"Thanks, I appreciate that," replied Ramon. "If there's no other business we'll let you men get back to work."

After the meeting ended, the others left and Denis stayed to help Ramon put things away and clean up the makeshift conference room. While they were talking, Ramon told Denis, "I had to sell Storm." He couldn't finish the sentence and he meant to say, "I had to sell Storm because I didn't have time to exercise him." Ramon choked up and couldn't say the last part of the sentence. Ramon wasn't acting, he really could not finish the sentence. When he started to tell Denis about Storm he thought he could speak without getting emotional. He didn't guess how much he would miss Storm or how much he hated seeing the empty pasture.

Denis saw tears in Ramon's eyes and suggested, "Like I was telling you Ramon, you have to learn how to manage your money." After Denis said it, he wished he didn't. On second thought, he realized he was being too cruel to Ramon. Now that it was said, there was no taking it back. Denis would have to amend things with Ramon by giving him an easier time about money in the future.

Several weeks later, Ramon called Thomaz from his farm to have one of their private telephone calls. Whenever Thomaz received an evening call from Ramon, he always knew the topic would be about Jane. Ramon started, "I may be playing the poverty card too well. Just to give you the heads-up, I was telling Denis that I sold Storm. I got so choked up that I couldn't explain that I sold Storm only because I didn't have time to care for him. He is under the impression that I sold Storm because I needed money. So, if that ever comes up when you are around, just go with it."

"Not a problem," answered the sleepy attorney. "Ramon, it is not healthy for you to be out on that farm all by yourself. When are you going to find yourself a wife?"

"If I don't have time for a horse, then I don't have time to look for a wife. Also, being single in Britania is like being a bug under a microscope. Everyone in town watches me. I have no privacy here and dating is out of the question. There are times when I really miss the big city. I may have to use some vacation days during my next business trip to Rio."

"Ramon, that's entirely your call. Don't feel so trapped about being in Britania. Do you want to come over to Goiania to work out of this office for a while? There are certainly beautiful women in Goiania."

"No, not really, so don't spend your time trying to find blind dates for me. If I ever marry again I have my mind set on a Carioca or maybe an American."

"Ramon, I never knew that you were once married."

"It was a long time ago and a very sad time in my life."

"Then I won't pry into your affairs, but if you ever need someone to talk to, you know I'm always here for you."

"Thanks Thomaz. Enough talk about women. I would be better off getting a dog right now. Actually, I do have business to discuss with you."

"I'm all ears," replied Thomaz.

"I think we need to give the men a raise. Inflation is killing our personal income and we need to see if Jane can index our salaries monthly to the American dollar. The men have been working hard enough and they deserve a raise. Let me be the ringleader to bring it up and I know the men will help me explain the justification for the raise. Don't commit to them with an answer. Just tell them that you will have to wait to discuss it with Jane the next time she calls."

"Yes, and I hope Jane will remember that inflation is also killing the retainer of her attorney."

"I'm certain that Jane will understand your position when you talk to her. Jane is feeling pretty deflated lately after buying all those new tractors but I'm sure she still has some funds left for us."

"Ok," replied Thomaz. "I'm not near my calendar, are we meeting in Britania this Friday or next?"

"Our next meeting time is next Friday, see you then. Oh, and I'm sorry I woke you up."

"No problem. See you then."

At the next meeting of the Templeton Farms management team, Denis gave an impressive update on the acreage currently growing soybeans. The new tractors were all in place and were busy planting and harvesting soybeans on a rotating schedule. Denis was now responsible for 100 men working the soybean fields and eight more working as teachers to help the new farmers.

Dalton reported a large amount of processed milk shipped out on a daily basis. Dalton had just nine men working the dairy with him and he explained that he needed more men to help manage the growing herd. He asked for and was given permission to recruit some Gauchos from Rio Grande do Sul to help with the cattle.

Marcio reported the mulching plants working efficiently, but needing more organic material. He proudly read off a long list of plants available as seedlings from the nurseries.

Ramon gave his report and in typical "Ramon Style" it was all about Ramon. He started, "With the inflation that the country is experiencing, I can't make ends meet. Thomaz, will you please ask Jane if she can give all of us a raise. I have only a decrepit old farm to care for, but these men all have families. I think it's time for a raise and we deserve it. I will leave it up to you to try to sell this to her. Please convey to Jane our sincere appreciation for our jobs and the opportunities here. Try to convince her based on our needs and don't portray us as money grubbing dolts."

"I would never do that," asserted the attorney. "You can rest assured that I will earnestly convey your requests to Jane the next time she calls."

Dalton added, "Mr. Rocha, so we don't have to go begging to Jane every other month for a raise, would it be possible to index our salaries to some standard and have automatic adjustments made monthly. I fully appreciate that the entire country is suffering from the current inflation. I've heard that some employers are doing that for their employees so they don't lose them."

"Yes," replied the attorney. "I've also read about that and it seems like a good solution. I will try my best to win her over to the idea of it. How receptive she is, probably will depend on her current financial situation. I have no idea if our inflation has affected her wealth. All I can do is to ask."

Denis added, "Raises for all of us would be great. I have an additional request item for Jane. She may not be too warm to this but it's a request I'm getting all the time. My workers all see these poor people getting free farms. Our farm package including the house, with well, road, fences, and utilities amounts to a $25,000 windfall for being poor. My workers are asking to be included as farm recipients. Personally, I agree with them and I wouldn't mind being in on the giveaway either. Several workers recently made reasonable suggestions to me. They aren't asking for a farm for weeks or months worth of work. They do feel if they serve the community over a number of years, then they should be rewarded, and I can't argue with that. In fact, I think all of us would like to be included in some similar fashion."

Thomaz replied, "Yes, I can certainly appreciate that coming from field workers who are making small wages. They probably feel they would be better off not working and poor, then they would get a free farm. Jane and I will have a very long conversation the next time she checks in. Thanks for bringing that to my attention. I will discuss all these issues with Jane and will let you know her response."

After the meeting, Thomaz stayed at the Home Office and reviewed specific items with all the management staff. All the men worked all evening long, knowing that Thomaz would be returning on the midnight bus. Ramon had no opportunity to privately speak to Thomaz. A day later, the two of them held another private evening telephone conversation to follow up the requests.

Several weeks later, the entire management team met and Thomas reported his most recent telephone discussion with Jane. "Jane was feeling generous when we talked. She has asked me to index your salaries to the American dollar so you will be getting automatic raises matching our monthly inflation statistics."

Thomas continued, "She also agrees with giving long-term employees farms. This gets a little sticky, and complicated, because we are dealing with the desires of our anonymous donor and the demands of the government. I'll get to the easiest part first. Jane thinks it's a good

166

idea for all of the management team to have farms together in a good location. That way, when we are old, we can all take care of each other. She has a vision of the six of us sitting on verandas sipping martinis. Andre, there will be some recordkeeping requirements needed from you."

"Certainly, whatever you need," replied the surveyor.

"The farms given to employees of any class, must come from the 49% of the tillable land owned by Jane. We just need to make sure that the records are straight on which hand owns what. So, Andre and the land supervisors should pick out a nice location for the six of us to have adjoining farms. The agreement is that Jane wants three years of employment for an employee farm."

Denis suggested, "I have a place in mind near the northeast boundary. Some weekend, we should all go out there to take a look at the area I have in mind."

Andre added, "That would be a perfect spot from my perspective since the farms in that area will not be assigned for a long time."

Thomaz continued, "That's the easy part. The next part makes this a bit more complicated. When we speak of employees we need to apply the offer to all employees. It is complicated because so many of the people working the soybean farm are natives. They were offered farms in the beginning. Some started farms and left, others didn't want a farm. Now that they have been working the land, they may want a farm. The natives will be receiving farms from the 51% of Templeton Farms reserved for residents. Andre, that means you will need to get involved in this to keep track of farms given under this program. If employees, natives or otherwise qualify for a free farm, then we must start reserving land for them. At their three-year anniversary, they get a farm if they want it. If they refuse a farm, then we need to be certain to have them sign a waiver and they have to understand what they are signing."

Denis suggested, "With the government pressing for land reform, there will be no shortage of land to give away. It just might be 200 miles away from here."

"Yes," answered the attorney. "And that's where people will get upset. They will expect a farm here in Templeton Farms. Denis, I will need you and Marcio to split up your work teams and talk to all your employees so they understand the program. Dalton, you don't have so many employees so I'm asking you to take care of your group. What I want is a signed "Reservation for Farm" form completed by all your employees. It doesn't matter if they have only worked three weeks, I want them to sign the reservations. If they refuse, and absolutely do not want a farm, then I want them to sign a waiver. You need to explain to the employees who sign the waiver that a farm in Templeton Farms will not be available to them in the future, if they change their minds. They must also understand that they must work any three out of five years to qualify for a farm under the employee arrangement."

Denis said, "That will make a lot of my people very happy. Andre, you will be plotting quite a few farms out of the communal land."

"No problem," replied Andre. "We have a lot of acreage setting idle. I will be certain to plot out more farms than we will ever need."

Denis asked, "Since the management group will all be farm owners soon, what do we want to grow?"

Thomaz answered, "I've always wanted to be a coffee baron."

Denis waived his index finger at Thomaz and said, "Too much work, too much expense. Besides, 400 acres in coffee is not going to make you a baron. Put the same acreage in macadamia nuts and then you might be a baron some day."

"Denis, I yield to your good judgment. Please plant my farm in whatever will bring the greatest return for the least effort. I don't think that you will be finding me working the fields though."

"That's the great part about nuts. Very little work and a huge profit. Marcio's team will even come around with their automated equipment and harvest your crops. Yes, I think if you let me plant your farm, you can spend your time sipping martinis on your veranda. Ramon, how about you?"

"Macadamia nuts are fine with me. Won't we glut the market if we all grow the same product?"

"No," answered Denis. "That's the wonderful part about macadamia nuts. They are for foreign export and bring the best prices."

Marcio added, "I'll start a lot of macadamia nut trees in the nursery so we can get our farms all planted soon after Andre completes the plots."

Ramon added, "Well, it does look like Jane's vision for us will be coming true. Imagine, all of us sitting around drinking martinis in the afternoon."

CHAPTER SIXTEEN

Three years after the first farming families arrived, the original three land supervisors and Andre Rondon were still on their jobs at Templeton Farms. Denis Brava was promoted to Superintendant of Land Projects, which made him in charge of all the day-to-day decisions. Andre Rondon and his team were still finishing the surveying project and they were near the middle of the property. Along the way, there were lots of frustrations but then there were a lot of success stories. Over 300 families had moved into Templeton Farms and the infrastructure would soon be complete to accept the remaining families. Fences were mostly completed for an additional 5,200 farms but not all of them would be immediately assigned to families. The team had always worried about density so they copied the plan from the American railroad development and filled farms in a checkerboard design. The planned vacant farms would be saved for future generations of the original families. Not counting this reserve, Templeton Farms would be assigning homesteads to slightly over 4,000 additional families.

A big success story involved the soil augmentation plan and the recycling business. To get enough garbage for recycling, the Foundation also had to buy out all the trash-hauling companies in Brasilia and several other surrounding cities. It was expensive to haul all the material by truck but the farmland needed it. The garbage business in Brasilia had its own mulch processing plant so the trucks hauled over only material ready to be applied to the fields. The recycling of glass and metals paid the workers' salaries but the communal farm income and profit from the garbage business had to be used for transportation costs.

The two original mulching plants on the Templeton Farms turned out to be operations that required workers 24 hours a day, seven days per week. The plant workers alone brought money and life back to Britania. Ramon spent weeks in Rio meeting with the company that designed and constructed the two mulch-processing plants and the one limestone crushing plant. He chose a company that designs tunneling equipment. He thought that a company that made equipment to chew through granite should be able to reverse engineer equipment to chew up and spit out trees and brush.

Ramon made a good choice picking Yorki International as the company to supply the processing plants. The company was used to making all kinds of large grinding equipment so Ramon's application was new to them but not beyond their scope of ability. The grinders turned out to look like six-story grain elevators. Inside, a series of sharp blades and rotating drill bits slashed away at the material to be processed. The processing plants were placed in areas providing a ten-story vertical drop in elevation. Roads were made to the top of the elevation where trucks dumped material on to a large metal grid. The plants worked on two different cycles. Small items found in garbage went right through the eight-inch grid and came out as fine bits in the bottom. After the first cycle, different grinders were turned on and the grid was mechanically removed to allow trees and large items to fall through.

Trees or garbage, it didn't matter much to the huge grinders. Either cycle took only a minute and then dumped the material into 5,000-gallon mulching barrels waiting underneath. A cycle of trees was distributed among several barrels because sawdust alone does not make good mulch. The 5,000-gallon barrels rode on train tracks and moved around by a small electric locomotive. The grinder operator remotely controlled the locomotive. The large black-painted barrels cooked the mulch in only a week with the help of the heat and humidity. The barrels were designed so they automatically rotated several times per day to mix the material. After cooking for a week, dump trucks spread the material over fields between plantings.

Safety was a big issue that was engineered into the design of the mulching plants. The mechanical grinders had no brain and it didn't matter what was sent through the grinder, it all came out a minute later as sawdust. A dump truck or a person going through the grinder ended up as small chucks in a minute. While the equipment had the capacity to do its work quickly, the safety concerns slowed the process.

All three processing plants were fabricated in Belo Horizonte and trucked over to Britania. The mulching plants were specially designed from the bottom up and Ramon spent hours discussing the types of material that might go through them and what was expected from the output. The limestone processing plant was standard issue from Yorki and simply involved trucking it to Britania and setting it up.

After the garbage was cycled through the process, it no longer looked or smelled like garbage. The cooked material looked more like black, loamy soil than anything else. Tilled into the heavy clay soils of the fields of Templeton Farms, it lightened the texture and weight of the native soil.

Marcio Torres supervised all the functions of the soil augmentation plan and was involved in the recycling business. Additionally, his vast nursery supplied plants so farmers had access to healthy stock. As the men had predicted, nuts became a major cash crop for the community and most farms had some land planted in cashew, macadamia, or almonds. The soil augmentation plan had been so successful that crop yields for soybeans were 60 bushels per acre, nearly the same as from North American farms, but Templeton Farms had the advantage of getting three harvests per year.

Andre Rondon managed to find a new and challenging project for himself. While checking out the large lake that Denis told him to reserve as a natural area, he found a massive canyon that ended in a tight narrows. The massive canyon was just a couple mountains farther north from the big lake. The area was perfect for building a hydroelectric plant that could power Templeton Farms and sell excess to the nation's grid. Andre realized that Jane did not have millions to spend on a big hydro project, but he wanted to reserve the entire area in case the government might someday have the funds to build it.

The soybean fields were bringing in cash to help pay for new projects and more equipment. The communal soybean fields grew in acres and over time, they reached the targeted goal of 800,000 acres. That required 200 equipment operators working every day and night in the lowlands. The fields were constantly rotated and on any given day some fields were being planted and others were being harvested. Housing was built for the workers and there was a large shop and equipment field just to keep all that heavy equipment running. Each day trucks full of diesel fuel made the trek to the soybean fields and eventually a fuel depot was built. The loam soils of the lowlands did not require the super tilling of the hard clay of the highlands, but manure and powdered limestone were applied over all the fields between plantings.

With three harvests per year, with that acreage, the total value of the soybean harvests exceeded 150 million dollars per year. About a third of that amount was spent on costs to produce and ship out the harvest. Ramon wanted ten percent of the net profits from the soybeans, dairy, and cheese returned to the anonymous donor as repayment of the original funding for all the equipment. That meant that Jane should retain all of her original funds and grow by 15 million dollars per year. However, the need for new equipment was so great that Jane was not being repaid and she was critically low in funds. Ramon promised himself to make things right with Jane once all the necessary equipment was purchased. The good news was that between the soybean fields and the dairy, the net revenues to fund Templeton Farms exceeded all expectations.

On the negative side, Ramon's plan to resettle natives to the land was a haunting failure. The best thing was that the two French graduate students both earned their doctorate degrees from their work with the natives. Only several dozen native families agreed to take up agriculture. They were the first ones to be relocated into Templeton Farms and they were given farms in the lowlands of the western periphery of the property. This placed them closer to their home villages. Less than a dozen of the original native families remained and made the transition to farming. Twenty native families proved to be a thorn in the side of everyone. The men refused to wear any clothes at all, which wasn't a big deal. The native families were given milk cows and chickens for breeding. They never grasped the concept of delayed gratification and instead ate the animals before any breeding could occur. Worse, after they ate their own farm animals, they stalked and killed the livestock of all their neighbors. The Foundation kept replacing animals at an alarming rate. After one of the white settlers was killed trying to protect his livestock, most of the natives returned to their home villages. Ramon had 50 head of cattle moved to each of the native villages that sent people to the Farm. He hoped that one day they might grasp the concept of cattle breeding but that never happened.

Oddly, some of the native men saw the heavy equipment working the soybean fields of the lowlands and asked for rides. After riding on the big diesel tractors, they wanted to drive them. Soon, a handful of native men were working the soybean fields as heavy equipment operators. They used their earnings to buy cattle for their villages. Ramon thought in his wildest dreams he would never see people going from using a blowpipe one day to driving a big diesel tractor the next day. Some of the men who became equipment operators were natives who started a farm and then left. To them, there was no excitement about staying on one piece of land. All the land beyond the Araguaia River was their land anyway, albeit swampland. The natives who because equipment operators returned to their villages and recruited more equipment operators. Soon, many of the 200 men farming the soybean fields were natives.

Thomaz Rocha became tired of answering inquiries from all outsiders so he hired an attorney to help him. He recruited Julia Arcos because she had experience both as a lawyer and as a media specialist. Julia helped screen applicants for farms and gave tours to visitors. As the Templeton Farms became the favorite subject of news stories in the tabloids, more and more Brazilians wanted to tour the Farms. News of the success of the Farms spread worldwide and soon Julia was frequently hosting foreign visitors.

During the tours, foreign reporters called the Templeton Foundation the birthplace of communism in Brazil and repeatedly attacked Julia Arcos. The distracters focused on the fact that the farmers were slaves to the land and that they did not own the land they farmed. Julia tried to set the record straight but she did not have the skills or personality to defend the Foundation. Instead, everything she said only fanned the flames of criticism. She naively told the reporters that the planners at the Templeton Foundation had five-years plans to solve this problem or that problem. The "five-year plan" reeked of the infamous communist five-year plans, making her reply very inappropriate. At every turn, Julia Arcos was able to bring out something controversial about the Templeton Foundation. Whenever someone brought up something negative, she couldn't turn it around and instead was either dumbfounded or defensive.

The rumor mill in the tabloids was so great that the President of Brazil sent his Interior Minister, Gilberto Lima, to the Templeton Farms on a fact-finding mission. Fortunately, Thomaz Rocha got wind of his visit in advance and was able to head him off in Goiania. Thomaz met with the Minister and personally escorted him on a tour of the Farms.

After the tour, the Minister spoke candidly to Thomaz Rocha, "You must immediately start the process to ensure that all the landowners hold deed to their own farm. Avoid the squatter problem by putting a guard gate at the entrance to the farms and make routine patrols of the property. We can't have the tabloids saying that we have communism in Brazil because your residents don't hold titles to their farms. This is something that you have to resolve right now."

Thomaz answered, "Yes, we can do that. It will take money and resources away from other projects, but if the government insists then we will devote the time and energy to getting it done."

"On this issue, Mr. Rocha, you need to look at the larger picture. Get your house in order, here in Britania, and greater things will come to the Templeton Foundation. Believe me, it will be well worth your time and money to resolve the issues I'm bringing to you today."

The attorney asked, "By the way you say that, are there more issues?"

"Just one," replied the Interior Minister. "We fear this next issue may be the one that shuts down the Templeton Foundation. We've heard rumors that the people backing the project were responsible for the death of the former landowner and his family. If that is the case, then the President could not support the project even though he is very interested in its success. Will you allow us to send an investigator to talk to people working at the Foundation in order to put an end to these rumors?"

Calmly the attorney answered, "Surely. Send as many investigators as you like. There are no secrets here. The Templeton Foundation is an open book and its sole purpose is to do good for the people. If there are negative rumors out there, then by all means we need to investigate and put them to rest."

Picking up his papers, the Minister replied, "I will call you next week to tell you when and who to expect. The investigation will be soon." Gilberto Lima and Thomaz Rocha shook hands and the Interior Minister returned to Brasilia.

Early the following week Thomaz Rocha found out that Nelson Machado would be leading the investigation into the deaths of the Roberio Family. Nelson was a major investigator from São Paulo and few people had ever managed to escape unscathed from his scrutiny. When the investigator arrived in Goiania, it meant another long drive over the Britania. Attorney Rocha had to drop everything to drive the investigator over to Britania.

Nelson Machado was tall, white, and European. When he walked into Thomaz Rocha's office, he acted as if he owned the place. The attorney could immediately sense that this man would stop at nothing to get to the truth. During their initial meeting, the investigator asked Attorney Rocha what kind of background checks he did before hiring the current management team. The attorney replied, "Nothing except checking employment references. Britania is a small community and everyone knows everyone. If you are a screw up in such a small town then everyone knows all about you. There were no red flags with anyone that we've hired."

"You know that this is a murder investigation," boasted Nelson. "And the President will not be happy until the truth is uncovered."

"Well, you can ask me all the questions you want while we are driving out to Britania."

Nelson answered, "That won't be necessary on your part. There is no sense in taking your time just to chauffer me over there. Just lay out for me the players in the town, now and at the time of the massacre. Who are the current employees and how did you come to hire them?"

Attorney Rocha answered all the man's questions and then Nelson asked, "So who is this anonymous donor that runs the Templeton Foundation and what's his involvement in all of this?"

The attorney replied, "Well, I don't know her name actually. If I did, then she would not be an anonymous donor. She calls from time to time to check progress and asks about the status of certain things but I don't know her name, nor would I dare ask. I don't even have a phone number for her."

The investigator asked, "So, did she just call you out of the blue one day and tell you that you had millions of dollars to spend on this project?"

"Well yes," answered the attorney. "That's about it. I don't know why she chose this project or how she found my name. When someone hands you millions of dollars for a major project, you don't dare look the gift horse in the face. I simply told her thanks and explained all the good that the money would do for the community."

"Sounds suspicious to me," replied Nelson as he closed his notebook and got up to leave.

Nelson Machado rented his own car and drove to Britania by himself. He wanted the freedom to come and go and did not want someone interfering with his investigation.

Nelson had the names of all the players and where to find them in Britania. When he arrived in town, he wanted to talk to Denis Brava first. He told Denis, "You know this is a murder investigation into the events that led to the death of the Roberio family. Since you were working for the Roberio Ranch at the time, do you have any knowledge of the events that happened to the family members?"

Denis answered respectfully, "No, I don't have any knowledge about that. As you already know, I was working on the ranch at the time, so my days were spent overseeing the crop production and grazing operations. Carlos Roberio didn't spend much time communicating with me. He only yelled at me if something went wrong so it was my business to make sure nothing went wrong."

The investigator asked, "And how about Ramon Gobbey? I understand that he worked with the doctor who was murdered. Wouldn't he want to revenge the killing of his employer?"

"Perhaps, but I can't see it. Ramon is not the type. The Roberios were killed off by snake attacks. I know from firsthand experience that Ramon is scared to death of snakes. When we did the initial ranch survey, Ramon screamed like a girl anytime he saw a snake. I can't image Ramon knowing where to go get some snakes to kill people. I don't think he knows the difference between a harmless garden snake and a Jararacussu. Now, are you asking if he paid a Quimbanda priest to do the job then I might say 'maybe, but doubtful.' I don't think that he has the balls to do anything like that either. Plus, Ramon doesn't have that kind of money to pay for a major undertaking like that. Everyone liked Dr. Noqueira but I don't think he paid Ramon very well. Ramon still owes a lot of money to people in this town. He still goes around hitting people up for money until the next payday. That kind of job would have taken at least a couple thousand dollars to hire the priest and Ramon has never been close to that kind of money."

"So, who do you think hired the Quimbanda priest?" pried the investigator.

"That's where I take issue with what's in the rumor mill. I don't think that Mrs. Noqueira hired the Quimbanda priest. Sure, she ran out of town, but wouldn't you do the same thing? I think that if Carlos Roberio was bullying the town doctor, then you can bet he was doing the same thing to quite a few other people. I'm certain that some merchant was tired of getting bossed around by Carlos. When Carlos had the doctor murdered, then it just drove someone over the edge. I am certain it's some merchant or business owner who was just fed up with the town being owned and controlled by Carlos. Find that person and you will find who hired the Quimbanda priest. I think the priest just got a little crazy and decided to wipe out the entire family. Carlos was never a nice guy. I can say that from an employee perspective and as someone who has lived in this town a long time. He was never voted citizen of the year. I can assure you of that."

The private investigator next interviewed Dalton Santos. Nelson asked him the same questions about Ramon Gobbey. Dalton was just as open with the investigator as Denis Brava was and he disclosed, "I know Ramon pretty well and I believe that he has led a pretty sheltered life. His father raised him and he was an only child. I don't see him having any abilities for doing something like that. Besides, when we were out in the wild doing the ranch survey, he was like a sissy boy around snakes. I don't think he has really ever spent any time in wild like the others. He wouldn't eat this, he wouldn't eat that. There is just no way Ramon could go out and pick up snakes and throw them in cars. He wouldn't know what snakes to pick out and he would have no idea where to find them. Like I said, he is really squeamish around stuff in the wild."

The investigator probed, "Do you think he could have hired a Quimbanda priest to do the job for him? After all, Dr. Noqueira was his employer and I hear they had a good working relationship."

"No, I don't think that's possible at all. Ramon was just a maintenance man and he never would have had the money it takes to hire a Quimbanda priest. Ramon's never been able to keep his money. I suspect he spends it all on the girls. Just last week I had to loan him money for lunch."

"How about Mrs. Noqueira, do you think she hired the Quimbanda priest?"

"Of course she did. And everyone in this town thinks she had the right to hire a Quimbanda priest. But I'm pretty sure it was a priestess. That poison snake thing—that's more like a priestess. A Quimbanda priest would have been more direct, like guns."

Nelson next asked Marcio Torres what he knew about the murders. Marcio informed the investigator, "Yes, it was a Quimbanda priest but Ramon didn't hire him and neither did Mrs. Noqueira. It was Dr. Noqueira himself who hired the Quimbanda priest. The doctor was being threatened by Carlos Roberio to move out of town so his son could move in and take over the hospital. So, the only logical answer is that before Dr. Noqueira was killed, he hired a Quimbanda priest to go after everyone responsible should he be killed. He was murdered; the priest was engaged, and look what happened. Case closed!"

The investigator replied, "That's a different angle on the murders. Everyone in this town believes that Mrs. Noqueira hired the priest and that's why she disappeared overnight"

"Wouldn't you disappear overnight if someone just ran your husband out of town by killing him? Of course she ran. She had no choice."

Hoping for a resolution, Nelson asked, "Do you have any personal knowledge about Dr. Noqueira hiring a Quimbanda priest?"

"No, I don't have any personal knowledge. That's just my conclusion after thinking about all those events. I never spoke to the doctor and

I've never seen him as a patient. I'm a pretty lucky guy—nothing bad ever happens to me."

After introducing himself, Nelson finally interviewed Ramon Gobbey. He started by asking bluntly, "Do you know who killed off the Roberio family?"

"Of course I wanted to revenge Dr. Noqueira's murder but they were all dead before I could even think to do anything. When it all happened, I was in Goiania delivering tissue samples to the pathology laboratory there. Dr. Noqueira sent me there three or four times a month to deliver specimens to the laboratory. The tissue samples were important and the only way to get them there was for me to carry them over by bus. Sometimes I would have to wait for the report. On the day of the shooting, I was in Goiania and didn't know anything about it until I returned late in the afternoon. The police talked to me and they told me that a stranger was caught in a nearby village with $500 cash. They told me they were certain that the stranger killed Dr. Noqueira but they couldn't hold him for lack of evidence. If you ask me, I say that the police were in on it. I think they know who did all the killings but they were paid off."

After interviewing the Templeton Foundation employees, Nelson Machado wanted to get the perspective from the locals. He also wanted to make certain that the locals knew that an investigation was being made. Sometimes, good leads come from people in the community who have heard things.

Looking for the town's gossipmonger, he stopped a small woman on the street and asked how long she had lived in Britania. He was certain to impress upon her that the government had hired him, a famous private investigator, to do the investigation. Giving her a business card he asked, "Do you have any information about the killings of Dr. Noqueira and the Roberio family?"

Of the Roberio family she confided, "They were the biggest bunch of sinners in all of Brazil. I think that the Lord God struck them all down for being sinners. God sent his serpents to send them to hell. They killed our wonderful Dr. Noqueira. He was the best doctor this town will ever have. And those sinners had him killed. Now those Roberios all belong to the devil to receive their punishment."

Nelson quickly realized that the old lady was the town's church lady and gossip lady all tied up in one little package. Her fire and brimstone speech was quickly giving him a headache so he asked the one question that he needed, "Is there anyone left in town that used to work for Dr. Noqueira besides Ramon Gobbey?"

She replied, "No, I don't think there is. The nurses who worked at the hospital all took jobs in other towns. There was this nurse, Rosie Cadrenho, who is now working at the hospital over in Itapirapua. She was Dr. Noqueira's charge nurse and I think he confided in her more than anyone. You should go over there and talk to her. Its only 60 miles away but I bet she can give you plenty of information."

Nelson wrote down the nurse's name and thanked the church lady for her time. He walked over to the Britania Hospital hoping to get some information by looking at the site of Dr. Noqueira's murder. Nelson would have been impressed with the hospital had he seen it when Dr. Noqueira was alive but now it was in ruins. The roof had collapsed and all the doors and windows were missing. Any clues hidden in the hospital were now gone.

On the way back to his car, he stopped and asked a few more townspeople about the murders in Britania. His purpose was as much for letting them know about the investigation as it was for gathering information. The people he talked to all informed him that the Widow Noqueira hired a Quimbanda priest and it was the priest who went crazy and killed the entire Roberio family.

Nelson drove to the Itapirapua Hospital in search of Rosie Cadrenho. He went to the hospital administrator's office asking for the location of Rosie Cadrenho. Nelson explained that he was sent by the government of Brazil to do an investigation into the murders at Britania. A fat bald man wrote down the information that Nelson gave him and collected a business card. The administrator told Nelson that Rosie's shift wasn't over for two more hours, "But I will send someone up to bring her down here. You may use my office to speak privately to her."

Mrs. Cadrenho was a small woman in her late thirties with short black hair and tiny rimless glasses. Nelson explained the purpose of his visit and asked her "Do you have any information about the murders of Dr. Noqueira or of the Roberio family?"

She answered frankly, "Of course, yes I do. I was Dr. Noqueira's charge nurse at the Britania Hospital when he was killed. Actually, I was working the night shift when he was killed in his car just outside the hospital. We didn't hear the gunshots and he wasn't discovered for some time, almost morning as I remember. We were all in such pain when we found out. I almost fainted on the spot. There were two other nurses working with me that night. After we learned what happened we all became hysterical. I believe the patients thought we had all gone mad. Once the patients found out they were also hysterical."

Nelson asked, "Who do you believe killed Dr. Noqueira?"

"I don't know who pulled the trigger but I know who paid to have Dr. Noqueira killed. It was that Carlos Roberio. There is no doubt in my mind. Carlos and that no-good-for-nothing phony pharmacist, Davis Lemas conspired and hired a hit man to kill Dr. Noqueira. About a month before the shooting, they sent a man to beat Dr. Noqueira with the message to 'get out of town or die.' Dr. Noqueira wouldn't leave his hospital so they killed him."

Nelson quizzed, "Of the Roberio family, do you have any knowledge of their deaths?"

"No, I only know about the two theories," the small woman replied.

"What theories?"

"The ladies in my church group say that God sent serpents to them. I believe in the other theory, that someone hired a Quimbanda priest to take care of things."

The investigator pressed, "I didn't hear about Dr. Noqueira being beaten. What happened?"

"Dr. Noqueira left to go home after dark and on the way to his car some guy came out of the shadows and beat him up. He was hurt pretty badly. He broke his ankle and he had a bad laceration across his forehead. I was not working that night. He told the other nurses that he fell down the steps when he was leaving the hospital but he told me the truth. He came back into the hospital and did his own stitches. He couldn't walk for a week and when he came back to work he was on crutches for a while. Some doctor friend of his filled in for him until he was up and around."

Nelson asked, "Why did he confide in you?"

"Dr. Noqueira knew that I would keep his secrets to myself. He delivered both my sons so besides being his charge nurse, there was a special bond between the two of us," Rosie said as her eyes filled with tears. Her shoulders shook as she wept and she couldn't speak any more about the events that happened in Britania. Nelson Machado gave her a little hug and thanked her for her information telling her, "Your information has been very helpful."

On the drive back to Britania, Nelson Machado was mentally putting all the pieces together. The town's rumor mill was inaccurate about the events but several people he interviewed had unwittingly solved the mystery when their testimonies were pieced together. Of the people he interviewed only one of them had correctly solved the mystery of the murder of the Roberio family. The investigator now knew the answer. It was Rosie Cadrenho's testimony that was the turning point. She disclosed that Carlos Roberio threatened Dr. Noqueira and he kept his beating secret from everyone except her. When Denis Brava pointed out that it took someone with considerable wealth to hire a Quimbanda priest for a mass murder, then the list of suspects narrowed.

Actually, Marcio Torres was right on the money with his theory that it was Dr. Noqueira who hired the Quimbanda priest. The doctor had the cash to hire the priest. He had the motives, which were the threats and the beating. The doctor covered his trail by hiding the fact that he was being threatened and that he was beaten. Probably knowing the end was near, Dr. Noqueira sought the help of a Quimbanda priest and gave the priest instructions to kill anyone and everyone remotely associated with his death. By the time Nelson was close to Britania, he had a big smile on his face. He was proud that he solved the mystery of the Roberio family murders. There were just a few loose ends he needed to cover before he could be certain that his conclusion was correct.

Back in Britania Nelson Machado sought out Ramon Gobbey for a second interview. Hoping to make Ramon squirm a little, the investigator asked, "Do you know why I'm here again?"

"To tell me I'm right about the police being involved in Dr. Noqueira's death?" Ramon asked back.

"No, no, that's not it at all," replied Nelson. "I'm pretty certain that you are wrong about that. But, I do have a few more questions for you. Do you remember what happened to Dr. Noqueira a couple weeks before he was killed?"

"No, am I supposed to?" asked Ramon.

"You don't remember an injury that happened to Dr. Noqueira about that time?"

"Oh that," Ramon replied as he tried to anticipate the next question and recall who knew what about the doctor's beating. "Yes, he said he took a tumble down the front steps and cut his face on the handrail. Bad luck."

"And do you happen to remember the name of the physician who covered his practice for a few days while he recuperated?" inquired the investigator.

"No, sorry, I don't know if I ever knew his name," lied Ramon. "He was a good friend to Dr. Noqueira but he has never been back. I don't think there is anything suspicious about that. If you only came to a town to see a certain friend and he ends up getting killed, why would you ever go back to that town? You don't think he had anything to do with Dr. Noqueira's death?"

"Hey, I'll ask the questions around here," snapped Nelson. "No, his friend didn't have anything to do with his death. I just wanted to find that doctor to verify a couple of things."

"Ok, then are we finished?" asked Ramon.

"Sure, get out of here," replied Nelson. He had verified with Ramon the information that he was fishing for anyway. Ramon had just verified that Dr. Noqueira was hiding the fact of his beating from everyone. That was all the proof he needed to prove his theory.

Nelson Machado drove back to Goiania and met briefly with Thomaz Rocha before his flight to Brasilia to meet with the Interior Minister. The attorney asked, "Did you find everything in order in Britania?"

"Oh no," replied the investigator. "That town is in quite a shambles. I did get good cooperation from your management team over there. That's quite a smart group of fellows you have working for you."

Rocha beamed, "I'm glad you approve. So what did you discover?"

"Oh, it's pretty obvious. The doctor was hiding the fact that he was being threatened and even beaten. He was the only one with enough cash to pay for a mass killing. The doctor hired the Quimbanda priest, or priestess, before he died to revenge his own death."

"Awful, awful," replied the attorney. "But now that the truth is known, the community can move on to healing."

The private investigator got up to leave, shook hands with the attorney, and thanked him for his cooperation. Later that day Nelson Machado had much the same conversation with Gilberto Lima, the Interior Minister of Brazil. Glad to have the matter completed, Gilberto handed Nelson a check for $5,000. The Interior Minister asked, "I don't suppose there would be any point to chasing down the Quimbanda priest who carried out the murders?"

Nelson Machado replied, "No, that would be like chasing air."

"Yes, I suppose you are correct," replied the Minister. "I don't think even one of them has been found guilty of anything in the entire history of Brazil."

"Correct," answered Nelson. "Even if you make a good case against one of them, all their colleagues come to their rescue with alibis."

Minister Lima inquired, "You'll send the usual report for our files?"

"Yes," replied Nelson. "Just give me a week to complete it." With the conversation finished, the Minister walked Nelson to the door and slapped him on the back.

CHAPTER SEVENTEEN

One of the challenges of getting the Farms populated was the rumor that the land was infested with Green Darters. Potential residents thought that the land was too dangerous to occupy. The snake rumor mill was helpful in keeping out the squatters but it was detrimental to recruiting new farm families. In reality, the Green Darter phenomenon was still a danger. During the land survey, Andre's assistants marked the locations of Green Darter hives when they encountered them.

Ramon called a special meeting of just the four field men so he could tell them how to deal effectively with Green Darters. During the meeting, Ramon asked, "How many Darter hives have you found and where are they?"

Andre had a special map just for the Green Darter hives so he opened it up and pointed, "Mostly over here, just before you reach the lowlands. That's where we've found most of them."

Ramon replied, "You guys all know how much I hate snakes. There is a reason for that. On my father's farm, we had Green Darters. My dad made me help him get rid of them, and of course, he always sent me in to destroy the hives. We experimented with lots of different ways to kill them. We didn't have the money to buy the fuel to burn them so we had to invent different ways."

Denis said, "Ramon, you continue to surprise me."

"No, this was never anything that I enjoyed doing. See, there is a reason for everything. If you were forced to do what I did as a child then you would be afraid of snakes too. I am surprised that I lived through it."

Dalton asked, "If you didn't burn them out, what did you use?"

"We experimented with lots of different things. Physically removing the hive never worked because the ones out hunting rebuilt the hive quickly. We tried drowning them but that had no effect. My father tried agricultural lye, or sodium hydroxide. It very effectively killed every hive in a short amount of time."

Denis offered, "Ramon, you should have written up your secret and sold it to the ranchers around here. It could have saved people millions in fuel."

"My father was never one to think about things beyond his own farm. I want you men to spread the word around about this process. Take full credit for it and let the residents know how smart you are. Don't mention my name about this because I am never going to go out into the fields ever again to help anyone deal with Green Darters."

Marcio asked, "Ok, how did your father do this exactly?"

Ramon answered, "First step is the same. Get all the livestock out of the area and fence them out. Then plow a circle around the hive. Stay at least 60 feet away from the hive and make the plowed circle 50 feet wide. Then apply the powered lye. If the grass is too thick to plow, just use your flame throwers to make the circle around the hive."

Denis asked, "Is that all there is to it?"

"Pretty much. If it rains, you must reapply the lye quickly. After a month, the hive will starve. The lye burns the sensitive eyes and tongues of the tiny snakes so they will never cross it. The unplowed area next to their hive won't support them with enough food and quickly they start dying out from starvation."

Dalton offered, "Ramon, your father was probably the smartest man in the whole country to figure this out. I bet it didn't cost more than fifty dollars to kill off a hive."

"Yes, about that much," answered Ramon. "My father never had any money so he couldn't spend thousands to burn out an entire field. He had to use his smarts to find alternative methods for lots of different things."

While Ramon was dealing with the snake problems, Julia Arcos was creating some of her own. During the day, she spent hours on the phone talking to her mother. She spent most of her time telling other people about the difficulty of her job. When Thomaz heard her use the word, "overtime" he was about ready to yank the phone out of her hands.

Ramon and Thomaz met at the Goiania office and Julia was on her usual two-hour lunch break. Thomaz sent Ramon to find something on Julia's desk and Ramon returned with a large box of resident applications. Julia had gotten tired of processing farm applications so she just tossed them in a large box. All she had to do to complete the processing was to verify income and assets and call the social welfare agency with an answer. Julia was supposed to spend each Friday over at Britania, giving tours and she frequently made some excuse not to take the bus over.

Thomaz received a visit from Vitor Pedrino, a reporter for the Goiania newspaper. Vitor had some information and he wanted more. Vitor inquired, "I know that the anonymous benefactor of the Templeton Foundation is Jane. I need to know her last name and what she does, where does she live, and why is she giving money to the Templeton Foundation?

"That's interesting," answered Thomaz. "And how did you learn of the name Jane?"

"Julia, your tour guide," replied Vitor. "She made the announcement on the tour bus last Friday. I heard it myself. I just thought that if the anonymous donor was willing to give out her name then perhaps I might have some more information about her."

Thomaz replied, "I don't know the identity of the anonymous donor. It could be a man, a woman, or some organization. That's the thing about philanthropy, sometimes people like to give to good causes but they don't want to be known. I'm sorry, but there really is no information for you. Julia overheard us using the name Jane because it's just shorter than saying, 'anonymous donor' all the time. 'Jane' is just our internal code word for 'our anonymous donor.' That's the whole story and hardly worth telling your readers."

Vitor pressed, "Don't you think the community deserves to know the identity of the donor who is helping Britania so much?"

"Absolutely not," replied a grouchy Thomaz. "As I've already said, people who give large sums of money sometimes do not like to have their lives scrutinized. I feel certain that if we probe into the donor's identity and discover it, then that person will cease contributing. I don't have to tell you what that means to Britania if that happens." Thomaz looked at his watch and got up from behind his desk to escort Vitor to the door. Vitor kept asking questions until the front door of the law office closed behind him.

Thomaz wrote out a severance check to Julia and asked her to clean out her desk immediately. He stood there while she gathered up some fingernail polish and makeup. An indignant Julia demanded to know the reason and Thomaz simply said he needed someone trustworthy who could maintain confidences. He said, "Overhearing and then giving out the name Jane indicates that we can no longer trust you. Here is a fair severance check." Thomaz escorted Julia to the door, turned to Mrs. Pedrinho, and said, "Never let that woman in this building ever again, not even for a second!"

Ramon told Thomaz he was glad he fired Julia before she could do any more damage. Thomaz explained that he scrutinized her resume and Julia appeared to meet all the requirements. While he was defending her hiring, he shoved a half dozen folders towards Ramon saying, "Here, help me choose her replacement and maybe the two of us can do a better job picking out the next person."

The two men decided on a young lady with experience in public speaking who knew many different languages. They planned to interview Bridgette Suzuki and if she could think on her feet and meet all the other criteria, she would be hired. Bridgette Suzuki was not an attorney. She had just graduated from the University of Rio de Janeiro with majors in communication and journalism. Raised by missionary parents, she spent time in many different countries while growing up. Along the way, she learned to speak Portuguese, Spanish, English, French, Japanese and Chinese.

Ramon had other tasks waiting for him in Britania and he asked Thomaz to do the interview with Bridgette Suzuki. Thomaz interviewed Ms. Suzuki and called Ramon to tell him that the young college graduate would be a great addition and she was young enough to mold into the person needed for the job. Thomaz assured Ramon that he had quizzed her about loyalty and trust issues and Bridgette was confident in selling her attributes. Thomaz told Ramon that she really needed to be a direct hire from the Templeton Foundation rather than an employee in his firm. Ramon understood, but he wanted to avoid developing a corporate hierarchy within Templeton Foundation. Until now, the payroll of the Templeton Foundation included only field personnel and the management team. He knew that hiring Ms. Suzuki would lead to other corporate hires for activities that he and Thomaz had been able to do until now.

The petite, dark haired, Ms. Suzuki was hired and given the title of Director of Public Relations. Her quick wit and perky personality proved to be a valuable asset for the Foundation. Overnight the negative distracters disappeared. Those who did ask pointed questions were given factual answers by Bridgette Suzuki. Her charming personality won over all challengers. Bridgette had a spectacular skill in turning something negative into a positive. She didn't tell lies nor spin the facts; she just saw the world with a glass half full instead of half empty.

Soon after her hire, Bridgette asked to sit in on the meetings of the field supervisors so she could know the operations and be prepared to answer questions. At her first meeting, Thomaz Rocha introduced Ramon Gobbey as the "Chief Executive for Operations." In attendance were the three land supervisors but Andre Rondon was out supervising survey teams. The meeting was routine with section reports from the field staff. Bridgette was not at all shy about asking questions and making suggestions.

Not long after Ms. Suzuki joined the Templeton Foundation she gave a tour of the Farm to a large group of foreign dignitaries. She immediately recognized the President of Brazil sitting in the front row of the bus. Next to the President was a high-ranking general. On his first tour of the Farms with Bridgette, O Presidente took out a small notebook and made notes of everything she said. At first this made her a little nervous but she realized that if O Presidente was going to quote her, then at least he would have his facts correct.

Soon after the President began escorting busloads of foreign dignitaries to the Templeton Farms, the government of Brazil sent a task force to Britania to dress up the town. Ramon's efforts brought back residents and businesses to the town. Streets were paved and a new coat of paint was applied to all the buildings. By the time the task force was finished, the town sparkled better than ever before.

The hospital was still in ruins and medical care was only available in Itapirapua or São Luis de Montes Belos. The government's team came to Britania a couple months later and restored the hospital to its former glory. The government team put on a new roof and replaced the doors and windows. The medical equipment that had all been looted was replaced with new equipment. A new young doctor was sent to serve the town. The Templeton Foundation still held title to the hospital. Ramon thought he would just hold on to the title. It might come in handy as a reward some day to keep the doctor from leaving Britania. Or, it might be needed as an incentive to lure a new doctor some day.

At a subsequent staff meeting with the field supervisors, Bridgette gushed as she told her story about the President participating in the tours of the Farms. Thomaz Rocha gave a sly wink to Ramon who was sitting at the opposite end of the conference table. Ramon could not hold back a grin because both men knew they made the right choice in hiring Bridgette Suzuki.

After the meeting, Thomaz Rocha had a short conference with just Ramon to bring him up to date on the progress of getting land titles to the current occupants of the farm. The attorney explained that the title work was creating too much paperwork for his firm and there was a backlog of titles to be completed and delivered. Thomaz told Ramon that he wanted to catch up with the existing occupied farms before the next wave of new farmers arrived. Ramon knew that much of the land title business did not require an attorney so he asked Thomaz to hire Wescley Silva as an intern to help with the title searches. He told Thomaz, "Wescley used to work as a delivery boy for the pharmacist in Britania and now the town doesn't have much opportunity for him. Please put Wescley to work learning the land title business as an intern. If he doesn't work out after a year then you can just terminate the internship."

Thomaz asked, "What if the boy doesn't want a job?"

"You won't know until you make him an offer," replied Ramon. "As one of the few remaining original residents, Wescley is tied down there by having to care for his elderly parents. You will have to help him make some arrangements for their care while he comes to Goiania as an intern. Perhaps we should do the title business out of the Home Office. Obviously, you'll need to train him in Goiania. I hope he sees the opportunity."

"I will try my best," replied the attorney.

During their private meetings, Thomaz Rocha frequently asked Ramon, "How is Jane doing?" or "How did Jane do last month?" Even Ramon started referring to his wealth as "Jane." To put a different twist on it, Ramon would sometimes make it Aunt Jane. Ramon had no living relatives so he could freely talk to Thomaz about Aunt Isabel or Aunt Luci and Thomaz knew the code. The aunts always seemed to be going somewhere. If they had just taken a trip to the north, say Recife, then the investments were doing well. If an aunt had just taken a trip to Porto Alegre, in the south, the investments lost money. If an aunt was staying put in Rio, then there was no change from the prior month.

The men escalated their code talk and could have a business meeting over lunch while discussing their relatives and their needs. A green Ford and a red Chevy for Aunt Luci meant buying a new diesel tractor and harvester for the soybean farm. Milk cows were children, and new farm residents were gifts. Sometimes it got a little confusing and Thomaz had to call Ramon late at night at the farmhouse to verify, "Did you really mean for me to negotiate purchase and delivery of 12 new tractors?"

This month Ramon's report was about bad news, "Jane is not doing very well. Initially when we started buying all the hard assets like the grinders, mulchers, tractors, and harvesters, Jane was down. Now, she is about gone. I do think that Jane is considering putting the Templeton Farms on a monthly budget. That way there will be a steady flow of payments. Special requests for funding will have to cease and the project will need to save up for major improvements or wait until there is crop revenue. I think that will work now that all of the known major improvements have been made."

Mr. Rocha added, "Jane should only send us part of her monthly income and she should maintain all of her original principle."

"Yes, I agree," replied Ramon. "That will help put Jane in a position to help with projects beyond the Templeton Farms."

After that meeting, Ramon called Mrs. Spencer at the Cayman Islands Bank and asked her to send an international money draft for $75,000.00 each month to the Templeton Foundation. Jane had just put the boys on a budget.

Several weeks later there was another busload of visiting foreign dignitaries and Bridgette Suzuki introduced herself and was about to start her tour monologue when O Presidente stood up in the bus and proceeded to give the tour for her. He had memorized her presentation word for word and he even cited the statistics correctly. Julia Arcos probably would have thrown the President off the bus but Bridgette Suzuki had no monster ego. Instead, she realized that the visitors paid much more attention to the President's delivery of the tour. She thought it was terrific that the biggest fan of Templeton Farms was none other than the President of Brazil.

During one of her farm tours when the President was listening, Bridgette inserted a request in disguise, telling the busload of dignitaries, "The communal soybean farm funds the infrastructure for all of Templeton Farms. With so many acres in production, we are fortunate to have a steady flow of income to build farm homes, wells, schools, and utilities. The entire annual income is at risk during a prolonged rainy season because the dirt roads and poor bridges prevent our trucks from taking the harvest out. With no assurance of income, the project must be very cautious about accepting too many new families. Because the project is building homes, wells, fences, and utilities, we cannot spend the money necessary to pave the road and rebuild the bridges to the soybean fields."

Bridgette never realized that her request had any success, but she started quite a process. The next day the President of Brazil called Paulo Dias, Senior Senator from Goias State. The Senator was not used to the President calling him. Usually it was the Senator calling the President. The President asked for an immediate meeting so Senator Dias rushed over to the Presidential Palace.

The President began, "Senator Dias, I am so glad that you brought to my attention the Templeton Farms project in Britania. I've made several trips over there with visiting statesmen and the project is doing very well. Their total agricultural production has even made a nice little positive contribution to our gross national product. Between their 150 million dollar soybean harvest and their exports of milk, cheese, nuts, and vegetables, their output is over 500 million dollars annually. When that family owned the ranch, their production in beef was only around 1 million dollars annually. Senator, I don't need to make it clearer, that's five hundred times the production under new management. And their soybean harvest is mostly an export so that improves Brazil's financial health. When those new farm owners become successful, they will be buying cars, ovens, and refrigerators, all made in Brazil. That is something they could never do when they lived in the favelas."

The Senator replied, "Yes, we all know that the project has been very successful. That's why you go there with bus loads of dignitaries."

"No," answered the President. "That is not why I go there. I go there to keep an eye on them. If their success continues, it may be the future of Brazil. I think from time to time, it's ok to give that project a discreet little push in the right direction. I understand that their soybean production is in jeopardy because the roads and bridges are so poor they cannot take out the harvest in the wet season. That's probably 60 miles of paved roads and a dozen new bridges. Costs on that project are going to be around 70 million dollars. Do you have any extra funds in your state budget that can take care of all or part of that expense?"

"I'm very sorry," replied the Senator. "We already committed our annual excess to cover school replacements for the southern part of the state."

"Will you go talk to them to see if they can come up with half that amount? I have some discretionary military funds that I can transfer but they need to come up with half the costs to complete the project. Please keep our conversation confidential. It's your state so tell them that you are watching out for them and keep my name out of it. I can justify the road and bridge expense from the military budget because it improves access within the interior. Additionally, I don't think that we are going to go to war with Columbia this year so the money will not be used anyway."

"I will go there tomorrow to speak with the leader of the project," assured the Senator. Back at his office, Senator Dias called Thomaz Rocha and requested a time to meet the following afternoon.

In Mr. Rocha's private office, Senator Dias explained, "We understand that your soybean harvest is in jeopardy because the dirt roads don't allow passage in the rainy season. I've calculated that it will require 70 million dollars to pave the road to the eastern edge of the soybean fields and to replace all the bridges. Can your anonymous donor be counted on to supply half that cost if the government can cover the other half?"

"I can only ask," replied Thomaz. "You know, our anonymous donor has made many financial sacrifices to ensure the success of Templeton Farms. I have to tell you that I will be somewhat embarrassed to ask for additional money beyond what has already been provided."

"Yes," replied the Senator. "I understand your position. Believe me, if Goias State had the entire amount I would ask that all of it be allocated to your project."

"Please understand our position, Senator Dias," replied the attorney. "Our anonymous donor has already paid for thousands of miles of fences, thousands of wells, thousands of homes, and other infrastructure costs. Our management team has already asked for funding for additional tractors and other heavy equipment to produce the crops. We cannot be in a position of losing the funding already earmarked for those projects. I will ask your question of our anonymous donor, but with all the other expenses, I feel that we have already drained the well quite dry."

"I'm sorry I have to ask you to have that conversation with your donor. I wish there were other options," the Senator said feeling somewhat embarrassed for pressing the issue.

"There are usually ways around these things if we put our heads together," replied the attorney. "Would there be a chance that the government could bridge the funding over two separate years? Perhaps spend the 35 million dollars by the end of this year to start the project. The Senate could make a new allocation for the coming year and complete the project in six months spanning two separate budget years."

"Yes, anything is possible, given the right priorities," answered the Senator.

"Now, about priorities and future needs," started the attorney. "I will give you this request in advance so you can be thinking where to place it in your funding priorities. Our work crews have discovered a vast canyon with a narrows at the end that will make an ideal hydroelectric project. The electricity generated will be sufficient to power all of Templeton Farms at its maximum size. There will even be plenty of electricity left over to route to Goiania and Brasilia. We are estimating that it will be a four-year construction project and will cost in the range of 200 million dollars. We already know that our anonymous donor cannot help in such a large project and it is somewhat out of her area of interest. Cheap supplies of electricity though, are a keen interest of the Federal Government. As Senior Senator of Goias State, I want you to start making funding requests for this project at the national level. You may want to send a team of government men out to tour the site with Andre Rondon, our chief surveyor. That way they can verify our estimates of the time and money for the construction."

"Yes, we can send a team out from the Corps of Engineers. I am certain that the federal authorities will want to look at it. However, with the massive debt on the southern dams, I'm not sure the country is in any position to take on any more debt for dam construction. Ask your donor about her resources for the road. I will do some additional investigating into other budget surpluses. I will call you when I find anything and will you please call me after you speak to your donor?"

"Yes, certainly." assured the confident attorney.

The next day, Senator Paulo Dias, called the President of Brazil using a telephone number shared only with the President's top aides. The Senator began, "I offered a crumb and the folks at the Templeton Foundation want the cake. They are asking for total funding for the road and bridges, plus an additional 200 million for a large hydroelectric project they want for their property."

"That's a lot to think about," mulled the President. "We are having a small State Dinner for our friends from Uruguay tonight. Why don't you come to the Palace at seven o'clock and before the dinner we can discuss affairs in Goias. Bring Mrs. Dias and she can visit with the First Lady while we have our discussion."

Paulo Dias was excited. Not about the State Dinner, but about the possibility of getting a large hydroelectric project in his state. Paulo was an honest politician by Brazilian standards. However, he was energized knowing that a big government project like the dam meant a one-percent finder's fee for him. The taxpayers called it kickbacks and in other countries, it's called embezzlement. In Brazil, such activity is just business as usual. The finder's fee on a 200 million dollar government project meant two million in the bank account of Paulo Dias. The money for the finder's fee is always built into the budget and is paid as upfront money to get things rolling. Actually, Paulo planned to work overtime to make sure that his project was approved and he intended to smooth the path as the project progressed.

That evening, the Senator and Mrs. Dias drove into the Menducci Porte Cochere of the old Palace and residence of the President. The Palace Guards opened the doors of Senator Dias' Mercedes and led them into the Palace. Mrs. Dias wore a long green evening gown and Paulo wore his black tuxedo with a white shirt and black bowtie. The First Lady immediately saw Mrs. Dias, escorted her away, and motioned to Paulo to meet O Presidente in a room off the grand ballroom.

Paulo entered and immediately found an agitated Chief Executive. The President blasted, "Now, I want that project in Britania to be successful but the federal budget will not allow any new major construction projects for several years. The interest on our existing debt from major projects is killing us. We've got to find private sector money to make this work."

There was a knock at the door and a man wearing a formal dinner jacket entered. Paulo recognized the young Minister of Finance, Mikel Lundee. The two men shook hands and slapped each other on the back. The President continued, "Paulo, in two weeks, I want you to take Mikel and Chief Andrade with you to Goiania to get the finances of the Templeton project settled out. I've asked the Corps of Engineers to expedite the exploration of that hydro project and before two weeks are up we will know the costs and the returns on it."

Mikel added, "Paulo, you know that we are heavily in debt for other hydroelectric projects. The Federal Government is not in a position to carry the debt on any more projects. We need to go talk to them to see if there is any way to put this back into the private sector."

On the way home that evening, Senator Dias was quiet and barely spoke to his wife. He was not listening as she told him all about her visit with the First Lady. Paulo was upset. He had spent the afternoon calculating what do to with the extra two million dollars from the big government project in his state. Now, if it's handed over to the private sector, there will be no finder's fee paid. During his visit with the President, he just lost two million dollars.

Men from the Corps of Engineers spent all week following Andre Rondon around the big canyon in the highlands. Chief Andrade of the Corps was impressed with the canyon site that Andre found. Damming the narrows would create a lake of 320,000 acres and provide electricity and water for the region. Several million years ago, erosion worked away at a small fissure in the granite mountains. Now there was a very tight opening at the bottom of the canyon. The high walls were perfect for a tall concrete dam. The eight hundred foot drop in elevation ensured the generation of many megawatts.

Soon after the Corps of Engineers left Templeton Farms, a lengthy report was hand delivered to Thomaz Rocha in Goiania. Thomaz quickly flipped through the pages of maps, drawings, and calculations. He picked up the phone and called Ramon. Ramon happened to be in the Home Office and picked up the phone one the first ring. The attorney asked, "Ramon, what are you doing tomorrow afternoon?"

"Marcio has some ideas to double the output of the mulchers so I was planning on spending the day with him. Why?"

"The Corps of Engineers just delivered this ten-pound book to me about our proposed hydroelectric project. They want a big meeting over here in Goiania next Friday. The two of us need to study this before then. I was planning to take the 8 a.m. bus tomorrow to Britania and returning on the midnight bus."

"That's fine. I'll just reschedule with Marcio for the next day."

"I've been busy pushing my friend in the Senate for money for the dam and I think they are about to dig their heels in. The government wants us to pave the road from Britania to the eastern edge of the soybean fields to make sure we can always get the harvest delivered. They're pushing a 70 million dollar project and they want us to pay for half of it. There's a lot we need to discuss."

"I'm all ears."

"No, I'd rather discuss this in person with the reports in front of us both. I'll see you around two o'clock tomorrow afternoon."

Thomaz walked into the Home Office shortly after two o'clock the following afternoon. The gutted interior was partially renovated and the only furniture consisted of a conference table, chairs, and six desks. There were many priorities and remodeling the Home Office was not at the top of the list. However, the upstairs apartment for the field staff was completely remodeled.

Thomaz pulled out the heavy dam report bound in plastic with wire straps through the top-of-page hole punches. Thomaz made a second set of copies bound with a large rubber band for himself. Ramon and Thomaz sat at opposite sides of the table and discussed the report. Thomaz started, "I think they are going to be looking at us to fund this hydroelectric project. That will put Jane in the electricity business. Does she want to go there?"

"Absolutely not," replied Ramon. "I can tell you that Jane cannot pay the 35 million dollar share of the road, nor can she fund 200 million for the hydro project."

"Page 18—revised government estimates to build out is three years and $160 million," replied the attorney.

"It doesn't matter, Jane doesn't have either amount."

"Let's not dismiss this as a lost cause too quickly," advised the attorney. "There are two separate issues here and they are getting in the way of each other. First is the roads. Personally, I don't give much of a priority to that. What do you think?"

"I agree. Our trucks have had minimal problems getting fuel and supplies to the soybean fields. Certainly, a dozen places in that road need elevation. Two of the bridges are in bad shape and do need replacement. That can all be done for far less than 35 million dollars."

"On that issue, let's take the 35 million dollars from the government," replied the attorney. "We'll explain that our anonymous donor has depleted almost all her funds and we'll ask the government to finish the project in another budget year."

"Ok, if they will give us the money, or complete the work, yes. Let them replace the worst bridges, elevate the lowest part of the road, and pave what can be done to finish off their 35 million dollars."

Thomaz asked, "Are we finished discussing the road?"

"Yes, on to the dam. Upfront, Jane does not want to be in the electricity business. She knows nothing about that, doesn't want to know, doesn't want to be hounding the residents to pay their electric bills."

Thomaz replied, "I understand all that, but let's look at the facts before we dismiss it. This is why I rushed all the way over to see you today. Now, pay attention to this! It's all about the numbers and I know you are good with numbers. Let's just say that the hydro project, with over-runs, ends up at $180 million. At 80 percent of capacity, the plant will supply 600 million megawatts annually. That's four times more that the local grid requires. The local grid will bring in 21 million dollars annually at the retail level. The rest will go to the national grid and will bring in 27 million dollars annually at the wholesale level. That's all at today's prices. Realize that financing of the project will be locked in at today's prices and will be fixed for the duration until it is paid off. Let's say that we can get attractive financing for 15 years, the annual repayment installment will be 17 million per year. Operating costs for the hydro project and for your newly created electric company are going to run 12 million per year. To summarize, you will earn 48 million each year, operating costs and financing will take away 29 million per year, leaving you with an annual profit of 19 million. Then, after 15 years, you own the entire project with no loan, and you earn 36 million in profit per year."

Ramon studied the notes on the attorney's legal pad and said, "If it's such a good deal, why isn't the government jumping on this project?"

"Normally they would," answered Thomaz. "Right now, the Federal Government is so far in debt for the hydro projects in the south, they don't want anything to do with government financing of major projects. They will be looking for the private sector to complete this project."

"And what will keep Jane from getting in the same spot that the Federal Government is in now?"

"Payback. It's all about payback. Those southern hydroelectric plants are all on flat land, which took a thousand times more dirt to move than our project. They do not have the elevation that we have, so their electric generation is far less than ours will be. We have a 'no lose' project here."

"If it fails to make a profit, Jane will be bankrupt. Are you willing to bet the farm on this?"

"Absolutely," answered Thomaz.

"Ok, but humor me. Tell me what happens when there is a year with crop losses and the residents of Templeton Farms cannot pay their electric bills. We lose the entire retail revenue and cannot make expenses. Jane is bankrupt because she has no reserve."

"Those are good concerns," admitted the attorney. "The residents of Templeton Farms will make up less than 2% of your retail customers. For all I care, you can give them all free electricity. The other 98% of your retail base includes the towns and villages in Goias and Tocantins. The rest are the big ranch owners who will always pay their bills."

Ramon asked, "Do you have the historical numbers for the collection write-offs from the current supplier?"

"No, but I can get that."

"Yes, please make a note to call me when you find that."

"I know this isn't sexy, it's not fun. It's just a good investment," advised Thomaz.

"And what about Jane's lack of reserve and down payment?"

"We finance it. Build your first-year profits into the principle. That way Jane gets back her reserve. As far as a down payment, we'll be asking the government to issue bonds in the name of your new electric company, backed by the government of Brazil. The bonds will provide the down payment and the construction loan."

The two men spent the rest of the afternoon and evening planning how to work the meeting with the government people the next Friday. Ramon fully divulged Jane's current condition so Thomaz could negotiate from the best position. Ramon agreed to come to Goiania a day before. He wanted to be well rested for his role in the meeting. Thomaz added, "I want you to look like you just came from working in the fields. Spend a couple days outside before coming over. And, do not wear your suit. Do you have one of those khaki shirts that I saw Denis wearing? The ones that say 'Staff – Templeton Farms' stitched in red."

"Yes, I have two of them. Blue jeans, khaki staff shirt, and field boots. Ok?"

"Perfect," beamed the attorney. "Just make sure to clean up the boots."

The next Friday, the government men out numbered Ramon and Thomaz. Senator Dias and Mikel Lundee brought along Chief Mauricio Andrade from the Corp of Engineers to explain the construction details of the hydroelectric project. Gilberto Lima, the Interior Minister, was sent along as spokesman for the President. Mr. Lima knew the President's leanings towards land reform but he would never disclose such knowledge. Mr. Lima was the power person from the government team and he was there to push things through. All the government men wore expensive suits and Ramon was glad that he cleared dress code with Thomaz in advance.

Thomaz Rocha led the meeting and started by introducing Ramon Gobbey as the "Chief Executive for Operations." The attorney opened by suggesting that they discuss the road issue first and then the hydroelectric project. The attorney argued, "Yes, some improvements to the road are needed but paving the entire length of it is not one of our priorities right now. We would be delighted to accept the government's offer of 35 million to improve the bridges and elevate the lowest parts of the road. If there is money left, then it would be great to have part of it paved."

"And what about your anonymous donor," replied Mr. Lundee, the Finance Minister. "Can your donor be counted on to supply the other 35 million to complete the project?"

"She cannot," asserted Thomaz. "She has given away all of her millions and millions to this very project and she has nothing else to give."

As if he didn't believe the attorney, Gilberto Lima turned to Ramon and asked, "Mr. Gobbey, do you believe that your donor has any money left at all to help with these projects?"

"I wouldn't hazard a guess," answered Ramon. "I've only spoken to her on a couple occasions about operational issues. She confesses her financial health only to Mr. Rocha. I'm here at the meeting today just to listen in to see how either of these projects will impact the residents of Templeton Farms. The financial issues of this project are in the hands of Mr. Rocha here."

With that said, Ramon practically dealt himself out of the meeting, which is just what he wanted to do. He wanted the ball to stay in Thomaz' court unless it involved something affecting operations of the Templeton Farms.

Thomaz asked, "Do we have a commitment from the government to spend the 35 million on road improvements?"

Gilberto suggested, "Let's put that issue on the side for right now and move on to the hydroelectric project. The Federal Government is more interested in completing that project. As you all know, the government has over extended itself financing the large projects in the southern part of Brazil. Unfortunately, it will be some time before the government will be able to tackle directly any large projects. The government wants your hydro project built since there are too few hydro plants in the central part of the country. Brasilia is projected to have huge growth in the next ten years and we do not currently have sufficient grid access for that growth. Your project will solve that problem."

Thomaz suggested, "Before we jump into finances, let's have Chief Andrade bring us all up to date on the specifics of building the site."

The Chief gave a boring half hour lecture about the details of the construction, how many workers, how many months, trucks, tons of concrete, and wattage produced. The Senator and the Ministers looked bored. The government men had all heard the Chief's presentation several times. All they had to know was that the project was going to help solve Brasilia's energy crisis down the road.

After the presentation, the Finance Minister was more direct, "We know that your annual harvest is now up in the 150 million dollar range. After expenses, you are surely netting more than 90 million dollars. With that kind of annual income, Templeton Farms should be able to pay for the road and the hydroelectric project from earned income."

"It could," replied Thomaz. "If we didn't have to reinvest every penny back in to buying more tractors, harvesters, tillers, planters, and dairy equipment. After that, the money has gone to buy thousands of miles of fence, thousands of homes with wells, and the list is endless. Our anonymous donor had requested a return of 10% interest for money loaned to buy farm equipment. We have not been able to repay loans made to us from our donor. Nor have we been able to pay the annual 10% interest on the loans."

Mikel responded, "I had no idea this project was such a money drain."

"It's really not," answered the attorney. "It's just that we have been reinvesting every penny possible to improve our crop yields and in the long run it will do well. That and the sheer size of this project require the investment."

The Finance Minster replied, "Templeton Farms was supposed to be a split of 49% to 51% between the owner and the new residents. Has your anonymous donor not been keeping 49% of the profit from the soybean production and the dairy?"

"Absolutely not," replied Thomaz. "As I said, we haven't even repaid promised interest."

Gilberto Lima asked, "Mr. Gobbey, would you please bring us all up to speed on all the divisions within Templeton Farms? Please tell us for every area approximately what percent of the required equipment has been purchased."

Ramon straightened up and answered, "For the resident's homes, we are at 60% completion. The same percent for their fences, wells, and roads. The major survey work is 90% complete with the 10% remaining only for some common areas that will never be developed. The soil augmentation equipment is 90% in place and exceeds expectations. We just made the decision to buy some expensive deep tillers when money is available from the next harvest. The nursery is the same, 90%. The dairy could use a few more delivery trucks but those are for outside sales and can be purchased from future profits. The soybean farm has been our priority and it is100% complete on the equipment."

Gilberto asked, "Would you mind if I make a suggestion?"

"Not at all," replied Thomaz.

"I think you have relied too heavily upon the generosity of your anonymous donor. Draining every dollar from that source has left you with no contingency backing. Now, because there is no cushion, your organization cannot take advantage of opportunities that might come to you. I think you should make it your top priority to repay from the next harvest or from dairy profits, all of the interest owed to your donor. Furthermore, I don't understand why your donor is not being paid 49% of all net profits from all operations. From the communal operations, the residents should receive 51%, going directly into the Templeton Foundation account for community improvements."

Thomaz answered, "Our donor has never been involved in this project for a profit. However, we did not intend to bankrupt the donor due to our needs. It was our intention all along to pay the donor the 49% of net profits but it was not done due to the need for major equipment. Additionally, because of our agreement with the government, we have been timid about returning funds to our donor. The project is, in essence, a quasi-government project."

Mikel jumped in, "Your agreement with the government should not interfere with your obligations to your donor. To clarify the situation, would you prefer to have a Stipulation from the Cabinet authorizing payment of 49% from all net profits from all communal activities?"

"Certainly," replied Thomaz. "That's an excellent idea and will keep our donor safe and will keep me out of trouble. I should have thought of that myself a long time ago and we could have avoided the problems we are in right now."

Gilberto said, "With that issue solved, let's move on to discuss financing for the hydroelectric project. I sidelined the road project because I want you to think about this. Instead of using the 35 million for your road, let's say we spend 5 million to do minor elevation work and repair the bridges so you don't kill someone driving one of your trucks. With the 30 million left, we use that for the dam instead of a construction loan. It won't be a loan, it will be a gift in exchange for future generation of wholesale electricity for Brasilia. We will want some written agreement that you will sell to the national grid and not to Bolivia or somewhere else."

Mikel, the Finance Minister added, "The 30 million for construction will last you during the first two years of construction and will cover the excavation phase. In the next 24 months, you will need to earmark the remaining 130 million from your soybean harvest and dairy profits. Remember, that this also is a joint project. So, you will be saving from the entire harvests. That should be easy but you may have to give some promissory notes to your donor to accomplish it. Also, when the project is generating electricity and cash, that same 49-51% split will be stipulated. The good side of that is, if you have to get loans to finish the construction, the resident community fund will be paying their 51% of the principle and interest."

Gilberto added, "There is a major reason why Templeton Farms should build this project. The government allows private electric coops to charge farmers less than other users. Your residents will be able to take advantage of cheap electricity. The government also sets the rates that you can charge the nation's grid and that is why the wholesale rate is so low. Most of your income will result from selling at the retail level to villages and towns in the two-state area." The Interior Minister added, "Mr. Rocha, do we have an agreement?"

Thomaz replied, "Yes we do. Will you draw up the legal agreements or do you want me to do that?"

"No," replied Mikel Lundee. "We'll draft the first document and you can mark it up for revisions. I will also send along a draft of the Stipulation we discussed. I should be able to get both documents prepared and sent to you by courier in just a few days. I'll call to advise if there is any delay."

Chief Andrade asked a question that caught Ramon's attention. It wasn't the content of the question which caught Ramon's attention, it was how he spoke when he asked the question. Ramon had heard that tone of voice before, but where? What was it about the tone of the voice? Where had he heard that tone in questioning before? Ramon thought for several minutes and knew he could show no emotion after he remembered where and when he heard that voice.

He had an answer but it couldn't be possible. Chief Andrade spoke again and this time Ramon listened intently to every syllable. Yes, it had to be. But how? No, it couldn't be possible. Ramon had spoken with this person before. Chief Andrade and Nelson Machado, the famous private investigator, were the same person. The Chief had crew cut gray hair and black eye brows. Nelson had black hair—he could have worn a wig. Both are tall, pasty-white Europeans.

Ramon wondered why he was being played. Was this all a big setup for payback? If the government wanted to get rid of him, they could have just killed him at any time over the years. If Chief Andrade is a plant, then what about Gilberto Lima and Mikel Lundee. Not possible. He had seen the two ministers in dozens of newspaper photos. Had the Chief been working all these years as a double agent for the President? But why?

After the government men left, Ramon had to hide his doubts from Thomaz. Ramon and Thomaz were like a couple of kids who had just been given the keys to the candy shop. Ramon burst out laughing first, followed by Thomaz who also clasped his hands together and pointed skyward while saying, "Thank you Jesus!"

Ramon asked, "How the hell did that happen so well? I was prepared to use the theatrics we planned but they just gave us everything we wanted without having to ask."

"I think I know the answer," Thomaz said in a serious voice. "When the President tours the Farm with the foreign dignitaries, I assumed it was only to benefit his popularity and for the photo opportunities. I think I gravely underestimated him. He obviously cares about our project. He just sent his two top Cabinet members here to make sure we had everything we needed. It could not have gone better!"

"So now I only own half of the electric plant. That just lost me 9 million a year."

"Don't be too greedy," Thomaz teased. "Besides, you didn't want to be in the electric business anyway. Now you are in the electric business for only 49%. You lost 9 million a year on the electric plant but you just gained 50 million per year on the harvest split with the Stipulation."

"Yes, now that most of our capital equipment needs have been satisfied, it won't be difficult to pay for the hydro plant from earnings. Since we are doing our own financing on the project, I'm guessing that we just saved in the neighborhood of 100 million on interest that we won't be paying."

"Smart boy you are," answered Thomaz. "That Stipulation just gave us the authority to have more control over your money. You can donate it back to the Templeton Foundation anytime you want but now you have more control. Additionally, if we are ever discovered, the Stipulation covers us. When I get their draft, I will add some additional protections so the both of us are entirely protected against any future action. The President is protecting us now, but he will not be in office forever. The generals will not be able to control election results forever. It will be important to get our protections in writing. Also, we can now wire funds to the Cayman Islands Bank for our anonymous donor with no fear of discovery because of the Stipulation."

Within ten days, Thomaz finalized the deal with the government and the construction of the hydroelectric dam started immediately. The Corps of Engineers is responsible for all dam construction and Chief Andrade had the project on his hot list waiting for signatures on the agreement. Purchase and installation of the generators and other equipment were the responsibility of the new electricity company. At a town hall meeting, the residents decided to call the new company Araguaia Electric.

CHAPTER EIGHTEEN

A year later, more families moved into the newly plotted and
fenced farms. Ramon's garbage businesses could not keep up
with the demand for organic material for the fields. The dairy
was producing organic matter by the tons and all of it was allocated to
the soybean fields. The soybean fields needed all the dairy material to
maintain the high crop yields because that meant cash for roads, fences,
schools, and an endless list of other necessary items for the growing
community. Ramon sent Marcio Torres to meet with the owners of
surrounding farms to see if they might be willing to let Templeton
Farms have their unwanted organic matter instead of burning it. Marcio
was successful in getting a number of farms to donate material.

In one of the field staff meetings, Bridgette Suzuki shared that
during her tours of the Farm, reporters frequently asked about the
environmental damage caused by having so many farms on land that
used to be tropical forest. During the conversation, Bridgette coined
a term that would come to common use. She was describing how the
soil augmentation plans were allowing the farms to have three or four
annual harvests of most crops. The harvest yields were as good as North
American harvests and the climate allowed for additional harvests. She
called the high yield farming, "hyper production agriculture, or HPA."
Her question for the group was this, "Do HPA methods return to
the atmosphere the same or greater amount of oxygen than tropical

forest land?" No one attending the meeting could answer how the two different landscapes compared in oxygen generation. Bridgette asked if she might have some small budget to find and entice a study group from the University at Rio de Janeiro to seek the answer.

Whenever Bridgette or anyone else at the field staff meetings had requests that required money, Thomaz Rocha was in charge and always gave the final approval or denial on proposals. If Thomaz couldn't already read Ramon's mind, he looked at Ramon. The two men had their hand signals synchronized and they had more kinds of signals than a major league baseball team. A pen in hand with the point up meant approval and a pen pointed down towards the table meant denial. Bridgette got the 'point up' from Ramon and Thomaz told her to proceed and asked her to keep a conservative lid on the money for the project. Thomaz scolded her bit saying that he did not want to see a lot of money spent on a propaganda campaign. Bridgette was used to working with restrictions and the attorney's sour warning did not daunt her.

Several months later Bridgette reported the findings of the volunteer team from the University of Rio de Janeiro. They found that HPA farming with three or four harvests per year of most crops produced 80% of the oxygen compared to the same acreage of tropical forest. Bridgette now had some facts to work into her tours of the farm. She beamed when she told Thomaz Rocha that volunteers from the University conducted the research and the entire project cost the Templeton Foundation absolutely zero.

The success of the HPA farming techniques did not escape the attention of the landowners of the surrounding ranches and farms. A group of landowners got together and asked to meet with the management of the Templeton Farms to learn their exact methods of increasing harvest yields. Ramon asked the three land supervisors to meet with the group of farmers. At the meeting, the farmers were not surprised to see Marcio Torres since he had recently asked each of them for their trash vegetation. However, Denis Brava did most of the talking in the meeting. He told the group that they could get the same yields by adjusting the pH levels of their soils and adding composted organic material on a regular basis.

Denis went out on a limb and suggested that the Templeton Farms may be able to sell them pulverized limestone at cost. The farmers wanted to receive the lime in exchange for their organic material and Denis explained that the cost to transport and process the limestone was great, but if they continue donating their organic material then they could receive the lime at cost. The farmers realized that they also needed composted organic material so they told Denis that they would be keeping their organic material for their own fields. Denis explained to them that the organic material had to be composted and they needed heavy equipment like the processing plants on Templeton Farms.

Soon after the meeting, the area farmers and ranchers stopped donating their organic material to Templeton Farms. The topic of the next field staff meeting was about the ranchers outside of the Farm. Denis explained his offer and told the group that the outside farmers were no longer donating any organic material. Ramon went to the blackboard and calculated the cost to compost organic matter. It wasn't just the cost of running the large composting bins; the cost also had to include the operation of the giant grinders that ground everything from tree stumps to palm fronds into sawdust. Ramon's blackboard calculations indicated that the group could return to the farmers 20% of their composted matter and still break even on the process.

Ramon knew that the land supervisors were already busy with other projects, but he asked them to divide the ranches into equal numbers. Each land supervisor personally delivered Ramon's proposal that contained two parts. First, those who continued to donate organic matter would receive back 20% of their donation as composted matter. Second, those who participated in the donations would be allowed to purchase processed lime at cost from the Templeton Farms.

About half of the farmers stopped donating material to the Templeton Farms and they did not buy the lime for their fields. The remaining half continued their donations, purchased lime for their fields, and received their compost for their fields. This group of farmers saw a marked increase in harvest yields while the others continued their usual farming methods.

O Presidente was still making trips to the Templeton Farms whenever there was an important group taking a tour. He continued giving his personal tours and now Bridgette felt free to speak up to add new information whenever the President paused. She had to work hard to keep finding new information because the President always added her new information to his next presentation. At the end of one of the tours, the President asked to speak to the Director of the Board of the Templeton Foundation. Bridgette explained that he should speak to Thomaz Rocha on his return through Goiania. He asked her to call Mr. Rocha to inform him when the presidential motorcade planned to arrive in Goiania.

It was the middle of the evening when the President's motorcade arrived in Goiania. The President's car and his security force stopped at Mr. Rocha's law office while the tour bus continued down the street to find a restaurant before completing its trip back to Brasilia. At his office, Thomaz had a meal and wine waiting for the President. The President, a big man in his fifties, thanked the attorney for the meal. While eating, the President asked, "Did you get everything that you needed from Mikel and Gilberto concerning construction of the hydroelectric project?"

"Yes," assured the attorney. "They were very helpful and they brought some new ideas to discuss and we are very happy with the outcome."

"They are the problem solvers on my Cabinet. Some of the others just bring up the problems, but I send those two out when I need a solution."

"Yes, they are very good men to have on your team."

"Now to the reason why I interrupted your evening, I have some offers and a request for the Templeton Foundation. The request is to help relocate homeless citizens from the favelas of Rio de Janeiro, São Paulo, actually anywhere. As you know, during each rainy season, many homes in the favelas end up sliding down mountainsides. Each year mudslides kill many and leave even more homeless. The Federal Government wants to send you some of these displaced families for you to turn into farmers. The social agencies will pre-screen potential new residents. They will all be people who have lost their homes from the mudslides or from some other catastrophe. Allowing Templeton Farms to help in this area is an important option for the government. Do you have any concerns so far?"

Thomaz answered, "As you know, we've been doing our own

screening from applicants sent to us through the social agencies. We try to prioritize those applicants who are willing to work. They don't need to know anything about farming, we just want people who will work at something. Then, when they come here, it's their choice about what kind of farming they want to do. We don't lock them in. If they start out wanting to grow coffee and they find out later they like cashews better, we help them make that change. It's just that we need people who will actually work." After he said the words, Thomaz wondered why he bothered. He was talking to the biggest fan of Templeton Farms, the guy who gets up at the front of the bus during tours and gives the tour presentation.

Holding up his hands, the President exclaimed, "Oh, I understand that perfectly. The government knows and appreciates the productivity of Templeton Farms. No question about it! Just write up your screening protocols and we can pass them on to the social agencies. If they send some bad people to you, just return the people if they do not meet your qualifications. No, we're not looking for a dumping place for criminals and derelicts. As I promised, these will all be poor working people from the cities who have lost their homes. I believe that your existing selection criteria will be perfect for our use."

"Yes," replied Thomaz. "Those are the people we have sought to relocate here."

"Now, in return for your help in relocating people, the government will pay to send the families to Britania. Additionally, the government will provide and build the homes for the families that the government sends to Templeton Farms. We will provide all of the other related expenses for the wells, fences, and other items. In a short matter of time, we will send you sufficient families to occupy the remaining 3,100 farms."

The President continued, "Templeton Foundation is doing a far better job at helping people than any agency of the government. After the work at Templeton Farms is finished, there will be additional land available to repeat the mission elsewhere in Brazil if your team is up to it. Please understand that all my offers of assistance are conditional upon your acceptance of poor people directed to you. The government will assist with the completion of the infrastructure of the Farms. We will pay the costs for the final build out of the internal dirt roads, the fences, and wells to complete the project. We will finish the road paving and bridges to your soybean fields. The government will take over all responsibilities for building and maintaining schools. Finally, we will place a moratorium on property taxes for each new farmer for three years and a five-year moratorium on property taxes for property owned by the Templeton Foundation."

"Mr. President," Thomaz replied. "Your offer could not have come at a better time. Our anonymous donor has depleted all funds and Templeton Farms has had to stop processing new applications because the project's funding is solely dependent on crop harvests."

"That is not the reason for my offer," declared the President. "The reason is that we simply need a solution to the problems of the homeless in our cities. We made a big mistake when the government tried land reform by dumping people in the jungle. We learned a bad lesson from that. You must do it the way you are doing things right here. You help the new residents all the way through the process. You have teams that go out to train the new people in everything that they need to know. You keep checking on them to see if they need help with any aspect of their farm. That is the way land reform must be managed. I don't need to remind you that there is an election coming and I need the support of the people for another term. Until now, my hands have been tied and I could not say anything in favor of land reform. Those large landowners control most of the generals in the army. Since I serve at the pleasure of both the people and the generals, it's been a difficult balancing act. With my opponent promising massive land reform, I must now make my feelings known on the subject."

"We'll certainly promote your re-election campaign in any way we can," promised Thomaz.

"Thank you. I will hold you to that. There should be a few thousand residents here who should know what way to vote."

"We'll keep reminding them, sir."

"Now about your repayments to your project's donor, Mikel and Gilberto reported that they have helped you with that. Not in terms of money, but with a plan. Is that accurate?"

"Yes, many things were clarified in our meeting and they provided a Stipulation signed by your Cabinet which defines the financial responsibilities to our donor."

"And are you happy with all of that?"

"Yes, very much so. We knew that it was the correct direction to go, we just needed the support of your team to help push us a little."

"And one more nudge if you don't mind. This is not a condition; it is just a personal recommendation from me. Now that we have clarified the 49/51% split on all of the land ownership and of the hydro plant, I think you should consider expanding your board of directors to include membership from the residents."

"Yes, you are correct and we will work in that direction," replied Thomaz.

"And one more thing," added the President. "Will you please ask Ramon Gobbey to come to the Palace this coming Friday at 9 p.m. and report to the south gatehouse. I would like to have a little chat with him."

Mr. Rocha thanked the President for his generous offers and explained that he would call an immediate meeting of the board of directors of the Foundation in order to get their approval. He assured the President that the Foundation was in no position to turn down such generous offers of help. He told the President to expect his call in the morning to convey the acceptance by the Foundation board of directors.

As soon as the President's motorcade pulled away from his office, Thomaz called Ramon to tell him all about the President's visit. Neither man could contain their joy over the President's generosity. As far as the "request" of accepting families, that just made the job easier for the Foundation. Additionally, the generous offers made by the President were a godsend. The entire package was a 100% benefit to the Foundation. Thomaz added, "By the way, O Presidente wants you to come by for a 'little chat.' I suppose he wants to thank you for all of your hard work. You're to report to the south gatehouse of the Palace at 9 p.m. this coming Friday."

The next morning Thomaz called the Presidential Palace, thanked the President, and told him that the Foundation was looking forward to receiving families sent by the government. He followed the phone call with a letter to the President telling him how happy the Foundation was to have the support of the President and of the Brazilian government.

CHAPTER NINETEEN

The next Thursday Ramon was in Brasilia ordering a rental tuxedo. No, he didn't need a tuxedo just to meet the President Friday night. He was going to crash the State Dinner at 7 p.m. instead of reporting to the south gatehouse at 9 p.m. Ramon thought that he might have a good relationship with O Presidente but he wasn't going to bet his life on it. Too many people disappeared after reporting to the Palace under one pretext or another. If O Presidente had something to say to him, then he could just say it in public. Ramon suspected that Chief Andrade snooping around as Nelson Machado probably had something to do with his invitation for a "little chat."

Ramon had never been to a State Dinner before but he knew something about the protocol. Tickets were not given to attendees nor were guests announced. Instead, the Chief of Protocol stood a mere shoulder width away from O Presidente and whispered any forgotten names. O Presidente took great pride in addressing every guest by his or her full name, even if he had to be reminded.

Ramon did his homework in advance of the State Dinner and knew who would be there. He couldn't just walk into the Palace by himself. He needed a confirmed guest to get him past the guards. He studied old society pages and looked for female guests who attended prior dinners alone. Friday's event was being held for delegates from Peru, Panama, and Honduras. Photographs of Elana Barbarro showed a young and attractive woman in her mid-twenties who frequently attended alone. Ramon called all over town and found her staying at the Crown Tudor Hotel. He explained that the Palace asked him to escort her to the State Dinner on Friday night.

Ramon rented a chauffeur and limousine for Friday night. With Elana on his arm, he easily made it past the guards and into the Grand Ballroom. While making small talk with Elana, he wondered what exactly he was going to say to O Presidente when he came around to greet them. He didn't have long to wonder. "Elana Barbarro, how wonderful to see you. And you brought a date with you."

O Presidente almost choked on his champagne when he extended his hand to Ramon and then recognized him. "I almost didn't recognize you in a tuxedo, young man. You really didn't need to dress formally tonight."

Ramon answered, "Oh, I just wanted to make a good impression, here in public, in front of all these important people."

"Yes, I see your point but you needn't bother. Elana, will you please excuse us? I have some urgent business to discuss with your date."

O Presidente walked Ramon to his private office off the Grand Ballroom and gave a nod to two guards who came to his aid. Once inside O Presidente's office, the guards pushed Ramon into a chair and handcuffed him to it.

"You will please wait here," ordered O Presidente.

"Well, if I have a choice can I attend the dinner?"

"No," ordered a frustrated Commander-in-Chief.

Left alone in the office, Ramon surveyed it to find a way of escape. The ironwood chair was so strong that he could try all day to smash it but it would never break. The guards overdid their duty and he had handcuffs on both of his wrists and both legs. He thought to himself, "So, this is how O Presidente's political opponents end up. I wonder if they will find me floating face down in some river tomorrow."

Ramon squirmed and tried to pull his wrists through the handcuffs. The more he struggled, the more his wrists swelled. Now he was sweating and his wrists were wet but that didn't help him. The cuffs were very tight around his wrists. He was hopelessly bound to the sturdy chair.

Shortly after 9:30 p.m., O Presidente entered the office. The boss was not in a good mood. He went to a file cabinet and pulled out a folder, which he slammed down in front of Ramon. "It's Brazil 1137—your file, my filing system. It doesn't do anyone any good to come in here to rummage through my personal files. Yes, I have the goods on all the generals and everyone else in Brazil, but they can't find their own file. And if they did, I write in the obscure Indian language taught to me by my caretakers as a child. It was never a written language so my personal writing is entirely my own secret code."

"What's so special about file 1137?"

"Yes, it's special. Eleven is Goias State, at least in my numbering system. Thirty-seven, well, that's you. Problem number 37, which I have been following for many years."

"Why?"

"Mostly because it's so interesting. You earn ten million dollars selling snake venom but you spend none of it for yourself. You kill off an entire family in Britania by snakes and then you buy their property to give it all away. You singlehandedly destroyed an entire town only to rebuild it better than before."

"You seem to be a fan from the beginning. I guess I will have to fire my confidential off-shore banker."

"No, don't blame your banker. No secrets were disclosed. It's just that our Foreign Service gets curious when the Treasury is asked to convert almost ten million of our dollars into foreign currency from the Cayman Islands. My staff also alerted me when the Director of the Instituto do Viperidae reported some unusual happenings in Goiania and Britania."

"So, you were following my trail all along?"

"Yes, and unfortunately I've linked myself to you. How do you think you were able to purchase the Roberio Ranch for pennies on the acre? Why were you set up to make a fortune from the Araguaia Electric Company?"

"Sounds like I've had a silent partner all these years."

"Yes, and that's the point of my little chat with you tonight. I just want to make certain that those links between the two of us always remain between the two of us."

"Well, I have no plans to publish my memoirs if that's what you're after. Tell me, are all of your cabinet members double agents or just Chief Andrade?"

"You're very astute. No one has ever made the connection between Chief Andrade and Nelson Machado. We didn't think that you caught on. Actually, the Chief is very versatile and has a number of undercover personalities. Actually, he really does have multiple personalities; we just have a use for all of them."

"How does he have time to cope with the workload of all his personalities?"

"As Chief of the Engineering Corps his position is mostly ceremonial. He makes many speeches. He has hundreds of men under him who actually do the work. His other jobs are 'part-time' positions."

"If you knew all about me from the beginning, why did you bother sending Nelson Machado to Britania? What was the point of his investigation?"

"I had to know that you would hold by your story and not fold at the first sign of pressure. It also gave me something for my files. Yes, I have a report from Nelson Machado that says you didn't do it. I had you investigated and the famous investigator found nothing bad about you. It saves my hide—not yours. If you are ever discovered, then I scapegoat Mr. Machado and run him out of the country. I sacrifice him and it saves my hide. Chief Andrade has lost a few of his multiple personalities over the years due to similar sacrifices. Ramon, I've worked very hard to keep our crossed paths hidden."

"Congratulations, you've done a wonderful job. I had no idea that you even knew I existed."

"If the press or the generals ever got wind that you are a mass murderer and that I knew you, or helped you in any way, I would be a dead man. Killing the Roberio men, I understand that. As an employee of the Noqueiras, guarding their safety could be considered within your job duties. Killing women and children, now that's a different story. Why did you do that?"

"I did it all for the protection of Vanessa Noqueira. I had to know that she would be safe for the rest of her life. I expected her to live a long and beautiful life. I was a complete failure."

"Don't be so hard on yourself. Since the murders you've obviously repented and paid for your mistakes."

"Gilberto Lima and Mikel Lundee, are they real or are they your double agents as well?"

"No, they're both the real deal. They are the best men that I have on the Cabinet. That's why I sent them to help you out."

"Thanks, I appreciate it. Now can I go?"

"Yes, certainly. I will get the guards and they will help you. I also just wanted to thank you personally for the work that you've done at Templeton Farms. You know, I really have been a fan of that project from the start. If you had come to the gatehouse as requested, we could have had this little chat without the chains."

"Sir, I'm just happy that I get to live. I am going to get to live?"

"Oh, you think I am the monster. You need to look in the mirror young man. Whatever we are, we're the same. Yes, I've sent a select few of my political opponents to swim with the fishes. As you know, it's unavoidable on the journey of doing good for the masses. I understand that you were protecting Dr. and Mrs. Noqueira, but killing women and children, now that's a low standard even for me. So please, no lectures from you about the evil I've done in my lifetime."

The Palace guards unlocked Ramon and escorted him out a side exit to his limousine parked in the Menducci Porte Cochere. He helped himself into the back seat and was surprised to find Elana Barbarro there waiting for him. She smiled and purred, "Let's get out of these clothes and have some real fun."

"Oh, wait. I'm not sure I'm in the mood after what I've been through tonight."

"You poor man, why don't you let me make it all better," Elana whispered in his ear as she jumped to his side while rubbing his inner thigh.

"No, no, no," Ramon protested as Elana started undressing him in the limousine.

Elana had prepared the driver in advance by telling him that she had special plans for her date. The driver drove around until the couple finished their back seat romp and then pulled up to the Crown Tudor Hotel. While biting Ramon's ear Elana slipped her phone number into his shirt pocket. "Here, call me anytime. I'm always here."

"You're not from Peru?"

"No, I work for O Presidente. And, oh, by the way, don't pay the driver tonight?"

"Why not?"

"Because he is my driver and my palace guard."

"What did you do with my driver and my limousine?"

"We sent them away."

"And why do you get a palace guard assigned to you?"

"Because I'm the President's daughter."

"But you don't have his last name."

"I didn't say I was his legitimate daughter. Sure, I wasn't born to one of his wives but he cares for me just like his other children. Maybe a little more because he uses me in official business and the press ignores me except for the society pages."

"Yes, that's how I found you."

"I know. I was flattered when you called me. I wanted to see my father's face when you brought me into the palace. It's hard to get a reaction out of my father. He's seen everything so almost nothing fazes him."

"Oh, I think we got a reaction out of him tonight. He was really pissed at me. I was supposed to see him at nine o'clock but I decided to crash the State Dinner for the sake of my safety."

"Oh, you have nothing to fear from my father. He's just a big teddy bear. Please, come up to my room for a nightcap. I do love a man in a tuxedo."

CHAPTER TWENTY

With the government's help, the remaining 3,100 homes and farm sites were put on a priority for completion. Within two years, the Templeton Farms were fully occupied except for the farms set aside for growing families.

In a private meeting with Thomaz Rocha, Denis brought up a concern he had about Ramon. He started bluntly, "I don't know what to do with Ramon."

"Yes," echoed the attorney, "What to do about Ramon?"

"Now that the project is nearly complete, Ramon has lost interest. The rest of us all have our families and Ramon has no one except this project. I think we need to get him off his family farm and send him to the big city to find a woman."

Thomaz asked, "What do you propose?"

"I'm trying to get a friend of mine to make an offer on his farm. Ramon really needs to get out of that place. There are too many lonely memories for him there. Did you know when he first started working here; he had to sell his horse just to make ends meet while he was trying to fix up that place?"

"No, really," replied the shocked attorney. "If we could just go buy a wife for Ramon then everything would be fine. Unfortunately, he has to find someone. Yes, I agree with you, I don't think that he is going to find a good woman staying around here. And, I can understand why he is bored. Ramon loves new challenges and Templeton Farms has solved all of its challenges."

"I have an idea," answered Denis thoughtfully. "Jane took Ramon out of college in America to come here to help start the Templeton Farms. Now that the project is nearly finished, I think that Jane needs to send Ramon back to finish his degree."

Thomaz inquired, "Where would you send him?"

"Anywhere he wants to go," answered Denis. "If he wants to return to America or go to Rio de Janeiro, that's his choice. Jane just needs to give him a premium scholarship so he can live well. I know that we give small scholarships and stipends to our high school graduates, but in Ramon's case, Jane needs to do much better. If he is a poor college student then he won't be able to find a woman from a good family. If he attends college here in Brazil then Jane won't have to pay tuition since the government pays that for all students. But if he goes to America, Jane will have to spend a lot for that. Plus, the cost of living in America will be so much more. Obviously Jane is good for it and Ramon has devoted much of his life to this project."

Thomaz replied, "I will speak to Jane, I'm sure she will agree with us about paying Ramon's college expenses. How are you going to get Ramon pushed into college?"

"Yes," replied Denis. "Push is the correct term. I will just keep pushing him until he enrolls."

"I just hope that Ramon doesn't feel guilty leaving us," said Thomaz. "He may feel that way as we start the new project for the government. You push him and I will encourage him. Maybe between the two of us we can put Ramon on a new course."

Denis found a buyer for Ramon's farm and he managed to push Ramon into college. Ramon had mixed feelings. He wanted to return to Rio for a social life. However, Ramon felt that he might be too old to complete his degree but he soon discovered that being older was an advantage in college. He quickly discovered that he was much smarter than the eighteen-year-old students attending the university.

O Presidente became embroiled in political battles in Brasilia and stopped making tours to the Farm. In his place, he sent the Secretary of State, then it was the Vice-President, and finally it was the Minister for Agriculture who ended up making routine visits to the Templeton

Farms. However, the President did complete his promise and deeded a large tract of land to the northeast of Britania for the next Templeton Foundation project.

With only five of the six men of the management group left, they were thankful that the project was only about 1.5 million acres. They all agreed that their first project was too big and that they all deserved a break before starting the next project.

While Quimbanda was given credit for the demise of the Roberio family, Umbanda (white magic) must have been working overtime for Ramon Gobbey. Before the fall of Brazil's currency in the mid 1980's, Ramon's American friend, Gary Bennett, introduced him to international banking and investing. Ramon also discovered that buying coffee futures low at a new harvest was a guaranteed profit when sold before the next harvest.

From his investments, Ramon became one of the wealthiest men in Brazil. Somehow, he always managed to have his money in the right place at the right time. He had a total cash position before the stock market crash of 1987. A decade later, he was too diversified to be affected by the fall of dotcom stocks. He was fortunate because he never acknowledged his wealth and he continued to live as a typical middle class urbanite. He never sought fame, nor did it find him. His average looks still let him meld into the masses. He used very little of the earnings from the secret snake laboratory, instead he lived on the salary of the jobs he did. He was happy just knowing that he was able to do some good for people.

CHAPTER TWENTY-ONE

With Ramon in college, only the four original field men were left working in Britania to finish the Templeton Farms project. Thomaz Rocha called Ramon in Rio every Sunday night just like a parent. Thomaz told Ramon about the events of the week and asked for input on certain projects. Thomaz always asked Ramon about his classes and Ramon told about his latest projects. He told Thomaz about his decision to continue graduate studies. Whenever Thomaz asked Ramon about girl friends, there was always a different one. Thomaz suggested, "You know, we all sent you to Rio to find a good wife. We care less about how many degrees you obtain. We just want you to find a good wife."

Ramon responded, "There are too many choices. It will take me a long time to decide. There is one girl I really like. Her name is Elana Barbarro. We met when I had my meeting with O Presidente. Turns out, she is a daughter of O Presidente."

"Sounds like you are keeping good company. You should marry her."

"No, I'm in no hurry for that."

Ramon said his goodbyes to Thomaz and turned his attention to a news magazine. A story caught his immediate interest. It described a horrific poison called vx, developed as weapon of mass destruction. The article said that just one cup of vx could kill everyone in the eastern half of the United States. Ramon's gut told him that someone, somehow, got their hands on a batch of Max Schuman's trilex. Destroying laboratories in Frankfurt and Tuscany did not put an end to Max's poison. Someone found his formula and just put a new name on it. Ramon remembered telling Director Strubble that Max's name of trilex probably meant that it contained the chemical compound of Green Darter venom along with three additional compounds each beginning with one of the last three letters in trilex. Vx probably meant that someone added two additional poisonous compounds to make it even stronger.

The story about the weapon brought a rush of memories back to Ramon. Long ago, his mind permanently erased the vision of Greta, dead in the trunk of her Audi. Nor could Ramon remember his subsequent emotional breakdown. Over time, Ramon transferred his guilt about Greta to blame placed on Max. Had Max not developed trilex, Greta would still be alive.

Over the years, he cherished the pleasant memories of Greta; the happy days they spent together. He remembered their honeymoon and spending time together on long walks on the beaches in Jamaica. Ramon smiled as he remembered Greta's happy times with him. They say you only have one true love in life, and for Ramon, Greta held that love.

Ramon remembered how Greta helped him destroy Max's warehouse and how excited she was to put one over on the authorities. He recalled helping Director Strubble in Munich find the perfumery laboratory in Tuscany. He wondered if Strubble was still the man in charge there. He remembered Greta's brother beating him at the hospital. He remembered his role in killing off the town of Britania after the death of Dr. Noqueira. The memories were starting to get unpleasant so Ramon closed the magazine and went to work on his studies.

In Britania, Andre was finished surveying all the individual farms and now just needed to take his team back to finish some work around the hydroelectric project and around some other open spaces.

Denis Brava was in charge of the daily details and work orders. His work had become routine. Like Ramon, he was beginning to lose interest in the project now that the end was in sight. Thomaz Rocha was busy negotiating with the government over the new 1.5 million acre tract that the Templeton Foundation planned to take on next. This time, the attorney wanted the government to pay for all the infrastructure of the new project. Thomaz was also busy negotiating contracts for the equipment to generate electricity for the hydro project.

Dalton and Marcio were both happy and busy. Dalton supervised the large dairy and grazing operation. Along the way, he became interested in making cheese and yogurt. He had his workers making many new products and soon the operation became a big commercial success. He applied to Jane for funding for a cheese factory and soon they were making a dozen different kinds of cheese that were shipped out to sell in Brasilia and Goiania. The dairy operation produced an excess amount of milk and it was being transported out of the area for sale. Jane was making an excellent profit on the milk and cheese shipped away.

Marcio was probably the happiest of all the original men on the project. He got his hands dirty every day and now he had big trucks with which to play. If any of the men could be accused of having an insider's relation to Jane, then it had to be Marcio. Whatever he requested, he received. Frequently he asked for one piece of equipment he received two. Through Thomaz, Jane told Marcio that he was being too frugal and needed to be more aggressive on his requests for equipment. The soil augmentation plan was so successful that the group decided to take it to another level. The men calculated that in another twenty years of augmentation, there might actually be black soils in all of the fields of Templeton Farms. Their normal tilling equipment moved the organic material into the top 12 inches of the soil. They needed a super tiller to break up the hard clay down to an additional two feet. This required bigger equipment and heavier tractors to pull it. Breaking up the hard clay down to three feet meant that rain and irrigation water stayed in the soil rather than running off.

Marcio was in a nurseryman's heaven. Now he had a half dozen nurseries spread around the property. He even had a nursery in the lowlands. Actually, the natives preferred living in the lowlands because it was their homeland. The natives who made the transition to farming did very well and some of them became rich cashew producers.

Jane saw fit to give Marcio an unlimited budget for anything he might want to plant in the nurseries. Marcio didn't have to turn in any spending requests for the nurseries at all. If he needed something, his men picked it up and the bills were sent to Denis for payment. In the tropical nursery in the lowlands, he was growing exotic fruit and nut trees. In the highland nurseries, he grew almond, walnut, pecan, and citrus trees. He also grew seedlings of small bush plants such as chu-chu and pena. Additionally, Marcio supervised the planting of the clover fields and the settlement of the first bee keeping families into the Farms. There were now 60 beekeepers and they were ahead of schedule for the targeted bee population. When the visitor's center was built at the entrance to Templeton Farms, it was Marcio who lined the road with royal palms and provided spectacular landscaping around it.

Ramon was busy in college with his nose to the grindstone. His course of study required that he take most of the classes required of architects. Most of that came naturally to him since he had been calculating load bearing requirements since he was 16 and working as Dr. Noqueira's contractor and builder. Some of it was a challenge. He had to prepare models made from foam board and art class was foreign to Ramon. The eighteen-year-olds made much better building models but he aced all the written tests. He always found math easy, so calculating load bearing and electrical requirements was a simple task for him.

Long ago, Jane stopped paying the same salary to all the men. She now paid based on what comparable jobs earned in the outside world. This meant that Dalton, as head of a major dairy and cheese factory made the most money. Denis was not disturbed by this and he felt it was only fair. His own salary had grown considerably since the time he was a malcontent in the first meeting in Mr. Rocha's office many years go. Marcio probably put in the most hours, worked the hardest of the four, and made the least. Andre's salary was competitive with other master surveyors. When Denis and Thomaz pushed Ramon into college, they asked Jane to provide money for Ramon's books and living expenses. Ramon lived very well as a student in Rio de Janeiro.

Things were going well for the Templeton Foundation. That was not the case in other parts of Brazil. The swelling ranks of the homeless in the big cities were igniting the fires of activists declaring that Brazil must make land reform the only priority for the salvation of the country.

Ramon was a third-year senior and about to graduate when a university clerk found him in a classroom and handed him a note which read, "Emergency in Britania, please call immediately." The sender was Wescley Silva. Ramon looked at his professor and the professor nodded at him excusing him to leave. Ramon left the classroom and called the Home Office from the nearest phone. Wescley was very upset, "This morning the men were having their usual Thursday morning coffee meeting when strangers broke into the office and took all four of them away. I had to call you because there is no one else left. I called Thomaz Rocha and Mrs. Pedrinho says that Thomaz has also been kidnapped. They did not get me. Bridgette was helping me put away some legal documents in the upstairs storage area. We heard the commotion and we saw all of them leave together. Our men had their hands tied behind their backs and were blindfolded."

Ramon asked, "When did all this happen?"

"No more than twenty minutes ago," replied Wescley.

"I will go to the airport right now and take the first flight to Goiania and then rent a car. It will be dark before I get there."

"We're not going anywhere," whispered Wescley. "It's not safe for us. We will be in the upstairs storage area with the lights off. When you come to the Home Office, don't park your car in front. Just leave all the lights off and come find us upstairs in the dark. We will be hiding here. I called my wife and told her to take my parents to stay with relatives who live away from here."

"Ok Wescley, just hang out there, but it will take me at least 12 hours to get there so don't be surprised when I come wake you up in the middle of the night."

"No, you won't wake me. I will be wide awake."

"Well, try to get some rest," Ramon said calmly. "We may be in for some sleepless nights ahead."

Ramon left the university campus by taxi. He went straight to the airport and used his credit card to purchase a ticket for the next flight to Goiania. While in the Goiania airport, he called Mrs. Pedrinho to get any information she might have about Mr. Rocha's abduction.

"Oh my God, Ramon," Mrs. Pedrinho shouted into her phone. "It was horrible, just horrible. Some guy just stormed into the office with a gun and demanded that Thomaz leave with him. He tied Thomaz' hands behind his back and blindfolded him."

Ramon asked, "Did you get a license plate or description of the car?"

"Yes," replied Mrs. Pedrinho with a shaky voice. "It was a small white pickup truck and I could only read the first letters on the license plate before it raced away. It was MB8. I'm sorry I couldn't get all of it. It was too far away for me to read the registration location on the plate."

"Do you remember anything else about the guy who came into the office?"

"No, he was wearing a handkerchief over his face. Nothing special, average build, average height. Nothing that would draw any attention."

Ramon thanked Mrs. Pedrinho and lied by telling her that her information was helpful. Practically every other person in Brazil drives a small white pickup truck and with no description of the intruder, he had nothing to go on. While still at the airport in Goiania, he called Wescley to say that it may be morning before he would arrive in Britania. He had one more stop and he planned to drive through the night.

Ramon picked up a compact car at the rental agency and drove to the next stop before going on to Britania. Long ago, Thomaz introduced him to a person of questionable character. Vicente Viera did jobs for Thomaz when the attorney didn't want to get his hands dirty. Vicente applied pressure, threats or actual physical harm, to persuade people. Vicente was a black market moneychanger, money launderer, weapons dealer, and minor crook. Vicente had been working at his vocation for a long time and never saw the inside of a jail so Ramon guessed that he had to be good at his job.

Ramon went to Vicente's house in a residential area near Mr. Rocha's office. Ramon had been there once before but could only guess if Vicente would remember him. It was nine o'clock at night and there was a chance the man would not come to his gate. Lights were on in the house so Ramon stood at the iron gate of the wall surrounding his house. Ramon clapped his hands several times very loudly and then again. A minute later a porch light came on and then a small door in the gate opened and Vicente shouted, "What do you want?"

"My name is Ramon Gobbey. We met before with Thomaz Rocha. I need your help. Thomaz has been kidnapped."

The gate swung open and Vicente motioned for Ramon to come in. Vicente was wearing only his boxer shorts and he asked Ramon to have a seat at his kitchen table. The fat little man pulled two beers from his refrigerator and placed one in front of Ramon. Ramon took only a couple sips of the beer since he had a long drive ahead.

Vicente asked, "What the hell happened?"

Ramon filled him in on the details and asked, "Do you have a few automatic guns and some ammunition for sale?"

"You are making a big mistake," replied Vicente. "If you go after the kidnappers with guns they will just kill your friends. Yes, I have a whole room full of guns for sale but that is not the correct route to go."

Ramon asked, "What would you do?"

"There is only one way to help your friends," replied the short fat man. "You have to use Quimbanda. If you use guns, the guys who took your men will have more guns. A Quimbanda priest will go after them with the element of surprise. The kidnappers will all be dead and your friends will all be alive. I guarantee it."

"No thanks," replied Ramon. "Britania has had bad luck with Quimbanda priests."

"Then you were not using the right Quimbanda priest. They are better than the police at solving crimes. You know what they say about Quimbanda priests, 'They are one part hit man, one part private investigator, and one part air.' Why don't you take my Quimbanda priest to Britania with you? It can't hurt and he will solve the crime for you."

With no real clues and no plan, Ramon relented. Vicente phoned his Quimbanda priest and asked him to pack his bag because he would be starting a little trip tonight. The priest told Vicente that he would be at his house in 30 minutes. With time to kill, Ramon asked to see some guns, saying, "Ok, I will try not to use them and I will let the priest do his work first, but I want to have three automatic pistols as backup just in case."

Vicente led Ramon to another room in the house. From floor to ceiling, there were guns of every make and model hanging on the walls. Handing Ramon some night vision glasses, he said, "Here, take two of these, you might need them. Anything that you take and don't scratch up you can bring back and I will only charge you for rental."

Ramon replied, "I'm a poor college student and I have no money. After we save Thomaz Rocha, he will pay you."

"That's quite all right, I understand," replied Vicente. "Thomaz and I go back many years. God forbid if something bad should happen to him, I know that Mrs. Pedrinho will pay the expenses."

"Well," replied Ramon, "With the Quimbanda priest, you have assured me that nothing will go wrong."

"No, I cannot make that assurance," replied Vicente. "If you take these guns then I can make no promises. Just make certain that you return my Quimbanda priest to me unharmed."

Ramon picked out three automatic pistols, two rifles with night vision scopes, and ammunition for all the guns. Ramon saw a case of hand grenades and took them as well. He thought if he was going to fight a war then he should be well supplied.

The two men heard clapping at the gate and Vicente left to let in the Quimbanda priest. Moises looked more like a reefer than a Quimbanda priest. In fact, Ramon could smell marijuana on his clothes. Moises looked just like a throw back from the late 1960's. He was jet black with a short Afro. He wore a tie-dyed T-shirt and over that a navy blue suit. His beads and rose tinted rimless glasses firmly put him in the 1960's but Moises was young, maybe in his mid-twenties. Moises was short and thin. Most of the Quimbanda priests that Ramon knew were big hulking guys and most looked pretty rough. If Moises had dreadlocks, he would be mistaken for a Rastafarian.

Moises helped Ramon load the weapons into the trunk of Ramon's rental car. In Vicente's weapon room, Moises checked out on loan a couple small pocket pistols. He put one of the small pistols in his pants pocket. Moises took the other pistol and put it under the passenger seat of the rental car. Moises noticed that Ramon had picked out three automatic pistols so he picked out two for himself. While Ramon was still choosing weapons, Moises asked, "What town are we going to and does it have an airport."

Ramon replied, "Britania, 60 miles beyond Itapirapua. It has an airfield five miles out of town but it's pretty rough because no one uses it."

Moises used Vicente's phone to call and in a hushed voice he said, "Yes, I will back in two days. I need you to do a favor. Yes, as early as possible, right now or early in the morning. Find a bush pilot out of Goiania or Itapirapua and have them waiting for me at the airfield outside Britania by eleven o'clock. Make them wait there because I may arrive later. No, I can't do it myself. Please, I will call you in the morning to confirm that you found a pilot."

Vicente wished the men good luck and the two men were on their way to Britania. Three hours later Ramon stopped at the midway point, went to his usual vending machine, and purchased a cold cola. Ramon filled the gas tank of the little compact car and the two were back on the road. Back in the car, Moises resumed his questioning of Ramon. There would be no peace for Ramon tonight because he would spend every moment answering questions posed by the Quimbanda priest.

In the mountains between Goiania and Britania, it was beginning to rain. Ramon had to slow down quite a bit because the curvy roads were now slick from the water. Ahead, on the shoulder of the road was a sight that enchanted the former snake handler. It looked like a hand waving up from the pavement but Ramon immediately knew what it was. It was a big Gray Water Cobra. The big Cobra's head was fully flared and he was waving madly. Ramon slowed down to take a good look and Moises rolled up his window very quickly. Cobras are territorial and this one was mad that something had invaded his territory. Probably, the big snake was just mad that cars were passing by on the road. The Cobra's head was more than two feet off the ground, waving and hissing. Ramon had thoughts about putting the Cobra to use but he had no handling gear with him. Ramon drove on and the Cobra stayed at the side of road protecting its territory.

The darkest part of night occurs just before dawn and that's when the two men arrived in Britania. As directed by Wescley, Ramon parked the car two blocks away and the men walked to the Home Office. Ramon still carried his entry key and he entered with Moises and locked the door behind him. In the dark, they felt their way around furniture and made their way to the stairwell to go to the second story to find

Wescley and Bridgette. Ramon shouted softly, "Wescley, Wescley." Ramon was beginning to get worried. After his eyes adjusted to the light of only the streetlights, Ramon saw Wescley slumped over a desk. Ramon shook him and Wescley jumped and gasped. They woke a very nervous Wescley. Bridgette also jumped when Ramon put his hand on her shoulder.

Wescley said, "Come back here, there is a small room in the back without windows. We can turn on the light in there and talk."

They made their way in the dark to a tiny office in the back and Wescley closed the door and turned on the light. Wescley took one look at Moises and asked, "Who's the Rastafarian?"

Ramon answered, "This is Moises. He is an investigator and he is going to help us."

Correcting Ramon, Moises made his own introduction, "I am Moises Proetto, High Priest of the Order of Quimbanda." Moises extended his hand to Bridgette and then to Wesley.

They shook the priest's hand nervously. Quimbanda priests have that affect on everyone and that was why Ramon introduced him as an "investigator." There were only filing cabinets in the tiny room so they all sat on the floor to decide what to do next. Moises started by asking all kinds of questions.

Ramon interrupted, "Tell us everything you saw about the guys, did you see the car they were in? What did the guys look like? Were they from around here?"

Wescley answered, "I couldn't see who the guys were. They all wore handkerchiefs tied around their faces. I did see the two cars they drove away in. One was a dark green Mercedes sedan, very unusual for around here. The other was a gray minivan. From up here we couldn't see any plate numbers."

Being more direct, Ramon asked, "Did you guys really piss off one of the neighboring ranchers?"

Bridgette answered nervously, "No, not that I know about. Things have been really quiet around here lately. Nothing new or unusual at all. You know that Thomaz has been busy negotiating with the government for additional funding for the new project. I can't image some environmental group kidnapping people over that."

Moises answered, "You are correct about that. However, there is something that you do here that is attracting attention. In an hour, when there are people on the streets, I will go out and start asking questions. Ramon, now that it is light out, please go to the manager's office and look through his papers and checking account to see if you can find anything unusual. If you find anything at all that looks like it might be out of place, please flag it for me to see."

Ramon went to Denis Brava's desk and started with the checking account while Moises stayed with Wescley and Bridgette to continue his interrogation. Ramon scanned the checkbook entries and made a few notes about things. There wasn't anything suspicious, just a couple of entries that he didn't know the supplier and couldn't guess what items were purchased. Before sorting through all the other papers on the desk, Ramon went to the windows and closed the blinds. Back at the desk, Ramon found the drawers full of documents so he started reviewing them one by one.

As he started reading through the documents, Moises came downstairs and told Ramon he would be out interviewing people on the streets. Ramon thought to himself, "Hell, those people don't have a clue. He won't come back with anything." Ramon continued to read the papers and Wescley and Bridgette came down to talk with him. Wescley said, "Moises said that you have several pistols. May I have one of them?"

Ramon asked, "Do you know how to use it?"

"Sure, sure," answered Wescley. "My uncle used to take me target shooting. Actually I'm a pretty good shot, at least at stationary objects."

"Ok," replied Ramon. "But just be careful with it around me!"

"No, honest, I'm good," assured Wescley.

Ramon could see that Bridgette was tense. Recalling his disastrous involvement in protecting Vanessa Noqueira, her presence was making Ramon nervous. Ramon suggested to her, "Bridgette, we need to send you away until this is over. Do you have anyone who can sneak you out of town?"

"Yes, I have a friend who can come get me. I will return to Rio to be with my parents. When it's safe to return, call me there."

Ramon replied, "Good. Consider this paid vacation time. Go have some fun and forgot about this place for a few weeks."

Moises quickly questioned several dozen residents and had the information he needed. Moises had excellent interrogation skills and could immediately determine if someone had useful information or not. When a Quimbanda priest walks up to you, most people answer quickly. They don't want the priest finding out that they withheld any information. Quimbanda priests are known for their ability to extract revenge even for the most minor infractions. Therefore, people are glad to spill their secrets because they know that the priest will eventually find the truth. With the mystery mostly solved, he owed a visit to the local Quimbanda priest and an apology for walking in on his territory. He went to the home of Gomez Cruz and explained that he was there helping with the investigation into the kidnapping of the men from the Templeton Foundation. Gomez was angry that he was not consulted first. Moises asserted, "But you are being consulted first. I am your client and here is your fee." Moises handed the man $500.00 and the priest continued holding out his hand so Moises placed another $500.00 in the palm of the older priest.

Gomez started by saying, "OK, you tell me what you have first and then I will tell you the missing pieces that you need."

Moises answered, "The crew of the Templeton Foundation have no idea that they have disturbed the natural order of things. That natural order belonging to the owners of the giant ranches around Goias and Tocantins States. There is not a problem with the ranch owners locally; it is with those who own ranches with many millions of acres. They are hearing the chants from the activists demanding land reform. They see the success of the Templeton Farms as the way that the government will repopulate people from the cities to their ranches. Now that the government has given the Templeton Foundation a new major project they are scared and the only way for them to turn around the trend is to kill off those making the projects successful."

"Yes," replied Gomez. "That is most of it. But have you narrowed it down to the exact location of where the men are being held?"

"No," replied Moises. "I just got into town three hours ago."

"Then you have done well," replied Gomez. "The name of the group you seek is called the Enterragato. It's a very private and secret club. You won't find ENT spray-painted on any wall. They are the owners of the largest 18 ranches in these two states. They keep to themselves so I am surprised that you could find anything about them. The Enterragato never come into Britania. They all own planes and fly their supplies in from Brasilia and beyond. They always have others do their bidding. These families are so rich that they home school their children until age 12 and then send them off to boarding schools in Europe. All of these families got their giant ranches from their fathers who got them by bribing government officials in the 1950's. These are the people who will lose everything if land reform happens. They have a lot of wealth to lose. They are desperate and they will stop at nothing. Just use the clues you already have and you will find the location of the kidnapped men."

The two priests shook hands and Moises returned to the Home Office. He helped himself to a desk with a phone and dialed out. Gomez had helped him solve the case and the older priest was a bargain at twice the price. Moises drummed a pencil on the desk while he waited for an answer on the other end. Ramon could hear Moises talking, "Hi honey. I got one for you. I need a Goias or Tocantins registration for a white pickup truck with plates that start MB8, yes I will hold."

Moises continued drumming the pencil's erasure on the desktop and humming to himself. Ramon wondered if it could really be that easy for Moises to find the men.

Moises continued talking to his contact at Vehicle Registration, "Porto Alegre, no honey, wrong state. A green Fiat, no, not that one either. Yes, jackpot!" Moises grabbed a sheet of paper off the desk and began writing down the driver's registration information. "Now can you cross-reference that to find a green Mercedes and a gray minivan registered to the same person or to someone in the same or nearby area? Yes, you can have all the time you want, just make it within the next half hour. Here is my phone number, just call me back when you have the information."

Moises then called another person and in a completely different tone of voice he asked, "Yes, did you find a bush pilot for me and will he waiting at the airfield in Britania by 11 o'clock? Ok. Thanks, love ya." Ramon guessed that the first call was a girlfriend and the second call was to his wife.

Moises asked Ramon and Wescley to pull up chairs so he could update them. "I am still pinpointing the exact location where the men are being held but I can now tell you who captured them. They are being held by a group of wealthy landowners that go by the name Enterragato. Also known as the ENT. These landowners are desperate because your Templeton Foundation is showing the government that responsible land reform does work. In other words, your people were too successful. We cannot use the local police because they have all been paid off and they are owned by the ENT. We must first rescue your men and after they are safe we can call in the Federal Police."

Ramon asked, "And you learned all of this in just the three hours you've been here?"

"Yeah," replied the priest. "I'm a little slow today because you kept me up all last night. Do you want the good news or the bad news next?"

Ramon replied, "Oh, hell, give us the bad news first."

"Unfortunately these men do not want money," Moises replied. "That means that they will kill your crew unless we act very fast. In fact, tonight we will be on our way to save your men. Do you have anyone else who can go with us?"

"No," replied Ramon. "Not anyone I would trust with my life. It's just Wescley and me. What's the good news?"

"While these people are very rich, there are not many of them. That makes finding their hiding location much easier. In fact, I may know the location any minute."

Ramon said, "If that is true, then you missed your calling in life. You should have been a police detective."

Moises answered with a laugh, "Haven't you heard about Quimbanda priests? We are one part grim reaper, one part detective, and one part air." Ramon didn't say anything but thought to himself, "Yes, airhead, or rather pothead." Still, Ramon had to admire Moises' detective skills. Moises just did in three hours what it would take the police three weeks to accomplish. Ramon just kept his fingers crossed hoping that Moises was correct and not just full of hot air.

Handing Ramon a list of supplies, Moises added, "Here, we will need these additional supplies tonight. Also, we cannot use your little rental car out there. We have to bring back five men with us so we will need two large vehicles."

Wescley offered his own personal jeep and an extended cab truck owned by Templeton Farms. Ramon and Wescley looked over the list of items. Many of the items were available in the hardware store and Wescley offered to get them.

Ramon asked, "Why so much gasoline and why so many containers of it?"

Moises answered, "We don't know how far we will be driving tonight and we may have to make some distractions."

Ramon worried quietly to himself. Kidnapping with intent to kill is quite different from the sort of thing that Max Schuman did to him. Ramon never told anyone about being kidnapped by Max and now he considered it more of a "difficult business transaction" than a kidnapping. His kidnapping was not a Brazilian kidnapping. Max was a foreigner. Brazilians are expert at kidnapping and Ramon knew that they would be lucky to get all the men out alive. He had a sinking feeling about the trip tonight.

Moises was back on the phone with his contact at the Vehicle Registration, "Yes, yes, I have it. Thanks honey for dropping everything to do that. I owe you. Yes, when I get back you'll have that and more. Gotta run honey. *Tchau.*"

Moises told Ramon, "I hope this is as easy as it looks right now. We're looking at two adjacent ranches. The owners of the ranches are Jose Rodrigues and Henri Couto. Two of the vehicles belong to the Rodrigues ranch. We'll do a secret raid on that farm first. The men will be tied up in a barn at one or both of these farms. The challenge is that these farms cover millions of acres and we don't know how many out buildings and barns might be on both these properties. My guess is that we're going to be lucky tonight and find all the men. In fact, we must find all of the men. If we only get some of them, the rest will surely be killed."

Wescley came back from the hardware store with the items for Moises. All of the supply items were in the back of the pickup truck. Ramon asked Wescley to discretely unload the weapons from the trunk of the rental car and to return the car to its parking space away from the building. Moises asked Wescley to evenly divide the containers of gasoline to stow them in both vehicles.

Moises needed to change clothes for the operation and Ramon told him to make himself at home in the upstairs apartment. Moises returned wearing his ninja outfit of black jeans and t-shirt. Gone were the hippie beads and rose colored glasses. He wore the same style of rimless glasses, but these were tinted light yellow.

Moises was trying to hurry Ramon to put his things in the truck but Ramon had one more job to do. He addressed an envelope to Mrs. Pedrinho with a note saying, "I am leaving with Wescley to rescue Thomaz and the rest of the men. If we are all killed, I owe Vicente Viera several thousand dollars—maybe as much as $10,000, but he will tell you a fair amount. Please find a way to pay him from Templeton Foundation funds. We also have Moises Proetto with us and if we do not return, pay some money to his widow and to the widow's of all the men. Give these names to government investigators and tell them that these men killed us: Jose Rodrigues and Henri Couto." Ramon quickly folded the note, shoved it into the envelope, and placed a stamp on it.

Moises carried with him a large and heavy backpack that included dynamite, explosive detonators, and a host of spy gear. He reached into the pack and handed walkie-talkies to Wescley and Ramon while pointing out places on a map. He said, "Keep these on all the time. I may have to use them to contact you. You'll be taking Route 164 to Route 153 and stopping at this airfield 80 miles south of Gurupi. I will be waiting for you there after I finish my aerial surveillance. The first farm north of Gurupi belongs to Jose Rodrigues. It will take us nine hours to get there so we must hurry to have time to finish the job tonight. It's now noon and I want to be at the first farm by nine o'clock tonight. Ramon drove the pickup truck and Wescley followed them his own jeep. On the way out of town, Ramon pulled up to a mailbox and mailed the letter to Mrs. Pedrinho. Ramon dropped Moises off at the airfield and made sure that the pilot was still waiting for him. Five minutes later the men were on their way to Gurupi and the small Cessna carrying Moises passed over them.

Mrs. Proetto had negotiated a fee of $500.00 for four hours use of the airplane. The pilot, Paulo Reis, told Moises it would be an extra $150.00 for every hour or part of an hour beyond four hours. Moises fished around in his backpack and between flashlights, hand grenades, and pistols, pulled out $500.00 in large bills and handed them to Paulo.

During Paulo's pre-flight check, he handed a headphone set to Moises so the two could talk over the noise of the engine. Paulo finished his flight check and then asked Moises for directions. Moises said, "I need to do some surveillance of two farms just north of Gurupi."

Paulo thought he could smell marijuana on Moises so he joked, "Did someone steal your marijuana plants?"

Moises laughed and replied, "You know, I get that all the time! It must be my glasses. I am Moises Proetto, High Priest of the Order of Quimbanda."

"Sorry sir, I didn't mean to offend you," replied Paulo nervously.

"That's quite alright," replied Moises. "You probably know about the kidnapping of the men from the Templeton Foundation in Britania. I have been retained by the Foundation to find and rescue all five men. My powers of Quimbanda intuition tell me that it's very likely that they are all tied up in a barn or out building on the ranches that belong to Jose Rodrigues or Henri Couto. The ranches are north of Gurupi and just west of Route 153. Unfortunately, I cannot have you fly around in circles to look for them because the kidnappers will get nervous. I need you to make a high pass over the farms and when I see something suspicious we can fly out and come back later for a lower pass. I am looking for new tracks in mud to the out buildings I described. I believe that these out buildings will be away from the owner's ranch house by a half mile but no more than four miles away."

Paulo asked, "And your Quimbanda powers told you all of that?"

"Yes, certainly," answered the small black man. "We all have such powers of intuition."

"Wow," replied Paulo. "The next time I lose something I will have to hire you." Paulo reached behind and gave Moises a pair of large binoculars saying, "Here, you will need these to see from the higher altitude. I won't fly in circles but I will bank so you can be looking straight down."

Paulo had never been so close to a Quimbanda priest so he decided to use the time to ask about Quimbanda. Moises replied, "Yes, it's true that Quimbanda works from the dark side. The dark side of God. Remember, it be God's own true words, 'an eye for an eye.' Quimbanda seeks to return to the true and natural order of things in this world."

Paulo asked, "Then why is it that you only hear about the Quimbanda doing evil deeds. Why don't they ever do something good?"

"Quimbanda gets the credit for almost anything bad that happens in Brazil. As priests, we do good deeds but those are never known. A Quimbanda priest will never divulge his work after he is finished. Quimbanda has a lot of competition in Brazil from the Umbanda and others. Any of them eagerly attribute bad things to the Quimbanda in hopes of generating interest for their own organizations."

Paulo asked, "These men who were kidnapped, why did their families hire you instead of going to the police?"

"The police are not available to help them. In this case, the police are owned by the people who organized the kidnapping. Even if the police were involved, it would take them weeks to solve the crime. This matter must be solved tonight before it becomes a murder investigation. The Federal Police will get involved in a kidnapping. It's something they would like to stop in Brazil. Murders in Brazil are given a low priority for investigation. Most murders are never solved by the police. There are too many cases and too few investigators. That's why people turn to Quimbanda. We are problem solvers and we use our powers of intuition to quickly solve crimes. Yes, most people who hire us want retribution and we are amply gifted to administer that as well."

Forty minutes later the Cessna was flying high over the two farms. The big binoculars were helpful and Moises could see the Rodrigues ranch house. There were several barns in close proximity to the big ranch house and one appeared to have recent traffic through the mud to it. At the Couto ranch, there were a couple of out buildings but they were too close to the ranch house. Henri Couto would not want his family members discovering his role in a kidnapping by walking into a nearby building. There was a large equipment barn but it was more than four miles away from the ranch house. In typical Brazilian style, the barn was merely an elevated metal roof suspended over a field with walls around the perimeter. Moises thought it might be worthwhile to get a good look into the barn on the lower fly over. Moises guessed that the kidnap victims would not be farther than four miles away from the ranch house based on people being lazy and not wanting to go too far out of their way even to hide a crime. After they passed the farms, Moises explained to Paulo which buildings he needed to see at the lower altitude.

On the low fly by, Moises saw something and he immediately knew the location of the men. He told Paulo to leave the area and follow Route 153 to the south. He told Paulo he would look for his colleagues and try to find a landing field close to their current location. The little Quimbanda priest soon located Ramon and Wescley and hailed them on the walkie-talkies, "Ramon, Wescley, we're just above you and there is an airfield on the right about ten more miles ahead. Just keep going and you'll see the plane."

Minutes later, the men reunited and Paulo was quickly back in the air returning to his home base. Moises said in a panic, "We must hurry now more than ever. We have almost no time left." The priest did not want to panic the men more but he had to give them some warning. He did not tell them how he found the exact location. Moises knew the exact location because he saw a backhoe digging a hole for a mass grave near one of the out buildings on Jose's ranch.

During the surveillance, Moises made many mental notes about the location and the surrounding terrain. Before getting back into the vehicles, Moises quickly drew out on paper the layout for Ramon and Wescley. Moises laid out his plan, "The out building housing the men sits out on a spit of land surrounded by a lagoon. Beyond the lagoon is a grove and beyond that is a hill. Near the out building is a shack that houses workers. I'm certain that the men who will do the killing tonight are in that shack. Wescley will stop first and hide his jeep away from the lane that leads to the workers shack. Ramon will let me out next, close to the worker's shack. I will run a trip wire at the door of the shack and the first person who comes out will be one less person for us to worry about. The blast should also knock down anyone else in the building and that will give us more time. Ramon, you will take the truck and park it beyond the grove and behind the hill."

Ramon asked, "So the first person there cuts them loose and we make a run for the truck?"

"No," answered Moises. "We need all our fire power together. With our automatic pistols, we can take out an army. We will regroup just behind the out building, on the side that faces the lagoon. There is a side door here, and I will enter first to see if they are being guarded. If there is no guard, then we cut and run. If there is a guard, I will take him out quietly. Ok, let's go"

Two hours later, the men approached the Rodrigues ranch. Wescley turned off the lights on his jeep and stopped. Ramon pulled up behind him. In one of the bags of supplies, Ramon found the duct tape that

Wescley purchased. The men used the tape to cover their brake lights. There was only a tiny crescent moon so it was difficult to see the road without headlights. Moises told them, "We won't return on Route 153, they will be looking for us there. Instead, we will drive north to Palmas and take Route 10 all the way back to Brasilia. It will be a long two-day trip but we can go directly to the Federal Police when we get there."

After driving another mile, Wescley pulled off the road and Ramon drove a little farther to let Moises out. Ramon could now see to drive in the dark. Instead of parking at the agreed spot, Ramon decided to hide the truck in the almond grove.

While Moises was setting up the trip wire, he heard the men arguing inside the shack. Some of the men wanted to shoot the guys in the out building and take them to the hole, and the others wanted to walk them to the hole and then shoot them. Moises was muttering under his breath that he should just blow up the whole damn shack and get rid of all the idiots inside. He could have blown up the entire shack but he had plans for some of the workers. After the trip wire was set, Moises went to the back of the outbuilding and waited. He listened for a long time trying to hear if there was a guard in with the men. He could just hear the men inside trying to talk. They were gagged so he couldn't understand what they were saying. Wescley came over to him crawling on all fours. They didn't hear Ramon approach and they both jumped when Ramon put his hands on their shoulders.

Moises and Ramon put on their night vision glasses and told Wescley to stay put and to back them up. Moises peeked his head in first from the side door. He saw the five men all tied up together in the center of the room. There were no guards inside. Moises whispered to Ramon, "They all know you, go untie them."

Ramon went to the men and while cutting ropes he said, "Hey guys, did you think I would let you rot out here? Let's get out of here."

All the men got up except Thomaz. He was still on the floor. Denis whispered, "They broke his leg really bad. He can't walk at all."

Moises said pointing to Denis who was the largest man there, "Ok, you and Wescley carry him out to the jeep which is parked nearby."

The gunmen inside the shack finally made their decision and were coming out to kill the prisoners. Moises heard a screen door open for a second and then a loud explosion. The men not killed in the explosion didn't wait very long to get back up. They came running out of the shack with their guns firing. By now the captives were all outside and Ramon yelled to Moises, "Change of plans, head for the lagoon and let's go swimming."

When Ramon made the decision to cross the lagoon, it was because there was no way to carry Thomaz away without being shot. Thomaz could swim across the lagoon with the men and then they would just have to carry him through part of the almond grove. Ramon would have preferred walking around the lagoon. The murky water was the perfect home for a dozen or more different kinds of poisonous water snakes.

The men entered the lagoon, which was ink black. The marshes surrounding the lagoon prevented clear sight across the water so they were completely out of sight while they were in the water. In fact, they couldn't even see each other. The men were all treading water quietly and Ramon whispered, "Is everyone here?" He heard all the men answer except Moises. Ramon whispered again, "Moises, where are you?" There was no answer.

Shots were being fired into the lagoon from the area around the worker's shack. Ramon saw a flash of light and looked back. Two explosions just took out the vehicles owned by the workers. Another flash of light and explosion finished off the worker's shack. Now the almond grove was lighted by all the fires and explosions set off by Moises. Moments later they could hear the cross fire of automatic weapons. The men struggled out of the marsh on the far side of the lagoon. Denis and Wescley carried Thomaz into the almond grove. Ramon led the way to his truck. While the men were racing through the grove, the bullets from automatic gunfire sprayed the trees. Every few minutes there was another flash of light and loud explosion. By the time all the men reached the truck, the gunfire ceased.

Denis and Wescley put Thomaz in the center of the front seat and Wescley rode shotgun, literally. Andre and Denis sat in the back cab, and Marcio and Dalton rode in the bed of the truck. Before he pulled out of the grove, Ramon gave his automatic pistol to Dalton saying, "If anyone comes up on us fast, don't be afraid to shoot." Wescley knew that he just lost his jeep in the raid because it wasn't safe to go back for it. Ramon followed Moises' directions and drove to Palmas.

CHAPTER TWENTY-TWO

Ramon was nervous driving into Palmas. It was in the heart of the Enterragato territory. Ramon told the men, "I don't like the fact that all of us are in just one vehicle. If we bought a second vehicle in Palmas, the dealer would just turn us over to the ENT, or just describe both our vehicles to them. Any suggestions?"

Denis answered, "They know what the five of us look like. You and Wescley could take buses to Brasilia since they don't know you."

Wescley said, "I think we need to stop and get Thomaz to a hospital."

"No, you're not stopping for me," replied Thomaz. "Besides, I wouldn't be safe in any hospital around here."

Wescley asked, "Why did Moises tell us to take Route 10? It winds through the mountains and will take forever. If we go beyond it, Route 20 is a major highway and it will cut our time in half. Either route goes though land owned by the ENT so I don't see an advantage to going by Route 10."

Ramon answered, "I agree. It will be harder for them to ambush us on a major highway. I'd prefer to stay out of the mountains."

After driving all day, they arrived very late at night in Brasilia. They took Thomaz directly to a hospital and then went to the Federal Police to report their kidnapping by Jose Rodrigues and Henri Couto. The President of Brazil quickly heard about the kidnapping of some of his favorite people. He sent guards to the hospital room to protect Thomaz and he assigned a guard detail for the rest of the men. The government of Brazil took swift action and locked up Jose and Henri. They also pulled their families and workers off the farms. The Rodrigues and Couto ranches would be the first ranches in a long list to be destined for land reform.

The Federal Court of Brazil gave due process to Jose Rodrigues and Henri Couto. It turned into a long, drawn out process over several years. During the trials, the ENT murdered two of the judges. With the assault on the judiciary, the Brazil legislative and executive branches declared war on the ENT and all the ranches obtained illegally in the 1950's. This process literally moved owners off hundreds of millions of acres of ranch land. The total land mass for redistribution amounted to an equivalent of the states of Texas and Montana combined.

After two days spent debriefing the police about their kidnapping, the men from the Templeton Foundation all drove back to Britania with a military escort. Thomaz and Ramon stayed in Goiania while the rest continued on to Britania. Thomaz was on crutches and decided that he would return to work in a few days. Ramon had some business to conclude with Vicente Viera so he borrowed a car from Thomaz and returned several boxes full of gear and weapons to the gun dealer.

Vicente was glad to see him, "Oh, I'm so happy that you and all your friends are safe. That was quite a big write up about the story in the newspapers."

Ramon replied, "I'm returning the guns, grenades, and one pair of night vision glasses. I know I promised to return your Quimbanda priest to you but I'm sorry to say he didn't make it."

"No, you are wrong on that," Vicente said quietly. "He was here by ten o'clock the next morning to return his night vision glasses, the pistols, and a few hand grenades. He told me you were separated and that all your men were safe. Here, he left this bill for you. He wants you to wire the money directly to his bank."

Shocked, Ramon replied, "How did he know all the men were safe? It was pitch black when we separated. And, how did Moises get to your office by ten o'clock the next morning? We were in a gunfight at midnight and Goiania was 14 hours away. That just doesn't add up."

Vicente assured Ramon, "It doesn't have to add up. Moises is a Quimbanda priest. He is part air. That's how they do things."

"Of course," answered Ramon. "He had the night vision glasses so he could tell we all made it out. He obviously had that bush pilot of his come get him and fly him back here to Goiania. See, there isn't any magic to Quimbanda. Everything has an explanation."

Handing a large box of supplies to Vicente, Ramon said, "We used all the guns we took with us and most of the ammunition. Here are some hand grenades. The night vision glasses are still in good shape."

Vicente made some notes on a piece of paper while saying, "That was quite the gun fight you were involved in. Yes, you were all lucky to get out alive. It's a good thing that I made you take Moises with you."

"Yes, without Moises we never would have found the men. I am so relieved that he is alive and I cannot believe he made it back to Goiania so quickly. I am still shocked by that. I am so happy about Moises, I was sure he was killed."

Vicente started adding up numbers on the sheet of paper and handed it to Ramon. The bill was for $6,500.00 and he handed it to Ramon saying, "Just give this to Thomaz for me and he will pay me when he is up and around."

Ramon also glanced at the bill from Moises, it said, "$7,500.00 – Moises Proetto," and it included a bank name and account number.

Ramon returned the attorney's car and gave him the bills from Moises and Vicente. Thomaz asked, "Why is this bill from a Quimbanda priest so much? What did he do?"

Ramon answered, "He saved your life. He saved all us. I keep forgetting that you never saw him. I'm sorry, you must be under the impression that I saved you. Well, yes, Wescley and I did come rescue you but it was all with the help of Moises Proetto. Fortunately, you introduced me to Vicente Viera and I went to him for some guns. Vicente recommended that we take Moises with us. Without Moises, we never would have found you. What a strange little Quimbanda priest he is! Do you know that those people dug a mass grave for you and they were getting ready to come shoot you when we arrived?"

"Yes, of course, we could hear the men in the shack arguing. And yes, I know Moises Proetto. We call him the Rastafarian, of course, not to his face," replied the attorney.

"Of course not," smiled Ramon. "Do you know that he solved your kidnapping in only three hours after arriving in Britania? And, he pinpointed from an airplane the exact spot where you were being held. He also blew up all the bad guys so we could escape. No, without Moises, Wescley and I would still be in Britania scratching our heads."

"Well yes," answered the attorney. "That's what a Quimbanda priest is supposed to do."

An exacerbated Ramon replied, "And you think that $7,500 is too much for saving seven lives?"

Thomaz replied, "No, I was just wondering if you felt that $7,500 is the right amount. Maybe we should pay him more?"

"Yes," replied Ramon. "Pay him more. I don't know how much more. Why don't you ask the men for their input and Jane will pay Moises what the group decides. Please remember that only Wescley knows what I know about Moises. You and the field men were probably thinking that I saved you because I came in and cut your ropes, but that's not nearly the whole story. "

"Good idea, I will consult with the men in Britania," replied Thomaz.

"And Wescley," continued Ramon. "For a title clerk, he sure made a good commando. Perhaps Jane should consider paying everyone involved in this trauma a nice big bonus."

Thomaz asked, "What does Jane want to do?"

"Maybe $100,000 each for all seven of us," replied Ramon.

"It's difficult for me to turn down money," replied the attorney. "That much money may be a life altering experience for the men. It may not bring happiness to them. I also fear it might be seen as a payoff because the Templeton Foundation provided nothing for their security."

"Yes, I see your point," replied Ramon. "But do give all seven of us and Bridgette a December bonus of $5,000 for any year that we are still employed. Consider my employment as "contractual" as in having to skip all my classes to come rescue you."

The attorney replied, "Ramon, whenever you need money you can just write yourself a check from Jane. You don't need my permission to spend your money. Don't be so silly."

"No, it's not silly," answered Ramon. "I live month-to-month on my college scholarship and I have no money left at the end of the month. It doesn't matter how much money I access on a monthly basis, I will always be broke at the end of the month. Denis was correct. I cannot manage any money that I can access. As for the bonus money, it will make me feel like I'm still part of the team. When you are handing them out, be sure to let the men see that you have a check to send to me."

Thomaz replied, "No problem, I can make that happen. But about your money, you should spend for yourself whatever you want. Only you know the amount currently held by Jane, but you should be able to spend whatever you want. Last year, the soybean crop alone netted over 120 million dollars."

"Yes, but almost all of that belongs to the Templeton Foundation," Ramon answered with a smile. "No, I must live within the boundaries I set for myself. I will never change my mind about letting the money control me. If I had access to it, I would spend it foolishly."

Thomaz tried to help by saying, "If you are broke at the end of every month, please let the Templeton Foundation increase your monthly scholarship."

"Perhaps," replied Ramon. "Do not go overboard; maybe just a little more would help. Now, about security, I do not have the time to personally oversee this because I am flying back to Rio to resume classes. Besides, you have Denis, and he can do this just as well as I can. I think you need to brick up all those extra doors at the Home Office. All of those extra doors from the original storefronts look odd anyway. Just put in one main door and of course a fire exit door that is always locked on the outside. Even before the new main door is built, hire two armed guards during work hours and one nighttime guard. Reduce the size of the windows in the front of the building and put in bulletproof glass. As long as you are making the Home Office look like a bank, you might consider asking one of the banks in Goiania if they want to lease space for a branch in the Home Office. We will never use all the space that is there, and a bank could help pay for the guards."

"Have a security expert come talk to the men about personal security. If any of them want to carry automatic pistols, Jane will buy them. And now, for you Mr. Rocha. Until this is all settled, with land reform in Brazil, you will be a target. Come to Rio, buy yourself a nice

European car, and then have them install bulletproof glass, solid rubber tires, and a big engine. When you get your car, you will need to hire an armed driver who is an expert marksman. You may have to have guards at this house. You should speak with the security expect who talks to the men to see if he has recommendations for you. Just send all the bills to Jane. Let me know if all this will require Jane to send a one-time check to cover the extra expenses."

"That's a lot to do. I wish I didn't have these crutches to slow me down," said the attorney.

"Call me when you come to Rio," said Ramon. "We'll go to this great steakhouse I know. Ok, I'm off to Brasilia to catch an evening flight back to Rio. Take care of yourself."

When Wescley Silva returned to Britania, he was scratching his head. Parked in front of the Home Office was his jeep. It was dusty and had a couple bullet holes in the side of it. He found the keys to his jeep on the desk in the upstairs storage area—just where Ramon and Moises found him. He wondered how the little Quimbanda priest got the jeep back to the Home Office and how did he enter the locked Home Office and put the keys on the desk. Wescley sat at the desk and thought to himself, "Maybe they are part air."

Ramon returned to his classes at the university and when he graduated he continued to work on his doctorate degree. Ramon's goal was to graduate with a doctorate degree in urban and environmental planning. He liked the work he initially did with the Templeton Foundation. He knew he liked the initial planning of a project and was less interested in the day-to-day building and running of an operation. He hoped to get a government job where he could have some impact on the future development of Brazil.

Leaders of the ENT were rounded up one by one and prosecuted. Their land was confiscated and the families and workers were removed from the ranches. During the gunfight at the Rodrigues Ranch, Moises Proetto managed to take two prisoners alive. Somehow, he managed to get them turned over to the Federal Police without involving himself in the case. The two prisoners quickly turned state's evidence in the prosecution of the Enterragato. They were the only two that managed to escape alive that night from the worker's shack. The two men had enough information to implicate all of the Enterragato in a conspiracy case involving kidnapping and attempted murder. Jose Rodrigues and Henri Couto would spend the rest of their lives in jail. The other members of the Enterragato received harsh jail sentences for their involvement. The families of all these men were dual citizens with grandparents in Italy or Germany. Brazil allows their naturalized citizens and their children to retain dual citizenship. The families thrown off the ranches quickly fled back to Europe.

Following the lead of the Templeton Foundation, the government sent in surveyors to divide the ranches into smaller farms. Andre Rondon was recruited to supervise the major surveying task. A massive project was undertaken by the government to research the titles of all the large ranches in the interior. The titles to all the ranches purchased by bribes to government officials were declared void and the owners were removed and some were jailed.

Just before Ramon graduated with his doctorate degree, a personal emissary of the new President and a high-ranking general came to him with a job offer. The emissary explained that the President personally picked Ramon for the position and he would be extremely disappointed if he did not accept the job offer. In circumspect language, the general made it sound like Ramon was drafted for the position. The emissary explained that the job was a perfect match for Ramon's skills and experience and the country of Brazil required his service. The job was to oversee and create teams to go to the confiscated ranches to help relocate poor people to the newly created farms. The President of Brazil wanted Ramon to organize teams to conduct relocation in the same manner that he did in Britania. It was the same job that he did with Templeton Farms except on a much larger scale.

Occasionally the original four field men and Wescley got together for a reunion and some beers on a Sunday afternoon. In the privacy of one of their homes, the men would always retell some aspect of their kidnapping. Wescley always choked on his beer when he retold what the Quimbanda priest looked like. Since none of the other men saw Moises, Wescley was free to embellish that part of the tale. Marcio or Dalton would retell some part of their initial survey of Templeton Farms and the stories usually included some aspect of Ramon and his lack of camping skills.

Eventually the conversation turned to the mystery of the identity of Jane. Denis explained that he finally solved the mystery, "Jane has been elusive and now I've solved the puzzle."

Dalton interrupted, "Remember, in the beginning, you thought that it was Ramon or Thomaz. Then we learned that they didn't have a clue. I should have bet you a week's wages on that one."

Marcio added, "Then it became clear that Thomaz was just a poor working attorney and Ramon never had enough money for lunch by Fridays. I think Ramon still owes everyone here for lunch money."

Denis said, "Don't worry about it. Ramon will come around some day and pay us all back with interest. Now that he has just gotten a good job with the federal government he will have money to pay us back. It just took Ramon a long time to finish that last degree and get a good job."

"I'm glad for Ramon," said Marcio sincerely.

Wescley said, "Yes, we're all glad for Ramon. Denis, please, finish your theory on the identity of Jane."

"Jane was never known because Jane was set up by the government of Brazil to test the feasibility of land reform. Just think about it and you will realize that I am correct on this. The government had millions of people demanding land reform and they had a couple hundred land owners sitting on half of Brazil. The government wasn't going to be foolish and throw out the big ranch owners unless they knew for certain there was a good way to get poor people out of the cities and onto the land. The Templeton Foundation was a government funded experiment to test land reform."

Dalton slapped Denis on the back and said, "What would we do around here without you to solve the mysteries of the universe?" At that cue, all the men raised their beer glasses saying, "Here, here!"

Marcio asked, "Knowing that, don't you resent that we were all used like lab rats in some social experiment?"

Wescley chirped in, "Yes, well-paid lab rats at that!"

Denis answered, "No, I don't resent it at all. Wescley is right. We were all paid handsomely for our work. The best part of it is that we all became part of a larger good, a good for the people of Brazil."

Dalton added, "And look where the project has taken us individually. All of us have benefited from the existence of the Templeton Project.

We all have great prospects for our own futures. So, it really doesn't matter if Jane is the government or if Jane really exists as an anonymous donor. I don't see that anything but good came from the project. If any of you doubt this, just think what you would be doing now and who you would be working for if the Templeton Foundation never existed."

CHAPTER TWENTY-THREE

It's late afternoon and time for another language lesson from my friend Dr. Rosa. Before I knock on his open door, he hears me coming and shouts in English, "Come in, Come in."

I ask, "*Como vai?*"

"*Tudo bem, e você?*"

"*Tudo bem,*" I reply.

Speaking English, Dr. Rosa corrects me, "No, you must say the opposite, not the same. They're supposed to be mismatched pairs. If I say bem, you say bom. If I say bom you say bem."

"Oh, is that how that's supposed to work? I always thought people were correcting me and I didn't think I would ever say it right. So it doesn't matter who says what first, you just reply with the opposite one?"

"Yes, see how easy. So what have you been up to?"

"I went in to Essenada this morning and on the way back I saw something very strange. Down by the bridge, before getting back on the island, there was a barefoot guy jumping around with a club so I went over to look. He was trying to kill a very long green snake. I've never seen such a long snake be that thin. It was like a ribbon six foot long. The snake was really mad it and was chasing him around."

"It was probably a Tree Cobra."

"Yes, that's what he said it was. I waited until after he killed the snake to ask him about it. The man was really jumping around. Usually Cobras have big thick bodies, like those Gray Water Cobras we see all the time down by the lake. This one had a big head but its body was long and thin."

The old doctor warned, "You must be very careful around them. They are extremely poisonous."

"I hate all snakes, I won't be playing with any of them. Every time I come up the path by the bridge, I will be looking in those trees to make sure there isn't some Tree Cobra waiting for me."

Moving on to the language lesson for the day, I show him a page from a recent news magazine. Above the story headline is a paste up cartoon picture showing the President of Brazil with his cabinet members at his side in the style of Da Vinci's "*Last Supper*." The President is portrayed as Jesus in the middle of the picture and in front of him is an empty plate with a napkin of a stylized Brazil flag over it. Surrounding the President are his cabinet members and in front of each cabinet member are stacks and stacks of money, representing their stolen fortunes while in office.

I am amazed at the picture because all of the cabinet members are white males of strictly European descent. While there are large pockets of Europeans in São Paulo and elsewhere, the majority of Brazilians are not white. Most are somewhere between white and black. Marcus tells me, "Never use the word mulatto because it is offensive. Say *prata* which means silver, but in the case of race it means gray, neither black nor white."

"No, I would never use the word mulatto. It's not really a word in my vocabulary—sounds vulgar and reminiscent of slavery. In the States, you are either white or black. Brazil even makes race a complicated issue."

"No," replied Marcus, "That's not true. You just don't understand. You and I are of different races."

"No Marcus," I reply. "We are both white."

"Yes, surely we are different races," bellowed the old man. "Here, put your arm next to mine. See, your skin is pink and mine is olive. I am Mediterranean and you are northern European."

"Actually I thought I was tan but now you point out that I am albino. Yes, I come from a long line of albinos from Ireland. I thought that the notion of Germans, French, and Spaniards all being from different races died out during the Inquisition."

"We are all different, both physically and culturally," answered Marcus.

"Yes, but native Europeans are all white. There are not 60 different flavors of white. After all, we all came from the same black monkey-person who walked out of Africa only 2,000 generations ago."

"That is all nonsense," yelled the doctor. "That is just what the hippies want you to think!"

"And I suppose you and I came from a white monkey-person and black people came from a black monkey-person."

"We did not come from the same source," snorted Marcus.

"You are totally wrong on that. They now have the DNA evidence that links all humans to a single ancestor. Everyone on the planet came from a creature that walked out of Africa. They have even chartered the migration courses from that common ancestor. Anthropologically speaking, race doesn't mean anything. Race just has cultural and economic impacts for most people, but that is a temporary condition in the larger picture of evolution."

"No, you are wrong on all of that," asserted Marcus.

"No, you are wrong. That magazine, National Geographic, they did a study of DNA and found a point in central Asia where most of our ancient ancestors either went east or west. Those who went west became Europeans. Those who went east populated the rest of Asia and eventually populated the Americas. Mediterranean people took the direct route out of Africa and did not go to Asia first. All race is simply a matter of skin exposure to the sun. Obviously, my ancestors, the albinos, never had any sun exposure."

The old man has stopped listening to my rant so I continue to read aloud the magazine article that seems to go on and on about government corruption. As I read, Marcus corrects me as I translate into English. Now after my tenth winter in Brazil, I can actually read Portuguese pretty well but I am still horrible at speaking and hearing the language. I read the captions that are in large print so he can follow my reading. The story describes how cabinet members embezzle money from government-funded projects by overpricing and accepting kickbacks. The article claims to follow the money trail on several big projects right back to the cabinet members. I flip through another issue of the magazine and it's pretty much the same issues about the government. I read a little more and Marcus continues to correct my pronunciation and translation. In between readings, he shouts his usual slogan, "See, I told you, they are all stullers! Every one of them is a snake in the grass! Snakes in the grass! They all wear thousand dollar suits and steal from the government."

I stopped reading to ask, "If they know who has stolen what, why don't they just arrest the politicians and put them on trial for embezzlement?"

Marcus answered, "It's just the way things are done in Brazil. It's been that way forever and no one is going to change it. Before, when the military ran the government, it was exactly the same way, only the generals got the money instead of the bureaucrats. The generals still get whatever they want. Brazilian politicos are scared to death of the military. From my government pension, I must pay a third of it back to the government in taxes. Retired military in Brazil receive much higher pensions than doctors and they pay no taxes on their pensions."

"I understand that the voter turnout rate is pretty high in elections here. Why can't the common people run some of their own who are honest?"

"Oh, they do occasionally, but as junior bureaucrats they have little power to change things and by the time they are in office very long they become corrupted. Brazil has many problems with corruption and drugs. A lot of this is the legacy of the former military rule, the old dictators. Additionally, the bureaucracy we carried over from Portugal does not allow for much modernization of the government. Many things make no sense at all. There are so many careers in Brazil that I could never do because the government does not allow the best jobs to be done by those not born in Brazil. I could never have been a judge, a lawyer, or a higher government official. I didn't want to, but I was not allowed to serve in the Brazil military because I was not born here. Still, every country has its negatives and positives. I loved living in America because people were so free to do what they wanted. However, in Chicago it was too cold, no palm trees, and Americans don't eat a good diet because there is no good produce. There are times I dream about working and living in America. If I had worked there my entire career as a facial plastic surgeon I would be rich and living in Miami right now."

"Yes, but would you be any happier living in the States? Americans deal with a lot of stress. If you think politics in America is perfect then you are wrong. Living in the only super power is a drain on everyone and the U.S. still thinks it has to police the world! Enough politics! Please hand me that National Geographic and I will read from it for awhile."

I notice my old friend sitting back and sipping his wine. I can see the wheels spinning in his mind. He looks at me and asks, "What do people in town call you, people who do not know your name? Do they try to guess your nationality?"

"Yes, they always guess that I am German."

The old man raised his glass of wine and said, "I've just proven my point. They never guess that you are Italian because you are not Mediterranean. You do not have the right color for being Italian."

"Ok, I concede that I can't get a good tan, but that doesn't make me a different race from other white people."

"No, I've shown that my viewpoint is correct. There are different races of white people," bellowed Marcus.

Changing the subject slightly I tell him, "Sometimes people call me gringo, which I find offensive because that's what Mexicans call us just before they are about to cheat us. I usually snarl back when they call me 'boy' or 'gringo.' I also get pissed off when some little old lady comes up to me and asks why I am so ugly."

"You must learn to defend yourself," replied Marcus. "When someone says such nonsense you must learn some unkind words to say back to them. Portuguese does not have as many curse words as English. Americans have plenty of foul words. The British curse words are too polite, but the Americans have swearing down to a science. I will teach you all the words you need to know so you can defend yourself."

I grabbed my language notebook and wrote as he explained the use of all the curse words in Portuguese. Sadly, many of my favorites do not have a translation in Portuguese. However, there were plenty related to bodily functions and sex. After Marcus explained them all I asked him to tell the "birds and bees" talk that every father gives his son. It was the typical tale with many words being nearly the same in either language.

After the sex explanation I asked, "I don't understand about sex in Brazil. At the beach, I frequently see a hammock full of teenage boys and girls. They are all twisted together like a bunch of snakes having sex. Instead of having sex, they are all there just talking. I can guarantee you that if you put American teens together like that they would be having sex even in public. At the very least, the boys would all be in tumescence. What's with all of that?"

"You are just seeing the difference in personal space. Here in Brazil we are always touching and kissing so it's never a big deal. I had a horrible time adjusting to American standards. People kept backing away from me when I spoke to them. At first I thought I had bad breath."

I poured some more wine into his glass and I could tell that Marcus was finished with the language lesson and now it was story time.

"When I worked as an obstetrician in Rio I worked many consecutive hours and then had part of the week off. With my free time, I studied art at the University and eventually earned a Bachelor's Degree in Art and Architecture."

"You won't believe this, but there are lots of rules when working with nude models. They are there all day long sitting naked and the students come and go. The students are required to negotiate amongst themselves for priority of position changes. You just can't walk in and tell the model to change positions. First, you have to ask the group when they will be finished and then you have to wait until it's your turn. Then, you must ask politely for the model to change positions. You cannot approach or touch the model at all. You must describe how you want the model to move. It's ok with some models to mimic the position you want, but some models are very picky about how you speak to them."

"One model was especially strict with the students. Her name was Madame Zundee. I have no idea why she called herself Madame, perhaps she was French, or maybe she just used it as a stage name. She wore only a colorful cotton handkerchief tied over her hair. The college professors loved her because she was extremely difficult to draw in charcoal. If you could render Madame Zundee in charcoal, you then passed on to the next, more difficult drawing classes. She was so difficult to draw because her skin was jet black and light reflected off her skin. In the light of the studio, her skin was so shiny that there was a glare of light bouncing from her skin. She had a lot of skin to draw—she was a very large woman. To draw her, you had to master the use of negative space and light. Some students never made it past Madame Zundee."

"If a student didn't say 'please,' Madame Zundee would not move. If a student didn't say 'thank you' afterwards then she would just ignore that student forever. After a session, you had to say, 'Thank you Madame Zundee, that was very good.' Then she would give you a wink and a smile and you knew that you were still in the good grace of Madame Zundee."

"We had a new student enter at midterm and I have no idea why he was taking art classes. He was a General in the Army and he came to art class in his uniform thinking he could do anything he wanted. I'm sure the General suffered from the 'Little Napoleon Complex' for he was short, with black hair and a mustache. He never smiled and always had a scowl on his face. He was never a happy person. When he set up his easel, he just shoved other students out of the way. He was rude, arrogant, and he bossed everyone around. Even the professors were afraid of him. I'm sure he was allowed to enter at midterm by bossing his way through the professors. He thought his paintings were wonderful but actually, they were horrible. He couldn't even make flowers look attractive."

"One day he entered a session where Madame Zundee was the model. He did his usual routine of shoving other students aside and he did not wait his turn to ask Madame Zundee to take a new pose. He didn't say please or thank you, nor did he pay attention to the fact that Madame Zundee's frown was growing by the second. She was changing positions too slowly so he went up to her and grabbed her arms and started shoving her into a position he wanted."

"Madame Zundee outweighed the General by a couple hundred pounds and she knew how to literally throw her weight around. She grabbed the General's arm and twisted it so hard behind his back that the little warrior was screaming in pain. With the General under her, she marched him to the door. By now, she had a good hold on the back of his neck and the back of his belt. Like a big sack of flour, she threw the General many feet down the hall. The General hit the concrete floor hard and kept rolling. Still naked, she returned to the General's easel and gathered his things. She then marched back down the hall and threw all of his art supplies on him. She told him if he ever came on campus again, he would have Madame Zundee to deal with in person. The dazed General gathered his supplies from the floor and ran away. When Madame Zundee returned to her perch in the classroom she was greeted with a round of applause from the students."

"That was a good story," I reply. "Did you ever have any beautiful women as models?"

"Yes, many. Rio is full of beautiful women so we had many to choose from."

"And did you ever date any of those models?"

"Yes," said the old man remorsefully. "I was married at the time and it was the reason for my divorce. I wish I did things differently."

I reply to him, "You can't change your past, only your future. Ok, I am leaving so I will see you later in the week. *Tchau*."

CHAPTER TWENTY-FOUR

All summer long, my old friend mixed language lessons with his personal stories. His favorite stories included those that happened when he was an itinerant physician serving the jungle population in the State of Tocantins. I had heard dozens of stories about a town named Britania that dried up after the murder of his friend. Snakes attacked the town and the citizens moved away. Now, in a more serious tone, he wanted to tell the end of the story about his friends from Britania.

"Frankie, I will tell this story to you mostly in Portuguese so you will get your language lesson that way today. When I use words that I know you don't know, I'll say the English word after it."

Continuing his story, old Dr. Rosa explained, "Years ago I was completely retired from the medical business and I foolishly purchased a part ownership in a business in Rio. Between the hyperinflation of the early 1990's and the poor decisions made by my partners, the business started to fail."

"I was busy designing a new product when our secretary interrupted to let me know I had a visitor. The visitor walked in behind the secretary and he had not given his name so she made no introduction. Ramon Gobbey and I had both aged considerably since we last saw each other and there was a moment of awkward silence before we talked. So many years had passed that neither of us recognized the other, but as soon as he spoke, I could mentally see the young man I knew so long ago."

"We ended up talking over coffee all afternoon and late into the evening. Ramon filled in all the details about the Templeton Foundation that I have shared with you. Other information about the Templeton Foundation I know from reading the newspapers over the years. Anyone in Brazil who reads the newspapers or listens to news on television knows all about the Templeton Foundation. During my friendship with Dr. Noqueira, I knew nothing about the snake laboratory or about the circumstances of the deaths of the Roberio family members. After the murder of Dr. Noqueira, I never returned to Britania, not once. Someone told me that Vanessa was in Brasilia but I never saw her again after my last visit when Roberto was still alive. Of course, Ramon never confessed to murder, but he gave me enough information to know what happened. I had never before known about the events in Britania after Dr. Noqueira's death. After our talk that afternoon, I knew everything."

"At the end of our conversation, Ramon said, 'Roberto Noqueira was the best friend I ever had. You would never know this, but when you and Roberto were talking at the Britania Hospital, I listened to every word. I hope that I learned a few useful things from my eavesdropping. I never forgot something that you told Roberto one day. You were telling Roberto about things you learned during your internship and residency experience in America. You said that in North America, Native American Indians made decisions about the land and plan for all impacts and contingencies out to the next seven generations. I have never forgotten your words. In all my work, I've tried to incorporate that thinking into every aspect of my planning. In everything that I do, in every decision I have ever made, I've always tried to maximize the positive effects upon the land for the next 200 years. That single thought you shared with Roberto so many years ago has been my guide for everything that I do.'"

"Ramon stood and handed me a large envelope saying, 'Roberto would have wanted you to have this. It's two first class tickets on Air France, good for any and all travel for one year. If you don't use them within a year, you will need to reschedule. The tickets are not refundable for cash so you will have to use them. You'll find plenty of spending cash in different currencies in the envelope. Roberto would not want you spending your government pension to use his gift.'"

"Ramon left my office that night and I never saw him again. The following day I sold my interest in the failing company to my partners at a bargain price. I took a taxi to the Air France office and scheduled my itinerary. I left the next week and traveled the entire year using as many flights as I could. I visited the United States, Europe, Asia, and the South Pacific. I traveled on the Concorde many times."

"I loved living in Greece. Ramon didn't know that I was divorced, or maybe he assumed I had a girlfriend, but I needed only one ticket so I was able to exchange the extra yearlong ticket for five round trip flights between Rio and Athens. I used those five flights to go to Greece once each year for five years. I lived six months of the year in Greece. I had a friend there who helped me find an inexpensive place to live and I painted and earned a good income when I lived in Greece. The island in Greece where I stayed was a wonderful place to spend half of every year, thanks to my friends Roberto and Ramon."

"I lived frugally in Greece and never spent the second set of spending money that Ramon gave me. When I stopped going to Greece I settled here in Essenada and purchased this condominium with the money from Ramon."

"As for Ramon, Denis Brava did make him grow up. Denis pushed and prodded Ramon to finish his degree in urban planning. Actually, Ramon's only prior college experience was the fabricated story about Ramon taking classes in Florida. When Denis signed off on the approval for the Templeton Foundation to give Ramon a college scholarship, Denis never guessed that he was giving money back to his boss. Ramon entered the University of Rio de Janeiro fearing he might become a dropout but he finished his Bachelor's Degree quickly and went on to complete his Doctoral Degree in Environmental and Urban Studies. He used his work experience at the Templeton Foundation as the basis for his doctorial dissertation."

"A new President of Brazil made an election campaign promise to redistribute lands illegally transferred to the land grabbers in the 1950's. Certainly, the Roberio Ranch would have become part of that redistribution. Perhaps it really was the success of the Templeton Foundation that became the marching chant for land redistribution in Brazil. The government hired Dr. Ramon Gobbey to head up that major project which he did for several years. Dr. Gobbey's success in land management caught the attention of the United Nations and their relief organizations hired him for similar projects in the southern hemisphere."

"As for the four field men, Wescley Silva, and Thomaz Rocha, they are all still alive and doing very well. Andre Rondon is still supervising that endless surveying project of redeveloping the ranches taken back by the government. Denis left the Templeton Foundation to work for the government as a supervisor in the same redevelopment project. Dalton Santos became very rich from his cheese factory. From his good salary, he bought out Jane's interest in the factory in Britania. Now he is busy setting up another factory in Belo Horizonte. Marcio Torres is coordinating the development of nurseries and soil augmentation in the new projects."

"Wescley Silva left Templeton Farms long enough to earn a law degree in Rio de Janeiro and then returned as junior partner with Thomaz. Thomaz trained Wescley and then left Goiania to retire and he now lives with his wife in Rio. Bridgette Suzuki fell in love with one of the young generals escorting the President. They married; she is now an executive with the national television network. She works in Brasilia."

"O Presidente lost his bid for re-election. His opponent made a stronger case for land reform and won with a large margin. In his retirement, O Presidente now serves on the Board of Directors of the Templeton Foundation. With his authority as a long-term president, the Templeton Foundation now has considerable influence on the future of Brazil."

"I never thanked Ramon for his gift. I wish I could have told him all about my travel experiences. Ramon was in Kenya working for the United Nations trying to export the Templeton Experiment to the African Continent. In 1998, his plane crashed and he was killed. He was only 54 years old. Ramon Gobbey was a very private person so there is no memorial or marker to remember him. He wanted all the credit for the Templeton Foundation to go to Dr. Noqueira so there is a nice bronze memorial to Roberto Noqueira in the Visitor's Center at Templeton Farms."

"Thomaz Rocha, Andre Rondon, Wescley Silva, and the three original land supervisors at Templeton Farms were the closest thing that Ramon had for a family. They spread his ashes on a vista overlooking Britania. Ramon's will left a few personal items for each of the men and his vast wealth went to the Templeton Foundation. Thomaz had prepared a will for Ramon years earlier and with the will, Ramon left instructions for Thomaz to contact the Cayman Islands Bank upon his death. Mrs. Spencer of the Cayman Islands Bank quickly and secretively delivered Ramon's vast fortune to the Templeton Foundation. Ramon kept the secret of his vast fortune even after his death. Now there is only the memory of Ramon Gobbey held by a very few us who were allowed to know him. He left no family, no children. His deeds, both good and bad, are his only legacy."

POSTSCRIPT

Atlanta is dark and cold. We landed at 4:20 a.m. and when I passed through Customs, it seemed like the middle of the night. As I sit here drinking the last of my coffee, I recall that it was only two evenings ago that I said goodbye to my Brazilian neighbor and friend, Dr. Marcus Rosa. I knocked on his door and entered with a bottle of wine, which I purchased as a parting gift to him.

"Come in, Come in." he shouted in English, for he knew that I was coming to say goodbye.

"Here, I bought you a bottle of your favorite wine. What are you doing tonight?"

A frail Dr. Rosa replied, "I'm starting a painting for my wife. Can you tell yet what it's going to be?"

"Well it looks like grape leaves to me, but when has there been a Marcus painting that didn't have grapes or grape leaves in it?"

"Correct you are," Marcus answered. "But can you see that this is going to be a river and a pond? The light will be reflecting from over here."

"Ok, I think I see it. Why are you painting a landscape for your wife? I thought you divorced her decades ago."

"Yes, I did, but the love never dies. She is still the mother of my son. She deserves something to remember me."

"Are you talking about the same wife that you refused to talk to on the phone last month and the same wife who later cleaned out your checking account?"

"Of course, but I don't want to talk to her. I haven't spoken to her in more than 30 years and I don't need to talk to her now. As for the money, she is entitled to it. That is a joint account and if she needs money then it is hers to take. She had some good reason to take it, so that's fine."

"Marcus, you are very strange. You won't talk to your ex-wife, but you are making a painting for her. That makes no sense at all."

"You think you have all the answers, but if you were in my shoes you might see the world in a different light."

'Ok, you're right. I have to go soon to finish packing. Is there anything you need from the States?"

"No, I'm fine. I have everything that I need and thank you for the wine."

"So what else have you been doing today?"

"Here, let me show you," Marcus said while handing me a hand-drawn map of the solar system. "I am calculating, using only math, the axis rotations of all the planets. I have calculated how they all spin when seen from their northern poles. I just need to verify. Do you know the directional spin of Venus and Jupiter?"

"Sorry, that's beyond my knowledge base. If I ever knew it, I've forgotten it long ago."

"When you get home, please look up the answer on the internet and drop me a note so I can see if my calculations are correct."

"Ok, I can do that. You will have to save your notes because it will take a couple weeks for my letter to get to you. Well then, I will see you again in nine months so take care of yourself."

When I shook the old man's hand, I felt certain it would be my last time to see him. A few evenings before, he told me that he had the mind of a 25 year old and the body of a 90 year old. He said confidently that he was going to live until he was 95. Now at 90 years old, he frequently fell.

Nine months later, I returned to Brazil and had some business matters to conclude in Rio de Janeiro before going on to Essenada. When I finally checked in at the condominium office, the staff asked me to wait a few minutes for the manager to return. Rogerio returned and sadly explained to me that our mutual friend, Marcus Rosa, died two days earlier. Rogerio explained that a month ago, Marcus fell and broke his hip. He never made it out of the hospital.

His death closed forever the details of the events in Britania that took place so many decades ago. No one will ever fully know the true facts of the events that once destroyed the town of Britania.

Printed in the United States
145753LV00004B/51/P